OLD MURDERS

D0807102

FRANKIE Y. BAILEY

An Imprint of The Overmountain Press
JOHNSON CITY, TENNESSEE

Hardcover ISBN 1-57072-217-X
Trade Paper ISBN 1-57072-218-8
Copyright © 2003 by Frankie Y. Bailey
Printed in the United States of America
All Rights Reserved

1 2 3 4 5 6 7 8 9 0

ACKNOWLEDGMENTS

As with my first two books in this series, I owe a debt of gratitude to the Wolf Road Irregulars—Joanne Barker, Caroline Petrequin, Christopher Myers, Audrey Friend, and Emer O'Keeffe—for their careful reading and critiques of various drafts of the manuscript. They have saved me from many a pratfall along the way—including rambling on when I should shut up and get on with the story.

Special thanks to Joanne Barker, who one evening, over dinner, put on her lawyer hat and suggested I think "malpractice suit." Thanks also to University Police Chief J. Frank Wiley, who again came to my assistance by answering my technical questions about campus policing. However, I should note that any errors regarding legal or policing practice in this book are my own.

To my friend, Joycelyn Pollock, who in the midst of classes to teach, presentations to prepare, book deadlines looming, and her own busy family life, again found the time to read my manuscript—thank you, Joy.

To my friends Alice Green and Charles Touhey, thank you for the information about marathons. Thank you, Alice, for the cover photo and for the recipe for collard green lasagna. Thank you, Olivia Raine Green—although you're too young to know it, you have contributed that marvelous white streak in your hair, a sign of luck, to one of my characters.

Thanks also to my friends and colleagues at my own university for their kind words and encouragement in my "other career."

A very special thank-you to the librarians, bookstore owners, and readers I encountered during the year, who have let me know that my books have an audience.

As usual, my thanks to the family and staff at Silver Dagger Mysteries, for their hard work and attention to detail. I am honored to be one of your authors.

AUTHOR'S NOTE

On August 16, 1912, Virginia Christian became the only female to die in the electric chair in the state of Virginia. According to a newspaper report from Richmond (*Danville Register*, August 17, 1912):

> On account of the public clamor against the execution of the woman the penitentiary officials withheld details of her electrocution, but it is known that the young negress went to her death without showing a particle of fear. She walked unassisted to the chair and made no statement whatsoever.

Christian, who was 17 years old, was executed for the murder of her employer, Mrs. Ida Virginia Belote, a widow and the mother of eight children.

I first read about this case while doing research on women and murder. Christian's name appeared on an Internet site devoted to women and the death penalty (maintained by law professor Victor L. Streib). Later, I read Derryn W. Moten's dissertation about the case, and then I visited The Library of Virginia. At the Library, I found documents about the case in the Virginia Governors' Records. I also read newspaper coverage of the trial and execution.

But although the case was my starting point, by the time this book was completed, I had moved in another direction, changing many details, including the year of the execution. The characters who people these pages are products of my imagination. The story is a "what if."

Therefore, I would send readers who are interested in the facts of the Christian case to the primary sources and to Moten's dissertation and forthcoming book.

P R O L O G U E

SUNDAY, MARCH 4
Gallagher (Virginia) *Gazette*
Letter to the Editor

<u>Reject Project Renaissance</u>

We've all seen or met him by now. He's been out there shaking more hands and greeting more people than a politician running for office. Howard Knowlin, tycoon, multimillionaire real estate developer. The man talks a good game, but do we really want to depend on him for our salvation? After the Civil War, Yankee carpetbaggers arrived on horseback, by train, and by ship. Knowlin didn't come that way. He flew into our municipal airport last year on a sleek corporate jet. But his motivation is the same. Greed. If we let this man come in and tell us how to go about restoring the vitality of our downtown, if we let him come in and buy up our prime riverfront property, including the abandoned Mercantile Mill buildings, we will live to regret it. We're smart enough to save our downtown without the likes of this carpetbagger from Maine. What about the project Sloane Campbell proposed? Campbell's project barely got looked at by the development committee after Knowlin arrived. It's true Campbell doesn't have Knowlin's big bucks or his high-flying resume. But he does have good ideas, and he's one of our own. Instead of signing on to Knowlin's "Renaissance" scheme, we ought to send him back where he came from. Let's use our own local talent and know-how to bring downtown Gallagher back to life.

Janet Nichols,
Owner, Daily Bread Bakery
Gallagher Native and Proud of It

* * *

After it was over, I came across that letter that I'd clipped from the newspaper because I'd been amused by the reference to carpetbaggers and wanted to share it with my students.

After it was over, that letter had a more ominous ring.

The letter writer had not been referring to murder when she wrote we would "live to regret it." But that was what happened. A "carpetbagger from Maine" came to town, and someone was murdered.

C H A P † E R · 1

The debate on the local radio talk show this evening was about Howard Knowlin. Callers were divided between those who thought he was the answer to Gallagher's prayers and those who swore he was in league with the devil. As with most radio talk shows, the people who bothered to call in did not reflect the middle ground of people like me, who saw both pros and cons and hadn't yet made up our minds.

When I turned in to my driveway, a caller was raising the issue of the environmental impact of the proposed project. He predicted grave damage to the Dan River.

I gathered up my things and locked the car. I knew George had heard me arrive, that he was listening for my key in the front door. But he would stay silent, waiting. Waiting while I put down my shoulder bag and briefcase on the chair beside the hall table. Waiting as I walked down the hall toward him. Waiting, lurking there on the landing at the top of the stairs, until I opened the second door.

Then he would spring out at me. That was his game.

Tonight was no exception. I opened the basement door, and George, my yellow Labrador-and-dash-of-whatever houseguest, charged out. Barking, tail wagging, he engulfed me in doggy enthusiasm.

Tonight, unlike the first time he'd played his game, I didn't have a grocery bag with a dozen eggs to drop to the floor. Tonight, I laughed, hugged him, and dodged a wet kiss. "Hi, boy! I missed you too."

Satisfied that he had expressed his delight at seeing me—and his pleasure at being released from the basement—he trotted off toward the kitchen and stood waiting beside the counter. The large dog biscuit I held down to him disappeared in two chomps. A quick snack on his way to the back door.

After four days—not counting our week together back in December—I was well trained. He barked twice. I unlocked the door and held it wide. He bounded down the steps and into the fenced-in yard. I flicked on the deck light. When he was outside at night, I liked to be able to see him.

But he was all right alone for a few minutes.

I pulled my U Albany sweatshirt over my head and went to check the messages on my answering machine. Quinn had said he would call me when his stepfather came out of surgery and they knew how things were going. I had almost skipped my workout at the gym to come straight home. But when he'd called last night, he'd said it would probably be late because today would be hectic and he would be busy with his mother.

Nothing on the first three messages. Telemarketers. I hit the delete button to erase the three hang-ups, then went on to the next message.

Doug Jenkins's exuberant voice filled the hallway.

"Lizzie! Doug here. Calling about the pasta blast-off on Friday evening. I've been going over the list of folks who plan to attend, and your name is conspicuous in its absence. But I expect to see you there, lady. In fact, as your coach, I'm going to insist that you be there. You can't walk a half-marathon when you're low on carbs, and pasta is the official premarathon meal of champions. So I'll see you on Friday. No excuses accepted. And between now and then, I want you to remember what I told you. Don't you lose one more ounce, ma'am. A leggy five feet seven inches and 118 pounds might work for runway models, but you're walking for diabetes research, not struttin' your stuff for Calvin Klein."

Laughing, I erased Doug's message. A public relations consultant by profession and a jock at heart, he had volunteered to serve as coach-trainer for the walkers in the marathon. Even though I was doing only the half-marathon, he was monitoring my progress as strictly as those who were going for the full 26.2 miles. He'd been lecturing me about carbs, proteins, and energy levels—and about the nine pounds that I had lost since I started training three months ago.

Another telemarketer. This one left an 800 number and urged me to call within the next twenty-four hours to claim my "fabulous free vacation." Delete.

I propped my foot up on the edge of the chair and worked at the knotted lace in my Nike. Then I pulled off the other shoe and hit the PLAY button again. Warmth enveloped me as I heard Quinn's rough-textured voice.

"Lizzie? Are you there? It's after ten o'clock, so I hope you're not still in your office. I know you want to get your manuscript finished. But, babe, you can't train for a half-marathon and put in twelve-hour days at your computer too. Or is this one of your evenings at the gym? Well, even if you have been out building muscle, get some rest tonight. As in eight hours sleep, Lizabeth." He paused. I heard a tired sigh. I could almost see him massaging the back of his neck the way he did at the end of a long day. "Ben came through the surgery. He's in intensive care. The cardiologist is being cautious, but Mom's sure he's going to be all right. I think so too. Ben Kerchee is one tough Comanche." Another pause. "You know how much I want to be there to see you cross the finish line on Saturday. But I'm not sure I'm going to make it back. Marielle needs to go home tomorrow. She's been here since early last week. Angus is with the kids, but he has a conference in Houston that he needs to attend. He's one of the speakers. So she's gotta get back to Santa Fe. And if she goes, I should hang around here for a while. Anyway, I'll be home as soon as I can. I'll talk to you tomorrow. And thanks for taking care of George. I hope he's not making a pest of himself." An audible yawn. "Sorry, I've been up since 4 A.M." Then he laughed, a low-pitched sound that rippled down my spine. "And I'm about ready to fall asleep and dream about you." A pause. "I would say that I love you. But I know how skittish that makes you. So, good night, Professor, darling."

Babe, huh? As a good feminist, I should object to being called "babe." But "Professor darling" was acceptable. The "I love you" part was quite nice too. It didn't make me nearly as skittish as Quinn thought it did.

I sat down on the chair beside the table and hit the button to replay. It was the last part of Quinn's message that I wanted to hear again. I played his message back three more times to hear that last part again. Definitely nice.

However, it did require thought—as in resolution. I sat there staring down at my feet in their white socks, daydreaming about how the present situation between John Quinn, formerly of Philadelphia, and Lizabeth Stuart, formerly of Drucilla, Kentucky, might be resolved. Not all Yankee carpetbaggers were the same. This one said all he wanted was me.

And I was forgetting George. Neither one of us had eaten dinner yet. I grabbed my shoes and headed toward the bathroom for a five-minute shower. It was too late in the evening for a full meal. If I ate a big meal now, I'd toss and turn all night. So soup tonight, and tomorrow I would heed Doug's nutrition lectures and have a real breakfast. . . .

TUESDAY, MARCH 13, 1:08 A.M.

I jerked up in bed. Moonlight seeped beneath the blinds. But the floor beneath the bed was pitching. The brass handles on the dresser clattered against the wood.

I fumbled for the lamp on the night table, and my hand struck the stand holding the handcrafted ceramic heart that Quinn had given me on Valentine's Day. I grabbed for it as the table moved, but it spun away and onto the floor.

I found the lamp and switched it on.

George stood stiff-legged beside the bed. "George?"

He whimpered. We both held still in place. But nothing else happened.

An earthquake? It couldn't have been an earthquake. We were in Gallagher, Virginia, not L.A. I reached for my robe and threw back the covers.

"Let's go see what that was, George. But first, let me find my heart."

I got down on my hands and knees to feel around on the floor beneath the bed. George nudged me with his head. "Just a minute, boy. Let me . . . oh, no!"

The light from the lamp fell across the ceramic heart and threw in relief the crack that I had felt with my fingers.

"Oh, dammit, George! It's broken." I stood up, cupping the zanily lopsided, multicolored heart in my hands. Now there was a crack down its center.

How was I going to tell Quinn? He had been so pleased that he'd given me a gift that had delighted me.

George butted up against my leg. "All right . . . it's all right, boy. We'll go see what that was all about. There'll be something on the radio."

Clutching the heart in my hands, I started for the door. George followed, hard on my heels.

"It couldn't have been an earthquake," I said. "We don't have earthquakes in the South." George gave an uneasy half-bark in response to my attempt at reassurance.

TUESDAY, MARCH 13, 2:33 A.M.

According to the news bulletin on Channel 13, the quake had been centered over 150 miles away, to the northwest of Gallagher. Close enough to be scary, but not life threatening.

I clicked off the big-screen television that belonged to my globe-trotting landlords. "Let's go back to bed, boy. There's nothing else we can do tonight."

George followed me down the hall so close behind me that I would have trod on him if I had turned. Our 5.1-on-the-Richter-scale tremor had spooked Quinn's dog. It had spooked me too.

"Just when you think life is finally settling down, right, George? Well, first thing tomorrow I need to get to Madeline's Attic and ask her if the person who crafted my heart might be able to repair it." I climbed into bed, but instead of putting the heart back on the night table, I tucked it beneath the opposite pillow. "Thank goodness I have a few days before Quinn comes home. Remind me tomorrow, George, that I need to send him a St. Patrick's Day card."

George had settled down again on the throw rug beside my bed. Quinn had told me not to let his dog get used to sleeping in my bedroom. But George and I had ignored that mandate. He liked my throw rug, and I liked his gentle snuffling sounds.

Especially tonight. Reaching out a hand, I let it rest on the dog's head. He stretched out, preparing to go back to sleep. I hoped I could do the same. If the earth had opened up and swallowed us, I would have been thinking, *I wish, I wish. . . .* Or maybe it would have happened so quickly that I wouldn't even have had that last fleeting moment to feel loss and regret.

CHAPTER · 2

A slobbery tongue swiped across my cheek.

"Okay, okay." I threw up my hand to block a follow-up swipe. "Stop. I'm awake."

George sat back on his haunches, and I reached out and ruffled the fur on his neck. "Even minor earth tremors don't make you sleep in, do they?"

He tugged at the edge of the blanket and let go. Just enough to make his point. Another trick in his repertoire.

Giving up any hope of distracting him, I threw back the covers and swung my feet to the floor. Rubbed at my sleep-sticky eyes and fumbled my toes into my bedroom slippers.

George barked, impatient for me to get up and open the bedroom door. When I did, he ran past me into the hall, in a sprint to the kitchen. I was content to let him win. He stopped by the back door, tail wagging. Squinting my eyes against the sunlight, I unlocked the door and held it open. He bounded down the steps and across the yard, muzzled the dew-damp grass, and shook his head. Then he trotted over to his favorite of the two apple trees and raised his hind leg. That done, he planted both front paws on the tree trunk and barked at the squirrel who was perched on one of the branches. The squirrel glanced down and swished its tail, not at all concerned about a silly dog who couldn't climb trees.

I turned back inside and closed the door. And heard myself humming. A lilting little ditty that kept bubbling up from my throat while I showered and shampooed and dried. That glided my footsteps as I went back down the hall and into the kitchen to make breakfast.

When I went so far as to execute a twirl between sink and stove, that move brought me up short. I had experienced being tentatively, cautiously, almost happy. But giddiness, as in waltzing around the kitchen, was not me, Lizzie Stuart. Giddiness, as Hester Rose, my grandmother, would have said, went before a fall.

Or if he had cared to stroll out of history and into my kitchen, Lord Byron might have informed me that waltzing itself went before a fall. Byron—influenced more perhaps by class snobbery than by prudery—had pronounced the waltz an improper dance. By bringing male and female bodies into such close proximity, the waltz left little mystery for "the nuptial night."

Not that the mystery of the nuptial night was of immediate concern to me.

But breakfast should be. The half-marathon I had signed up for—a walk for diabetes research that I was doing in my grandmother's name—was coming up on Saturday. Four more days of training and workouts. Between now and then, I should focus on taking to heart the lectures that Doug had given me.

Especially since I had also gotten input from another quarter. After planting a zinger of a farewell kiss on me as we were saying good-bye at the Greensboro airport, Quinn had frowned and reminded me to stop for lunch on my way home. "Remember, you need to eat more when you're training," was how he'd put it. A tactful way of saying that he'd noticed that the few curves I did possess were in danger of disappearing.

So now I would have a good, healthy breakfast. I had a recipe I had been wanting to try for spinach soufflé. Add broiled pink grapefruit, turkey bacon, and whole-wheat rolls. And strawberries for dessert. Since I didn't have to be on campus until afternoon—wouldn't have gotten any useful work done even if I'd gone—I might as well have a leisurely meal and then do the errands that needed doing.

"George!"

Leaving the squirrel in the apple tree to get on with its business, Quinn's dog dashed back across the yard. He raced up the steps and shot past me into the kitchen. Breakfast was George's favorite meal. I set his plastic bowl down in front of him. He wagged his tail and bent his head to sniff. Then he dug in.

"The chef accepts your compliments," I said and went back to the preparation of my own breakfast.

I was turning from the oven with the soufflé dish in my mittened hand when Sharon Markas, the Channel 13 morning news anchor, said, "And now we have a really tragic story out of Baltimore. Last night, a 4-year-old child shot his father to death as his pregnant mother looked on in horror."

I did not want to hear about a child shooting his father in front of his pregnant mother. That was not how I wanted to begin my day. I had turned on the television to hear more about the earthquake and to get the weather report. But I was holding a hot soufflé dish, and the remote for the portable TV was on the other counter.

Before I could reach it, Sharon Markas went on with her story. "The father," she said, "the 32-year-old owner of a sporting goods store, had apparently taken the handgun from the locked box in which it was kept, to clean it." Pause. "When his wife, seven months pregnant, returned from the supermarket, he left the gun unattended on the kitchen table while he helped her to unload the car.

Unobserved, their 4-year-old son picked up the gun. As his father came back through the door, the child pulled the trigger." Markas paused again. "We have a portion of the frantic 911 call made by the boy's mother. The child's voice is also audible on this tape."

Then the voices and the scrolling transcript of the 911 call:

"Help me! My husband's been shot. He's bleeding . . . there's so much blood. . . ."

"Ma'am, try to calm down. We'll get help right out to you. I need you to tell me—"

"He's not breathing! He's not breathing!"

"Ma'am—"

"Mommy . . . Mommy . . . what's wrong with Daddy?"

"What did you do? Oh, dear God, help us. What did you do?"

"Mommy, I didn't mean to. . . ."

Sharon Markas came back on the screen. "A tragic story," she said. "And now for the rest of this morning's news. This evening the Gallagher city council will hold a second public hearing on 'Project Renaissance,' the proposal for the development of the downtown riverfront area—"

I pushed the OFF button on the remote and turned back to my breakfast soufflé. It had puffed up high and golden brown. Too bad I had lost my appetite.

Several months ago, a few weeks after Richard Colby was murdered, Quinn and I'd had a conversation about his—Quinn's—gun. Now, standing there by the kitchen counter, staring at my spinach soufflé, I replayed that conversation in my head.

We'd been in the middle of a chess game, a quiet interlude that had seemed the perfect opportunity to bring up the subject. To ask if he always carried his gun. To ask if even then he had a weapon of some sort somewhere on his body, under the bulky sweater he was wearing or strapped to his leg under his blue jeans. There were holsters that allowed people who carried guns to conceal them in various places on their person.

He didn't look up from the chessboard when I fumbled out my question.

"I have one gun," he said. "I wear it in a hip holster when I'm on duty."

"One gun? That would be the gun you were wearing that night at the Halloween party?"

"Yes," he said.

"And when you're not on duty?"

"When I'm not on duty, I don't usually wear it. But I do usually have it with me."

"You do? Now?"

"Yes. Outside in my car."

"And when you're at home? What do you do with it then?"

"I put it in a dresser drawer. Your move."

I glanced down at the chessboard and saw that he had taken my bishop.

"Wouldn't it be safer to lock it away?"

"Yes," he said. "But since I live alone, I don't think that's necessary." He looked up and his silver gaze held mine. "Lizzie, I've been around weapons since I was a kid. I know how to practice gun safety, if that's what you're worried about."

"I'm not worried about anything. I was just wondering. I was on the Internet today looking for sites about frontierswomen in the Old West, and I ended up in a Web site for gun owners. Then I went to this chat room where they were talking about the various ways of 'carrying' and when they carried, and I just wondered—"

"If you were playing chess with a man who's armed and dangerous?"

"Armed," I said. "Not dangerous."

"Well, I'm powerful pleased that you don't consider me a threat, Miz Lizzie."

"Don't. Please, don't do Southern. My ears can't take it."

He laughed and indicated the chessboard. "Still your move, Lizabeth."

Since that conversation, as I adjusted to this "courtship" that John Quinn and I were having, I had been doing my best to push the matter of his gun to the back of my mind. After all, it wasn't as if I ever saw it. He didn't bring it into my house. I never saw it when I was at his house. When he returned from Oklahoma, he would go back to spending his days in his office at the university police department. He did not go out on patrol with a gun strapped to his waist.

And I was certainly not afraid that I would ever be in any danger from him because he had a gun handy. In spite of any psychological trauma he might have experienced because he'd shot a 14-year-old boy and been shot himself or because of the double-whammy ending of his marriage, I knew Quinn was emotionally stable. He might shoot off occasional sparks of half-amused, half-frustrated irritation when he thought I was being impossible, but he was rational and balanced and hardly likely to go off his head and shoot either me or both of us.

So, what—come right down to it—was my problem with his gun? He was a cop. Cops carry guns. Quinn was not the kind of cop who would go out looking for opportunities to shoot people. And he would never be careless enough to leave his gun on a table where a small child could reach it.

Assuming a small child was ever in his house. If his sister, Marielle, and her family came to visit, he would lock his gun away.

So there was no reason for me to create a problem where one didn't exist. No reason to throw up another barrier between us, as he had said I was prone to do. I had been doing a bang-up job of throwing up barriers. True, all of the issues I had raised had deserved discussion and careful thought. But we had reached a point in our relationship when Quinn would be justified in wondering what the hell else I had left to think about or talk about.

I scooped up my broiled grapefruit half and put it into a bowl.

Sometimes—even at the ripe old age of 39—you just had to decide to let it go and grow up. It was way past time that I did that.

"Getting hurt is one of the risks you take when you get involved with another person," I said to the dog, who had been watching me standing there, holding my grapefruit half. "There are no guarantees. And it isn't as if any woman outside of a melodrama ever died of a broken heart because she loved a man and he didn't love her as much. Or because he lost interest and stopped loving her. If that happens . . . well, an intelligent woman realizes that she's better off without that man. And she picks herself up and goes on with her life. Right?"

He barked. "I'm glad you agree with me," I said. "Now that we've gotten that settled, I'm going to sit down and eat my breakfast."

George thumped his tail against the tile floor. More in polite acknowledgment that I had addressed him than because he understood the import of my announcement. But I understood what I had said, and that was sufficient. When John Quinn returned, he was in for a few surprises.

C H A P T E R · 3

I LET GEORGE OUTSIDE again while I washed up my breakfast dishes and did some tidying. Then I changed into one of what Quinn had dubbed my "schoolmarm" dresses. That done, I escorted Quinn's dog down to the basement and provided him with a bowl of fresh water.

I came back upstairs, collected my briefcase, and let myself out the front door. As usual, I glanced across the street at the house that belonged to my neighbor, Mrs. Cavendish. When she was at home, I always complained that she knew my every move. But she was also talkative and funny, and I couldn't help wishing she were there now to poke her head out the door and ask where I was off to.

With Quinn in Oklahoma and Mrs. Cavendish in Florida visiting her daughter, I was feeling a little lonely. Not that I didn't have George for company, and Joyce Fielding and the two or three other faculty friends I'd made at the university. But I seemed to have gotten in the habit of having Quinn and Mrs. Cavendish around.

Quinn would be back in a few days. Between now and then, I had more than enough to do. First, see about getting the ceramic heart he had given me repaired. I was my superstitious grandmother's granddaughter. Cracked heart was not good. So that was at the top of my list. Then, I needed to shop for a dress that was a bit—a lot—sexier than anything I had in my closet. I also needed to buy candles, flowers, and wine, and I needed to decide what to make for dinner.

I took a deep breath as I stood there in the driveway. The morning smelled of spring, even though the calendar hadn't quite reached that point. Humming my giddy waltz tune, I climbed into my beige Focus that should have been cheery blue because I was in a very good mood. I had survived an earthquake, and I was about to claim my man. Luckily, he wanted to be claimed.

The dark gray waters of the Dan River flowed over the dam and fell churning white into the river basin below. The silver bridge supports glistened in the sun. Sunlight also sparkled off the glass windows of the abandoned buildings of the Mercantile Cotton Mill. Months ago the mill had been forced to cut back in order to tighten its fiscal belt. After over 125 years in continuous operation, the company had closed the downtown facility and either transferred the employees uptown to the main facility or laid them off.

The city of Gallagher was hoping that would be the worst of it. The mill was lifeblood to the city's economy.

But the new twist in Gallagher's economic drama was that Howard Knowlin had arrived with his proposal to renovate the abandoned mill buildings and make them the centerpiece in a riverfront complex—"Project Renaissance"— that would include shops, restaurants, and condominium apartments. The city council meeting that Sharon Markas had been talking about on the morning news was another opportunity for the public to comment on the proposal.

The question in everyone's mind was whether this Yankee from Maine would or could do all he promised. Could he lure the residents of Gallagher—particularly faculty and students from the university, who patronized the shops and restaurants along Riverside Drive and in Piedmont Mall—back to a new and improved downtown? Could he fill the office space and the shop space in this complex he was proposing? Would he be able to persuade upscale home-seekers to buy his riverfront condos?

Doug Jenkins, my walking coach, was excited about the project. His agency was handling Knowlin's PR campaign.

The people who remembered Gallagher's once-bustling downtown, and were willing to do whatever it took to bring back those days, were excited about the project too.

But there were also vocal expressions of resentment and dissent.

I headed away from downtown toward upper Main Street. There was a more direct route to the Boulevard Shoppes. I could have taken the uptown bridge. But I enjoyed driving through "Millionaire's Row," the several blocks of Victorian houses on upper Main. Along with the Gothic church that stood adjacent to the city's Civil War museum, the houses were a Gallagher tourist attraction and listed in the historic registry.

Even though I knew firsthand that there was an unattractive—a downright ugly—underside to Gallagher's history, I couldn't deny that the city had a certain appeal.

The forest-green pickup truck and I came from opposite directions. We were both headed for the same parking place, the last remaining unreserved slot in front of the plaza. The driver of the pickup stopped. I stopped too. Then he waved me in with an impatient hand.

Not above accepting his chivalry, I waved back a thank-you.

So much for being a good feminist. Oh, well. Next time, I would yield to a male driver.

I reached for my shoulder bag and the damaged ceramic heart that I was taking to Madeline Oliver. As I got out of my car, I heard the argument that was taking place a few spaces down. A woman's voice soared upward in anger, "Are you blind?"

The man in the pickup truck had parked in one of the four handicapped-parking spaces. A woman with straggly white hair confronted him. She was clad in a pink jogging suit and black loafers, and she clutched a large paper cup from Tasty Freeze in one hand and a rolled newspaper in the other. "Can't you read that sign?" she said. "You're not supposed to park there. You aren't handicapped."

The man—dressed in worn blue jeans and a black cotton shirt, long sleeves pushed up on his muscular arms—listened to her rant. His face revealed nothing, but his hands were anchored to his belt, clenched on the turquoise-studded silver belt buckle. He was no more than an inch or two taller than her five-eight or five-nine. But his stillness should have given her second thoughts about pushing him too far.

Her voice took on a sing-song quality. "My father had bad lungs, and he couldn't breathe when he had to walk. He would turn red in the face, and he couldn't breathe. He's dead now." She shook her newspaper. "That parking place is reserved for the handicapped."

The man looked back at her. His eyes were as dark as his thick head of hair. Not young, not old. A brooding air about him. A miscast Hamlet to her withered and loony Ophelia in this little drama.

"I know who this parking space is reserved for," he said, his voice a low rumble. "I put the damn signs up. But I don't have the time—and I'm damn well not in the mood—to circle this lot looking for a place to park. In fact, old woman, I am in one hell of a foul mood right now. And since I happen to own this piece of property"—he gestured toward the arcade containing the Boulevard Shoppes—"I will park my truck wherever I damn well please."

With that, he turned and strode away, leaving her sputtering.

I tried to ease by behind her as she mumbled to herself. But she turned and saw me and glared. "People who can walk should think about people who can't."

"Yes. I'm sorry about your father."

She lowered her chin, and tears appeared in her washed-out blue eyes. "He's dead now. I have no one else."

I reached out and touched her arm. It was bony beneath the pink jacket. "I'm sorry," I said. And I walked away too, fleeing her pain.

The rocking chair in Madeline's Attic was not one that would have been discarded among dusty boxes and forgotten toys. It was an elegant curve of gleaming oak. A heavy silk shawl was draped over an arm of the chair to show both items to best effect. An antique doll in blue velvet riding habit stood on a lady's writing desk nearby. A white porcelain bowl and pitcher graced a washstand decorated with hand-painted flowers.

Nostalgic, romantic. The shop also ran to the slightly naughty and unexpected. I turned for a second look at the mannequin. Wearing a shoulder-length blonde wig and a smile, she perched on the edge of an armchair, her black lace Victorian corset visible under her loosely draped black silk robe.

Who on earth would buy her? Or maybe only the corset and robe were for sale.

There was a book on display on the table at the mannequin's elbow. *The Bordello Cookbook: Food With Passion.*

I did need to come up with a menu for my romantic dinner with Quinn. Listening with one ear as Madeline eased her customer toward the door, I picked up the book and began to flip through it. It was a social history of turn-of-the-century "businesswomen"—upscale madams—and their ladies, who had catered to assorted male clientele in mansions staffed with chefs, who'd prepared recipes similar to those featured in the book.

I'd have to hide the book from Quinn, or he'd never let me live it down. But some of the recipes looked like they might work for our dinner. Oyster stew. Brandy Alexander pie.

Or I could opt for the Southern fried chicken served by a Dixie madam.

This book might also provide some useful material for my class on crime and culture. Now, if Madeline could help me get my heart repaired, I'd be all set.

I tucked the book under my arm. As I turned, I saw the teddy bear. Clad in a fedora and trench coat, he was perched on a rolltop desk beside a display of paperback detective novels in plastic jackets.

I was holding the teddy bear when Madeline Oliver finally got the woman she was trying to get rid of out the door and turned her attention to me.

"One hundred and seventy-five dollars?" I said, pointing at the teddy bear's price tag.

"His fur is cashmere," Madeline said, her silky voice amused. "He's a collector's item. An investment."

"He would have to be," I said, trying not to visibly hold my breath. Garlic.

She laughed, her eyes crinkling at the corners. "I know," she said. "Sorry about that. I've been so busy today I had to eat a salad at my desk. Hold on just a minute and let me get a stick of gum."

Her rose silk broom skirt fluttered around her ankle boots as she turned back to her old-fashioned counter, which featured a display of lace collars. A computerized cash register sat beside the collars.

As she fished for the gum and popped a piece into her mouth, Madeline said, "That woman who was just in here must have been about ready to fall over. But she was so snooty, it served her right. She had the attitude that she was 'Miz It' and I was supposed to have what she wanted waiting for her to buy. And at the price she wanted to pay, mind you." Madeline held the pack of gum out to me. "Just being polite. You don't want this. It tastes awful. But it's the only thing strong enough to overwhelm garlic." Her full-lipped smile flashed. "And I do love garlic. Lately, I've been craving Caesar salads. Between that and the shrimp scampi, my honey Doug can barely stand to be around me after dinner. He has to hold his nose to kiss me."

I returned her smile. "I'm sure he manages."

"Well, you know it's true, he does. It's so nice to see you again, Lizzie. What can I do for you?"

"I'm surprised you remember me," I said.

Or maybe I wasn't. People did these days. But our actual meeting had been the briefest of encounters when she and Doug passed Quinn and me—one couple leaving, the other arriving—in a crowded restaurant foyer. Introductions tossed at each other with smiles and waves. That had been almost three months ago, just after I started to train with the other walkers.

"I do have a good memory for faces and names," Madeline said. "And if I'd forgotten, I would have been reminded when that good-looking man of yours came in here shopping for your Valentine's Day gift. He kept mumbling your name whenever he stopped to look at something, like he was conjuring you up to tell him if you'd like it. At one point, he said right out loud, 'Dammit, Lizzie, what am I going to get you?'"

I laughed. "He says 'dammit, Lizzie' a lot."

"But he was feeling a little frustrated at that point. It took him a while to settle on what he wanted, once he got here. He said he'd already been to four other stores."

Sorry about that, Quinn. But it had taken me a while, too. Shopping for a Valentine's Day gift was no easy task.

Madeline picked up the teddy bear. "This fine fellow here was his original choice."

"Until he saw the price tag?" I said.

"No, he'd already seen that." Her eyes crinkled again. "He was sighing with relief and handing it to me to ring up, when I made the mistake of remarking that he and the teddy bear had the same rakish smile."

"And what did he say?" I asked, imagining Quinn's reaction to that observation.

"He flushed scarlet and put the teddy bear right down. He mumbled something about it being 'too cutesy.' So he was even more relieved when he turned around and saw that heart that he bought for you." Madeline tilted her head. "For your information . . . so you'll know he's not a cheapskate . . . the heart cost more than the teddy bear."

"More?" I said, thinking of that crack. "More than $175?"

"Yes, ma'am. Considerably more. RaeAnne—the artist who designed it— has started to make a reputation for herself. She was working for a jewelry designer, but he closed down. Since then, she's been venturing into other forms. In fact, I've been trying to talk her into doing an exhibition of her work as soon as I move out of here into a larger space." Madeline wrinkled her nose. "But that's another story. What I was getting at, is that RaeAnne makes one-of-a-kind ceramic pieces. With a sense of endearing whimsy."

She said that last phrase with a grin.

"Oh," I said. "Well, I'm afraid I have a slight problem."

Madeline glanced at the tissue-wrapped object that I'd picked up from the table. "Don't tell me that you're returning it."

I shook my head. "The earthquake last night. It fell off the table." I pulled back the tissue paper to show her the crack. "Do you think RaeAnne could repair it?"

Madeline ran her rose-tipped fingernail along the fissure in the ceramic. "She probably could. The shape and the surface itself is uneven and irregular enough so that some patchwork wouldn't be obvious. But the problem is, catching up with her."

"Catching up? You mean, she's so busy that she—"

"I mean, I haven't been able to reach her in the past three or four days," Madeline said. "She hasn't returned my calls. And I've got customers who want more of her work. Two women from Greensboro made a special trip just to see if I had anything of RaeAnne's in." Madeline fluffed her fingers through her dark, wavy hair, lifting it up from her neck. "I had to tell them no. And I do hate sending people out of my shop empty-handed."

I laughed. "What about the snooty woman who was in here when I arrived?"

"Now, with her, I was pleased to make an exception. She was rude and abrasive, and I had no desire to have her ever come in here again. But these two women from Greensboro are good customers. The kind that tell their friends about me. I like that."

She was smiling as if she meant what she said. Madeline might look and sound like an old-money Southern belle, but she wasn't afraid of a little garlic. Or of revealing her enjoyment of hearing her cash register ring. Which probably went some of the way toward explaining how she and Doug had come to be together. She liked business. He liked business. And they both did it with charm.

"If you want to leave the heart with me—" Madeline started to say.

"Charlotte, I need to be getting back to my office," said a male voice, strong but with a slight quiver of age. The legs of two people appeared on the open stairs coming down from the loft. "If you haven't found anything yet—"

"Good lord, man, I found what I wanted two minutes after we walked in," the woman said. "I just wanted to have a look and see what else Madeline had in her inventory."

"You mean you've been wasting all this time looking?" the man said. "We've been here over an hour."

"I told you yesterday morning when I called that I would need you to escort me this afternoon. I don't know where your mind is these days, Jebediah."

"My mind is right where it's always been. But I need to get back to my office. Abigail wanted me to be there when she got back from the courthouse."

I glanced at Madeline. She shook her head. "My father and his favorite client," she said. "They enjoy entertaining listeners with their little squabbles."

Charlotte was saying, "You left Abigail a message telling her where you'd be."

"I know I did, but I still don't want to be gone too long. That new secretary Abigail hired . . . she's still learning what she's supposed to do."

"Then being there alone should help her learn faster," Charlotte said as they came around the corner and into full view. "What I'm going to buy is in the back. But let me have another look at these first." She swung to her left, her wide-brimmed, black hat forcing him to duck his bald head.

"Charlotte, why the devil are you looking at baby spoons? You said you were buying a wedding gift. Is the bride with child?"

"Of course not. The bride is my goddaughter."

"What does that have to do with it?"

"Good lord, man, stop fidgeting." She turned from the display of silver baby spoons and gave him the full force of her stare. "If you can't trust this new girl Abigail hired to mind your office, then I suggest you fire her."

"If you would get whatever it is you're going to buy, I could get back to—"

"You're my lawyer, Jebediah. I pay you good money for your time. I expect you to make yourself available when I need you, and not spend the afternoon whining about having to accompany me."

"Charlotte, if this is your way of making me dance to your tune until you decide what you're going to do about that house, I'll tell you right here and now that I've—"

"We'll discuss the matter of the house when I reach a decision. In the meantime, I will go make my purchase. Then you may escort me to my car and return to whatever it is that requires your urgent attention at your office."

"Charlotte, you know I don't mind escorting you on these shopping trips. It's just that today . . . I told you what's been happening—"

"And it will not help matters to sit in your office and brood about it," she said and steered him toward the rear of the shop.

Madeline said, "I pay those two to stroll through and entertain my customers. As I was saying, Lizzie, if you'd like to leave the heart here, I'll try to reach RaeAnne about it."

"Thank you, I'd really appreciate that," I said. "Quinn is out of town for the next few days, and I was hoping to have it repaired before he gets back."

Madeline reached for a pad. "So this is an emergency. Let me get your contact information."

I gave her my home and office numbers as well as my E-mail address.

Madeline's father, a tall man with a slight stoop to his shoulders, and his client, a large woman who had that look that I always associated with the "horsey set," were returning from the rear of the shop. He was carrying a silver tea pot.

As they came closer, the woman's glance fastened on me. I saw recognition and felt a tingle of unease along my spine.

"And I'll take this cookbook," I said, turning back to Madeline.

Madeline smiled. "Guaranteed to add a dash of spice to your love life."

The shop door banged open. A petite, flame-haired woman sailed down the aisle. She flung her attaché case from her shoulder to Madeline's countertop. Spots of color flared along her creamy cheekbones. "I have had it this day," she said, "with people who do not listen to what I say. Do you hear me? I have had it."

Madeline accepted the cash I was holding out and said, "I don't know what your problem might be, Abigail Sims, but I would appreciate it if you would—"

Abigail planted her hands on her hips beneath her boxy jacket. "I would appreciate it, Cousin Madeline, if you would kindly endeavor not to sound like my mama. I don't have one, and I don't need one."

"Madeline. Abigail. Don't fuss," Madeline's father said as he and Charlotte reached the counter.

"Uncle Jeb," Abigail said. "I asked you to be at the office when I came back so that we could discuss. . . ." Her glance flickered from Charlotte to me before she continued, ". . . the case."

Jebediah said, "It's all right, honey. I've told Charlotte about it." His watery blue gaze touched me. "Of course, I expect this young woman would rather not hear—"

Charlotte's booming voice overpowered his. "I told your uncle that I think it's outrageous. Sloane Campbell's behind this. The man worked for him. Any fool would know Campbell's behind this ridiculous lawsuit."

"I'm not a fool, Charlotte," Abigail said. "But I happen to think it would be an awfully roundabout way to go about getting this revenge Uncle Jeb believes Sloane Campbell wants."

"It's not roundabout," her uncle said. "He wants to humiliate me before my peers."

Abigail sighed. "We've been all through this, Uncle Jeb."

"I know you think I'm a doddering old fool," he said.

"No, Uncle Jeb, I do not think that. But we have to decide what to do. And you need to talk to the insurance company lawyer."

"Outrageous," Charlotte said. "Suing an attorney because he was too busy to file some paperwork before a deadline."

Abigail drew a breath. "It's called malpractice," she said. "And this public discussion—" She looked in my direction again.

This time her glance lingered, became a frozen stare. I could have sworn she paled.

"I know you," she said. "You're that crime historian. The one who was involved in the murder case last year. The one who was poking into the Mose Davenport lynching." Her hand went to the crisp cravat at her throat. "If you're here because you—" She shot a glance at Jebediah. "If you're here because of my uncle, you may as well forget about it. We won't—"

A piercing whistle drew our eyes to Madeline.

"All right, that's enough," she said, directing her words at Abigail. "This is a place of business. Lizzie is a friend of Doug's, and she's here as my customer. I want you and my father to take this discussion about your lawsuit back to your law offices." She turned to me, handing me my change and the bag containing my cookbook. "Lizzie, I do apologize for my family's ill-mannered—"

"That's all right," I said. "We've finished anyway." I slid past Abigail. "Please excuse me, everyone. Madeline, I'll check back with you about RaeAnne."

"I'll let you know if I hear anything," Madeline said.

When I had put some distance between myself and the shop, I slowed down. Well, that had been strange, hadn't it? Go into a shop to get a ceramic heart repaired and get practically branded as a—what?

During the four months since Richard Colby's murder—especially those first few weeks—I had been recognized on occasion from my photograph in the *Gallagher Gazette* or my face seen on the local news. People had reacted with curiosity. They had pelted me with questions, wanting the "real story." On occasion, they had even asked intrusive questions about my private life.

But no one had ever reacted in the way Abigail had when she recognized me. Not with alarm. That was the emotion I had felt from her. First, alarm. Then confusion, and then a rush to arms.

I sat down on a bench facing the waterfall in the center of the plaza. From there I had a clear view of that end of the arcade, and could take off running if I saw Abigail coming in my direction.

Why on earth would she have thought that I was in Madeline's shop because of her uncle? Because of Madeline's father? I had never even heard of the man.

Or, rather, I didn't think I had. The name Jebediah was distinctive enough to be memorable.

He was a lawyer and he was being sued by someone. But why would that be of interest to me? And how did Sloane Campbell fit into it? That name I knew. Campbell was the local real estate developer. The one whose proposal had gotten tabled after Howard Knowlin arrived.

Oh, my gosh. Campbell owned the Boulevard Shoppes. This shopping plaza. It had been listed among his holdings in an article in the *Gazette*. That meant that the man in the green pickup truck had been him—he.

I sat there a few minutes longer trying to unravel the connections. Madeline Oliver, whose boyfriend, Doug Jenkins, was a PR man for Howard Knowlin, had her shop in a plaza that Campbell owned. Madeline's father thought the real estate developer was plotting against him.

And I had just stumbled into a minefield in the form of Abigail Sims, who thought I was up to something involving her uncle.

And then there was Charlotte—Madeline's father's client—who had looked as if she recognized me and was about to say something about it when Abigail swept through the door.

I watched the water gush over the miniature dam and into the pool below. Then fishing a quarter from my purse, I got up and flung it toward the waterfall. It landed among other coins. I would have to remember to look up that custom. Find out why people thought tossing coins into water would bring good luck.

I was turning away when I thought of something else. I fished another quarter from my change purse. I needed to amend my request.

"Make that love, happiness, and no nasty little catch-22s that I forgot to cover in that first wish," I said and tossed the coin.

I was superstitious, and I had recently accepted that fact. I had learned at my grandmother's knee to be wary of black cats who crossed my path and doves who cooed at midnight. Add to that the fact that I had seen more than my share of *Twilight Zone* episodes. Well-trained, rational social scientist, yes. But I still couldn't escape my deep-rooted belief that there was no harm in covering my bases.

As in the case of the cracked heart. So I hoped Madeline would manage to reach her elusive artist before Quinn returned. I made a mental note to call Madeline the next day and find out RaeAnne's last name and ask if I could try to reach her too. Maybe between the two of us, we'd be able to catch up with her.

The woman in the pink jogging suit had gotten the last word. The creamy, thick contents of her Tasty Freeze cup—apparently a vanilla milk shake—had been deposited on the windshield of Sloane Campbell's pickup truck. Now he was the one mumbling to himself as he surveyed the mess.

He glanced up as I approached. His deep-set, dark eyes narrowed. "Here she is," he said. "The woman I gave my parking space to. You know this is your fault." But he looked more amused than angry. He was obviously in a much better mood than he'd been in when he arrived.

I paused to look at the cleaning job before him. "Well, she did tell you not to park there, Mr. Campbell."

"You know who I am, do you?"

"I figured it out," I said, not considering it prudent to mention the discussion about him that had taken place in Madeline's shop.

He shook his head. "That old bat sure enough fixed me for being an arrogant jerk."

"Looks like it," I said. "Bye, now."

"Bye to you, too," he said. "And, please, don't even think about offering to help me clean this mess up."

I turned and gave him a big smile. "No, I certainly wouldn't think of doing that. I know you'd rather do it yourself."

He mumbled something that I probably didn't want to hear. I tried not to laugh until I was inside my car. That wasn't nice of me, considering he had been gallant enough to let me have the parking space. Of course, I was a customer in his plaza.

And why did Madeline's father think Campbell wanted revenge? Because Madeline's boyfriend Doug worked for Howard Knowlin? But that wouldn't explain why Jebediah would think he was the person that Campbell was out to get.

Definitely an interesting situation. Maybe I could find a way to ask Doug about it without appearing to be too nosy. Of course, given the way Abigail had looked at me—like I was a reporter from *Dateline* who had just turned up on her doorstep with my camera crew—I was entitled to some explanation.

The light changed, and I turned out of the parking lot of the Boulevard Shoppes.

There was something else about what had just happened. An objective witness might have said that I'd stopped one step short of flirting with Sloane Campbell. Interesting, because I'd never been comfortable doing or saying anything that an attractive male stranger might construe as an acknowledgment that I'd noticed he was male. What if he displayed interest in return? Good grief, what would I do?

But obviously, now that I had Quinn, I wasn't quite as worried about that anymore. I could simply say, "Sorry, I'm already involved."

Not that Campbell had given any indication that he was about to ask me out for a night on the town. But still, it was a revelation about how I was beginning to feel about myself as a woman. I had felt confident enough to be playful, and that was good. Definite progress, Dr. Cage would have said. Coming out of my cocoon, as he would have put it.

Except for his bald pate—shaved in his case—Dr. Cage bore no resemblance at all to Sigmund Freud. He was rust brown and broad shouldered, and his approach to therapy was summed up in what he had said to me at the end of our first session: "So all that happened, huh? Bummer. So now what are you going to do?"

Caught by surprise by his unsympathetic tone, I had stopped crying. He made a face. I laughed in spite of myself, and he handed me a bubble gum lollipop from the bowl on his desk. At the end of our seventh and final session, three weeks ago, he had said, "You aren't even halfway crazy. You aren't even neurotic enough to be any fun. Frankly, you're starting to bore me. I don't want to listen to you talk about your childhood anymore. And the Richard Colby thing is getting as old as the Cornwall thing. So unless you can prove to me that you're some kind of angel of death, I don't think we have anything else to talk about. Unless, of course, your relationship with the white cop heats up enough to get past its present PG rating." He stood up and gave me the Vulcan salute, one Trekkie to another. "Live long and prosper, Lizzie Stuart—and call me if you ever really manage to make yourself nutty."

Dr. Cage was not your usual therapist. I laughed every time I thought about him. I owed Pam Robinson, my friend over in African-American Studies, big time for recommending him.

And I was not going to let a chance encounter with Abigail Sims and company ruin my day. I pressed the SCAN button and ran through radio stations until I found one playing Otis Redding's "The Dock of the Bay." I sung along as I headed back down Main Street to do my other errands.

C H A P T E R · 4

"IS HE BUSY?" I asked, nodding at Amos Baylor's closed door.

"In a meeting," Amos's secretary, Greta, said. "He's got two administrators in there with him, talking about his budget request for the school."

I glanced again at the closed door. "Doesn't he usually go to their offices?"

"Usually," she said. "But Amos and the other deans wanted the provost and the assistant provost to come over here to Brewster Hall. They wanted them to see what we've been complaining about . . . including the fact nobody has enough room to swing a chicken." Greta tugged at a dead leaf on the plant on her desk. "You took the last office on this floor when you arrived. And now that Richard's office has been reassigned to the adjuncts. . . . Are you going to keep your office, by the way?"

"Keep it?" I said, pretending not to understand her question.

Gossip was Greta's middle name. Not malicious gossip. Simply the dispensation of all available information, including rumor. I wanted to tell Amos that I'd decided to accept his offer to join the faculty on a permanent basis before everyone else in the school heard about it.

Greta nodded her curled-gray head. "So you still haven't decided. You know you need to make up your mind soon."

"I know," I said. "Would you tell Amos that I'd like to speak to him when he's free?"

"That meeting in there could go on for a while. Better make an appointment for tomorrow morning. I'll put you down for eleven." She paused with her hand hovering over Amos's schedule. Her eyes behind her wire-rim glasses held a hint of cheerful devilment. "But that's too early for you, isn't it? Want to make if for after lunch?"

"No, eleven o'clock should be fine," I said. I was capable of being in the office and functional before noon, in spite of my reputation to the contrary.

I left Greta plucking another dead leaf from her plant. I headed to my office. When I turned the corner, I saw Keisha McIntyre sitting on the carpeted floor in front of my door. Her head was down on arms that rested on her raised knees.

She looked small and shrunken in her blue jeans and black leather vest. Even her wildly curly retro-Afro looked less militant than usual.

"Keisha? What's wrong?"

She scrambled to her feet. "Hi, Dr. Stuart. Could I talk to you for a minute?"

"Sure, come on in."

I stifled a groan when I saw the balled-up manuscript pages I'd left scattered across my desk. Not to mention an empty water bottle, protein bar wrapper, and the paper clips I'd spilled as I jumped up to race to my workout at the gym the night before.

"Excuse the mess," I said. I scooped up the bottle and wrapper and tossed them into the waste basket. Then I sat down behind my desk and glanced over at Keisha. She had curled up in my blue vinyl armchair. Head down, eyes closed, as if she were gathering her strength. She looked even more pathetic than she had out in the hall.

With any other student, my "Look out!" antenna would have been up and waving. But Keisha, who was still only BA/MA, was a better student than some of the regular MA students—even some of the first-year Ph.D. students—in my "Crime and American Culture" seminar. She did the readings before class. She thought about them, she dissected them. She didn't just contribute to classroom discussion, she sparked it with her questions and challenges to the other students'—and my own—mind-sets.

She also had been one of the students who had spearheaded the petition to Amos Baylor, dean of the School of Criminal Justice, to insist that he offer me a permanent appointment. Not that the matter hadn't come up when I'd first arrived, but after Richard's murder and my involvement, Amos had been gun-shy where I was concerned. He might have been happy to see me pack my bags and go away at the end of spring semester. But the student petition had helped to prod him in the other direction.

Between that and her classroom performance, Keisha was one of my favorite students.

That meant I needed to be careful not to give her favored treatment. I folded my hands on my desk. "You wanted to talk to me, Keisha?"

She looked up then, her brown eyes red-rimmed. "I've got a mess going on, Dr. Stuart. I'm not going to be able to get the outline for my research paper done in time for class tomorrow night."

Good grief, is that what all this fuss is about? The due date for the outline was only a marker intended to keep the students in the seminar on track toward completing their research papers. It wasn't that important. I was about to tell Keisha not to worry about it, when I realized how tensely she was waiting for my reply.

Her outline was going to be late, yes. But she wanted to tell someone about the mess she had going on, too. I had been elected.

This was the part of teaching I really hated. I had trouble keeping my own life in order. I had neither the warm and nurturing personality nor the training that would equip me to advise students about their lives. Of course, I could always refer Keisha to the counseling center.

But first, see what the problem was. I only hoped it wasn't something that would stop her dead in her academic career. She was too good for that.

"Do you think," I said, "you'll be able to get your outline to me by Thursday afternoon?"

"I don't know, Dr. Stuart, it's a real mess." Keisha leaned forward in the chair and licked at her lips. Lips that were missing their usual burgundy lipstick. "See, I had to move out of my apartment. My roommate's been making me crazy. She kept bringing these guys home . . . guys she'd just met. It got so I couldn't even come out of my bedroom at night without stumbling over one of them. And I seriously can't stand not being able to move around. I get claustrophobia. So we got into it about the guys and the other stuff she's got going on that I don't want any part of. I ended up telling her I was moving out."

I said, "Sometimes in the heat of an argument . . . but if you really can't get along—"

"See, I didn't know her that well when we moved in together this semester. But my roommate in the dorm decided that she wasn't going to come back after Christmas. I didn't like living in that building anyway. So when this girl told me she had a spare bedroom. . . ." Keisha licked her lips again and rubbed at her chin. "But I had to beg and plead with my parents to let me do it. They came down and looked at the apartment and everything. And now it's only been two and a half months, and here I am having to leave."

"Where are you staying right now?" I asked.

"That's the other part of the mess. See, I moved in with Marcus, my boyfriend, a couple of days ago. But I can't stay there long because my pops . . . my father . . . well, he would blow a gasket if he found out. I mean, not that I'm not old enough to live anywhere I want to. I *am* over twenty-one. But my parents . . . you know how parents are. I try to do what they. . . . They're working hard to send me to school . . . the scholarship doesn't cover everything."

"I know," I said. "I had a scholarship when I was an undergrad. So you're staying with Marcus—"

"But I've got to find someplace else." A smile curved her lips. "I'd have to, anyway. Marcus and me would be past tense if we tried living together long. The man sits there on his sofa at one in the a.m. watching this video he has of an autopsy."

"I suppose if he's studying premed—"

"Yeah, but, Dr. Stuart, I mean the man is crazy about 'ER.' He mumbles 'stat' in his sleep." Her moment of lightheartedness passed as quickly as it had come. "Anyway, that's the mess I got. And, see, I'd still be able to do my outline, except I left my notes back at my old apartment, and I can't get in there to get them until I know my roommate's gone out."

"She won't let you back into the apartment?" I said.

"She'd let me back in. But then we'd get into it again about me walking out and leaving her with the rent. I don't feel like getting into another argument, so I just want to wait until she's not there. She has a class tomorrow afternoon, one that she actually goes to 'cause she thinks the prof is cool. She keeps coming on to him, hoping he'll give her some time. So she'll definitely be gone tomorrow afternoon. Then I can go back in and get my notes. But I still won't be able to get my outline done before our class at 4:15."

"Okay," I said. "So let's shoot for Friday morning. Leave it in my mailbox. How's that?"

"That's great, Dr. Stuart." Keisha scrambled up from the armchair and grabbed up the knapsack she had deposited on the floor. "I'll have it to you, I promise. Thank you. I knew you'd understand."

"Keisha, do you think you'll have trouble finding another apartment? Maybe if you check with university housing—"

"Yeah. Well, I've got a couple of leads." Her face brightened. "And I got that job. Remember the one I was telling you about. As an intern for that independent filmmaker. It doesn't pay much, but—"

"But you'll get experience, and that's the important thing."

"That's what I was trying to explain to Marcus. He thinks I'm being frivolous because I'm interested in media. I keep trying to explain to him how powerful the media are and that we as people of color need to be making more films and getting ourselves into decision-making positions in newsrooms. . . ."

I nodded. Keisha's ambition was to be a combination Oprah, Ted Koppel, and Spike Lee, bringing media savvy to bear on criminal-justice issues. She just might pull it off too.

". . . but Marcus is so on this medical stuff, he can't see that," she said, winding down. "Anyway, I got to go, Dr. Stuart. See you tomorrow in class."

"Good luck with the apartment hunting."

She turned in the doorway. She looked at me, and then sent a darting glance around my office.

"Keisha, is there—"

"Thank you, Dr. Stuart. I promise I'll get my outline in by Friday," she said.

And then she was gone. I stared at my closed door. I was her professor, not her mother. She had come to me with a problem related to class, and we had dealt with it. I was not paid to pry into students' personal lives.

Picking up one of the crumpled balls of manuscript on my desk, I smoothed it out to make sure I really wanted to discard it.

Keisha had Marcus, who, on the couple of occasions I'd met him, had seemed to be a solid, if somewhat reserved, young man. And she had her parents, who were probably going to become aware of her living arrangements a lot sooner than she would like. Then they would step in to help her straighten everything out, including the irate roommate. Keisha would be fine.

Except I wasn't thrilled about that look she'd given me from the doorway. As if there had been something else she'd wanted to say. But looking at me and looking at my office, she hadn't been sure that I really would understand. Did my students think of me as prim and proper?

Well, if Quinn did, why wouldn't they?

Thinking of Quinn, I pulled a yellow legal pad toward me. I wrote "day spa" and circled the words. Did I have time to go in for a manicure and massage and facial and the total body treatment before he got back? I'd never had a pedicure. That would be fun.

Joyce Fielding stuck her streaked-blonde head around the door of the faculty lounge. "I thought I saw you headed this way," she said.

I took my mug of hot water out of the microwave and dropped in an herbal tea bag. "Come in and talk to me. I'm celebrating. I've actually managed to produce two whole pages of possibly readable prose in the past three hours."

"Congratulations," Joyce said. "Isn't it lucky that I have just what we need to celebrate?"

"What?" I said, trying to get a glimpse of what she was holding in the hand she had behind her back.

She held her arm aloft, displaying a bag I recognized. A bag from my favorite bakery. "Double-fudge-walnut brownies with mocha chocolate icing," Joyce said. "Baked less than an hour ago. Two for each of us."

I sighed, sniffing the air as she walked toward me. "Have I ever told you how much I value you as a friend and colleague?"

Joyce smiled. "Maybe you shouldn't do this. You did say you were going to be good until the marathon was over."

"I lied. Bring them here."

I was licking the mocha chocolate icing from my fingers and wondering if I'd be sick if I finished the last bite of my second brownie, when I noticed that Joyce still had a whole brownie left.

"So you were only leading me into decadence and excess?" I said. "You're going to practice discipline and restraint?"

"Huh?" she said, looking up from her coffee mug.

"Hey, are you okay?" I said, realizing for the first time how quiet she'd been while I rambled on about Keisha's apartment problem.

"Fine," she said. "Or maybe not. He doesn't know yet."

I reached for the paper towel I was using as a napkin. "Who doesn't know yet?"

"My doctor. He says I need to have a biopsy. I went in for my mammogram and . . . he says it could be nothing. But I've got to go in and make sure." She sat back in her chair and gazed down at her generous bosom in the turquoise silk blouse. "I'd hate to lose one of these guys. We've been together since I was twelve."

"You aren't going to . . . it's just a biopsy," I said. "Have you told Pete?"

Joyce smiled. "Pete and I don't have that kind of relationship."

"What do you mean you don't. . . ?" She and Pete Murphy, another criminal justice faculty member, had been involved for at least six months. "You mean you aren't going to tell him?"

"I mean he's not the first person it occurred to me to tell," Joyce said. "I thought of calling my mother. But she lives in Oregon. And it would have taken me at least an hour, at daytime long-distance rates, to calm her down and get her through her hysterics. So it just seemed easier to stop and buy some brownies. Then I thought about telling you. You don't do hysterics."

Oh, but I did. She'd never seen my private floor show when there was no one in the room but me. But that aside, there were three other women on faculty. Joyce had known them all much longer than she had known me. I wanted to say, *Why me?*

Then I saw the tears welling up in her eyes and the way her hand was clenched on the handle of her mug. "What can I do?" I said. "Tell me what I can do."

Joyce swiped at her eyes. "Split this brownie with me. We can't let it go to waste."

I reached over and broke the brownie in half. "So when is the biopsy?"

"Next week. Monday. I thought it would be the perfect way to spend spring break."

"Want to have lunch this Thursday? Seafood linguine at the Olive Tree?"

"You're on," Joyce said. "After lunch, let's play hooky and go to a matinee."

I thought for one fleeting moment of how much work I still had to do on my manuscript—my manuscript that had bogged down and was resisting all of my efforts to make sense of a murder and a lynching in Gallagher in 1921.

But one more afternoon wasn't going to make any difference. And there was something in the manual about when your friend was about to go in for a biopsy, something about doing anything she damn well wanted to do.

"I'll spring for the popcorn and Raisinets," I said.

On my fourth circuit around the track, I broke into a run. It was not a part of my prescribed training program for the half-marathon I was supposed to walk on Saturday. In fact, since my left knee tended to stiffen up when I ran—premature old age creeping in—running was not a bright idea. But I felt like running.

I picked up my pace and loped past the out-of-season football player who was moving in a lackadaisical jog. I ran until I had a stitch in my side. I slowed down and drank water and walked another lap to cool off. Then I headed inside to take a shower and change.

It was after seven, and the university recreation center was packed to the max. Students, faculty, alumni with membership cards. The rec center was state-of-the-art, and anyone who could find a way to gain privileges did. Through the glass, I watched a woman make a clumsy dive into the pool. But she made up for it with the grace and strength of her strokes as she sliced through the water. One of these days—when I overcame my fear of putting my head underwater— I was going to learn to swim. Maybe I'd sign up for the summer "swimming for scaredy-cats" class.

"Lizzie! Hi, I thought that was you."

I turned to find Doug Jenkins standing in the exercise-room doorway.

He rubbed his towel over the expanse of forehead and scalp left bare by soft, curling brown hair that had retreated to the rear. But he had lively brown eyes and a mustache that flowed into a precisely clipped beard, forming an arch around a strong mouth. The pleasant cast of his features and his eyes gave him an alert, ready-to-get-going, let's-take-off-our-jackets-and-do-this look, even when he was just standing there smiling.

That was attractive. So was his long-torsoed, narrow-waisted body that at the moment was shown to good advantage in his shorts and T-shirt.

Not that I was interested. I was simply noting what else—other than their shared commitment to doing business with charm—might have drawn a woman like Madeline to him.

Doug waved his hand. "Hey, in there."

I hadn't returned his greeting. I had been standing there staring at him. Sometimes I could sell grazing rights in my head. Invite campers in to pitch their tents.

"Hey, Doug!" I said. "Forgive me, I was wool-gathering."

He nodded at my soggy T-shirt. "But I see you've gotten in a good workout. Your coach approves."

He looked a little tired. Maybe he had overdone his own workout.

"And who is this lovely lady?" a voice, pure New England, said behind me.

I turned around. I had seen the man's face in the *Gallagher Gazette*. A bony, weathered face that went with the voice. This was Howard Knowlin, the real estate developer from Maine who was spearheading "Project Renaissance." Doug's public-relations client. That explained his presence in the university rec center. Doug was alumni and could bring a guest.

Knowlin looked as if he had gotten in a good workout too. But where my sweat-soaked T-shirt said TEACHERS KNOW THEIR LESSONS, his said HARVARD. He was using the white towel around his neck to pat his damp face.

"Howard, how'd the weight lifting go?" Doug said. Obviously a question intended only to acknowledge his client's manly vigor, because he moved into introductions without waiting for an answer. "Lizzie, may I present Howard

Knowlin. Howard, this is Dr. Lizzie Stuart. Lizzie's a visiting professor in the School of Criminal Justice this year, but we're trying to persuade her to stay on with us."

"How do you do, Mr. Knowlin," I said. "I've been reading about your downtown development proposal."

He smiled. "Have you, indeed? And what do you think about it?"

His blue-eyed gaze was attentive, giving the impression that he was interested in what I thought. Yes, the man would make a first-rate politician.

"I think that if the project is done right, it might be good for the city," I said.

He nodded. "So do I."

"Well, if you gentlemen will excuse me," I said. "I'm on my way to the shower and then home." I held out my hand. "A pleasure meeting you, Mr. Knowlin."

Instead of shaking my hand, he carried it to his lips. "I hope we'll meet again soon, Professor Stuart."

"Yes . . . uh, well . . . good-bye." I stuck my hand into my shorts pocket as I walked away.

That kiss on the hand had caught me off-guard. Howard Knowlin probably specialized in doing the unexpected and then observing people's reactions.

That no doubt explained why he had enough money to invest in a development project in Gallagher. He read people and made use of that information.

The city council was holding a public hearing this evening. Shouldn't he and Doug be there? Maybe Doug had thought it would be better if Knowlin didn't attend. But if they wanted to work out, why hadn't they gone to the Palmetto Athletic Club? That was where all the local CEOs were reputed to gather. Unless, of course, Knowlin just enjoyed hanging out with the regular people found on a university campus.

I'd have to remember to look up his bio tomorrow. If I ever met him again, I'd like to know enough about him not to be reduced to stammers.

CHAPTER · 5

"LIZABETH, I WAS HOPING you might have come home early tonight. Is everything okay there after the earthquake this morning? I called the office, and Sergeant Burke told me damage on campus was minimal. I've got to leave in a few minutes to take Marielle to the airport. Then I'm going back to the hospital to try to pry Mom away from Ben's bedside and bring her home to get some rest. Ben's doing pretty good so far, but I'm still not sure when I'll be able to—"

Quinn broke off, and I heard a female voice in the background.

"Lizzie, I've got to run. Marielle's afraid she's going to miss her flight. We've got plenty of time, but she can't wait to get back to her husband and offspring. And, just in case I haven't mentioned it, I can't wait to get back to you."

I wondered if his sister was standing there listening as he said that.

"I'll try to catch up with you again tomorrow. Sleep tight, love."

The man did know how to leave a phone message.

I played it again as I shuffled through the mail in my hand. I needed to go let George out.

The address label on the cream envelope said "Mrs. Enid Cutler." Mrs. Cutler, my eleventh-grade geometry teacher. I had sent her one of the diabetes society's fund-raising letters. To reach my goal, I'd sent a letter to everyone I could think of who knew me and/or had known Hester Rose, my grandmother.

Had Mrs. Cutler gotten confused about where to send the check? She wasn't that old. She had seemed middle-aged to me when I was seventeen, but she must have been only in her thirties at the time.

It had been over twenty years since the last time I saw her. She'd left Drucilla right after my senior year in high school because her husband had gotten a job in Virginia Beach.

But the handwritten condolence card she had sent me when she learned of Hester Rose's death had been precise and to the point and in the same firm hand that had written my name and address on this envelope. Mrs. Cutler was not the type of woman who would tolerate confusion. Whatever was in the envelope, I could be certain it was not a check that she had mistakenly sent to me instead of to the diabetes society.

It felt like a letter. I ripped open the side of the envelope and shook out two folded sheets of cream stationery.

Lizabeth,

I have sent a check in your name to the diabetes society. I am pleased to see that you are turning your grief for your grandmother to constructive use. However, I am writing this letter to you with regard to another matter. I have been pondering this matter since your grandmother's death. I decided to wait until the traditional year of mourning had passed before contacting you about it. Then, circumstances in my own life claimed my attention, and it was not until last autumn that I again thought of you. In fact, I was about to write to you, when I heard on the news the distressing report of the murder of your colleague at the university. Given the unsettling denouement of that case, I thought you would need time in which to recover.

But I surmise from your participation in this marathon that you have now sufficiently regained your self-possession to be able to have the discussion I believe we should have. I did not pursue this matter when your grandmother was alive. I was fully aware that she preferred you know as little as possible about your mother's departure from Gallagher and where she had gone. I will never forget that day when I, as a teenager, went to her with the postcard that your mother had sent to me thinking that your grandmother would be happy to know that her daughter was alive and well. Her reaction then silenced me for years afterward. Because of the way she reacted, I bit my tongue each time I was tempted to even so much as tell you that I had known your mother and that we had been friends of sorts.

Of course, if you had been thinking logically, Lizabeth, you would have realized that your mother and I were of an age, and had probably gone to high school together. But you were rather shy—painfully so— when you were a teenager. Even if it had occurred to you, I don't suppose you would have been able to work up the courage to question me. I remember quite clearly an evening when you were serving as an usher at a school concert. I came to the door and motioned you over so that I could ask if the other women inside were wearing hats. You stared at my hat and then at me and then stammered something unintelligible. I had to look inside and see for myself. As I said, you were a very shy young woman. But I always had great confidence in your brain power. And that is why I believe I should share this old (and perhaps now useless) information that I have with you and let you decide what, if anything, to do with it. I gathered from the news coverage of the Colby case that you do quite well with mysteries—particularly old ones.

I would like you to come to visit me. We live near Williamsburg. You should be able to make the round trip in one day. However, you are welcome to spend the night with us if you would like. We have a guest room. I should warn you, however, that since his retirement, my husband has become somewhat cantankerous. Too much time on his hands. He was never a reader.

I look forward to seeing you again, Lizabeth, and meeting the woman you have become.

Sincerely,
Enid Cutler

And below her signature, a telephone number.

I stared down at the letter. Then I walked down the hall to do what I had been about to do. I needed to let George out. I needed to. . . .

I sunk down on the floor with my back against the basement door.

Mrs. Cutler wanted me to visit so that she could tell me something about my mother.

As Mrs. Cutler had said, my grandmother had not been inclined to discuss her daughter. Or the man who had fathered me. It was only when she was on her deathbed and thought I was my mother that Hester Rose had revealed that she knew my father's identity. Then she died, and took the secret with her to her grave.

And now along came Mrs. Cutler, who had decided I was sufficiently self-possessed.

Dammit! I stood up and kicked the basement door and felt pain shoot up my instep. George gave a startled yelp and then began to bark.

I sagged back down on the floor with my hands pressed to my hot face.

"I don't need this, Mrs. Cutler. I have Quinn. He says he doesn't care who my father was. He says it doesn't matter. For the first time in my life, I am almost normal. And now you come along with your damn letter. . . ."

Just when I didn't want to know anymore what the secret was that Hester Rose had thought was too awful even to share with my grandfather, along came Mrs. Cutler.

"You can forget it, Mrs. Cutler. Thank you very much for your kind invitation, but I don't care to visit. You can keep whatever you have. I don't want to solve that particular mystery. I don't want to know. Oh, shut up, George! Shut the hell up! Here!"

I jumped up and flung the basement door wide. George charged out, barking. He stopped in mid-woof and dropped to his haunches, gazing up at me.

He must have known he was looking at a woman on the edge and found the sight fascinating.

"Joyce told me today that I never have hysterics, George. She should be here now. Then she could see me kick doors and rant and rave." I sat down on the floor beside him and hugged him. He licked at the tears on my face. "Oh, George, why now? Huh? Explain that to me. Why now, when I don't want to know anymore. I want a life, George. I just want a life."

C H A P † E R · 6

George and I went for a walk at dawn. I had been awake most of the night, and I couldn't stand lying there in bed anymore. When I got up, he wanted to be let out, so I pulled on wrinkled jeans and a sweatshirt and found his leash and announced we were going for a walk.

By the time we had made a long loop that had taken us through several adjacent streets and back, the sun was up and my neighbors were beginning to bustle as they prepared for the workday. I didn't know any of my neighbors other than Mrs. Cavendish. But she had filled me in on everyone else's lives and habits. Mr. Roth, who lived next door to me, was a confirmed bachelor, sung in his church choir, and rode his bike to his job as supervisor at the power company. I rarely saw him. He left for work before I was up, and I came home too late in the evening to see him tending his immaculate lawn.

Now he was coming down his driveway, pushing his bicycle, biking pants clinging to his narrow body, helmet already on his head.

"Good morning, Mr. Roth," I said.

He gave me a startled glance, then a smile lit his bespectacled face.

"Good morning, Professor Stuart," he said. "I don't think I've ever seen you out and about this early."

I pointed at George. "My houseguest felt like a walk."

Mr. Roth swung onto his bike. "And the morning air will do you both good," he said. "We must talk one day about your work. I'm very interested in forensics." With that, he waved and pedaled away, leaning forward like someone who could pedal for miles and miles.

There was a surreal quality to the morning. The sun was too bright for my blurry eyes. The sky too blue.

"Come on, George, maybe if we have breakfast, I can manage not to crawl back into bed."

I was responsible for George. I couldn't go off and leave him alone. So I might as well put Mrs. Cutler and her letter out of my mind until after the marathon on Saturday. Until after Quinn returned to take his dog. Of course, there was the question of whether I would tell Quinn about the letter or wait until after I had seen Mrs. Cutler and heard what she had to say.

But that was something I didn't have to decide now. What I needed to do was to pull myself together and get ready for my meeting with Amos Baylor.

"Give me half a second to splash some water on my face, George, and then I'll see what we have in the kitchen."

And after that I would go back to bed for a couple of hours. I had almost four hours before I needed to be on campus. I didn't want to nod off during my conversation with Amos.

"Lizzie, there you are," Amos said, with that hint of his native Ottawa in his voice that was a sure tipoff he was not happy. He was standing in the doorway of his secretary's office. "I was about to have Greta call you at home," he said. "To make sure you were on your way in."

I glanced at my wristwatch. "Is my watch slow? I thought our appointment was at eleven."

He made a visible effort to smile. "It is at eleven. You're on time. But something has come up."

"And you need to cancel?"

"No, we need to talk." Amos turned and glanced at Greta, then gestured me toward his office.

I sat down in one of his plush leather armchairs. He sat down behind his desk. His office had the feel of a study in a country manor: pipes on the desk, hunting prints on the walls, and leather-bound volumes on the bookshelves.

But the faculty rarely showed Amos the deference to which his title of dean and his gentleman's study office suggested he was entitled. In the School of Criminal Justice, the faculty, individually and collectively, thought quite well of themselves. Democracy sometimes ran riot. Quite often Amos could be seen with his bushy white brows furrowed in distress under his leonine mane.

I wondered in passing how yesterday's discussion about the school's desperate need for an increase in budget had gone when the provost and his assistant had been resting their bottoms on Amos's leather chairs.

I also wondered why Amos was shuffling the papers on his desk instead of getting to why he had hustled me into his office and out of Greta's hearing.

"You said something had come up," I reminded him. "And that we need to talk."

He looked up from his paper shuffling. His expression was interesting—half-wary, half-hopeful. Did he intend to head me off at the path before I could tell him that I had decided to accept his job offer? Well, in that case, I would just go on back to Drucilla.

"We have an invitation to lunch," Amos said.

"We do?" I said. "With whom?"

"Charlotte Wingate," he said.

"Who?" I said. "I don't know anyone named—"

Charlotte? The Charlotte who had been in Madeline's shop? Madeline's father's client?

Amos was saying, "She said she encountered you yesterday." His white brows went up toward his hairline in inquiry. "*Encountered* is the word she used. What did she mean? Where did you meet Charlotte Wingate?"

Obviously the woman was someone important, and Amos was concerned that I had met her.

"If she's the woman that I encountered yesterday," I said, "then it was in a shop, and we were not actually introduced—"

"Which would explain why she phrased it that way," Amos said. "What I don't understand is how this encounter led to an invitation to have lunch with Mrs. Wingate today at noon."

"Today?" I said. "Amos, would you please tell me who the woman is and why—"

"She's one of the wealthiest—if not *the* wealthiest—people in this city," he said. "Old money, her own and her husband's." Amos drew a breath that was audible. "When she called, she said she wanted to talk about a possible endowment to the school." His gaze fixed on me. "She wants me to bring you with me to lunch."

"Don't worry, Amos. I promise not to eat with my fingers or belch at the table."

"I wish you would try to take this seriously, Lizzie," Amos said. "Sometimes your sense of humor—"

"I would try to take it seriously, if I had any idea what it was about. If you would rather, I'd be happy to stay here while you go to lunch at Mrs. Wingate's. In fact, based on my encounter with her yesterday, I would be delighted to stay here."

Amos froze in his chair. "What happened yesterday?"

I almost said, *I stood on my head and sung "My Old Kentucky Home."* But, technically I was talking to my boss. I shook my head. "The truth is, I'm not sure what happened."

I told him—skipping the lawsuit discussion—about being recognized by Abigail Sims.

When I was done, he leaned his head in his hands. "All right," he said. "Mrs. Wingate knows about Richard . . . and your involvement in that. But for some reason, she is still considering making an endowment to this school. So we will go and have lunch with her."

"Amos, if she wants me to tell her all about Richard's murder, I'm going to get up and leave."

He frowned at me. "I'm sure, Lizzie, that Charlotte Wingate has more impor-tant ways to occupy her time than by indulging in morbid curiosity." He picked up one of his pipes and cradled it in his palm as he thought about that. "But somehow you're involved in this endowment discussion."

"So it would seem," I said and stood up. "Are we done? I have some work I need to do."

"Yes, go work. But we should leave here at around 11:40 to get there on time."

"All right," I said. "If you're sure you want me to come along."

No reply to that. But before I could open the door, he said, "Why did you want to see me?"

I was wondering if he'd ask. I turned and gave him a big smile. "Oh, that. I wanted to tell you, Amos, that I accept your offer. I would be happy to accept a permanent appointment to the faculty of this school."

He didn't choke. He managed to almost force his lips into a smile. "Fine. That's fine. I'm sure the students will be pleased. With Richard gone, having another minority faculty . . . not that we don't value you in your own right—" He put his pipe down and stopped trying to express his delight. "We'll discuss the details after our lunch with Mrs. Wingate."

Of course we would.

Poor Amos. After what Joyce had described to me as a "surprisingly on track and sensible" discussion of the matter, the majority of the faculty had voted in my favor. Amos had then duly offered me the position. Now, unless the lunch with Mrs. Wingate provided him with an unexpected out, he was about to be stuck with me.

Amos slid in a Mozart CD, and music surrounded us. The Volvo made quick work of the trip from the Piedmont State University campus on the north side of the river, across the uptown bridge, and into the old part of the city.

Amos and I were both silent during the drive. I was considering all the pos-sible ways this could turn out to be an embarrassing, humiliating, and/or annoy-ing experience.

But when I saw Charlotte Wingate's house, I decided it wasn't going to be a complete loss. She lived in one of the Victorian mansions on upper Main Street that I had been longing to see inside. In fact, she lived in one of my favorite houses in Millionaire's Row. A pale blue Queen Anne.

I got out of the car and stood admiring the architecture.

Amos hooked my elbow and turned me toward the front door. "Remem-ber," he said, "let me do the talking."

"Of course, Amos. I'll be quite happy to keep my mouth shut. But would you please ask her to give us a tour? I'd love to see the house."

I was joking, but Amos scowled. "Please, don't ask Charlotte Wingate for a tour of her house," he said. He didn't add *Sit where you're told and keep quiet.*

With Amos, I was always torn between bristling annoyance and mirth. But I really shouldn't tease him. He had no sense of humor and a difficult job.

The first person I saw when the uniformed maid showed us into the living room was Abigail Sims. She did not look happy to see us. In fact, she looked tense and sulky. But she must have been warned I was going to be there, because this time she didn't turn pale.

Her cousin Madeline swept toward Amos and me with a smile on her face. No garlic today, and she brushed her cheek against mine.

"Hello," I said, returning her greeting. "I'd like you to meet my dean, Amos Baylor. Amos, this is Madeline Oliver."

Madeline enveloped Amos in her smile and led him off to meet the others in the room. The others included her father and Charlotte Wingate. Minus the huge hat, but still formidable in black, she lumbered up from her chair to greet us.

And—coming from another room with a cocktail shaker in his hand—Doug Jenkins.

How did he figure into all this? Other than as Madeline's boyfriend? And why had Charlotte invited all these people if she wanted to discuss an endowment to the school?

Madeline concluded the introductions with her father.

Jebediah Gant? Yes, the Gant part sounded vaguely familiar. Maybe I had seen the law offices mentioned somewhere. But nothing that would explain Abigail's reaction yesterday.

"I expect," Charlotte said, her gaze on me, "you're wondering why I wanted you to accompany Dean Baylor."

"Yes, I am," I said.

"Have a seat, everyone," she said, gesturing toward chairs that were straight-backed and brocade-covered in a muted rose pattern that echoed the carpet. The sofa was covered in rose damask. Abigail and Jebediah claimed the sofa. It looked somewhat more comfortable than the chairs.

"Douglas, please, pour drinks for all of us," Charlotte said.

"Happy to oblige," Doug said with his usual good cheer.

The frosty, green liquid he was pouring into glasses was apparently Charlotte's drink of choice, and we were not encouraged to ask for anything else.

"Getting to the matter at hand," Charlotte said, "I've asked you here, Dean Baylor and Professor Stuart, because I would like to make an endowment to the school." She paused for effect. "I have a house that I would like to give to you."

"A house?" Abigail said, spots of color in her cheeks now. "Charlotte, you can't mean the Grant Avenue house? You know Uncle Jeb's been counting on . . . you practically promised—"

Jebediah coughed. "Actually, Charlotte—" he started to say. Then he turned to his niece and said, "Abigail, I should have mentioned this to you—but I've changed my mind about wanting that house for our offices."

Abigail gaped at him. "Changed your mind? But you've been going on for the past three months about how we need to move."

"We do need to move. With Sloane Campbell owning the property next door, we most certainly need to move," Jebediah said, his voice gaining firmness. "But you were right. That particular house—" He glanced in Charlotte's direction as he tugged at his bow tie. "No offense intended, Charlotte. But Abigail was right. That house might be off-putting for people who come to us as clients. It's a bit too imposing for common folks like Abigail and me."

"But, Daddy, you and Abigail aren't common folks," Madeline said in her lazy voice. "You're the best lawyers in this city."

Abigail shot Madeline a look. "Why, thank you for saying so, Cousin Madeline. But Uncle Jeb's right. We don't need that house." She shook her head at Doug's offer of a drink and turned back to her uncle. "I'm glad you've seen reason on this, Uncle Jeb. But you might have told me." Then to Charlotte. "And you might have just told us that you'd made up your mind, Charlotte. Inviting us here to lunch for this dramatic—"

"Now, Abigail." Jebediah smiled at Charlotte. "We're always delighted to receive an invitation, Charlotte."

"Yes, we all are, Charlotte," Madeline said. "And I guess your announcement means I'll also have to keep looking for a new location for my shop."

Doug said, "Of course, Charlotte, if you'd sold the house to Howard Knowlin—"

Charlotte narrowed her gaze on him. "As I have told you, Douglas, I do not care for your client. I'd rather do business with a cottonmouth. If you have any sense, you'll break off your dealings with him."

Doug smiled. "He's not quite that bad, Charlotte. He has an ego, but with his money and reputation, he's entitled. And it's my job to let other people know why he's entitled to feel good about himself and why they want to get on his bandwagon."

"Get on his bandwagon and ride to perdition," Charlotte said.

Doug laughed. "As I've tried to explain, Charlotte, his social blunder of inviting a few people to dinner on the same night you had your open house was completely unintentional."

Charlotte glared at him. "I don't dislike him because of that. I'm not that petty." Then her mouth twisted, and she smiled. An almost coquettish smile. "Don't try to get around me, Douglas."

"No, ma'am," he said. He glanced over at Madeline. "But, you see, I do have a lot riding on Howard's project. If I make enough money out of it, I might even be able to persuade that lovely lady sitting over there to have me."

Madeline looked up from regarding her rose-tipped nails. "Douglas, are you implying that I'm swayed by the size of a man's bank account?"

He smiled back. "No. Unfortunately, you do have your own."

Madeline wrinkled her nose at him. "So all I must want from you is your gorgeous bod."

Jebediah harrumphed as if his daughter's frankness had embarrassed him. Charlotte said, "Remember where you are, if you please, Madeline."

"Yes, please do." Abigail gave her cousin an irritated look. "We don't need to know about your sex life."

Madeline said, "Just because you can't find a man, Abigail Louise—"

"Girls," Jebediah interjected. "We do have— Charlotte does have guests."

"And you see why none of you are going to get the house," Charlotte said. "You fight enough among yourselves as it is. Better to give the house away and have no hurt feelings."

Maybe no hurt feelings. But her announcement had produced a variety of other emotions. Abigail, in spite of her obvious relief that her uncle had changed his mind about wanting the house, was still giving him worried glances. As for Jebediah, he kept tugging at his old-fashioned bow tie as if it were choking him. And Doug, as he handed me my drink, looked distracted. As if his mind was on having to tell Howard Knowlin that he wasn't going to get the house he wanted.

Madeline was the only one of the bunch who appeared unruffled.

Charlotte turned her attention back to Amos and me. "I'm giving you my house. But it's to be used for a very specific purpose," she said. "That is a condition of the endowment."

"What purpose did you have in mind?" I said, ignoring Amos's order that I keep my mouth shut.

"I want the school to establish an institute for the study of crime and culture," Charlotte said. "Focusing on the South."

Amos snapped to attention, beaming his pleasure. "I can assure you, Mrs. Wingate, that the school would be delighted to establish such an institute. We've been wanting to expand into an area that would give the school another unique—"

"Yes," Charlotte said, cutting him off. "There is one other condition, Dean Baylor."

"I'm sure we can meet any condition—"

"I want Professor Stuart to serve as the executive director of the institute."

Amos spilled his drink on his gray slacks. He grabbed for his handkerchief to dab at the stain and sent more of the green liquid splashing onto Charlotte's carpet. "I'm sorry," he said, flushing red. "Forgive me."

Charlotte said, "Don't concern yourself. It will be attended to later." Her voice was amused. "I take it that my stipulation concerning Professor Stuart comes as something of a surprise, Dean Baylor."

"Yes," Amos said. "Of course, if you feel . . . however, there are other more senior faculty who . . . not that Professor Stuart isn't fully qualified . . . but with such a challenging—"

"I want Professor Stuart as the executive director," Charlotte said. "I get her, or you forget the endowment."

"Of course," Amos said. "Of course."

"Why?" I said, finally managing to pry my tongue loose from the roof of my mouth. "Why do you want me as the director?"

"I followed your involvement in the Colby case," Charlotte said. "You're a crime historian, obviously a skilled researcher. And you're a woman. I want a woman in charge of my institute."

"But," I said, "if you give the school the house as an endowment, it will be the school's institute."

"With my name above the door," Charlotte said. Then she smiled. "Don't worry, Professor, I don't intend to be a shadow dictator. You will be in complete charge, with a board of directors, or whatever organization is required. However, I do want a person as executive director who I believe understands the nuances of life here in the South."

"And you think . . . based on the little you know about me . . . that I'm that person?"

"Oh, but I know more about you today than I did yesterday, Professor. I had my assistant collect some information on your personal background and academic credentials." She smiled. "When do you expect Chief Quinn back from Oklahoma, by the way? His background is rather unusual too. I'd like to meet him."

I stared at her. Then I stood up. "I am not interested in being the director of your institute, Mrs. Wingate."

Charlotte clapped her hands. "Bravo, Professor. You're a woman with spunk. Exactly what I want."

"What you want—" I started to say.

"Lizzie," Amos said as he stood up and grabbed my arm. "I think we should discuss Mrs. Wingate's offer."

"So do I, Dean Baylor," Charlotte said. "I'm sure Professor Stuart hasn't considered all the intriguing projects she could pursue with her own institutional base."

I opened my mouth to tell her that I didn't need to consider. But before the words could make their way past my lips, I was already thinking.

An institute for the study of crime and culture.

There were all kinds of things . . . even with the focus on the South. Especially with the focus on the South. There were so many aspects of Southern culture that had permeated the rest of American society. Like the argument that Fox Butterfield had made in his book about the relationship between the nineteenth-century white Southern ideology of honor and violence and the violence of young black men in urban ghettos. Whether or not you accepted his argument, there were still aspects of Southern culture that had been transported with the Southern migrants.

Tonight in class I was going to be talking about the impact of 1950s rock and roll, born in the South and—

"From the expression on her face," Charlotte said, "I believe Professor Stuart is beginning to consider the possibilities." She reached for her cane, and Amos rushed to her side. "Thank you, Dean Baylor. I have a touch of blasted gout today. Let's go in to lunch. Bring your drinks along if you like."

I left the green beverage that I hadn't touched on the side table and trailed behind the others.

Yes, directing an institute of crime and culture would be exciting. Challenging. A boom to my academic career. But the other side of the coin was Charlotte Wingate.

And Amos was suddenly looking way too pleased. He was probably already hatching some plan that would limit any control I might have, even if I were willing to accept the position.

We had lunch. A salad of field greens and pecans dressed with a raspberry vinaigrette. Cornish game hens with rice stuffing, served with asparagus tips. And for dessert, an unexpected and utterly delicious crème brûlée. I could have echoed Madeline when she asked if she could possibly get another serving to go. But I managed to resist swiping my fingers around the dessert dish to collect the last smidgen. I had promised Amos I wouldn't eat with my fingers.

Whatever else I might say about her, Charlotte Wingate knew how to hire kitchen staff. And I suspected *staff* was the operative term. I had seen so far the maid who'd opened the door and another maid and a manservant who'd served lunch. There must be a cook and a cook's assistant or two out in the kitchen.

Charlotte could afford to give away a house. But could we—and that meant the School of Criminal Justice—afford to accept the gift?

Amos seemed to think, yes. He was on Charlotte's left, regaling her with information about the school. Its ranking in the top five among criminal justice Ph.D. programs in the country. The faculty's impressive research and publication records. She let him ramble on, but I suspected she already knew all that and was just sizing Amos up.

No one but Amos and Charlotte seemed to be in the mood to do their conversational duty.

As coffee was being served, I asked if tea was available, and the maid came back with my favorite—peppermint. I didn't even want to think about whether that was a coincidence.

Charlotte ended her conversation with Amos and turned to me on her right.

"I understand from Douglas that you're taking part in the marathon on Saturday," she said.

"Yes." And then, to be polite, I added, "My grandmother had diabetes. I'm walking the half-marathon in her name."

Charlotte nodded. "You were raised by your grandparents, I believe."

As if she didn't know. She probably could also tell me how many days old I'd been when my mother left on that Greyhound bus.

"Yes, my grandparents did raise me," I said.

"I'm sure that helped to nurture your appreciation of the past. Old people pass on their stories."

"Yes, they do," I said. "When I was a child, I loved listening to my grandfather's stories."

"We must talk at greater length one day," Charlotte said. "Perhaps you could come to tea next Wednesday afternoon. Just the two of us."

Amos made an uneasy movement that Charlotte apparently caught from the corner of her eye. "Forgive me for excluding you, Dean Baylor. But I'm sure you would find an afternoon of storytelling boring."

He opened his mouth.

Charlotte said, "I mean, of course, since your area of research is juvenile justice administration rather than crime history." She signaled to the manservant, who came and pulled back her chair. "I know you all need to be elsewhere this afternoon. Thank you for joining me for lunch."

With that we were dismissed. Without a tour of the house. But if the living room and the rather stiff and dismal dining room were an indication of Charlotte's decorating taste, I would probably have been disappointed by the rest of the house anyway.

But what about the house on Grant Avenue? What was that like?

"Could we have a look at the house you want to give us?" I said as we reached the door. "If that would be possible."

How could I even ask to see it? I should be running as fast as I could in the other direction. But looking at the house did not constitute an obligation to accept her offer.

"Quite possible, Professor Stuart," Charlotte said, leaning on her cane. "I'll arrange for you to receive a key. I think you'll find the house intriguing. It was built in the nineteenth century, and it passed through a number of hands before my husband purchased it the year before his death. I leased it briefly to a young couple who wanted to provide a foster home for troubled teenagers. But I finally had to put them out." She drew herself up. "They had no control whatever over those children—" She broke off. "But as I started to say, you'll find it particularly interesting because during Prohibition the house was used as a private club and speakeasy. Inside the house there was a secret entrance to the basement, and another entrance was concealed outside for bringing in the liquor."

"Really?" I said. "Do you know how long the club operated?"

Charlotte's smile said she knew she was hooking me. "An interesting question, and not one I've looked into. But I'm sure if you wanted to do a bit of research . . . ." She let the suggestion drift off. "I'll get the key to you later today," she said.

"Thank you," I said. "Dean Baylor and I will have a look at the house. But, in case I haven't made it clear, Mrs. Wingate, I don't appreciate your little background check. I would find it impossible to serve as director of an institute knowing that you consider it your right to pry into my life."

"Lizzie—" Amos said.

Charlotte said, "Not my right, Professor Stuart. But I did feel my interest was justified by the offer I intended to make. We can both be pleased that there's nothing in your past that is worthy of concern."

"No dirt?" I said. "No nasty little secrets?"

She smiled. "By today's standards, nothing that would be considered scandalous." She nodded her head. "You needn't concern yourself about future inquiries, Professor Stuart. I'm satisfied."

Wonderful. She was satisfied.

Amos said, "Thank you, Mrs. Wingate, for your generous—"

"We haven't closed the deal yet," Charlotte said. "You'd better work on getting Professor Stuart to agree to my condition."

She turned away and began clunking down the hall, back toward the others. They were apparently lingering until Amos and I were gone so that they could voice their opinions.

The maid nodded at us and opened the ornate front door, then closed it behind us.

"We need to discuss this, Lizzie," Amos said.

Amos used the time on our drive back to campus to explain to me how important the endowment was to the school.

"We're in a tight budget year. Do you know how little of the university's budget is coming from the state these days? Since the mid-1980s, spending on prisons has been increasing faster than spending on higher education. It's the same all over the country. That's why endowments from people like Charlotte Wingate are so important."

I nodded. I had heard this before in faculty meetings. All the units in the university were hearing it from their deans and chairpersons. They were passing on the message that they were hearing from the president and other administrators. In this brave new world of state reduction in academic funding, we had to take on more responsibility for bringing money into our units.

Maybe we should ask Howard Knowlin if he'd like to throw some cash our way.

Amos was still talking. "This endowment could lead to other things. With this new institute, we would be able to go after funding from sources that we haven't tapped before."

"Amos, are you honestly willing to have me in charge as executive director?"

He was silent for a moment, focusing on his driving. Then he turned his head and astounded me with a grin. "Lizzie, if that's the price of Charlotte Wingate's endowment, then I'll have to learn to live with it. You're academically capable. More than that. I wouldn't have you on my faculty if you weren't." He sighed. "And it isn't as if last semester's fiasco—and that doesn't begin to describe it—was really your fault." He threw another glance in my direction. "One benefit of this arrangement is that you'd be too busy with the institute to have the time to become involved in any more unfortunate—" As he said that, he seem to rethink it.

"Yes, I would be very busy," I said, smiling back at him. "If I decide to do this."

Amos frowned. "I suppose you have conditions of your own," he said. "Of course, you would be appointed as a tenured associate professor, and your salary would reflect—"

"I need time to think about it, Amos. This is a big decision."

"All right," he said. "But I want your answer as soon as possible. I want to get back to Charlotte Wingate before she changes her mind."

"Or decides to give or sell the house to someone else," I said.

Amos made a sharp turn onto College Avenue. "We can't let that happen," he said. "The school needs this endowment."

"Are things that bad, Amos?"

"Bad enough," he said. He turned into the parking lot of Brewster Hall. "President Sorenson is thinking of running for political office. If he does, the school will lose its strongest supporter."

I reached for my door handle. "I really will give Mrs. Wingate's offer serious thought. I'll let you know by next Monday. How's that?"

"Monday?" He frowned, not pleased by the delay. "All right, I'll expect your answer by then."

Assuming I had an answer by then.

This was a big decision, and I wanted to talk to Quinn about it. Not because I needed his approval, but I did value his opinion. Especially about unusual and unexpected developments. He has a cop's instinct for things that smell wrong. I couldn't smell anything, but something about all this was making me nervous.

Maybe I was reacting to the way the other people at Charlotte's luncheon had reacted to her announcement about the house. Especially Jebediah, who didn't want "that house" anymore, much to Abigail's surprise and relief. Was he an elderly man who had gotten an idea into his head, but then come to his senses and realized that his niece was right all along?

Or did Jebediah know something Amos and I had yet to discover?

Why had the house passed through a number of hands, as Charlotte had put it?

Maybe the teenage foster kids Charlotte had been forced to evict had been out of control because of the house. Maybe the house had possessed them.

And maybe while he was at the house, Jebediah had had a paranormal experience. But he hadn't told the others because then they would be sure he was getting senile. And all that bow tie tugging had been because he was imagining what would happen to our unsuspecting faculty when we tried to set up an institute in that house.

I turned my head, about to share my flight of fancy with Amos. But I realized in time he would not be amused. Besides, we had nothing to worry about. Howard Knowlin had wanted to buy the house. Multimillionaire real estate developers don't buy haunted houses.

C H A P T E R · 7

THAT EVENING I looked up from what I was saying to my class and saw Jebediah Gant in the doorway.

He said, in a bone-dry voice with the slightest quiver, "Now, some witty fellow once said that 'naked is the best disguise.'" My students twisted around in their seats to see who was there. "Speaking personally, I've always preferred to preserve my dignity by at least wearing my boxer shorts."

My students laughed.

He smiled and stepped from the doorway, into the room. "Professor Stuart, I hope you don't mind my dropping in like this. I was hoping we could talk after your class is over."

"My class won't be over for another half hour, Mr. Gant."

"I know. I wanted to arrive early to be sure I wouldn't miss you." He sat down in one of the desks near the door. "I promise to sit here quiet as a church mouse."

He seemed more together than he had the last time I'd seen him. In fact, he seemed to be in good form. But he was disrupting my class.

I turned back to the students in my grad seminar. We had been in the middle of an impromptu discussion of clothing and crime. Impromptu because it was supposed to be next week's topic. But I had made passing reference to clothing as I was discussing images of crime in rap music.

That had prompted Ted Cerulo, one of the state police officers enrolled in the master's program, to recall the less-than-helpful description the victim of a convenience store holdup had once given him of a young perpetrator. "How do I know what he looked like?" the store owner had said. "He was dressed like one of them gangsta rappers. You know, with the baggy pants and the sneakers."

The class had been discussing the status of baggy pants and sneakers as the equivalent of a youth uniform that could serve as a kind of disguise, when Jebediah joined the conversation.

I needed to get things back on track. "Does anyone recognize Mr. Gant's quote?" I said.

I was leaning against the front of the table that served as a teacher's desk, because being behind it made me feel I was too far away to connect with them. The room was not ideal for discussion; it was set up in rows of seats like a standard classroom. But somehow I had ended up with twenty-three people in my class, and it was either this room or spend three hours upstairs crammed together in the largest seminar room available.

I walked over to stand in front of Keisha McIntyre, who was tapping on her lower lip with her pen. Was she hearing music in her head? "Recognize the quote, Keisha?"

"No, but it sounds like it should have come from a mystery novel or something like that," she said. "Sherlock Holmes?"

"Good guess. You may have seen a book about Holmes with that title. But the original quote comes from William Congreve's *The Double-Dealer.*" I glanced at my other students. "A play written in the late seventeenth century. If I recall correctly, the full quote is, 'No mask like open truth to cover lies, As to go naked is the best disguise.'"

Ted Cerulo grinned. "Way to go, Professor."

I bowed from the waist. Jebediah Gant had irritated me into a one-upmanship display of erudition. But it did bother me that he thought he could walk into my class and make himself at home.

The question was why he had dropped in. Had Charlotte Wingate sent him as her ambassador? With the key to the house? Or maybe he had changed his mind about not wanting the house for his law offices. Maybe he was here on his own behalf to try to subtly discourage me from agreeing to Charlotte's condition. It would have to be subtle. She was his client.

"Getting back to tonight's topic," I said. "We were talking about music. Anyone an Eminem fan?"

Keisha McIntyre groaned. "He is such a misogynist." Several of the other women in the room nodded in agreement.

"Oh, come on, Keisha," Jim Taylor said. "You listen to black rappers. Cut the guy some slack."

The debate during the next twenty minutes was lively. For the most part, I let the discussion flow, intervening only to play referee. As for Jebediah, he kept his mouth shut as promised. But from their glances in his direction, I had the feeling my students were all aware of his alien presence in our Wednesday evening seminar.

I waited until Betsy Anderson had finished what she was saying, then pointed at the clock.

"Let's call it a night, folks. Please turn in your research paper outlines before you go."

I glanced up from tucking the stack of papers into my expanding folder and saw Keisha's red sweater still draped over the back of her chair. I thought she might come back for it, but I'd better take it along to my office in case she didn't.

I closed my briefcase and looked at my visitor, seated in his suit and bow tie in a student desk. He hadn't offered me a key yet. What did he want to talk about?

"What can I do for you, Mr. Gant?"

"You said at lunch that you grew up listening to stories, Professor Stuart. Perhaps you'd humor me by listening to a story I'd like to tell you." He turned sideways in the chair and crossed his legs in his perfectly creased gray pants. A watch fob dangled from a pocket of his vest.

Did he cultivate his image of Southern lawyer? If he did, he was certainly doing a better job of carrying it off now than he had the other times I'd seen him.

Maybe he went in and out. Good days, bad days. His mind sometimes less dependable than it used to be. My grandmother, Hester Rose, had begun to have problems with her short-term memory before she died. Still sharp in other respects, but sometimes a little foggy around the edges.

I sat down in the chair across from his. "All right, Mr. Gant. But I'm afraid we'll have to keep this short."

He smiled. "Brevity has never been a virtue I could lay claim to. But I will do my best to oblige. I know you must be tired after your class. It was very informative, by the way."

"Thank you," I said. "The story you wanted to tell me, Mr. Gant—"

"Jebediah, please." He touched his watch fob. "This happened back in the 1950s. An era I heard you refer to as I was listening out in the hall."

"Were you listening for your cue to make your entrance?" I said.

"Lawyering does involve quite a bit of acting. If you're any good at it, you develop a sense of the dramatic. Of timing. But back in the 1950s—the year was 1955, to be precise—I didn't know much about being a showman yet. I was a young lawyer, only a few years in practice. And I was given a big case. A case that nobody else wanted."

In spite of myself, he had my attention. Was this what Abigail had been so disturbed about when she recognized me in Madeline's shop? This case of her uncle's from 1955? And, if so, why was he about to tell me about it now?

"Why did no one else want this case?" I said.

"Because it involved a young colored girl . . . pardon me, a young African-American girl—she wasn't a woman—who'd killed her white employer. The employer, Blanche Campbell was her name—"

"A relative of Sloane Campbell's?" I said.

Jebediah frowned. "You know Sloane Campbell?"

"I've read about him," I said. "I know he's a local real estate developer."

"He was a boy back then. Ten years old. Blanche Campbell was his mother."

"And she was killed?"

Jebediah nodded. "Blanche was a widow, the mother of four young children. Sloane and his sisters, who were twins and about six years old. And a baby, not yet a year old. The baby died on the same day as his mother."

"The girl who killed Blanche Campbell killed the baby too?"

"Yes, but that was an accident. In fact, it was all a tragedy that might not have happened but for a missing skirt and blouse. Blanche Campbell accused her mother's helper, Verity Thomas, of stealing the garments. Verity did not take the accusation well."

"And that was why she killed her?"

"No, not then. She left when she was accused. She walked out of the house in the middle of the laundry she was doing. She intended never to go back."

"Why did she?" I said.

"Because her family sharecropped on a piece of the Campbell farm. Her parents feared that if Verity didn't go back, Blanche would put them off the land."

"But why would Blanche Campbell have taken her back if she believed she was a thief?"

"Blanche had four children and she needed help. And maybe she wasn't as convinced Verity had stolen the skirt and blouse as she seemed to be when she was yelling the accusation at her. The garments had been hanging out on the line outside. Dog could have taken them. Or a passing tramp. At any rate, two days later, Blanche drove over to the Thomases' run-down little shack and asked the parents to send their daughter back to work for her."

"And Verity agreed to go because of her parents?"

"She was the oldest child," Jebediah said. "The oldest, at 17, of eight siblings. The father tried, but he was a luckless man. The sharecropping system made his luck worse. The mother had worked for Blanche herself, but now she was bedridden. Much of the burden fell on Verity."

"So when Blanche came to ask her to come back, and her parents wanted her to go—"

"She gave in and went. Even though she felt ill-used by Blanche. Unjustly accused and no apology. And Verity had been thinking that she might be able to find other work. Maybe even get on at the mill. But her parents—as they told me later—were scared of Blanche Campbell's temper. Scared of being thrown off the land. So they pleaded and argued, and finally the girl agreed."

I felt my skin crawl. I hated stories like this. "And that turned out to be a fatal mistake?"

He nodded his bald head. "Yes, it was. Things went along well enough that first week. Then something happened. Another argument between them . . . although you must understand there were two or three different versions of this story. The prosecutor who accused Verity of killing her employer in cold blood said that Verity walked over to the farm with the intent of stealing from Blanche Campbell. She had expected her to be gone—it was Blanche's day to drive into town. But Blanche came back. She had forgotten a piece of cloth she wanted to take in to match up. She found Verity in her house. The two of them argued, fought, then Verity grabbed a piece of the broken broom handle that was being used to prop up a window. Of course, Verity claimed Blanche had grabbed for a piece of that broom handle first, and they both had a piece. But, however it happened, Verity, who was younger and stronger, beat Blanche, who was a tiny woman, about the head until she was on the floor and begging for mercy. Then Verity took a sock from the laundry she'd done the day before and rammed it down Blanche's throat with that broken broom handle. She left her there on the floor, bleeding, and Blanche choked to death on her own vomit. According to the prosecutor, Verity scooped up everything she might be able to sell and then stole Blanche's car."

"The baby," I said. "You said he died on that same day."

"His mama had left him in the car while she ran back inside the house to get her strip of cloth." Jebediah fingered his watch fob. "Verity stole the car with the baby still in it. She'd learned how to drive in her daddy's old pickup truck. She managed to drive Blanche Campbell's Cadillac."

"And the baby? What happened?"

"Verity lost control of the car. She got scared when she saw a county sheriff's vehicle. She thought they must be looking for her and, even if they weren't, when they saw a black girl driving a brand-new Cadillac, they'd surely suspect she'd stolen it. In her panic, she crashed into the side of a bridge. The car went into the water. She managed to scrabble out and dog paddle to the river bank."

"But she left the baby?"

"She said she couldn't get to him. Said she was so scared when the car went in the water that all she was thinking about was getting out. Then she remembered him, but the car had sunk. The police car that had frightened her pulled up as Verity was crawling up on the bank. She started babbling, and they knew something was seriously wrong. They took her to the jail and started checking."

"And that was when they found out that Blanche Campbell had been killed?" I said.

"The boy and his younger sisters had found their mother when they returned from school. He called their nearest neighbor, who came and summoned the sheriff. Then word of the car and the drowned baby came in." He told the story like someone watching from a distance. In a voice that held more than a trace of irony.

"And Verity Thomas was charged with murder," I said.

"And the judge assigned the case to me, the only young fool in the county who would take it." He smiled slightly, then cleared his throat. "But I did do my best for Verity Thomas. I put witnesses on the stand—including Blanche Campbell's own young son—to testify about Blanche's temper. I tried to introduce evidence of self-defense. When the jury convicted her of murder, as we all knew they would, I stood up again and argued that she was 17 years old and it would be a dark stain on the history of the commonwealth of Virginia to execute a poor, ignorant, semi-retarded child."

"Was she executed?" I said.

"She would have been. Would have been the second woman in modern Virginia history to be executed. The other one was black too, back in 1912. But Verity was luckier. She died of pneumonia two weeks before her death sentence was to be carried out." He paused. "Her mama fell to her knees and thanked her god for showing her daughter mercy."

And, I wondered, *blamed herself for sending her daughter back into the situation that had led to her death?* "That's a very interesting story," I said. "But I don't understand why you told it to me."

He smiled, revealing crooked and slightly yellowed teeth. "Because I knew you'd appreciate it. I admit to you that when I took Verity Thomas's case, I was seeing myself as a budding Clarence Darrow. I thought even if I lost that case . . . as I knew I would . . . people would know my name. And they did. I rose quite quickly after that. I'd gotten myself a reputation."

"And no one held it against you that you'd defended a black girl who'd kill her white employer?" I said.

"But, you see, I had no choice in the matter. The judge had appointed me. Made it clear that he would be displeased if I refused. So I took the case and did my best. I spoke eloquently in my client's behalf. And bowed my head in resignation and sorrow at the inevitable outcome of those tragic events." He smiled. "As I recall, I used that phrase, 'these tragic events.' The *Gazette* printed up my closing argument."

"And that's what you want me to know? That you spoke eloquently for Verity Thomas."

"There is another matter that I—" He broke off as something fell with a thump in the hallway. "Who's there?" he said, twisting around. "Who's out there?"

I got up and started toward the door.

"It's just me, Dr. Stuart," Keisha said as she stuck her head around the door. "Dropped my book." A moment later, the rest of her appeared. "Excuse me, I forgot my sweater."

She shot Jebediah a glance as she passed en route to her seat at the front of the room.

"Good night," she said on her way back out.

"Good night, Keisha," I said. And how long had she been standing out there in the hallway?

I turned back to Jebediah. "You were saying?"

"When you get to be my age, loud noises can be startling." He straightened his shoulders, reaching for his dignity.

"At any age," I said.

He nodded. His fingers went from his watch fob to his bow tie. "What I want you to know, Professor Stuart," he said, his voice not as smooth or as dry, "is that you're dealing with people with their own agendas. I had mine back in 1955. Charlotte's got hers now. She likes playing queen and having power over us ordinary mortals. But that don't mean she don't wanna do good." He paused. "So I reckon I came here to tell you to accept the house and the position."

"You're sure you and your niece no longer want the house?"

He glanced away, seemed at a loss for a moment. Then he said, "Abigail was right. The big gate out front would scare our clients away. Besides, Charlotte's made it clear we aren't going to get it. Neither is Madeline. And Howard Knowlin would only get it over her dead body." He smiled. "And then she'd probably rise up from her grave and bring the roof crashing down on his head."

"I've met Mr. Knowlin," I said. "He seemed pleasant enough."

"That's why Charlotte doesn't trust him. The other part of it is that there's only room for one monarch in this town. Charlotte may rule her queendom with discretion, but she does not care for would-be usurpers."

"That would explain her antipathy toward him."

Jebediah uncrossed his legs and heaved himself up from the chair. "I brought the keys to the house. The address and directions are in the envelope. Go have a look at it."

I stood up too, accepting the envelope he had taken from his jacket pocket.

"Thank you," I said. "And thank you for telling me about Verity Thomas." I watched him for a change of expression as I asked, "Is that story the reason your niece was so upset when she recognized me in Madeline's shop?"

He cleared his throat. "What Abigail was upset about is the lawsuit we have pending. Lawyers don't like to be sued. It isn't dignified."

"How did it happen?" I asked. "The lawsuit, I mean?" A question which he might choose not to answer. It was certainly impertinent, but since he seemed so anxious to share. . . .

He said, "This will become public knowledge soon enough, so I might as well tell you about it so that you'll understand my present dilemma."

"What dilemma, Mr. Gant?"

"The man who initiated the lawsuit worked for Sloane Campbell on his construction sites as a stonemason. This man came to me with a lawsuit he wanted me to file against the city. A traffic light had malfunctioned, resulting in his serious injury." Jebediah flushed. "But due to an oversight on my part, the papers were not filed on time, and he lost his opportunity to pursue his claim. Now he is suing me for malpractice."

That sounded reasonable to me. "And you think . . . if I understood correctly what I heard in Madeline's shop . . . that Sloane Campbell put this man up to the lawsuit as a way of getting revenge?"

Jebediah's back stiffened. "If you had seen that 10-year-old boy when I had him on the witness stand questioning him about his mother . . . he hated me then. I saw hate in his eyes. Now he's finally in position to pay me back."

"Pay you back for calling him to testify?"

"Pay me back for much more than that. Pay me back for the insult . . . the assault . . . by me on his mother's reputation and good name. I made him admit his mother was a hot-tempered, sometimes violent woman."

I shook my head, looking at him, trying to imagine that courtroom scene. "I'm surprised that the judge let you call a 10-year-old boy . . . I mean in 1955 . . . in that kind of trial when the defendant was black and he was the victim's son."

"The judge had no choice. He had to let me have something. He and the prosecutor both knew it was the safer course."

"Why?"

Jebediah smiled. "Because there was more to the story that might have come out. What did come out was enough but not too much. They were willing to sacrifice the boy to keep any more from coming out and casting doubts."

"Casting doubts?" I said. "Are you saying that there was . . . that Verity Thomas might not have been—"

"No. No. She was guilty all right. Verity Thomas killed Blanche Campbell. She confessed it to me. But there were other things not directly related to Verity, things about Blanche—" He shook his head. "But I've said enough so that you can understand my concern about Sloane Campbell and what he's up to. He bought the Boulevard Shoppes where my daughter leases space. Then he bought the two buildings on either side of the building where my niece and I have our law offices. He's had those buildings razed. We haven't been able to find out what he intends to do with the properties."

Which sounded like suspicious behavior. But I couldn't reconcile this supposed vendetta with the man I had met in the parking lot. Arrogant, yes. A slow-burn temper, yes. But he hadn't struck me as vindictive. Or, at least, not toward old women who dumped milk shakes on his windshield.

"If he wanted revenge," I said, "why wait so long?"

"Because he hasn't had the money until now." Jebediah frowned. "Of course, my niece doesn't want to believe it either. She got that from James. He always wanted to believe people would forgive you if you did the right thing." He glanced toward the window. "Truth is, if you do the right thing, you'd better know where the bones are buried."

An unsettling philosophy for a champion of justice. "James?" I said.

His glance came back to me. "What did you . . . oh . . . he was Madeline's husband. Partner in our law firm. Died of a heart attack. My daughter told him he ought to get out of the office and go play golf. He was fool enough to listen to her."

"But she couldn't have known he would have a heart attack."

"She knew he exercised about as often as an atheist goes to prayer meeting. Both of them should have known he didn't need to be out there on a hot August afternoon playing golf." He shook his head. "Sometimes people are damn fools."

"On occasion," I said.

He looked at me. "There is another matter I wanted to speak to you about, Professor Stuart. The other reason I came here tonight. Actually, it's the reason I told you that long-winded story about Verity Thomas. I was hoping to spark your interest."

"Spark my interest in what?"

He stood there, looking a little embarrassed, a little uncertain, fingering his watch fob. "I've been talking to Doug Jenkins, and he suggested this might be a real good time for me to write my memoirs. Unfortunately, I never have been as fluent with a pen as with my tongue. I'm hoping perhaps I might persuade you to work with me . . . help me to tell the story of this old country lawyer's life and times. Including the Verity Thomas case."

Good grief! "I . . . Mr. Gant . . . I am flattered that you . . . but right now, I really already have too much on my plate."

"Well, perhaps we can talk again in a month or two. This lawsuit is likely to be a protracted affair unless we settle . . . which is what my niece thinks we've got to do. So does that damn insurance company attorney. But I'm thinking there may be another way to skin this cat. And getting my memoirs out there . . . the story of my illustrious career. . . ." A crooked smile. "Can't but help my cause."

"It might not make Sloane Campbell happy," I said.

"Probably won't. But I don't intend to tuck my tail between my legs and slink on away like a beat-up old cur." He nodded his head. "Good evening to you, Professor Stuart. I've enjoyed our conversation. And I'll speak to you again in a few weeks about my proposition."

I stepped out into the hall and watched Jebediah walk with determined briskness toward the elevator. I decided to take the stairs up to the fifth floor.

As I unlocked my office door, I thought again of Keisha. She'd been lurking out in the hall, listening to my conversation with Jebediah. Maybe she'd even left her sweater on purpose so that she'd have an excuse if she were caught. She'd obviously wanted to know who Jebediah was and why he was there.

Keisha, my militant crusader for truth and justice, would take to the Verity Thomas case like a hound scenting spoor. But since Verity Thomas was long in her grave, there wasn't a lot Keisha would be able to do for her cause.

CHAPTER · 8

I spent the first hour after getting out of bed sitting at my kitchen table. After a bowl of Cheerios with banana slices and two cups of tea, I'd had plenty of time for a mental replay of my conversation with Quinn the evening before. He'd told me that (a) his stepfather was getting stronger every day, so much so that his cardiologist was predicting an excellent recovery, and (b) when he and his mother had been talking on the drive home from the hospital, she had said that it was past time that she met me and that he was to bring me with him the next time he came to visit. He, by the way, was "in complete agreement."

It had been a lovely conversation. Somehow I hadn't quite gotten around to mentioning (a) the ceramic heart he had given me for Valentine's Day had been cracked, (b) Mrs. Cutler's letter, or (c) Charlotte Wingate's endowment offer and the attached condition.

The question was whether I hadn't told him any of those things because I wanted to wait and talk to him about everything in person. Or whether I was simply a coward and afraid that our relationship was still so new and fragile that anything might rip it apart. The mystery of my mother's whereabouts and the prospect of a challenging new position counted as big anythings.

As for the cracked heart—he would probably shrug that off.

But I wanted it repaired. All of this had started when the heart was cracked, and, superstitious or not, I'd like to have the crack mended before things went any further.

I went into the hall and looked up the number for Madeline's Attic in the telephone book.

Madeline was talking to someone else, a customer it sounded like, when she picked up the telephone.

"Hi, Madeline, it's Lizzie Stuart. I won't keep you, it sounds like you're busy."

"Lizzie, I was going to call you. I haven't been able to catch up with RaeAnne yet. Nobody's answering her phone, and she's not returning my messages."

"Do you think it would be all right if I tried to reach her?"

"Sure, I don't see any problem with that. Hold on a minute, I'll get you the number. I'll give you the address too. You might want to drop on by there. You could leave her a note if she's not there."

"That's a great idea. Thank you, Madeline."

"Think nothing of it. I know how much you want to get that heart repaired, and I like satisfied customers. When you catch up with Ms. RaeAnne Dobb, would you tell her Madeline would appreciate it if she'd return her calls?"

"Will do," I said.

When I hung up with Madeline, I headed for the shower. I didn't want to be late for my lunch with Joyce. It was symptomatic of the upheaval in my life that I had given Joyce and her pending biopsy very little thought. I hadn't even looked for her yesterday at school because I was still too floored by Charlotte Wingate's offer. This afternoon, I would try to be a better friend.

The telephone rang while I was in the shower. I heard it over the spray of warm water, but I was not inclined to hop out and run and see who it was.

I should have. The message that had recorded was not a telemarketer's hang up. It was Keisha McIntyre and she'd had a lot to say:

"Dr. Stuart, it's me, Keisha. I hope you don't mind me calling you at home. I really needed to reach you. When I came back for my sweater last night, I heard what that Mr. Gant said about Verity Thomas. I went over to the library and looked up the newspaper for 1955. Then this morning I went out there, out to the Campbell farm."

She was talking fast, as if she wanted to get it all in before she was cut off— or I picked up the telephone.

Her message continued: "Marcus was in his eight o'clock chem lab, so I borrowed his car. I wanted to see where it happened, you know. The newspaper had this sketch of the position of the two houses on the farm. The cabin where Verity and her family lived . . . it's all falling down now with cobwebs and stuff . . . but it's still there." She paused for breath. "I climbed over the fence, and I guess he saw me, because this man—a caretaker or something—came. He had these two big dogs and a shotgun. I explained how I was with a film company and we were thinking about doing a documentary. I was kinda scared, but he just told me to get off the property. Then he watched to make sure I was gone." A breath. "But I bet J. T. could get him to talk. He looked old enough to have been around when it happened. And we could do interviews with the other neighbors. Verity Thomas's family left town, but we could track them down. And maybe you could get Mr. Gant to do an interview."

Maybe I—as in Lizzie Stuart—could?

"Anyway, that's why I'm calling. Because J. T., the independent filmmaker I got the job with, told me he'd been wanting to do a criminal justice documentary. This morning when I called to tell him about Verity, he was really excited.

He said we could do a conference today at 11:30, and he thought it would be really great to have you as a consultant. So please come, Dr. Stuart. The address is 524 Van Buren." Another pause. Then more subdued. "J. T. really wants you as a consultant. He says you'll give us credibility. So, I'll see you there, okay, Dr. Stuart?"

I reached for the telephone book intending to find this J. T. and his film studio and inform the person who answered that I would not be joining the morning's conference. I was running my finger down the listings, looking for the number, when I began to think better of it. I should go, first because I needed to speak to young Keisha about eavesdropping and about volunteering me for projects. I should also go because I needed to warn Keisha and her boss off this particular project. I needed to tell them that something might be going on between Jebediah Gant and Sloane Campbell and that they would be wise to steer clear of it.

Keisha would be disappointed, but maybe I could suggest another criminal justice topic. Not something I had any intention of consulting on, but something that would be worth doing. I had gotten into a chat with a woman at Miss Alice's church the last time I was there. She was a hardworking, well-spoken woman with two sons serving time in Virginia correctional facilities. There were other mothers and wives of men in prison. It would make a marvelous documentary to talk to them about how they saw the criminal justice system and how having men in prison affected their lives. A much more useful documentary than one about an almost-fifty-year-old crime.

Or was it? There were all kinds of issues that were still relevant in the Verity Thomas case. Including the execution of juvenile offenders.

Would I be discouraging Keisha from pursuing the Thomas case if my own position wasn't still tentative? No signatures yet on the dotted line for the faculty position or the endowment.

I sunk down on the chair by the telephone and thought about that for a moment.

Yes, I would still tell them to leave it alone. At least, for now. Definitely when it came to making a documentary.

J. T. was a few years short of 30. He wore glasses, a serious expression, and a Grateful Dead T-shirt. From all of the camera equipment, some of which I couldn't identify, it was clear that he was a professional—or wanted to be.

In fact, his film-school credentials sounded impressive. He explained that he had done an apprenticeship and then, a couple of years ago, had started his own company. He had a partner, and they had three employees. Two full-time and Keisha, who would be working part-time.

I let him talk, glancing from his earnest face to Keisha's eager one. When he was done, I took a deep breath and said what I had come to say.

Keisha's smile faded, her lower lip dropped. She looked as if I had stabbed her in the back. It probably did feel that way to her.

I stood up to go. J. T. stood too and shook my hand. "Thank you, Professor Stuart, you've given us something to consider." He glanced at Keisha's downcast face. "I know K's all excited about the Thomas case, and I admit I was too. But we don't want to create trouble for ourselves if we don't have to. And I really like this prisoner family idea you pitched. If we decide to do it, would you be willing to—"

I knew what was coming, and I braced myself for Keisha's—K's—hurt look when I said no. But before J. T. could finish, the heavy, metal door slammed inward. Sloane Campbell strode in with one of J. T.'s employees running after him, waving her arms at J. T.

"I couldn't stop him," she said.

"Are you in charge here?" Campbell demanded.

J. T. stepped up to him and held out his hand. "James Taylor Prentice, III. May I help you?"

"You can help me all right," he said. "You can keep your staff off my property." Then he saw me. "You again. What game are you playing? How do you fit into this?"

I shook my head. "I don't. Our meeting in the parking lot was purely coincidental, and this—"

"Don't give me that bullshit. Did they send you over to look around the Shoppes?" He turned back to J. T. "Stay away from me. Stay off my property. Or you're going to get a camera rammed down your throat."

Keisha's mouth fell open. She turned and looked at me. I could see that she was as stunned as I was that Campbell would talk about ramming anything down anyone's throat. Or maybe it was because of how his mother had died that he'd made that reference.

He strode out the way he had come, leaving a definite impression behind him.

J. T. sat down at his conference table and fiddled with his glasses. "I don't think we'll be doing that documentary, Keisha."

"You're going to let him intimidate you like that?" she asked.

"Yes," J. T. said. "I like my throat the way it is."

Keisha was arguing the point, reminding him about truth and integrity in filmmaking, when I tiptoed out the door.

I was glad to see Campbell's pickup was nowhere in sight when I stepped out into the parking lot. I would do well to look out for that truck if I ever needed to go back to Madeline's shop. He was not likely to give me his parking space the next time we met. He might even call security and have me towed away.

But, on a brighter note, Campbell had ensured that J. T. would not change his mind again and that I would not have the awkward task of calling Jebediah Gant to explain that one of my students was working on a documentary inspired by what she'd heard while eavesdropping outside the door.

Joyce dug into her seafood lasagna and grimaced. Not at the food. At the account I had given her of my morning and my day before. "Your life is fascinating," she said.

I forked a cucumber slice from my salad bowl to my mouth. "But enough about my life. We're supposed to be cheering you up."

"Except I'm not sure we can do that. I think distraction is the best we can hope for."

"Did you tell Pete yet?"

Joyce shook her head. "I'm going to wait until I get the results. There's no reason for him to have to rack his brain trying to figure out what to say. Sensitivity is not Pete's strong point."

I had to agree with that. "He might surprise you," I said.

"He probably wouldn't. So no reason to put us both in that uncomfortable position."

Still, I did think Pete would want to know. But I could see from her tense shoulders, hear in her voice, that she did not want to talk about it.

"So what movie do you want to see?" I said. "We're playing hooky and doing a matinee, remember?"

"Let's skip the matinee and go see your house," Joyce said.

"Charlotte Wingate's house. And we're supposed to spend the afternoon doing something fun."

"This will be fun. You have the key with you, don't you?"

I nodded. "Yes, but I still think—"

"Please, Dr. Stuart, please," Joyce said. "I want to see the house."

"Okay. If you insist. I'd like your opinion anyway."

"And if we find some bootleg liquor setting around, we can get drunk as skunks."

I took a sip of my iced tea. "I wonder where that expression came from."

"Skunkweed," Joyce said. "Skunks eat it and get intoxicated."

"They do?" I said. "But isn't skunkweed a cabbage? No, I guess it isn't really, but the name—"

Joyce giggled. "Has anyone ever told you that you're gullible, Lizzie?"

"Well, it sounded right for a moment," I said. Then I giggled too.

And then we were both laughing at Joyce's joke and my gullibility and all of life's assorted absurdities.

The house on Grant Avenue was enough to leave us both too stunned to laugh. It sat back from the street in its own acre or so of real estate with a gated entrance. I got out and used the key to unlock the gate. Joyce kept saying "wow" as I drove up the driveway under majestic oaks and parked in front of the house.

"Can you believe it?" she said. "Who in the world designed this place?"

"I think several people must have had a hand in it," I said.

We got out of the car and stood staring up at the tower that seemed to have been a later addition. The original structure combined the most eccentric gingerbread features of Queen Anne with bay windows and a wraparound porch that featured white colonial pillars. The entire structure—except for the pillars and the gray brick Gothic tower—was painted shocking pink. There was also a touch of dashing black in the form of the shutters on the windows of the two lower stories and what appeared to be a third-floor attic.

Joyce craned her head back to peer up at the shingled roof. "You did say, didn't you, that people wanted this house as a place from which to conduct serious business activities?"

"I'm not sure why Howard Knowlin wanted it," I said. "But it would work for Madeline's Attic. Her customers would be attracted to a place like this. If Jebediah Gant and his niece had gotten it for their law offices, I guess they would have painted it a somber gray. But for some reason, Jebediah changed his mind about wanting it."

"I wonder why," Joyce said.

"It isn't that awful," I said. "It's rather impressive in its own screwy way. And with all this land around it right in the city, you would definitely have privacy."

"Ideal for a 1920s speakeasy," Joyce said. "Any drunk who staggered out of this place and looked up at that tower must have staggered right back in for another drink."

"I think they would have been more discreet than that. Charlotte Wingate said it was a private club. Probably wealthy people who came and had a high old time, and maybe slept over if they were really drunk." I swept out my arms. "This place must have loads of rooms."

"Loads of something," Joyce said. "Let's go see the inside."

When we stepped into the foyer, Joyce let out another "wow." There was a sweeping staircase with a banister that seemed to be made of brass.

But there was also the smell of dust and old stale cooking odors and maybe a decaying mouse or two. The rose-patterned wallpaper in the foyer had a waist-high gash across it as if someone had slashed at it with scissors or a knife. The hardwood floor had black scuff marks.

"The kids that were living here," I reminded Joyce. "Remember, Charlotte Wingate leased it to a couple who were running a foster home for teenagers."

"I wonder how she got that bright idea," Joyce said, fingering the gashed wallpaper.

"Being Lady Bountiful, I guess." I glanced into the large room off to the left. It contained a bare fireplace, a ripped velvet love seat, and two battered armchairs. The rest of the room was empty except for an old potato chip bag under one of the chairs. "I wonder why she didn't send someone in to make repairs after she evicted her tenants."

Joyce sat down on the stairs. "I'm sitting here because I've got to send this dress to the cleaners anyway. Speaking of which, you'd better hope a cleaning service, repairs, and appropriate furniture come with the endowment."

"They must," I said. "Charlotte Wingate can't expect the school to pay for renovations."

"What about upkeep?" Joyce said.

I dropped down on the step beside her. "I dunno. Doesn't that come with the endowment of a building? An annual stipend for upkeep?"

She shrugged. "Don't ask me. I've never been endowed."

I leaned back on my elbows and looked up at the high ceiling, which featured cherubs and peeling gilt paint. "Would you like, Professor Fielding, to be the assistant executive director of this institute?"

"Sure, now that you know you're getting a pink elephant."

"Seriously," I said. "I don't know if I want to take this on alone."

"And you also don't know if you can choose your second in command."

"I could make it a condition of acceptance."

Joyce said, "Thank you for the invitation. I'll let you know after next week."

I sat up and hugged her shoulder. "I'll take that as a tentative yes. Let's go see the rest of the place."

We made our way through a dining room that was in no better shape than the living room and foyer.

Joyce snorted when she saw the kitchen. There was a huge fireplace built into one wall, as if the original owners had thought "medieval" when they got to this part of the design and had visions of servants roasting the occasional pig for dinner.

The furniture in the room consisted of a rickety wood table and two matching chairs.

"Well, at least, it looks like someone scrubbed the kitchen floor before they left," I said looking down at the white and gray tiles.

"Maybe it was so gooey, they couldn't bear to walk on it," Joyce said.

There was an impressive butler's pantry that still contained a torn bag of coffee and assorted cans of beans, vegetables, and soup.

Joyce pushed open the door leading from the kitchen out onto the wrap-around porch. "Now, this is better," she said.

"Move so I can see too," I said.

What we saw was a rolling lawn that ended on the bank of a stream. The water sparkled in the sun. The lawn featured a gazebo and a picnic table and a brick barbecue pit. Someone had actually bothered to care for the lawn.

"Look," I said as the water reeds parted down by the stream. "A duck. Two of them." I looked closer. "I wonder if they have any babies yet."

"Uh-huh," Joyce said. "That means when you stroll down to the stream, you're going to be walking in duck poop. But the back lawn does make up some for the house."

"We haven't looked upstairs yet. Let's— Oh! The basement." I swung around, scanning the kitchen walls. "Where do you think the secret door is?"

"We could walk around tapping the walls until we reach a section that sounds hollow," Joyce said. "Standard Nancy Drew."

"Or we could use a process of elimination. Standard Sherlock Holmes. Shucks, why didn't I think to ask where? Let's try out in the hall. Basement doors are usually there."

"And since the hall is paneled in wood, concealment would be easier," Joyce said, her voice profound.

We spent the next ten minutes or so running our hands along the pine wall, pushing at knobby sections, tapping. We even tried the door to the tower. There was enough light coming in from the narrow window slits to make our way up the stone steps to the tower room. Which was utterly and completely empty.

"Not even a prince waiting to be rescued," Joyce said as we went back down again.

"It has to be here somewhere," I said. "Where would you put a secret basement door?"

"The living room or the foyer. Or the—"

"Under the stairs," I said. "There's enough space."

But it wasn't there, or in any of the other downstairs rooms we tried.

"Upstairs?" Joyce said.

I turned toward the staircase. "Wait! The butler's pantry."

We went back to the kitchen and into the pantry. "There's no place for a door in here," Joyce said.

"Let's try pushing at the shelves."

We both gasped when the pantry swung backward to reveal a dark staircase. Joyce peered down. "I am not going down there without a flashlight."

"Maybe there's one in the kitchen."

There was. Right on top of the refrigerator.

"If there are rats down there," Joyce said, "you're on your own."

"It can't be too awful. Remember, people were living here. I bet the kids even hung out down there." I started down the stairs, creeping, ready to retreat. "There must be a light switch. Oh, wait a minute, it's a pull-chain setup."

The single bulb flared on. Joyce and I stood there at the bottom of the steps, regarding the two small rooms. The larger one contained a dilapidated plaid couch with crushed cushions and a dartboard on the wall. The smaller room contained a washer and a dryer.

"Well, that was a whole lot of effort for nothing," Joyce said. "Nary a gin bottle in sight."

"And even in those days, they obviously didn't fit a lot of people in here at a time," I said. "So much for the secret basement. It is kind of interesting that it doesn't have any windows."

"Uh-huh. Let's go check out the second floor."

"What I really want to see is the attic," I said, reaching for the light chain. "Ever since the first time I read *Little Women*— What's that?"

"What?" Joyce said.

I swept the flashlight beam under the staircase again. "I saw something glint."

"Aha," Joyce said. "We've found treasure."

I bent down frog-fashion, trying to avoid getting on the dusty floor as I edged under the stairs. "Not treasure. It looks like some kind of dental thing. A mouth guard?"

Joyce leaned over my shoulder and looked down. "It's called a night guard. Pete has one. His dentist made him get it." She laughed. "For which I'm grateful. Have you ever heard a man grinding his teeth in his sleep?"

"No, I can't said that I have." I pushed at the night guard with the flashlight. "What a strange place for this to be. Under a staircase in the basement."

"The people who lived here with the foster kids probably left it," Joyce said. "With the mess they left upstairs—"

"Yes, but wouldn't you think they'd miss it?" I said. "Aren't these things expensive?"

"If you get them specially made by your dentist. Pete was moaning and groaning about how his cost over $400. But I've seen ads in magazines for mail-order kits."

I fished a tissue from my shoulder bag and picked the night guard up. "But doesn't this one look like the dentist kind? It doesn't look like something you could put together with a kit."

"Yeah," Joyce said. "It's got the metal frontpiece like Pete's and the same kind of palate. But it could still have belonged to one of the kids. Kids lose things and don't have any idea where."

I took another tissue out of my purse. "Well, we'd better take it with us and see if we can find the owner."

I was edging back from under the staircase, when the flashlight swept over something else. "There's the case," I said, scrambling farther under the staircase. "Dammit!"

"What?" Joyce said. "Don't tell me if you found something really gross under there."

"Just old chewing gum. My knee landed in it."

I backed out, holding the night guard in one hand and the tangerine plastic case in the other. The case had been open. Someone must have dropped it from the stairs and the night guard had fallen out.

"They aren't grimy," I said.

"What?" Joyce said.

"It's really dusty and yucky under the stairs, but the night guard and the case aren't. I don't think they were there very long."

"Do we really care?" Joyce said. "If you're through rescuing people's dental paraphernalia, could we go back upstairs?"

"Okay, I'm done." I dropped the case with the night guard into the zippered side pocket of my shoulder bag. Then I swept the flashlight around the basement one more time. "Definitely a bit gloomy. Can you get the light?"

"Yeah. Just shine the flashlight so we don't break our necks going back up the stairs."

I was halfway up the stairs, leading the way with the flashlight, when I stopped. Joyce plowed into me.

"Geez, Lizzie!" she said. "Why'd you stop like that?"

"Look," I said, shining the flashlight over the wooden railing. "The railing support is almost splintered there."

"It looks like someone hit it with something. Don't lean against it. And would you please just keep moving up the stairs."

"It is kind of spooky, isn't it?" I said. "Maybe it was more fun to hang out in a secret basement when a party was going on."

"I'd need a lot of booze to want to party down here," Joyce said.

En route to the attic, we stopped on the second floor and walked through the six bedrooms, all of which were without furniture. Each bedroom had period wallpaper and hardwood floors. There were plenty of windows which provided attractive views. The two bathrooms had been modernized, but they were in definite need of scouring. That was about all that could be said of the second floor.

Upstairs in the attic, we found more dust and cobwebs and an odd assortment of broken and discarded furniture. I raised the window and leaned forward, peering out and down.

Joyce opened a hatbox to look inside and came up with a sagging lilac lace concoction. "Had enough?" she said, dusting off her hands.

"Yes," I said, pushing the window down and locking it.

We locked up as we were leaving. Back door, front door, gate behind us as we drove out. Not that a thief would find much worth stealing in the house. But someone might decide to take up residence.

"Are we still playing hooky?" I asked Joyce.

She had found a moist wash pad in her purse and was scrubbing the dust from her hands. She held one out to me. "Definitely. What did you have in mind?"

"An errand I need to do. I want to stop by the address that Madeline gave me for RaeAnne. Remember, she's the artist—"

"Who made the heart that Quinn gave you. I'm riding, you're driving. Go wherever you like."

"Thanks, this shouldn't take long. If I can find the place."

"What's the address?" Joyce said.

I handed her the card I had taken from my purse.

"I think I know where this is," she said. "It isn't one of Gallagher's better neighborhoods."

It wasn't bad as The Row, down by the railroad tracks, but it was more dismal. In this neighborhood, the residents were losing their battle to maintain their working-class respectability. Three young white men who should have been at work—maybe at the mill—were sitting on a stoop drinking beer. They eyed the car as we drove by. A couple of discarded toy scooters were scattered among the yellowed grass in the yard next door. That was the address we were looking for.

"I'm glad I brought you along," I said. "I think I'm a little out of place in this neighborhood."

"I'll have you know this is not my natural environment either," Joyce said with mock outrage.

"But you have less of a pigmentation problem. Come on, you're coming with me. Maybe the guys next door will think we're social workers."

They eyed us as we picked our way up the rutted walk. One of them stood up, still sipping his beer. Watching.

On the porch, I rapped on the door with my knuckles. The doorbell was pulled loose and obviously not working.

"Are you certain you wrote the address down right?" Joyce asked, examining the peeling white paint. "It doesn't look like a place that would inspire creativity."

"No, it doesn't. But it's the address Madeline gave me." I rapped one more time. Then I dug into my shoulder bag for a pen and paper to leave a note.

The front door creaked open half an inch.

"Hello," I said, trying to see what I could of the face peering through the crack. "Are you RaeAnne Dobb? Madeline Oliver gave me your address, Ms. Dobb. I want to talk to you about—"

"I ain't RaeAnne," the woman said, opening the door wide enough for us to see that she was middle-aged and wearing a housedress. "RaeAnne's not here."

"I'm sorry," I said. "Do you know when she'll be back?"

"It better be soon. I can't stay here much longer with her kid."

Her kid? Well, that explained the toys on the lawn.

"Are you the baby-sitter?" I asked.

"I'm RaeAnne's aunt," the woman said. "Who did you say you were?"

"I'm Lizzie Stuart. The name won't mean anything to your niece. My . . . my boyfriend bought something at Madeline's Attic that RaeAnne made. That's the shop in—"

"I know where it is," the woman said. "Not the kind of place I'd spend my money even if I had any. But some people are fool enough to pay them kind of prices."

Joyce made a coughing sound. I ignored her.

The woman went on, "And you can tell her to stop calling here. She's already left three messages on RaeAnne's answering machine telling her to 'please call Madeline.' Between her and that kid who called and left two or three messages about RaeAnne having his jacket—don't they think if she was here she would've called them back by now?"

I decided to let that one lie. "About RaeAnne. Will she be back later today?"

"That's what I'm telling you. She ain't here. She's been gone since Monday morning. That's why I decided to come to the door. I thought the two of you might be lady cops."

"Lady cops?" I said. "Then you're expecting to hear bad news about—"

"I ain't expecting to hear she won the lottery." She reached up and snapped the cover of one of her pink plastic curlers into place. "RaeAnne's a sweet girl. Real talented with her art." She waved her hand toward the inside of the house. "She's got herself a studio set up back there." The woman shook her head. "But sometimes she ain't got the sense God gave her. Especially when it comes to men. If she did, she wouldn't have that kid in there. The only thing she can be grateful for is that his daddy finally shot himself up with too much dope and died."

"But RaeAnne—" I said. "She isn't . . . you don't think she's off somewhere—"

"Nah," the woman said, studying her slippered foot as if it might have the answer. "I don't know where she is, but RaeAnne ain't never touched dope. But she's gotta be somewhere she don't want to be, or she'd be back here. She's nuts about that kid of hers. Me, I ain't got that much patience. Terrible twos, they call them, and there's a reason. Only time he's quiet is when he's sleeping."

Since the house behind her was silent, I assumed he must be having a nap.

"Have you thought of calling the police?" I said. "If RaeAnne has been gone since Monday morning, maybe you should call the police and file a missing person—"

"Nah," the woman said. "If the two of you ain't them, I'll just wait. I might be wrong. She might be staying with one of them girls she met at school."

"At school?" I said. "What school?"

"Piedmont U. She's going there part time. Got this idea in her head about learning to teach art to handicapped children. Special needs, I think you call 'em."

"But if she were with one of her friends from school," I said, "wouldn't she have called to let you know? So that you wouldn't worry about her."

"I ain't the worrying kind," RaeAnne's aunt said. "It ain't worth it. Nothing you can do about most of the things you worry about."

"That's true," I said. "But if RaeAnne is missing—"

"I don't know that she's missing. I told you, sometimes RaeAnne ain't got the sense God gave her. Anyways, she knows I ain't going nowhere until she gets back. Maybe she's off studying for an exam or writing a paper or something."

"Maybe," I said. "But still, it might be a good idea to call the police and—"

"If I call the police, next thing you know, them child welfare people will be around here again. They'll accuse RaeAnne of deserting her kid. That's the way they work. I'll wait until I hear something. She'll turn up sooner or later. I gotta go back in now. I got some stewed fruit for the kid on the stove."

With that she closed the door, leaving us there on the porch.

"Let's get out of here," Joyce said. "Those guys next door are on the move."

I glanced toward the house next door. The other two had joined their companion. They were all standing now, staring in our direction. One of them, the tallest one, stretched. Then he tossed his beer bottle in the general direction of a plastic garbage can. It missed and shattered on a stray brick.

"We could ask if they know anything about RaeAnne," I said. "But I think we probably don't want to stop and chat."

"No, we don't," Joyce said, edging toward the steps. "So, walking briskly but not showing fear, we get ourselves back to the car."

We didn't quite make it. We were a few yards away, when the three of them, obeying some silent signal, starting running toward us. Before we could get to the car and tumble inside, they were there in front of it.

Three young white men in their late teens or early twenties clad in white T-shirts and blue jeans. Flash back to the '50s, and they could have played extras in any Hollywood gang movie.

The sky was blue, the March sunshine was warm. It was all right. No need to panic. They wouldn't dare do anything in broad daylight right out on the street. They were just trying to intimidate us. And it was working.

"Hey, guys," Joyce said when they didn't speak. "What's happening? We were just visiting with RaeAnne's aunt. Now we're leaving."

"So if you wouldn't mind moving so that we can get to our car," I said, taking a step forward.

Which brought me a step closer to them. Because they didn't budge. Or speak.

The tall one, who seemed to be the leader, did fold his arms. I thought of telling him that I was really good friends with a cop who did that when he was pissed. And he really would be if they messed with us.

But Joyce and I were adults. We should be able to get ourselves out of this without evoking the name of an absent male. "We'd really like to leave now," Joyce said.

No response. We could always scream for RaeAnne's aunt.

"This is ridiculous," I said, trying not to let them see that I was sweating. "We don't have time to stand here all day, even if you do. What do you want?"

The tall one said, "What'd you want with RaeAnne's aunt?"

"We were looking for RaeAnne," I said.

"Why?" he said.

I told him. Then he said, "That all you want with her?"

"That's all," I said. "But her aunt says she hasn't been home since Monday morning."

The shortest of the trio nudged him. "I told you," he said

"Shut up," the tall one said. "That don't mean nothing."

"What doesn't?" I said.

"She was crying," the middle-sized one said. "Randy saw her crying."

"When was that?" I said.

They exchanged looks again. Then the short one, who must be Randy, said, "Last week. Thursday. She was walking along crying. I asked her what was wrong, if someone had been messing with her, and she shook her head and told me she was okay."

The tall one glared at him. "Yeah, she told you she was okay. And the next day when you saw her, she was smiling and laughing like always. Women cry over stupid stuff."

"Not RaeAnne," Randy said. "And where is she, if everything's okay? I told you I hadn't seen her in a while."

"Since Friday?" I said.

"We were gone on Saturday and Sunday," he said. "Went to Charleston to—"

"Randy, shut your trap," the tall one said. "Don't be telling our business."

"I'm not telling our business," Randy said. "I'm worried about RaeAnne."

"She's probably off with some guy or something," the tall one said, but he sounded as if he was trying to convince himself.

"Is she dating someone?" I asked.

"Nobody that ever comes here to get her," Randy said. "And I'd know. I live right there, next door."

The middle-sized one dug into his back pocket. He came out with a wallet. "See, here she is," he said, pulling out a photograph. "With the three of us. We were at a picnic."

Joyce and I leaned closer to stare at the photograph. RaeAnne Dobb was beautiful. Slender with a kind of Audrey Hepburn elegance in the tilt of her head. More generously curved, but still with a kind of fragileness about her. Laughing at the camera as she stood with her arms around Randy and the middle-sized one. The tall one sat at her feet. The three of them were laughing too. Sharing her joy.

"We all went to school together," the tall one said, his voice grudging. "From the first grade on. We watch out for RaeAnne."

"Yeah, she's like our little sister," the middle-sized one said as he put the photograph back into his battered wallet.

"What about the guy she . . . the father of her child?" I said. "I've heard he—"

The tall one glowered at me. "We couldn't do anything about that."

"Yeah, we tried to tell her the guy was scum," the middle-sized one said.

"Anyhow, he's dead now," the tall one said, with a hint of a suggestion—just a hint—that they had taken care of the problem.

Was he playing tough? Or was it the truth?

"So what are you going to do?" the short one, Randy, asked. "You going to tell the cops she's missing?"

"Why don't you?" I said.

He glanced toward the house. I turned around and looked too. I couldn't tell if RaeAnne's aunt was at the window.

"You do it," the tall one said. "Come on," he said to the others. "We got better things to do than stand here."

The other two hesitated, looking at Joyce and me. Then they followed him. Departing with swaggers meant to suggest they didn't give a damn. Except they obviously did when it came to RaeAnne.

Joyce said, "Okay. Fine. Now, let's get in the car and go."

By the time I had found a place to turn around, the trio were back in their lounging positions on the stoop. They all had fresh bottles of beer.

Joyce waved through her rolled-up window. "Bye, guys."

They didn't wave back.

"Thank you, Lizzie," Joyce said as we stepped out of the elevator at Brewster Hall. "As distracting afternoons go, this one was a beaut."

"I did my best," I said.

"Don't forget to give Amos a report on your pink elephant," she said as she sauntered off down the opposite corridor, toward her office. "And let me know how the RaeAnne thing turns out."

C H A P T E R · 9

IN MY OFFICE, I sat down at my desk and pulled the telephone toward me. I debated with myself for another few minutes, then I punched in the number for the university police department. I gave my name to the officer who answered, and asked for Sergeant Burke.

The sergeant came on the line with a brisk, "Yes, Professor Stuart, what can I do for you?"

That was when it occurred to me that he might interpret my call as a special request from the woman who was dating his boss. But it was a perfectly legitimate request. I would have made it even if I hadn't been dating Quinn. I just wouldn't have known to ask for the officer that Quinn considered his right-hand man. Sergeant Michael Burke, somewhere around six-three, tawny brown of skin, and unflappable of manner. He had seemed to find me acceptable on the several occasions when we'd encountered each other at the university police department. So maybe he wouldn't take my request as a presumption on his time and my relationship with Quinn.

"Professor Stuart, are you there?" he said.

"Yes, Sergeant Burke, I'm sorry, I know you must be busy. But I wonder if you could check on something . . . or rather someone . . . for me. Her name is RaeAnne Dobb, and she's a part-time student here. In art education, I think."

"What do you want me to check about her, Professor Stuart?"

"She seems to be missing. I wonder if you could find out if she's been in her classes this week."

I told him what I knew about RaeAnne Dobb's absence. What Joyce and I had learned from her aunt and from Randy and his friends.

Sergeant Burke said, "What's your connection to RaeAnne Dobb, Professor? I thought I understood you to say that she's an art education major. Is she in one of your criminal justice classes?"

"No, I've never met her," I said. "Aside from being a student here, she's also an artist. I have one of her pieces. A ceramic . . . a ceramic piece . . . that she designed and that someone gave to me. It has a crack, and I was hoping that she could repair it. That's why I went there, to her house. Because the owner of the shop where this ceramic piece was purchased couldn't reach her and suggested I stop by RaeAnne's house."

Sergeant Burke was silent for a long moment. Was he writing this down? "Okay," he said. "I'll let you know if I come up with anything."

"Sergeant, I don't want to . . . as I've told you, her aunt is worried about child welfare becoming involved. That's why she hasn't reported her niece missing. I'm assuming that you won't have to call them. I don't want to get RaeAnne in trouble."

"We'll treat this as a routine attempt-to-locate request," he said.

"What does that mean exactly?" I said.

"It means that we'll make an attempt as time permits to contact Ms. Dobb's professors, any known friends or associates, and her place of employment if she has one. Normally, we would also contact her family, but since you'd already spoken to—"

"Yes," I said. "Please don't contact her aunt."

"We won't for now. But we will send a teletype to local law enforcement agencies."

"No, you can't do that. I told you, her aunt's concerned about—"

"Child welfare," Sergeant Burke said. "We won't contact any social service agencies."

"But does that mean they won't become involved?" I asked. "Once you begin contacting other law enforcement agencies—"

"I can't promise you that won't happen, Professor. What I can tell you is, now that you've made me aware of the fact that a student enrolled at this university might be a missing person, Chief Quinn would expect me to act on that information."

I felt a chill seeping through my body. "To act in case something really has happened to her."

"Let's hope nothing has," Sergeant Burke said. "But if it has, it would be preferable for this department if we can show that we didn't ignore the information that you provided. I'll get back to you, Professor."

"Thank you," I said.

"Just doing my job. If you don't mind my asking, is this ceramic piece you wanted to have repaired the heart that Chief Quinn gave you for Valentine's Day?"

"I . . . yes . . . it . . . he showed it to you?"

"Chief Quinn was having second thoughts about his choice. He asked me if I thought you'd like it."

"I did like it. I do like it very much. But it fell and cracked during the earthquake. And I wanted to find RaeAnne Dobb, who designed it, to see if she could repair it."

"I'll do what I can to track her down, Professor Stuart."

"Thank you, Sergeant Burke. I . . . of course, now I'm also concerned about the fact that she's missing."

"Understood," he said.

"Good-bye, Sergeant. Thank—" And then I remembered that Quinn had been calling his office to check in. "Sergeant, if you talk to Chief Quinn . . . I want to try to have the heart repaired before he—"

"I'll try to avoid mentioning that aspect of our conversation, Professor. Unless it becomes necessary."

"Thank you," I said. "I'll check back with you tomorrow."

"We may not have anything by then," he said.

"I'll check back anyway."

Having done what I could about RaeAnne, I decided to go to the university library and do some research on the Verity Thomas case. Even though I had done my best to discourage Keisha and J. T. from making a documentary about the case, there was no reason I shouldn't see what else I could find out about it. I could incorporate it into my class lectures. As a juvenile-death-penalty case, it was worth discussion. Besides, I wanted to read Jebediah's summation to the jury.

Before I walked over to the library, I decided to do a quick Internet search to see if there was anything on-line about Verity Thomas.

The answer was, not much. There was brief mention of her on a Web site devoted to executions prior to *Furman,* the 1972 decision that had sent the states back to their drawing boards to come up with a two-step process that satisfied the majority of the Supreme Court's sense of due process in capital cases. The entry for Verity Thomas on this list of pre-Furman death-sentence cases appeared under the state of Virginia:

Verity Thomas, age 17, sentenced June 12, 1955. Died while awaiting execution.

Well, now I knew that the killing of Blanche Campbell had occurred during the first half of that year. That would help as I was going through the *Gazette,* looking for articles about the case.

The sparsely populated library reminded me that we were only one day away from spring break. Many of the students who lived on campus had already departed for home.

I found the microfilm that I needed and set it up on the machine. As I did, I reminded myself that I was not here to read every article in the newspaper. That was one of the hazards of this kind of research, the temptation to meander through yesterday.

On the other hand, I also knew from experience that it was important to look at a case against the background of what had been happening when it occurred.

So skim, but don't get bogged down.

January 1, Churchill had been prime minister of England. *Shane* was playing at the movies, and there were at least seven different movie theaters in Gallagher, including three drive-ins.

The new Congress had opened with a record number of the "fair sex" among its members. But it was still 1955. In an article in the *Family Weekly* Sunday supplement, Edith Neisser warned the perfect housewife and mother about the dangers inherent in trying to "remake" one's less-than-perfect spouse.

An ad for a Ford Thunderbird. What kind of car had Blanche Campbell owned? Hadn't Jebediah Gant said it was a Cadillac? A new one. Had she purchased it after her husband's death? How long had she been widowed before she was killed?

The Senate Juvenile Delinquency subcommittee urged federal funding for a school building program and for public housing to combat the "spiraling rate" of delinquency.

Virginia told the Supreme Court that school integration was impossible because of Negroes' lower level of educational attainment.

Here it was. The first story about Verity Thomas in the April 8th edition of the *Gazette:* 17 YEAR OLD NEGRO GIRL HELD FOR BRUTAL MURDER OF MOTHER, DROWNING OF BABY.

In the front page story, the reporter described Verity Thomas's apprehension by the county sheriff's deputies. Then noted: "The sheriff reports that feelings are strong in the county against the Thomas girl. Extra guards have been placed on duty at the jail to ensure no disorder occurs prior to her arraignment."

Understandable that the sheriff had been concerned. It was the year after the 1954 *Brown v. Board of Education* decision shook the segregated South. It was the year when the Civil Rights movement would hit its stride when Rosa Parks refused to give up her seat on the bus. A year when anything might happen. Including a black girl killing her white employer and a mob dragging her from the jail.

But it was fascinating that Verity Thomas, a 17-year-old girl, had struck out . . . or back . . . at her employer in that year that had symbolized postwar concern about juvenile delinquency. In 1955, *Rebel Without a Cause,* a movie about alienated white teenagers, also had been playing at theaters nationwide.

Verity Thomas's case had gone to trial in June, attracting "much attention," according to the reporter assigned to the case. The *Gazette* had given the trial extensive coverage, including portions of the testimony of various witnesses.

Witnesses for the prosecution had included the neighbor who'd been the first to arrive at the farm after Blanche Campbell's children called him. The medical examiner testified as to Blanche Campbell's death from asphyxiation. He also described the damage that had been done to her head and body during the struggle. But it was the description of that sock shoved down her throat that had "shocked those in the courtroom."

When Jebediah's turn came to present Verity Thomas's defense, he had called her aunt, Helen Thomas, to the stand. The aunt testified that she had been at her brother's house that day, in the early afternoon, when her niece announced that she was going to walk over to see Mrs. Campbell.

The reporter—bless him—had transcribed the rest of her testimony and included it in his article:

> "For what purpose?" the attorney asked. "Why did Verity want to go see Mrs. Campbell?"
>
> "To ask for the wages that Mrs. Campbell owed her," replied the aunt.
>
> "Was it her regular payday? Verity's, I mean?"
>
> "No, sir. She didn't have no regular payday. Was whenever Mrs. Campbell felt like giving it to her."
>
> "Why did Verity want her wages on that day?" Attorney Gant asked.
>
> "Because her mama was ailing. Verity wanted the money so that she could buy her mama's medicine."
>
> "Wasn't Verity aware of the fact that Wednesday was the day that Mrs. Campbell drove into town to do her shopping?"
>
> "Yes, sir. She knew that. But Mrs. Campbell had told her she weren't going until the next day 'cause she had too much to do. She'd asked Verity to come over and help her. So Verity thought if she went and worked a little while, Mrs. Campbell might go ahead and pay her."
>
> "She went," Attorney Gant said, "with the intention of offering her services to Mrs. Campbell?"
>
> "Yes, sir. That's why she went."

According to the reporter, the prosecutor had then subjected Verity Thomas's aunt to a "keen cross-examination, touching upon discrepancies in her story." But she continued to maintain that her niece had gone to Blanche Campbell's house expecting to find her at home and to work for her.

Jebediah's next witness had been Blanche Campbell's 10-year-old son, Sloane.

I thought for a moment of the man Sloane Campbell and tried to imagine him as a boy called to testify by the lawyer who was defending his mother's killer.

According to the *Gazette* reporter, he had been compelled to testify over the prosecutor's "vigorous protest." His testimony had seemed to "first help, then harm" the defense's case. Described by the reporter as "a thin, somber boy who answered the defense counselor's questions in a steady voice," young Sloane Campbell had answered, "I don't know," when Jebediah asked, "Did you ever see your mother lose her temper?"

Jebediah had persisted, "You must know. Did you ever see your mother lose her temper?"

The prosecutor had stood up and "yelled out" his objection to this "badgering of a child."

But the judge had allowed Jebediah to go on. Had instructed young Sloane Campbell to answer the question. The article continued:

> "Yes, sir," the boy said. "Sometimes she'd get mad."
> "Did you ever see her strike Verity Thomas?" Attorney Gant asked. "That happened, didn't it?"
> "Yes, sir. When they were arguing about the skirt and blouse she said Verity stole. Verity said she didn't, and she slapped her."
> "Did Verity strike her back?"
> "No, sir," the boy replied. "Verity just left."

But then it was the prosecutor's turn to cross-examine. With statements that were worded as questions to the boy, he reminded the jury and the courtroom spectators that Blanche Campbell had been tiny, barely five-two and all of one hundred pounds. Verity Thomas had been a "strapping, stoutly built, and much younger woman." That final struggle, according to the prosecutor, had been "no equal contest."

The prosecutor asked Sloane Campbell if he had ever seen Verity Thomas show disrespect to his mother, talk back to her. The boy answered, "Yes."

After calling Helen Thomas and Sloane Campbell, Jebediah had rested his case. He had called no expert witness to testify about Verity Thomas's mental state or the semi-retardation he had mentioned to me.

Verity Thomas, herself, did not take the stand. Perhaps because he was concerned about the impression she would make on the jury or how she would stand up under cross-examination.

Perhaps Jebediah had thought that daring to argue self-defense and to attempt to show that Blanche Campbell had been both hot-tempered and physically abusive toward her employee was as far as he could go on his client's behalf.

But it was a strange defense. Call the victim's son and antagonize every white person in the courtroom by browbeating a child. Call the defendant's aunt who told a story that was inherently biased in the eyes of the jury.

Of course, as he had said, everyone in the courtroom already knew what the outcome of that trial would be. But the judge and the prosecutor had known that they had to let him have something. What had he meant by that? Why had they allowed him to go even as far as he'd gone? Things about Blanche, he'd said.

The prosecutor in his summation to the jury described Verity Thomas as a "savage young killer who destroyed two lives on that afternoon for no more than what she could steal."

In Jebediah's summation to the jury—which had indeed been printed in its entirety, but so had the prosecutor's—he asked the jury—presumably all white and probably male—to "show mercy to this ignorant Negro girl." He told them that she came of poor parents—sharecroppers who had done their best by her but, because of their own impoverished state, had not been able to teach her control or discipline. Because of that, "these tragic events" occurred. But, he continued—rising to that eloquence that he had spoken of with pride—"I urge you to spare this girl's life. Send her to prison and hard labor, but do not put a stain upon this fair state with the blood of this ignorant, hapless girl."

It had taken the jury less than an hour to find Verity Thomas guilty of murder (and manslaughter in the case of the baby). The judge, having anticipated the outcome, immediately pronounced her sentence.

I skimmed through the next few months. After her sentencing, Verity Thomas disappeared behind prison walls until the final report of her "death by natural causes." The story was headed 17 YEAR OLD NEGRO MURDERESS CHEATS ELECTRIC CHAIR. She had died around 5 A.M. in the prison infirmary, attended only by the chaplain.

I rewound the microfilm and glanced at my watch. I had been there longer than I intended. It was after eight. But if I hurried, I would have time to stop by the Orleans Café and see Miss Alice. If anyone knew anything about this case, she would.

"What you getting yourself into now, child?" Miss Alice said, regarding me with a narrowed gaze.

"Nothing, Miss Alice." I held up my hand in oath. "I'm just doing some research so that I can use the case in my class."

We were sitting at her table by the kitchen door. As usual, the café was packed with diners who represented a cross-section of Gallagher society. There was nothing like good food to achieve at least a temporary melting pot.

"Well, I can't tell you nothing about that one," Miss Alice said, rubbing at her arthritic knee. "I weren't here when it happened."

"You weren't?" I said, surprised.

She eyed me. "Didn't you think I ever went nowhere in my life?"

"Yes, ma'am," I said. "I know you've been to New Orleans and—"

"That's where I was then. Down there a lot that year. My husband 'bout talked me into moving down there. Going someplace exciting."

"But you changed your mind?"

"This old town . . . I'd leave it, but I'd always come on back to it. 'Sides, I knew in my heart I couldn't depend on them children of mine to keep this place going like they should. This was my daddy's place. I couldn't let it go down."

"Yes, ma'am," I said.

"So I ain't got nothing to tell you about that case you so interested in. But now that you're here, you might as well have some dinner." Her gaze fastened on my face, observing my expression. "Then you can tell me what you been doing with yourself. He back yet?"

"Who?" I said, trying not to smile.

"You gonna have to do something about that man, you know. Take him or throw him back. Men get restless you keep 'em dangling too long."

"Yes, ma'am. I'm going to do something."

"Not that I'm saying I approve of no stuff without the preacher," she said. "You just remember what it is you want."

"I'll keep that in mind, ma'am. Once I figure it out."

"You know already," she said. "Question is, can you get it? Robert," she called out to her waiter. "Bring this child some of my gumbo. Some of that corn bread too. She look like she ain't ate in two days."

I tried not to notice the grinning customers who turned to look at me and confirm Miss Alice's observation.

She turned back to me. "Men don't like no skinny women, no matter what them magazines say."

"Yes, ma'am," I said. Then I thought of something. "Miss Alice, have you met Howard Knowlin, the real estate developer who—"

"I know who he is," she said. "Come in here trying to talk to me. Talking about how good his project's gonna be for all us small-business people downtown. Smooth-tongued rascal. I told him this café been here since 1912 and still going strong."

"I take it you didn't like him," I said.

"Didn't like him, didn't trust him. Don't trust no man smiling at me like that, while his eyes shifting round looking at what I got and thinking about how he gonna get it away from me."

"Yes, ma'am," I said, then thanked the waiter as he set gumbo and corn bread in front of me.

I ate and sat and listened as customers stopped at Miss Alice's table to present themselves to her. Along with their shared dislike of Howard Knowlin, Miss Alice and Charlotte Wingate had that much in common. They were both local royalty, divas with attitude.

CHAPTER · 10

FRIDAY, MARCH 16

Keisha's outline was in my mailbox when I got to school at a little before noon. I carried it with me to the faculty lounge. I hadn't slept much the night before, and I was ready to snap at anyone who came near me. So I made my tea and left the lounge before any of the other faculty could walk in and expect me to engage in conversation.

Not that my bad mood was totally due to lack of sleep. A part of it was that Quinn hadn't called last night. I'd almost called his mother's house this morning to make sure everything was all right with his stepfather. But there was no agreement between us that Quinn would call me every night while he was away. If he missed one night, maybe he'd been busy or gotten in late. Or maybe he hadn't felt any particular urge to talk to me.

I unlocked the door of my office, stalked across to my desk, and set down my mug and dropped Keisha's outline beside it. Then I raised my arms in the first movement of one of the stress reduction exercises that I'd found in a health magazine.

A few minutes later, I slid into my desk chair. I didn't feel as if I'd had the "mini-vacation" the article promised, but at least I felt ready to cope. Keisha's paper topic was the depiction of John Brown's raid on Harper's Ferry in popular culture. I opened the expanding folder I'd started for the class and put Keisha's outline with the others.

Then I took another sip of tea to fortify myself and pulled the telephone toward me.

When Sergeant Burke came on the line, I said, "I'm sorry to bother you, Sergeant. But I was wondering if you've had a chance to do anything about checking on RaeAnne Dobb yet."

"As a matter of fact I have," he said. "She's taking three classes this semester. One of them was canceled this week because the professor was ill. The professors in the other two—Intro Psych and Biology 101—don't take attendance, and neither one of them even recognized her name until they checked their rosters."

"Well, that's understandable," I said, feeling compelled to defend my colleagues. "If they're lower-level, introductory classes, they're both probably large."

"That's what the professors said. Intro Psych has 120 students enrolled. Biology has 75. But the psych professor thought her teaching assistants—who actually talk to the students individually on occasion—might know more about RaeAnne Dobb. If one of them does, the good professor will have him or her give me a call."

I ignored the touch of sarcasm in the sergeant's tone. I was not up to trying to explain that if you met with a class of 120 students once or twice a week in a large lecture hall, you didn't get to know each one up close and personal. Actually, I did wish that my colleagues in psychology and biology had known RaeAnne Dobb as more than a name on their rosters. RaeAnne was one of the reasons I hadn't been able to sleep. I kept seeing that laughing young woman in the photograph, surrounded by three would-be tough guys who thought of her as a little sister.

"Professor?" Sergeant Burke said.

"Still here," I said. "Just thinking. Yesterday, you mentioned checking places of employment. Do you know if RaeAnne had . . . has . . . a job?"

"Work study in the School of Education. Her supervisor, one of the secretaries there, says RaeAnne hasn't been in this week. She was scheduled to work both Monday and Wednesday afternoons. When she didn't come in on Wednesday, the secretary called her home."

"Did she talk to RaeAnne's aunt?" I said.

"She talked to an answering machine. She left a message asking RaeAnne to call her. She said she made it clear that she needed RaeAnne to get back to her. She had a lot of copying that needed doing and no work-study student to do it. She wanted to know if RaeAnne would be in to work her scheduled hours on Friday—this afternoon."

"But RaeAnne didn't call back?"

"She hadn't as of this morning," Sergeant Burke said. "But you spoke to her aunt yesterday afternoon. So we know she wasn't there then."

"You said that you usually contact other police agencies. Have you checked with the Gallagher PD?"

"I'm about to do that, Professor. I wanted to see first what I could find out here on campus."

"Of course . . . I didn't mean . . . I know you know your job." I pressed the fingers of my free hand to my forehead and rubbed. "It's just that I'm beginning to have this really bad feeling."

"That makes two of us," Sergeant Burke said. "So I think it might be a good idea if you stayed away from this, Professor Stuart. If we do have a problem here, the chief is not going to want you in the middle of it."

"I'm not in the middle of it," I said. "I've never even met RaeAnne Dobb.

All I wanted to do was get her to—"

"I know what you wanted, Professor. But it looks like this might turn into a police matter. So if you wouldn't mind not asking anyone else any more questions about Ms. Dobb's whereabouts."

"Believe it or not, Sergeant Burke, I didn't set out to conduct my own inquiry."

"I know you didn't, Professor," he said. "And I will give you a call if I find out anything more. But in the meantime—"

"In the meantime, leave this to your department."

"If you wouldn't mind. I hope you understand why I'm saying this. If Chief Quinn were here—"

"He would want me to stay out of this. Understood. Have a good afternoon, Sergeant."

"You too, Professor."

I hung up feeling more than a little put out by that final exchange. The message the sergeant had been trying to convey was that if I stirred up another mess, Quinn would be blamed. Therefore, Quinn would expect me not to stir up another mess.

Somehow I had managed to miss that moment when Quinn had assumed responsibility for my behavior.

The really annoying part was that the sergeant was right. Because of our relationship, what I did affected Quinn.

Back in Drucilla, the only women who'd had that much pressure on them had been the wives of ministers. I was not married to John Quinn. So it was downright irritating.

Especially since the man couldn't even remember to call last night so I didn't spend the day worrying about whether everything was all right out in Oklahoma.

I hadn't brought the number along. I would have to get directory assistance to find his mother's telephone number. They were probably at the hospital anyway.

If he hadn't call by ten this evening, then I would try to reach him. Until then I would work on my manuscript and pretend RaeAnne Dobb wasn't missing. Pretend everything was fine and dandy and that I wasn't in the least uneasy about where all this was headed.

When six o'clock came, I persuaded myself that I should show up for the pre-marathon pasta blast. The banquet room in the Rathskeller, the restaurant in the Student Center, had been reserved for the event.

I edged my way through the crush of marathoners and their guests, marathon sponsors, diabetes-society officials, and assorted university administrators there to lend their support.

I said hello to the members of my walking group that I spotted and kept moving until I'd made my way to the food on the other side of the room. I was standing in front of one of the tables, debating with myself about whether I should supplement the green salad on my plate with ziti, vegetable lasagna, or a little of each, when Howard Knowlin materialized out of nowhere.

"I should tell you, Professor Stuart," he said, "I'm a man who is used to getting what he wants."

That announcement and the surprise of having him turn up beside me left me speechless for a moment. Then I tried for cool nonchalance. "Hello, Mr. Knowlin. What a pleasant surprise. I'm sorry, what did you say?"

He smiled. "I understand Charlotte Wingate has decided to donate her house on Grant Avenue to your school. I want that house."

"Why do you want that particular house?" I asked, turning back to the table and helping myself to the ziti.

"Because it's taken my fancy. It's a rather unusual house, wouldn't you agree?"

"Yes," I said, adding a scoop of vegetable lasagna to my plate. "But it needs a lot of work. Have you seen the inside?"

"Of course I've seen the inside." He picked up the tongs for the iced shrimp. "I make it a practice to examine anything I'm considering acquiring."

His words were innocuous enough. But his tone made me look up into his face. And into his pale blue eyes. He said, "Would you join me for dinner this evening, Professor Stuart?"

"We're having dinner now," I said, moving a few steps away from him to pick up a napkin and fork.

Knowlin glanced down at the shrimp he had put on his glass salad plate. He frowned, then picked one up between his fingertips. "You have to be careful about shellfish," he said, sniffing at the shrimp.

He dropped the shrimp back on his plate and set the plate down on the serving table. He plucked up a napkin and rubbed his hands. Then he dropped the crumpled napkin onto the discarded shrimp. "As for the rest of this display," he said, "you'd do much better to let me buy you a really superb meal. There are at least a couple of places here in town where one can trust the chef."

"Thank you," I said. "But I have a half-marathon to walk tomorrow. And if your invitation is intended as— I have . . . I'm involved with someone."

Knowlin moved a step closer, leaning toward me. "So I was told by Doug Jenkins. But I understand your someone is out of town at the moment." His fingertips brushed my forearm. "And there's no reason you should sit at home and be bored while he's away."

"I'm not bored, Mr. Knowlin," I said, setting my own plate on the table. "Please excuse me, I see some people I need to speak to."

"Of course. By the way, I enjoyed your article."

"What article?"

"Your article in the *Journal of Popular Culture* about race and ethnicity in film noir. But I did have some questions about your interpretation of Orson Welles's character in *A Touch of Evil*. Was he really that repulsive?"

Charlotte Wingate had said a cottonmouth. I would have said a cobra. But he had done Charlotte one better when it came to background checks. He had read one of my articles.

"I don't believe *repulsive* was the word I used to describe Welles's character," I said. "But he was quite clearly the villain of the piece."

"But villains can be rather complex personalities. Richard III, for example. Is he villain or tragic hero?"

"That depends on whose interpretation of Richard you—" I broke off, realizing he was drawing me into a discussion.

Knowlin shrugged his shoulders, and the smile he gave me could have passed for disarming. He was rather complex himself. But I was not going to stand there and chat with him.

"If you'll excuse me," I said.

"We'll see each other again," he said.

That was all too possible. In spite of protests from the "Yankee carpetbagger" faction at Tuesday's public hearing, an article in this morning's *Gazette* had reported that the city council was ready to go forward with Project Renaissance. Howard Knowlin would be around for a while.

But what was he doing here tonight? Doug Jenkins, his PR man, was here, of course. But did Knowlin go wherever Doug went? Or was this another opportunity he was taking to meet and influence people?

Or maybe he was here to check out his erstwhile competition for the house on Grant Avenue. I had spotted Madeline Oliver at a corner table as I was getting something to drink.

And her cousin, Abigail Sims, had just walked through the door.

Abigail stood there, glancing around until she saw Madeline. Then she headed straight for her. She obviously had something she wanted to say.

And I really had no one I needed to speak to. In fact, now that I had seen her and Madeline, it would be rude not to go over and say hello. I did have at least some excuse for wanting to know what was going on with these people. Their lives seemed to be spilling over into mine.

Madeline saw me coming. She waved.

I waved back but hesitated in my approach because I'd seen Keisha McIntyre. She was standing over by the windows with a plate in her hands, wearing one of those fake I'm-standing-here-by-myself-at-this-party-because-I-want-to expressions. Where was her boyfriend, Marcus? He was the one who was involved with the marathon. When I'd seen him a couple of weeks ago at the track, he'd told me he was going to be a volunteer at one of the water stations along the race course.

Maybe he was off talking to someone or getting his own plate. Wherever he was, Keisha didn't look as if she was enjoying herself.

But the cousins Oliver and Sims were closer at hand. I would get to Keisha in a few minutes.

"Hi!" I said, joining them.

Abigail was gripping the back of a folding chair so tightly that her knuckles stood out against her skin. As usual, she did not looked pleased to see me.

"Sorry if I'm interrupting," I said to Madeline, who was leaning back in her chair, clad in a sapphire-blue sheath and looking as relaxed as her cousin looked tense. "I saw you two over here and I just wanted to say hello."

"Sit down and join us," Madeline said. "We've got this table, but Doug's been working the room ever since we walked through the door. PR men are obsessive socializers."

"I guess that goes with the territory," I said.

Abigail said, "Madeline, if I could have your attention for another moment." A glance in my direction. "Excuse me, Professor Stuart. But I do need to finish this discussion with my cousin." Then back to Madeline. "Will you please talk to Uncle Jeb and try to make him see reason?"

"Abigail, if you can't persuade my father with your well-reasoned legal arguments, I hardly think that I can do any better."

Abigail leaned forward over the chair she was gripping. She pitched her voice to a near whisper. "Just tell me, have you ever once in your life thought of anyone besides yourself? You let James work himself to death. Now you won't even acknowledge that Uncle Jeb—"

Madeline struck back. "Just a dang minute. My father's a grown man. As far as I can see, he still has his right mind. As for my husband, James—the man that you mooned over like a lovesick puppy dog—you were there with him every day, working in the same offices. Why didn't you do something if you thought he was working too hard?"

"I tried. He wouldn't listen to me. You were the one who could have influenced him. But you didn't even notice that he—" Abigail paused. "Forgive me, it was your idea, wasn't it, that he play golf that day."

"I was trying to get him out of his office," Madeline said.

"Yeah," Abigail said. "You got him out of his office just in time to have a heart attack while he was trudging around on the golf course with Doug Jenkins, the man you're now bedding."

Madeline's eyes went wide. "James might have had that heart attack at any time. And whatever you're implying, Doug and I hardly knew each other when James was alive. It was James who introduced us."

Abigail leaned forward again, her voice still pitched low. "That was convenient, wasn't it? Your husband introduced you to his replacement."

Madeline said nothing. Tears welled up in her eyes. For a moment, Abigail looked uncertain, as if she hadn't intended to go quite that far.

Then she straightened and turned and saw the small group of interested spectators who had sensed an argument and had been edging closer to try to hear what was going on. "Get out of my way," she said, glaring them down. "Bitch on wheels coming through."

A moment of silence followed her departure. Then the spectators, who had parted for Abigail, averted their glances from Madeline and went back to their conversations. But if anyone had heard Abigail's taunt—that Doug had been with Madeline's husband when he died—that would definitely make the rounds.

"Sit down and join me, Lizzie," Madeline said again. She crumpled the paper napkin she had used to dab at her eyes. "I do apologize for that little exchange."

"My fault for standing there listening," I said, reduced to honesty. I pulled out the folding chair that Abigail had had her death grip on and sat down.

Madeline raised her plastic wine glass in a toast. "To lively and public displays of family animosity," she said with a smile. But her smile was brittle and her hand was shaking.

"Sometimes relatives say things to each other that they don't really mean," I said.

"Oh, she meant it all right. You'd never believe that Abigail and I were close as children. She came to live with us when she was four and I was ten. I thought of her as the little sister I'd always wanted. And she followed me everywhere, wanted to be like me."

Adoring little Abigail, huh? I thought. "What happened to change that?" I asked, taking a sip of my club soda.

"A man, of course. My father's new young law partner. Abigail was fifteen, and she loved him from the moment she saw him." Madeline smiled. "It took me a little longer. But eventually I did come to appreciate James Oliver's sterling qualities."

"And that was when you and Abigail—"

She nodded. "James thought of her as a child. She was a child. He did his best not to hurt her." Madeline drained her plastic glass. "That was his mistake. She got her law degree, and then they were working there together in the firm. During all those years, she never had a chance to get over him. To get past that teenage hero worship." A twist of her full lips. "I think my cousin was even more devastated than I was when James died." Her brown gaze sought mine. "But whatever Abigail believes, Lizzie, I did truly grieve for my husband. There were days—" She shook her head. "It took me a long time to pull myself out of that pit. If it hadn't been for Doug . . . it was his idea that I open the shop."

I thought of a thing or two I'd like to ask about that, but I'd been nosy enough for one day. "Madeline, what do you think of Howard Knowlin?" I asked.

She grinned and leaned toward me to whisper, "I think he's kind of sexy. Don't you?"

I remembered the intimate gaze, the brush of his fingers on my arm. "Victor Newman," I said, the realization clicking in. "That's who he reminds me of. Victor's a character on—"

"'The Young and the Restless,'" Madeline said. "I tape the show so that I can watch it in the evening." She glanced toward the center of the room.

I turned and looked too. Howard Knowlin, in conservative dark suit and white shirt, was talking with several of the diabetes society officials and a young man with spiky blond hair who seemed vaguely familiar.

But it was Knowlin that we were both studying.

"Well, he doesn't really look like Victor Newman," I said. "But—"

"But he does have that same air of slumbering power about him," Madeline said. "And power is definitely sexy." She tilted her head. "Now, I wonder how many ex-wives who can't forget him our Mr. Knowlin has."

"And how many enemies—corporate and otherwise—he's outfoxed and brought low," I said.

Madeline sighed dramatically. "My sweet Doug had better watch himself with Mr. Knowlin. And the two of us, Lizzie, have to have lunch one day. Shall we?"

"Yes, let's," I said, and meant it. I liked Madeline.

But I was also feeling a bit more sympathetic toward Abigail. Growing up in her beautiful cousin's shadow and then falling in love with the man who married Madeline couldn't have been fun.

I caught another glimpse of Keisha through a gap in the crowd. She was still standing alone over by the window and taking rather desperate sips from her plastic glass. *I'd better go check on her*, I thought.

"Excuse me, Madeline. I see one of my students over there, and she looks a little down in the dumps."

"Don't go yet," Madeline said. "You haven't told me what happened when you went looking for RaeAnne. You did go, didn't you?"

I nodded. And remembered Sergeant Burke's request. So nothing to Madeline about the fact the university police department was now looking for RaeAnne.

"My colleague Joyce Fielding and I stopped by there while we were out looking at Mrs. Wingate's house."

"What'd you think of— No, first tell me what you found out about RaeAnne."

"Her aunt came to the door. She said RaeAnne had been gone since Monday."

"Since Monday?" Madeline said, frowning. "What about her little boy?"

"The aunt was taking care of him."

"Had she reported RaeAnne missing?"

I told her what the aunt had said about child welfare.

Madeline nodded. "Her baby's daddy got them in trouble with child welfare because he left the baby in the car while he was in a bar drinking with his friends.

Somebody called the police on his sorry behind. And mind you, that happened when he was swearing up and down to RaeAnne that he was cleaning up his act."

"But the aunt said he's dead now."

"He is. And believe me, RaeAnne is better off without him. She's a really beautiful girl with a wonderful way about her. You've seen how talented she is. But she'd been messed up with that loser since her sophomore year in high school. Drugs, women—don't even talk about child support. And every time he came knocking at the door, she would take him in again." Madeline lifted her hair from her neck, the movement more irritated than smooth. "I did try to talk to her about him. But she was in love."

"Love does make fools of us all," I said.

Madeline looked at me and smiled. "Now that's a cynical remark, Lizzie Stuart. You having trouble with your man?"

"Not yet," I said. Then I realized how that sounded. "No, he's wonderful. Everything's fine. But I do need to go check on my student." I pushed back my chair and stood up.

"I'll call about lunch," Madeline said.

And Sergeant Burke would have been pleased to know that I'd managed to get away without saying any more about RaeAnne. Although, there were other questions I would have liked to ask Madeline. Like whether she knew of any friends or anyone else who might have seen RaeAnne. If she had known RaeAnne well enough to try to advise her about her love life, she might know other things. I'd have to suggest to Sergeant Burke that he contact Madeline.

I edged my way around the milling crowd in the center of the room, making my way toward Keisha. I was almost there when I came face to face with Doug.

"Lizzie!" he said. "I'm glad to see you made it." He was carrying a dessert plate loaded with a selection of miniature sweets and garnished with strawberries. For Madeline, no doubt.

I mustered a smile. "I saw in the *Gazette* this morning that Project Renaissance looks like it's being approved. You and your client must be pleased."

"We are. Speaking of my client, when I saw him a few minutes ago, he said he had invited you to dinner. He suggested you might be willing to join him if Madeline and I came along."

I shook my head. "Marathon tomorrow, remember?"

"That's what I told him. And I did remind him that you are otherwise spoken for."

"And since his invitation to dinner was prompted by the fact Charlotte Wingate has offered to endow the school with her house. Does he understand how strongly Mrs. Wingate feels about not selling to him?"

"I've tried to convey that to him," Doug said. "But when Howard makes up his mind that he wants something—"

"So he told me," I said. "But would you mind making it clear to him that I don't have any influence at all in this matter."

Doug's gaze was suddenly much shrewder than one would expect in a face that was usually so good-natured. "But, you see, that's the crux of it. You are the key to this. If you agree to Charlotte's conditions, then the School of Criminal Justice gets the house on Grant Avenue. And Howard doesn't."

I didn't like the way he'd put that. "But even if I don't agree, that doesn't mean he would get the house. Charlotte might give it to Madeline for her shop or do something else with it."

Doug shook his head. "Charlotte has decided she wants to endow an institute. She wants her name over the door, and she—for whatever reasons—wants you as executive director. Charlotte is stubborn too."

"But if I say no, she might find some other academic unit to give the house to and endow some other kind of institute. And unless my hearing is gone, she said quite plainly on Wednesday at lunch that she does not like Howard Knowlin, and she has no intention of selling her house to him. So will you please tell him to bug off."

As soon as the words popped out of my mouth, I glanced around to make sure no one was close enough to have overheard. But we were still in our own little oasis on the edge of the crowd.

Doug was grinning. "Do you really want me to tell him that?"

"No . . . just . . . I don't like being placed in this position."

"I know, and I'm sorry. But Howard is convinced that if her criminal justice institute idea falls through, he'll have another opportunity to persuade Charlotte to change her mind."

"I wouldn't count on it. Why does he want the house so much anyway?"

"Because he wants it," Doug said. "As simple as that."

But he was looking at something behind me.

The kid with the spiky blond hair who had been standing with Knowlin and the diabetes-society officials was coming toward us.

"Hi, Mr. Jenkins," he said. "Mr. Knowlin asked me to look for you. He's at your table and he wants to know if you can join him."

"Be right there," Doug said, and his features settled into their usual pleasantness. "Professor Lizzie Stuart, I'd like you to meet Tommy Irving, Piedmont U's star pitcher."

That was where I'd seen the kid. His face had been on the front page of last week's *Tattler*, the campus newspaper. Tommy Irving—a.k.a. "The Iceman"— was the Piedmont Rockets' hope for a winning baseball season. The kid was being described as a phenom. He managed to make good grades too, and had a double major in computer science and business.

"Hi, Tommy," I said. "It's a pleasure to meet you. Congratulations on the great season you've been having."

A smile lit up his rather homely face. "Thank you, Professor. I just hope I can keep it going until the end."

Nice kid. So why was he hanging out with Howard Knowlin? Did Knowlin like to surround himself with local celebrities wherever he went? Or maybe he was going to go Charlotte Wingate one better again and endow the university baseball team with a brand new playing field.

Doug said, "Lizzie, if you'll excuse me." He grinned. "Unless you'd like to join us."

"Thanks, but I was on my way somewhere else. Nice to meet you, Tommy. See you in the morning, Doug."

"6:30 A.M.," he said with a cheerfulness that made me grimace. Hadn't anyone ever heard of a late afternoon marathon? 4 P.M. to midnight.

I took another step and realized Keisha was no longer standing by the windows. Big surprise, as long as it had taken me to get over to her. She'd probably gone home.

I glanced at my watch. Almost seven. The pasta blast was supposed to end at seven-thirty, and I was ready to go home. But I might as well swing by the dessert table before I left. The plate Doug had been carrying to Madeline had looked tempting.

I sampled the miniature desserts—cheesecake, chocolate mousse, pecan pie. Then I started making my way to the door. My path happened to take me by Doug Jenkins's table.

But I'd only intended to sneak a glance and keep moving. What brought me up short was the sight of Keisha sitting there with Howard Knowlin, Doug, Madeline, and Tommy "The Iceman" Irving, the Rockets' star pitcher.

I walked over and smiled. "Hello, everyone."

"Hi, Dr. Stuart," Keisha said.

Doug and Knowlin had come to their feet. Knowlin said, "Won't you join us, Professor?"

Doug was staring toward the door. "I didn't think he'd show up for this," he said.

"What the hell is he doing here?" Knowlin said.

"He's one of the corporate sponsors of the marathon," Doug said. "I told you about that."

"I know what you told me. What I want to know is what he's doing here."

Assuming that Doug could read Sloane Campbell's mind.

Dressed in a business suit, Campbell stood in the doorway long enough to let everyone know he had arrived. His glance swept the room. He looked amused, as if he were anticipating something.

When his gaze fell on our little group, his expression changed. The smile went to blankness. His hands went to his turquoise-studded belt buckle. I glanced at Knowlin to see if he was having a similar reaction—two gunfighters squaring off.

But it was Knowlin who was smiling now.

Campbell strode toward our corner table.

When Campbell stopped in front of him, Knowlin held out his hand and said, "Mr. Campbell. A pleasure to see you here. No hard feelings I hope."

Campbell didn't shake hands. Instead, he punched Knowlin in the face.

Madeline jumped up and scrambled away as Knowlin crashed across the table in front of her.

"Keisha!" I held out my hand to her.

She started around Tommy Irving and toward me.

But Knowlin righted himself and charged at Campbell like a rutting ram.

Doug and I were caught in his forward momentum. I collided with Doug, and we both went sprawling. I heard Keisha cry out and Tommy Irving say "Sorry."

Doug cursed and scrambled to his feet. I scrambled up too. The strap of my shoulder bag was tangled around my wrist. I untwisted it and dropped the bag into one of the empty chairs at the table.

Three or four men had separated Campbell and Knowlin. Doug was doing his best to smooth things over. But the two combatants were glaring at each other. The men who had separated them were standing at the ready in case they should spring at each other again.

I glanced over at Keisha. She had tears in her eyes and a paper napkin pressed to her nose. "Keisha?"

"I fell against her," Tommy said. "My elbow hit her in the nose."

"It's bleeding," Keisha said.

I edged behind the men confronting each other and took her arm. "Come on, let's go to the ladies' room and put some cold water on it."

"I'm really sorry, Keisha," Tommy said again.

"Try dropping a key down her back," Madeline said. "That's supposed to work."

The ladies' room was empty. I wet some towels and held them out to Keisha. "Hold your head back," I told her.

I leaned against one of the sinks and watched her. She had two or three drops of blood on the white drawstring top that she was wearing with a short black skirt.

And how had she come to be sitting at that table? "So you know Tommy Irving?" I said.

"Sorta," she said. "Not *know* know. But I've met him a couple of times at parties my roommate . . . the girl I was sharing the apartment with—" A flick of her eyes toward me. "But he's okay. He doesn't get drunk or high or—" She took the wet towels away to stare at her reflection in the mirror. "Do you think it's going to swell up?"

"No, I don't think so," I said. "Where's Marcus, by the way?"

"On a field trip," she said, shoving the soggy paper towels into the trash receptacle. "His botany professor invited him and two other students. They're going to be gone all weekend."

"But I thought Marcus told me that he'd volunteered to work at one of the water stations along the marathon course tomorrow."

"He did." Now there was a decided pout to Keisha's burgundy lips, and she was looking me right in the eye. "But he got invited to go out in the woods and look for fungus or something. And he said it was an honor to get invited by this professor." A pause and a shrug. "So I told him I'd take his place."

"That was thoughtful of you," I said.

"No, it wasn't," she said. "I mean, it was . . . but he shouldn't have gone . . . when I got here tonight . . . I decided to come because of the food. But then I started thinking about Marcus's nerve to go off on a field trip when he'd said he'd do something else . . . I mean, he's going to be gone the whole weekend. He just went and left me. He didn't even ask if I minded being alone by myself in the apartment all weekend."

I tried not to smile at her outrage. "He probably thought you'd be safe."

"Of course I'll be safe," Keisha said. "I can take care of myself. But he should have at least thought about that."

I shook my head. "Sometimes, Keisha, men get preoccupied with—"

"Yeah, but they don't think we ever should."

I decided it was time for a change of subject. I was not really qualified to give advice on men. "About Tommy," I said, looking in the mirror to fluff—as much as I could—my own one-inch haircut. "I was a little surprised to see him with Howard Knowlin."

Keisha was scrubbing at the drops of blood on her white top and making a large wet stain. "I think Mr. Knowlin's into sports," she said. "You know how some old guys are? Like how they like being around young athletes and pretending like they're still jocks."

Old guys, huh? I thought. *Well, yes, Knowlin must be in his mid-fifties.* Which didn't seem quite so old to me now that I was a few months short of forty.

"I don't think that's going to come out like that," I said, referring to the blood on her blouse that she was still scrubbing at. "Maybe if you go right home and use a spot remover, then soak it."

"Or just throw it away," Keisha said, her voice resigned. "It's always like that when you wear white. Something always gets on it." A slow, mischievous smile spread across her face. "Black's a whole lot classier."

"Definitely easier to wear," I said, gliding around her racial play on words. "Come on, let's go back outside and see what's happening."

We were at the door of the ladies' room when Keisha stopped and whirled around. "Oh, Dr. Stuart, I didn't mean . . . I was just joking about . . . I forgot that you . . . I mean about you and Chief Quinn."

She really was a nice kid. "I didn't think you meant it that way," I said. "Black is classy. Now, please, move it, ma'am."

She grinned and pushed open the door. "I hope that Mr. Campbell's gone. When I saw him at the door, I was sure he'd found out about. . . ."

"Found out what, Keisha?" I prompted.

She turned to face me. "J. T. says he isn't going to make the documentary. But see, I still wanted to know about what happened to Verity Thomas. So I called the county courthouse to ask if they had the records . . . from the case, you know. And the clerk that I talked to said if it was a death-penalty case then some of the documents would be in Richmond at the state library."

I nodded. "And that's what you were afraid Sloane Campbell had found out? That you'd called the county courthouse?"

"I thought someone over there might have called him. So I was really glad when I saw he was there to punch Mr. Knowlin." She grinned when she said that. An impish grin.

I couldn't help smiling back. "But now you've seen concrete evidence of his capacity for punching people in the nose. And gotten somebody else's elbow in your nose in the bargain. So, Keisha, I think it might be a good idea if you—"

"But I come from Richmond, Dr. Stuart," she said, her tone both protest and plea. "And I'm going home on break. I was planning to wait until Monday . . . but now that Marcus is gone on his field trip . . . anyway, I could go check out the documents at the library while I'm there. Just to see what they have, you know?"

"And then what?" I said, gesturing for her to continue down the hall.

She made a quick adjustment of her step, a kind of hop and skip. "And then, couldn't I do a paper? For you? For class?"

Enthusiasm was Keisha's middle name. She was brimming with it at that moment.

If she had really given up the idea of the documentary, what harm could it do to let her look at the case for her research paper assignment?

"I just want to check it out, Dr. Stuart. Just to see what's there."

No matter what I said, when she got to Richmond, she would be off to the state library.

"We'll talk about the paper idea," I said.

We stepped back into the banquet room. The guests had dwindled to a handful. At Doug's table, Tommy was hovering, looking ill at ease. Knowlin was gesturing as he spoke to Doug and Madeline. He looked angry.

"We're back," I said, as Keisha and I walked up.

Tommy gave Keisha a searching look. "Are you okay?" he said. "I'm really, really sorry."

"No problem," she said, smiling back at him. "Just got to watch for the pitcher's elbow."

He grinned. And the next moment, a red paper rose was in his hand. He held it out to her.

Keisha's eyes widened. "How did you do that?"

"Magic," Tommy said.

Or sleight of hand, as my grandfather, Walter Lee, would have said. He too had been fond of magic tricks. In his few spare moments on his runs as a Pullman porter, he'd taught himself how to do them using secondhand manuals. He was quite good by the time I came along. I'd had many a nickel plucked from behind my ear before he explained how one created illusions.

"Thank you," Keisha said, cradling the rose in her hand and smiling at Tommy, the magician.

I retrieved my shoulder bag from the chair where I'd left it. "If you will all excuse me," I said. "I'm going home."

Knowlin seemed to remember his manners. He got to his feet. "Forgive me, Professor Stuart. I don't usually engage in brawls in front of ladies."

"He did punch you first. Any idea why?"

Doug said, "Howard bought some land that Sloane had bid on too."

Madeline looked up at Knowlin. "By the time Project Renaissance is finished, we could have real estate developers calling each other out."

He laughed. But the skin around his left eye was already beginning to change colors. "That would be more gentlemanly than throwing punches," he said.

"Let's walk out together, Keisha," I said. "See you in the morning, Doug."

"You may see Howard and Sloane too. They are both official corporate sponsors of the marathon."

Knowlin gave him a look that was not exactly pleased. Then he said to me, "But I promise you, Professor, that tomorrow I, at least, will be on my best behavior."

One could only hope. "Talk to you later, Madeline," I said.

"And you be sure to let me know if you hear anything from RaeAnne," she said.

"RaeAnne?" I heard Knowlin say as Keisha and I walked away. "That beautiful young woman I met in your shop?"

Madeline said, "No one's seen her since Monday. Lizzie needs to find her to get a ceramic heart repaired."

Thank you, Madeline, for spreading the word that a young woman was missing and I wasn't particularly concerned other than how it inconvenienced me.

"What kind of heart did she say?" Keisha asked.

"Ceramic," I said. "It was a gift. RaeAnne is the artist who made it. I'd hoped she could repair a crack."

"Where do you think this RaeAnne is?" Keisha said as we stepped out into the balmy March evening. "It's always creepy when someone just disappears . . . you know, just isn't there anymore."

"Yes," I said. "But hopefully she's fine and will turn up."

* * *

On my way home, I decided to stop at the mall to look for a dress for the dinner I was planning when Quinn returned. But you have to be in the right mood to shop. After wandering through a store or two, I gave up and went back to my car and drove home.

It was when I got to my front door that I realized that my keys were missing. The chain with my office and door keys was not in my shoulder bag. I sat down on the front stoop and dumped my shoulder bag out. No keys.

I went back out to the car and checked under the seats and even in the glove compartment. No keys.

I closed my eyes and tried to remember if I could have taken the key chain—with a large red letter L and two keys attached—out of my shoulder bag for any reason at the mall.

No. I'd dropped the black plastic remote with my car key attached into my shoulder bag as I was walking into the mall. I'd taken it out again when I came back to my car. My key chain with the house key should have been in the side pocket of my bag, and there had been no reason for me to take it out.

The last time I had physically seen or held that key chain was when I left my office to go to the Rathskeller. I remembered dropping it into my shoulder bag as I was speaking to a passing grad student.

So the only place I could have conceivably lost my keys was at the Rathskeller during the pasta party.

George would be wondering why I'd driven up and was now driving away again. It was a nuisance to have to drive all the way back to campus.

But the keys must have fallen out of my shoulder bag when Doug and I collided during the fight. That was the only thing that could have happened.

CHAPTER · 11

I CAUGHT A WHIFF OF GARLIC and roasting meat as I walked back into the Rathskeller. Too bad I wasn't there for dinner in the dining room, instead of a nervous search for lost keys.

When I explained to the maître d' why I was there, he gestured to a waiter named Andrew and asked him to go with me to the banquet room to look.

"We were sitting over here," I told Andrew.

The table had been stripped of its white cloth, and it was easy enough to see that there was nothing on the tile floor beneath it. But I bent down and looked anyway.

"Could it have been another table?" Andrew asked, as he peered around the legs of adjacent tables. "They all look alike."

"No, I'm sure it was this one."

"What you looking for?" a woman's voice said. She was wearing a white apron that covered her from waist to toes and a hairnet on her head.

"My keys," I said. "I was here earlier for the pasta blast, and—"

The woman was digging into her apron pocket. She held up my key chain. "These them?"

"Yes," I said. "Yes, thank you so much. Where did you find them?"

She gestured toward one of the long tables that had been used for serving. "Right beside the shrimp platter."

I stared at the empty table, trying to picture myself standing there, talking to Knowlin. Had I had my keys in my hand? Why would I have had my keys out when I was serving myself from the dishes?

"Is everything all right now, ma'am?" Andrew said.

"Yes, thank you," I said. "Thank you both."

But it wasn't all right. My keys should not have been beside the shrimp platter. They had been in my shoulder bag, not in my hand.

So how had they gotten there? Obviously someone had taken them out of my shoulder bag. Four people had been sitting at that table when I left my shoulder bag there on the chair. But which one? And why?

* * *

I told George about it as I was preparing his dinner. He thumped his tail against the floor, his gaze fixed on my hands as I opened canned dog food and added dry.

I set his bowl down in front of him. He sniffed and began to eat.

"Howard Knowlin sniffs his food too," I said. "The folks at Harvard never got around to telling him that food sniffing could be interpreted as rudeness when a human does it."

I sat down at the kitchen table and watched George eat.

"I can't really imagine Knowlin rifling through my shoulder bag," I said. "Even if he'd felt like it, the others would have seen him. Would they have ignored what he was doing?"

But Madeline . . . if Madeline had picked up my purse and started to go through it, the men wouldn't even have blinked. Men didn't pay attention to women's handbags. They would have assumed it was hers.

Or maybe none of the adults had been involved. There was Tommy. Tommy of the sleight of hand. But would he dare risk trying to steal my keys in front of three people. And why would he want them anyway?

"That leaves Doug," I said.

George continued with his meal, leaving me to ponder why Doug Jenkins would take my keys out of my purse.

A joke? Maybe the four of them had concocted a joke. Something that one of them had thought up when they saw my unguarded shoulder bag.

But that didn't seem likely. Knowlin had not seemed to be in the mood for jokes when Keisha and I came back from the ladies' room. He'd looked annoyed, angry. Had seemed to be expressing his displeasure to the other three.

I got up and opened the refrigerator. I had a half-marathon to walk tomorrow morning, bright and early. I needed to eat more than the miniature desserts I'd had at the pasta blast.

Quinn called as I was washing up the dishes. I grabbed a paper towel to wipe my wet hands, then snatched up the kitchen extension as he started to leave a message.

"Quinn! Hi, I'm here."

"You're home at a decent hour tonight," he said. I could hear his smile.

"I have to be up early tomorrow. Before daybreak in fact."

"So you're all set for—" he broke off. "Hold on a second." I heard voices in the background, muffled as if his hand was over the receiver. Then he came back. "Lizzie, I've got to run. I'll talk to you tomorrow, okay?"

"Wait, Quinn, I—"

"What?" he said. "What's wrong?"

"Nothing," I said. "Everything's fine. Is everything all right, there?"

"Fine," he said. "I'll talk to you tomorrow, Lizabeth."

And then he was gone. The receiver on the other end clicked down.

Of course, I wouldn't have told him about the keys anyway. He was in Oklahoma.

But it would have been nice to talk to him for a few minutes. Why had he bothered to call if he didn't have time to talk?

I went to bed and tried to fall asleep. I left the lamp on beside my bed because even with all the doors and windows locked and George stretched out on the floor beside me, I couldn't quite get out of my mind the fact that someone had taken my door key out of my purse. Would he or she have had time to have a duplicate made?

I dozed off and woke up again at a little after two. After tossing and turning for another half hour, I gave up and reached for my robe.

Still half asleep, George snuffed and thumped his tail. I stepped over him. But he was up and at the door as soon as he realized I was leaving the room. Luckily, he didn't think it was time to go outside. I sat down on the sofa in the living room and clicked on the big-screen television.

Creature From the Black Lagoon was on one of the movie channels. I reached for the other pillow and stretched out on the sofa. George stretched out on the floor. He went back to sleep. I drifted in and out of slumber. When I woke up, Sylvester Stallone was running up those steps in Philadelphia. Very appropriate for my morning marathon. I was going to need a dose of "eye of the tiger" to make it through my 13.1-mile walk.

"I hope you appreciate this, Hester Rose," I told my grandmother as I staggered up from the sofa.

And I heard her sharp voice say, *Well, I didn't tell you to do it.*

No, but it had been intended to lay our ghosts to rest. Except now there was Mrs. Cutler, who had a postcard she wanted to show me.

"I do not want to walk a half-marathon, George. I want to go back to bed and sleep and have everything make sense when I wake up."

But I had signed up and raised funds. I had sponsors. I'd trained for three months. So I was going to go walk. And then I was going to collapse. And Quinn would be sorry he hadn't even wished me luck.

CHAPTER · 12

SATURDAY, MARCH 17

The sun was not shining. It was drizzling and chilly. The marathoners milled around, doing stretches or jogging in place.

"Good morning, Lizzie," Doug Jenkins said, bright-eyed and cheerful.

I had watched him giving some of the other walkers in our training group a pep talk. But I hadn't been in the mood to listen, so I'd stayed off to the side.

"Hi, Doug," I said, in a voice that I hoped would discourage him from offering final pointers.

He studied my face. "You don't look good. Feel all right?"

"I've felt worse. I had trouble sleeping last night."

His grin flashed. "Excited about today?"

"Wondering about my house key."

He frowned. "Your house key?"

"Just a little mystery I was trying to figure out," I said. "So give me my pep talk and let's get it over with."

He did. By the time he had finished assuring me that after three months of training I was ready for this, I almost thought I might be. And he really wasn't behaving like someone who'd gone through my purse when my back was turned.

"Move around a little," he said, as he left to find the rest of his people. "You'll stiffen up if you stand there."

"Tell me one more time that I can do this," I said.

He gave me a grin and a thumbs-up. "You can do it."

Maybe I could. All I had to do was concentrate. Think of the finish line.

I started off in the middle of the pack. I tried to remember Doug's words of encouragement. But by the end of the second mile I was dragging, wondering if I'd even be able to do three miles, much less thirteen. The sun was beginning to peek out from the clouds. The sky was clearing. And my vision was blurry. My legs felt like they had lead weights attached to them, and all I wanted to do was sit down. Lie down. *Why did I even think I could do this?*

I stopped at the next water station, closed my eyes, and swallowed a few sips of water.

All right, I thought. *This is ridiculous.*

I'd trained for this. I was tired because I hadn't gotten very much sleep last night, but I was not going to drop out before I'd even gotten halfway. I just needed to keep moving.

For the next two or three miles, I struggled to put one foot in front of the other. Then I began to find my second wind—or more accurately, my first wind. The weights fell off my legs. I took in deep breaths of fresh morning air.

"How you doin', Lizzie?" said Bob, one of the guys from my walking group, as I came up beside him.

"I might make it," I said.

Nora, another member of our group, laughed. "Sure you're going to make it," she said. "If we can, you can."

They both had diabetes. If they were doing this, I could too. What was one missed night of sleep? I felt fine.

For the next four or five miles, the three of us kept pace. Talking as we walked. We followed the race course along a scenic route that took us through the forest preserve that the university owned and then out for a brief mile along the highway, winding back onto campus.

Along the course, cheerers and well-wishers, music and balloons. I swung along, buoyed up by the noise and the beautiful spring morning and my walking companions. I felt great. Until I hit mile nine. By mile ten, my surge of energy had evaporated.

But when I got to Keisha's water station, she handed me a cup and a "Looking good, Dr. Stuart!" After that, pride required that I keep going.

Another three miles. That was all I needed to do. I could ignore the blister on my heel.

But not the cramp in my midsection.

Nora and Bob had picked up their pace as we neared the finished line. Nora glanced back at me and said, "You okay?"

I had stopped walking and bent over from the waist. I nodded and waved my hand. "Yes. Go on. I'm coming."

"See you at the finish line," Bob said.

I straightened and breathed, stretching carefully until the cramp eased enough for me to move again.

Focus. Focus on the finish line. Ignore the blister on my heel. Ignore my aching midsection.

Mile eleven. I could do this.

Cheering spectators. The sun beating down. A blur of noise and color. Sweat dripping down my back.

Keep moving. Just keep moving.

Thirty minutes later, I crossed the finish line. I moved off to the sidelines and bent over, head to my knees. Exhausted. But I'd done it! Me, Lizzie, the bookworm. I'd walked a half-marathon!

"Way to go, Professor."

Straightening, I turned.

He was standing there smiling at me. That slow smile that started in his silver-gray eyes. I yelped and threw my arms around his neck.

"Dammit, Quinn, why didn't you tell me you were coming?"

He held me away from him and touched my cheek. "I wanted to surprise you."

"You did. I'm so glad you're here."

"Are you?"

I pulled his head down toward me.

"I think you missed me," he said, when the kiss ended.

I started to respond to that, then I glanced around at the crowd of spectators. They were too busy cheering each person who crossed the finish line to pay attention to our public display of affection. Not that I really cared at that moment.

"I did miss you," I said, hugging Quinn again, pressing my face to his shirt that smelled laundry clean. He smelled good too. "I'm so glad you're home."

And I must smell. . . . I'd just walked thirteen miles. "Oh—" I pulled out of his arms and stepped back, tugging at my damp T-shirt. "Is your stepfather better? He must be or you wouldn't be here."

"Ben's improving steadily," Quinn said. The sunlight shimmered in his dark auburn hair, picking out the touch of gray at each temple. "So my mother told me to get on a plane and come see you cross the finish line."

"I'll have to remember to thank your mother," I said, shoving my fingers through my own hair. It must be plastered to my scalp. *We haven't seen each other in over a week, and I look like something the cat—*

Quinn grinned. "Although I don't know if it was worth all that effort."

"What?" I said.

"Boy, are you a mess," he said, shaking his head.

I made a face at him, but I could feel myself blushing. "Easy for you to say, buster. I've just walked thirteen miles."

"Yes, you have, haven't you?" He caught the end of my T-shirt and tugged me toward him. "So I guess you might be entitled to be sweaty."

"Yes," I said as he nuzzled my neck. "But I'd still like a shower. I have a blister on my foot."

He laughed. "I don't think a shower will fix that. But if that's what you really want." He let me go and reached down to pick up his brown bomber jacket from the top of his suitcase.

"How did you get here?" I asked. "I drove you to the airport. I was supposed to come and pick you up when you got back."

"But since I knew you'd be otherwise occupied this morning," he said, "I hitched a ride." He pulled out the handle of his suitcase. "Ready?"

"Yes." I hooked my arm in his. "Let's go."

I waved to Bob and Nora as we passed them standing at the food table. They grinned, flashing victory signs.

"Hold on a minute," I told Quinn. "I just need something to eat. I'm starving. Do you want anything?"

He shook his head, and I darted toward the food table. "I could eat a horse," I told Bob and Nora as I scooped up a banana and a plastic cup of orange juice.

"With a cow on the side," Nora said.

Returning to Quinn with my hands full, I said, "Okay. I'm ready now."

"You're limping," he said, after we had been walking for a few minutes.

"That blister I mentioned," I said around the banana I was swallowing. "I'll survive."

"Then I guess we aren't going dancing tonight," he said.

I glanced up at him. "How about tomorrow night?" That would give me time to run out and find that incredible dress I had intended to buy.

And time to tell him about everything that had been happening. Or maybe I should wait until after we'd had our big evening out.

"Where are you parked?" he asked.

"In the Brewster Hall lot," I said, pausing to drop my banana peel and plastic cup into a trash can. "I didn't want to get caught in a traffic jam."

And I hadn't considered the fact that I would have to walk back across campus to retrieve my car after walking thirteen miles.

He pointed at the bench we were passing. "Sit there. I'll go get the car."

"I can walk," I said. But it was a halfhearted protest. That burst of energy I'd felt seemed to be draining away.

"You've walked enough for one morning," Quinn said, handing me his jacket. "Got your car keys?"

I reached for the tiny pouch that was dangling from my neck and pulled it over my head. I shook out the key attached to the plastic remote and handed it to him. My house key was in my shoulder bag, locked in the trunk of my car.

"Be right back," Quinn said and went striding off.

He ran five miles every day except Sunday. Of course, he also liked red meat, beer, and chocolate chip cookies.

I sat there on the bench, holding his jacket and wiggling my foot without the blister around in my shoe. It was nice to sit.

The campus green stretched before me. The stone chapel was at the other end. In the expanse between, cement paths crisscrossed the grass, providing passage between the dormitories on one side of campus and the administrative and classroom buildings on the other.

Even though the predawn drizzle had given way to late-morning blue sky, the drill field was desolate. No Frisbee players. No sunbathers. It was the first official day of spring break, and the 26,000 students at Piedmont State University were making themselves scarce. Gone south or home for mom's cooking.

I leaned my chin on my hands and closed my eyes, half-drowsing in the warm sun.

Quinn hadn't mention RaeAnne Dobb. Did that mean Sergeant Burke hadn't told him? Or maybe he was waiting until I'd had my shower and caught my breath before he started asking questions.

My car pulled up to the curb in front of me. Quinn got out.

"See that sign," I said, pointing to the NO STOPPING AT ANY TIME sign at the curb.

"So get in before one of my officers shows up and gives us a ticket," he said, putting his suitcase in the trunk.

Sloane Campbell would appreciate Quinn's attitude.

I climbed into the passenger seat. Quinn got back in and started the engine.

"Is the seat all right?" I said. "You might need to adjust—"

"Lizzie, sit back and relax," he said.

"Sorry, I'm just not used to being driven in my own car." I leaned back and closed my eyes. "Have you ever met Sloane Campbell?"

"We were once at the same reception. Why?"

"Nothing. I'll tell you about it later."

And about Howard Knowlin and the house on Grant Avenue.

That had been odd last night. Why had Campbell punched Knowlin in the eye? That couldn't be his usual response to being outbid for property. Had Knowlin done something to undercut him? Something that was devious and underhanded?

Good grief, if Sloane Campbell and Abigail Sims ever crossed paths, with the tempers those two had. . . . But they must have encountered each other now and then. They both lived here in Gallagher and were business people. Now Campbell had bought the property next to the building where Abigail and her uncle had their law offices. He also owned the plaza where Madeline had her shop.

So he and Abigail had probably not only met on occasion but in all likelihood had a run-in or two. But that afternoon in Madeline's shop, when Charlotte had accused Campbell of putting his injured employee up to bringing the malpractice suit against Jebediah, Abigail had shrugged off the idea. She obviously thought that was a figment of her uncle's imagination. An old man's paranoia.

Except, when Jebediah had come to my class on Wednesday he hadn't seemed that feeble or that senile.

What had Abigail wanted Madeline to talk to her father about when she came to the pasta blast-off? Maybe Jebediah was still resisting settling the lawsuit. Still convinced there was another way to skin that cat.

"Hey, remember me?" Quinn said.

I opened my eyes and reached over to touch his knee. "Of course I remember you. I was just thinking about some people I've met recently. I'll tell you about them later."

"You seem to have a lot to tell me later," he said.

I drew back my hand and straightened in my seat. "Sergeant Burke told you something, didn't he?"

"Only that you had brought a matter involving a student to his attention. I asked if it was anything I should be concerned about. He said he didn't know yet."

"And is that why you hurried right home?"

We had come to a traffic light. It was just as well, because he turned his head to give me the full benefit of his gaze. "What do you think?"

"All right. I didn't mean that. I know you came to be there for me at the finish line. But you— I am not involved in the situation with RaeAnne Dobb."

"Who's RaeAnne Dobb?"

"The student Sergeant Burke told you I brought to his attention. I went looking for her because of something I needed her to do." I sighed. "And now that we're on the subject, and since RaeAnne is still nowhere to be found. . . ."

I told him about the ceramic heart . . . about how it had been damaged during the earthquake. And how I had gone first to Madeline's shop and then to RaeAnne's house, trying to have it repaired.

"And that's the limit of my involvement in this. Whatever Sergeant Burke might have implied about my stirring up trouble."

The light had changed and Quinn was focusing on his driving again. "Sergeant Burke didn't imply that. In fact, he went out of his way to make it clear that you were inadvertently involved in the matter."

I took a breath and willed myself to relax. I was being childish. "I'm so sorry about the heart, Quinn."

He glanced over at me. Then he held out his hand. "Next time I'll buy you one you can wear on a chain around your neck."

I looked down at our clasped hands. Sometimes I loved him so much.

And I was not going to cry.

"Quinn, getting back to RaeAnne Dobb. She's been missing since Monday. She has a 2-year-old child that her aunt says she's devoted to. She wouldn't just go off and leave him."

"Sergeant Burke may have something by now," Quinn said. Meaning he wasn't ready to discuss it until he had more information.

We were driving along Riverside Drive. I said, "If you want to swing by your house first to pick up your car—"

He shook his head. "I'll drop you off and get George. Then we'll leave you to have your shower, and I'll come back later."

"But that means. . . . Wouldn't it be easier to. . . ." I tried to work out the logistics in my head.

"I don't want you driving until you've had a nap," he said.

"A nap. Quinn, I'm not 4 years old. I don't need a nap. In fact, I feel—" It was purely psychological—the power of suggestion—that I chose that moment to yawn.

"You were saying," he said.

I made a face at him and turned to look out the passenger window.

We'd covered RaeAnne. I might as well tell him about Charlotte Wingate and her proposed institute while we were at it. "Quinn?"

"Yes, Lizabeth?"

"I have a challenging new opportunity. Except it's a little complicated."

"Okay," he said. "Just let me brace myself."

I punched him on the arm.

"Ouch! That could count as an assault on a police officer."

I looked at my still-balled fist. "I did that without even thinking about it," I said. "I've seen other women do that. But if a man punched a woman in the arm—"

"Men punch harder," he said.

"But still . . . I shouldn't have hit you."

Quinn laughed. "Lizzie, you are. . . ."

"What?" I said, when he stopped.

"A lot of things. But getting back to your challenging, but complicated, new opportunity."

"Yes, about that. Maybe you *should* brace yourself."

As we drove up the hill from Riverside Drive toward my house on the north side, I told him about Charlotte Wingate's offer and Amos Baylor's eagerness to have the School of Criminal Justice receive the endowment.

When I had wound down, he said, "How do you feel about it? Is this something you want to take on?"

We had turned onto my street. I opened my mouth to tell him I wasn't sure how I felt about it. But before I could get the words out, I saw my neighbors. Four or five of them standing on my front lawn. And there was a blue-and-white Gallagher police cruiser pulled up to the curb in front of my house.

"What the hell?" Quinn said. He pulled into my driveway.

My front door was standing wide open.

As I hopped out of the car, Mr. Roth detached himself from the clutch of neighbors and came over. In place of his biking helmet, he was wearing a Boston Red Sox cap.

His eyes behind his spectacles were distressed. "I tried to reach you, Professor Stuart. After I'd called the police, I called your office, thinking you might be there."

"What's happening?" I said. "Why did you call the police? What are they doing in my house?"

"There was someone in the house," Mr. Roth said. "I'd been out biking. I go for a long ride every Saturday morning. And I came home and went in to change. I saw a white van in the driveway when I glanced out the window, but I didn't think anything about it until I heard your dog barking."

"George?" I said. "Where is he?"

"At the vet's. The police called one of their canine units to come and transport him."

"Why?" Quinn asked. "What happened to him?"

Mr. Roth gave him a wary look. "The man in the van . . . the one who broke into the house . . . I heard barking. I think the dog . . . George . . . tried to defend the house. When I found him, he was bleeding. His head and one of his legs, like he'd been hit with something."

Quinn cursed.

Mr. Roth said, "But he chased him out. The man ran out of the house. I'd be willing to bet he had a few dog bites."

Quinn said, "Good. That should help us to identify him." He shot a glance at me. "I'm going inside to talk to the cops." He strode off toward the door. It was just as well that the man who had hurt George wasn't inside.

"Thank you," I said, turning back to Mr. Roth. "For calling the police."

He flushed. "That's what neighbors are for. I hope your dog will be all right."

"Me too," I said. "Thank you again."

I walked toward my open front door. I didn't want to go inside. Quinn had trusted me to take care of George.

He and two uniformed officers were standing in the hallway. "This is Professor Lizabeth Stuart," Quinn told them. "She lives here."

The older of the officers introduced himself as Vaughan, his partner as Santiago.

I said, "Do you know how he got in?"

Vaughan said, "There's no sign of forced entry." He rubbed at his chin. "I don't suppose you might have left the door unlocked, Professor Stuart?"

"No, I didn't. I'm sure it was locked." I went over and sat down on the hall chair. "But I think my keys were stolen last night."

Quinn said, "What do you mean, you think your keys were stolen?"

"I mean that the chain with my house and office keys was missing from my purse. But then I found it again."

"Found it where?" Quinn said, scowling. "Where were you when—"

"At school." I stood up and gestured toward the living room. "Shall we go in and sit down and be comfortable?"

The three men followed me into the living room. "I'm sorry," I said. "Would you like something to drink . . . coffee or—"

"Lizzie, they don't want refreshments," Quinn said, his patience slipping.

I sat down on the sofa, gestured Vaughan and Santiago toward the armchairs.

Quinn went over to the picture window and looked out. Then he took up his stance there, his arms folded.

As I had noticed in our checkered past, he liked to stand back and observe when a suspect was being questioned. Obviously, I was now on the hot seat.

"You were saying about your keys?" Officer Vaughan prompted. He had his notebook out.

I told them about the pasta blast. About how my keys had disappeared from my bag and then turned up again beside the shrimp platter in the empty banquet room.

"Who were the people at the table?" Santiago asked, speaking for the first time.

I wished he hadn't. Because I really didn't want to get into that. "Keisha McIntyre," I said. "Doug Jenkins and Madeline Oliver."

Vaughan noted the first three names down in his notebook without outward reaction. But when I mentioned Tommy Irving, he said, "Hey, you don't mean that kid who pitches for the Rockets?"

"Yes," I said. "The only other person at the table was Howard Knowlin."

Vaughan looked from me to Quinn. Quinn said nothing. Vaughan cleared his throat. "Would that be the Howard Knowlin who's involved in the riverfront development? That Howard Knowlin?"

"Yes, that one," I said. "I'm certainly not implying that any of these people removed my keys from my purse. There was an incident. . . ."

I told them about the brawl between Sloane Campbell and Knowlin.

Santiago gave a low whistle and grinned. "Sounds like a really exciting pasta blast."

Vaughan said, "So that was when you left your purse unattended? After this fight?"

"Yes," I said, then explained about Keisha's nosebleed.

"So it is possible," Vaughan said, "that someone else passed by the table and—"

Quinn said, "If one assumes that four people would simply sit there and watch while a passerby went through Professor Stuart's handbag."

Vaughan looked chagrined. "I know, Chief Quinn. But these four people. This Doug Jenkins guy, I've seen his name too. And isn't the Oliver woman . . . isn't she Jebediah Gant's daughter? I remember seeing her name in the paper a year or two ago when her husband . . . he was a lawyer too . . . died out on the golf course. It just doesn't add up that one of them—"

Quinn interrupted. "But last evening Professor Stuart's key chain vanished from her purse. This morning, someone entered her house, apparently using a key."

"Yeah, but—" Vaughan glanced at me, his brow creased. "Professor, couldn't you have put your keys down on the banquet table when you were getting your plate?"

I shook my head. "I'm sure I didn't have my keys in my hand then."

Vaughan sighed and stood up. "Chief Quinn, could I speak to you out in the kitchen for a moment."

"This is my house," I said. "Or it is until my lease expires. Anything you have to say about this break-in should be addressed to me."

Quinn considered my expression. Then he said, "Officer Vaughan, Professor Stuart doesn't like being excluded from conversations that concern her. So if you wouldn't mind talking here."

Vaughan looked uncomfortable. He shifted his notebook to his other hand. "If that's the way you want it, Chief. I just want to know how you want us to handle this. I mean—"

"I know what you mean," Quinn said. "Let's do it strictly by the book, shall we? But I'll check in with Chief Anderson to discuss this."

Vaughan said, "That would be a real good idea. Once the newshounds get ahold of this . . . well, you know how that goes."

Yes, Quinn knew. We both knew. A break-in this time. Not a murder.

But I had just mentioned Howard Knowlin and a star athlete at the university in conjunction with my temporarily missing keys.

Quinn said, "If you have everything you need, officers. . . ."

Vaughan slid his notebook into his jacket pocket. "Yes, sir. That's all for now. But if you wouldn't mind calling the chief as soon as you can."

"Within the next half hour," Quinn replied.

"Thanks," Vaughan said. "Then we'll get out of here. We don't have to tell you about getting the locks changed."

"Yes, I'll call a locksmith," I said. "George . . . do you know which veterinarian the canine unit took him to?"

"Pet Med on Riverside," Santiago answered. "But, like we told Chief Quinn, he didn't look too bad. I think he'll be okay."

I nodded.

"We'll be back in touch, Professor Stuart," Vaughan said.

Quinn walked with them to the door. I didn't bother to strain my ears to hear what else they might say.

"Sloane Campbell was still there when I left to go with Keisha to the ladies' room," I said when Quinn came back. "What if my keys did fall out of my shoulder bag when Doug and I bumped into each other? What if he saw them on the floor and just reached down casually and picked them up as if they were his?"

Quinn sat down in the armchair across from me. "How would he know they were your keys?" he said.

"My key chain has a big red letter *L*," I reminded him.

"Okay. Now explain to me why Sloane Campbell would want access to your house."

I threw my hands up. "I didn't say it made sense, Quinn." And I needed to tell him about Keisha and the documentary. But not now. "For that matter, I don't know why anyone at that table would want to get into my house. Maybe Howard Knowlin is trying to unnerve me. To psych me out. I told you he wants Charlotte Wingate's house. Maybe he sent someone over to—" I stopped as something occurred to me. "George was in the basement. The man, whoever he was, opened the basement door."

Quinn scowled. "No burglar in his right mind would open a door with a barking dog behind it."

"But he wouldn't have known George was there. George has this game."

I explained about the game George liked to play with me.

Quinn said, "So our burglar opened the basement door—the wrong door—and George sprang out and went for his jugular."

It was a bloodthirsty image, but it seemed to please Quinn. He had a kind of grim smile on his face as he spoke.

"Unfortunately," I said, "our burglar seems to have made good his escape, and George got the worst of it. Hadn't we better get over to the vet?"

Quinn stood up. "First I need to touch base with Bob Anderson. Why don't you go have your shower. And pack an overnight bag."

"An overnight bag? Why?"

"You'll be spending the night at my place."

"But . . . I . . . if the locksmith can get here this afternoon, there's no reason—"

"Lizzie, we don't know what's going on."

"I know that. But that's no reason for me to—"

"Lizabeth, someone was in this house. George was beaten. What the hell do you—" He paused. "You are not staying in this house alone tonight."

"Then I'll go to a hotel," I said.

He looked at me and then shook his head. "Fine. If you'd rather stay in a hotel than with me, go to it." He went out into the hall.

A few moments later, I heard him on the telephone asking for Chief Anderson. I stood up, stood there, replaying what had just happened.

My reaction had been pure panic. Planning a romantic seduction was one thing. Being forced to take refuge with Quinn when I hadn't even had time to shop for something more frilly and feminine than my Garfield nightshirt was another matter entirely.

But if I went to a hotel he would never forgive me.

I waited until I heard Quinn wrapping up his call to Chief Anderson, then I went out into the hall. He hung up the receiver.

"If the invitation is still open," I said, "I would like to spend the night with . . . at your house."

He glanced at me, his silver gaze distant. "I have four bedrooms. You can have your choice."

"Thank you. I'll go shower and change and pack my bag."

As I turned away, he said, "It would be real progress in our relationship if you felt safe with me."

I spun around. "I do feel safe with you. I always feel safe with you."

He was flipping through my telephone book. He didn't look up. "Yeah. About as safe as you'd feel if you were dating Count Dracula."

I left him there in the hall. I didn't cry until I was in the shower with the water pouring over me. Ridiculous. Sometimes I was really ridiculous.

The tension between us was being played out in awkward silence. I fiddled with the radio. Scanning, seeking. Quinn, who had kept my keys when we walked out to the car, tapped his fingers on the steering wheel, impatient at every traffic light.

Luckily, the veterinary hospital on Riverside Drive was only fifteen minutes away even in Saturday afternoon mall traffic.

We pulled into the parking lot, and I opened my door and started around the car. I jolted to a stop when Quinn rounded the car and planted himself in front of me.

We stared at each other. Then he rubbed at the back of his neck. "I've spent the last eight days missing you like hell, Lizabeth. This is not the way—"

"I've missed you too," I said. "And I do trust you. I do feel safe with you."

"Lizzie, we can't go on like this. We've got to . . . you need to decide if you want . . . what you want."

"I have."

"You have what?"

"Decided," I said. "But I wanted—" I looked away from him at the woman walking past with a yellow tabby in a carrier. "I had planned this romantic evening with candles and wine and a special dinner . . . and now everything's gone wrong, and I . . . I wanted to get this right, Quinn."

He laughed and pulled me into his arms. "Don't worry about it. Don't worry about the candles." He rubbed his hand up and down my back. "And we don't have to . . . I can wait until. . . . You need to rest up from your half-marathon anyway. As long as I know that you are finally . . . at very long last, before I start baying at the moon . . . ready to. . . . Is that what you're saying, Lizabeth?"

I nodded against his shoulder. "Yes."

"Okay," he said, his chest rising and falling. "Okay."

He set me away from him and cleared his throat. "So let's go in and see George."

I tried to laugh. "We should have brought him a treat."

"Or the arm of that bastard who beat him," Quinn said.

* * *

George was awake. But he looked drowsy. He had a white bandage around his head and another on his hind leg. He licked at Quinn's hand and tried to thump his tail against the table.

I kissed his forehead. "Oh, George, I'm sorry."

Quinn turned to the vet. "How long do you need to keep him, Doctor?"

"A couple of days for observation," she said. "Then he should be able to go home, as long as you keep him quiet. He has contusions and a slight concussion, but he's young and strong and should be as good as new in a couple of weeks. Won't you, Georgie?"

George tried again to thump his tail.

"What was the weapon?" Quinn asked.

His use of the word *weapon* seemed to give the vet pause. But only for a second. She said, "A tool of some type, I would guess. Probably a hammer."

Quinn ran his fingers along George's rib cage. Then he looked at me and said, "Ready?"

"We'll be back to see you tomorrow, George," I said.

He licked my fingers.

"When I was in fifth grade," I said to Quinn as we were walking back to the car, "I made a voodoo doll because there was this boy that I hated."

"Did it work?"

"I never got a chance to find out," I said. "Hester Rose found it and tanned my hide before I could stick in any pins. And, of course, I wouldn't even think of wishing that something just slightly painful would happen to the person who hurt George."

He laughed. "Of course not."

CHAPTER · 13

I WAS UNPACKING the groceries we'd gotten at the supermarket, when the young woman from Express Lock and Key arrived with my new house keys. Quinn heard the doorbell and stuck his head out of his study long enough to ask if she'd made sure the house was secure after she changed the locks. She assured him she had.

He went back to his telephone call to his office. I wrote the young woman a check and added a cash tip for the delivery service.

When Quinn strolled into his sunny yellow kitchen a few minutes later, I said, "So, do you need to go to campus?"

"No, they have everything under control." He leaned against the counter, watching me shred zucchini. "Is that going into something we're going to eat?"

"Yes," I said. "Vegetables are good for you, Quinn."

"I eat vegetables, Lizabeth. I just don't like them sneaking up on me."

"Would you rather have a steak and a potato?"

"Now, that—"

The telephone rang.

"Max! What's up?" Quinn said by way of greeting. The response he received make him laugh. He listened for a moment, then he said, "I thought you were coming back by."

His smile faded in response to Max's reply. Quinn said, "That security check you were running on the South American? Why? . . . No, you can't be too careful when you're dealing with that kind of setup. . . . I'll believe that when I see it, Torelli." He glanced toward me. I pretended to be busy with my vegetable chopping. He turned away. "Yes, I did figure that out," he said to Max. "It was a little too much of a coincidence. Did he ask for a written report? . . . Yeah, tell him I said so." Another laugh. "You too, Torelli. Remember to keep your head down."

Quinn hung up the telephone and turned back to me. "That was Max Torelli, one of Wade Garner's operatives."

As in Garner International Security. The old Army buddy who had wanted

Quinn to take over as head of his Toronto, Canada, office.

"Oh," I said. "Was Mr. Torelli calling for Wade?"

"Ms. Torelli," Quinn corrected. "Max as in Maxine." He came over to the sink and picked up a carrot stick from the bowl. "I stayed at Wade's house in Arlington last night. I had a layover on the only flight I could get." He chewed and swallowed. "Then this morning, Max and I flew into Greensboro. She had an assignment in Martinsville."

I reached for the cucumber for the salad. "So she's the person you hitched a ride with?"

"Yeah," he said. He went over to the refrigerator, opened it, and took out a bottle of beer. "She was going to stop in Gallagher again on her way back to the airport, but something broke in the investigation she's been working."

"It's too bad she couldn't stop by," I said.

He took a swallow of his beer. "Wade sent her down here to assess the situation."

"To assess what situation?"

"He has more business these days than he knows what to do with. He still wants me to join the company."

"As head of the Toronto office?"

"As his partner," Quinn said, then took another swallow of his beer. "He's upped the ante."

I shook the water from the head of leaf lettuce. "It sounds like a tempting offer. Dinner will be ready in a little while, if you want to go into the living room and relax."

"Yeah, why don't I do that?" He walked out of his kitchen, and I reached for a paper towel to mop up the water I had spattered.

Dinner was as tense as the drive to the vet's had been. Quinn complimented me on the grilled salmon and vegetable medley. Responded with minimal information to my questions about Oklahoma and his family. I gathered up the dessert plates with the homemade apple pie and melting ice cream and took them back out to the kitchen.

He came and leaned in the doorway.

I looked up from loading the dishwasher. "All right. Do you want me to ask?"

He straightened away from the door and walked toward me. "Ask what?" he said.

"What you're going to do."

He took the dish towel out of my hand. "Take you to bed?"

My breath caught in my throat. "Quinn—"

"Please?" he said. A nerve was throbbing in his cheek, and I reached up and touched it.

To heck with candles and lace nighties. I wasn't going to be any sexier tomorrow than I was tonight. "Yes," I said. "Please do."

He swung me off my feet and up into his arms.

"Oh, wait, Quinn. Make sure the stove is off."

"Frankly, Lizabeth, I don't really care if the house burns down."

"You don't care if . . . because you won't need the house if you aren't going to be here? Because you're thinking of taking Wade Garner up on his offer to—"

"I'm thinking about the first time we met. You sneezed. Several times, as I recall."

"I was allergic to something. . . and you made me really nervous back then."

"And I don't now?" he said, walking toward the door.

"No," I said, tightening my arm around his neck. "I know you now."

As we left the kitchen, I reached over and snapped out the light.

CHAPTER · 14

The telephone was ringing. I dragged myself up through several warm, lovely layers of sleep and reached out for it—and almost fell out of the bed.

A brawny arm around my waist pulled me back. That woke me up. And reminded me of every moment of the night before. That had been me. Us. Wow! And he was still there. I turned on my side, toward him.

But my presence in his bed was not what was uppermost in Quinn's mind at that moment. One arm was around me, and his cell phone was to his ear.

His mouth was hard. His cop face. Then he said, "Is he still breathing?" A pause. "Right, I'll be there as soon as I can." He reached over and put the cell phone down on the night table on his side of the bed. Then he gave me his full attention. His expression gentled. "Sorry, love. I didn't mean for you to wake up like that. I had to leave the damn thing on in case of an emergency."

I pulled the sheet higher up around my shoulders. The room was chilly. "Is there one? An emergency?"

"You could call it that. Tommy Irving is at Gallagher Medical Center."

"Tommy?" I sat up. "What happened?"

"He jumped out of the window of his second-floor apartment when the police came calling this morning. He landed badly."

"Why were the police there?" I said.

"Because late last evening, Tommy went to a walk-in clinic in Martinsville, seeking treatment for several dog bites."

"Dog bites? Then Tommy was the person who broke into my house?"

"Unless he just happened to have a run-in with some other dog. Marcia Williams is at the hospital. She's going to try to question him as soon as the doctors are through bandaging him up from his latest mishap."

Williams was the detective who'd served as the Gallagher PD's liaison to the university last fall when Richard Colby was murdered. Quinn liked her. A good cop, he called her.

Quinn leaned over and kissed me. A brush of his lips across mine. "As much as I hate to leave you, Lizabeth, I do need to get over there. Why don't you go back to sleep?"

"Go back to sleep? Are you crazy? I'm coming with you."

"No, you're not." He shoved back the covers and climbed out of bed. "This is police business."

"That may be true—" I snatched my gaze away from his naked body to avoid being distracted. "But I'm involved in this, Quinn. I'm coming with you." I slipped out of bed, holding on to the edge of the sheet, and reached down to retrieve his discarded shirt from the night before. My robe was still in my overnight bag.

"I don't have time to argue," he said when I turned around to face him.

"Then don't," I said, ignoring the lurking amusement in his gaze. He might be perfectly comfortable standing there in all his glory. But I hadn't quite managed to shed thirty-nine years of self-consciousness about my body in one night. So he could just be amused. "I'll use the other bathroom," I said, "and be ready by the time you are."

He caught my arm as I passed. "All right, you can come. But you're not going to be able to go into his room. In fact, I should probably assign an investigator to this. I have a slight conflict of interest."

"But if Williams invited you to be there, she must not be concerned."

"She thought someone from the University PD should be present because he's one of our students. I'll get one of my guys to meet us there."

His gaze, which had gone to his cell phone on the night table, came back to me. "Believe it or not," he said. "I can do better than this."

"Better than what?"

"At being romantic. Our first morning together—" He looked down at his hand on my arm. "I was planning something other than having you hop out of bed to go with me to interview a suspect."

"Well, he is my suspect too. And all things considered, we were very lucky. Last night the house didn't burn down. And no one at all called."

"True," he said and kissed me.

I moved closer and kissed him back.

"Go get dressed," he said.

"You have to let go of me then."

"Yeah," he said. But he didn't let me go.

One of us had to make a move. Focusing firmly on his duties and responsibilities, I kissed his chin and wiggled out of his arms.

"That didn't help, Lizabeth."

"Oh, I . . . sorry." From the safe distance of the door, I turned to ask, "But why would Tommy Irving want to break into my house? And why would he risk going to a clinic . . . even one in Martinsville . . . knowing that the police would probably be looking for someone with dog bites?"

"Maybe he thought George was rabid," Quinn said.

CHAPTER · 15

"YOU MADE GOOD TIME, CAL," Quinn said to his investigator.

Detective Mayhew was standing in the fourth-floor corridor with Marcia Williams. "But you may not need me after all, Chief," Mayhew said. "Detective Williams here says the Irving kid is ready to make a statement."

Williams, clad in her usual pant suit, nodded her head. "Unless his attorney vetoes the idea. She's in there with him now."

"He has an attorney?" I said. "A private attorney?"

"His family does," Williams said. "Mom and Dad are in Honolulu, but the family attorney was available."

I remembered reading in *The Tattler*'s feature article about him that Tommy Irving was a Gallagher native. Father, a dentist. Mother, the owner of a modern dance studio. Yes, people like that would have a family attorney.

"How long has the attorney been in there?" Quinn asked.

Before Williams could answer, the closed door of Tommy Irving's hospital room opened. Abigail Sims stepped out.

As usual, she looked disgruntled. More so when her gaze fell on me. "Professor Stuart," she said. "Our paths do seem to keep crossing."

"Not by my choice this time, Ms. Sims."

Abigail turned to Williams and said, "My client wishes to make a statement." She glanced back at me. "It's just as well you're already here. He says he wants to explain to you."

"To explain—" I started to say.

"I'm not sure about that," Williams said. "I don't want my victim—"

"The dog was the damn victim," Abigail said. "And you're getting a confession. What more do you want? He'll make it. He'll sign it. Let's not play games."

"Is his confession contingent upon having Professor Stuart present?" Quinn asked.

"Yes," Abigail said. "As I said, he wants to explain."

"Okay," Williams said. "But I want one of the ADAs here. We're going to get press on this one, and one thing I do not need is my lieutenant asking me how I could have screwed up a confession."

"So get the ADA and let's get this over with," Abigail said.

Williams pulled out her cell phone to call in her request for an assistant district attorney.

"Why did he do it?" I said to Abigail Sims.

"The next step up from virtual reality games," she answered.

"What the hell does that mean?" Mayhew asked.

"He'll explain it," Abigail replied.

Forty-five minutes later, we were all—including an assistant DA—there in Tommy Irving's room. It was semiprivate, but he was the sole occupant. He lay in the bed, a sturdy kid with his left arm in a sling and cuts and bruises on his face. A gauze bandage swaddled his right wrist. Courtesy of George?

He looked at me as he started to talk. "I didn't mean to hurt the dog," he said. "I like dogs. I opened the door . . . I didn't even hear him . . . and he came charging out at me. He was barking and growling . . . and I pulled the hammer out of the tool belt I was wearing . . . to try to make him back off. But he started to snap at me." Tommy held up his right arm. "The dog did this. And I had to hit him to get out of there."

"Why were you in the house?" Williams asked.

"Not to steal anything. I just wanted to go in and look around." His gaze came back to me. "I read this article about how repairmen and mailmen, or anyone in a uniform is practically invisible to most people. Your purse was open, and I saw your keys. And I had the duplicator out in my van—"

"The duplicator?" Mayhew said.

"This portable machine for duplicating keys. I ordered it on the Internet when I started to think about going into places."

"Just to look around," Quinn said.

"Anybody can hack computers," Tommy said. "But to really walk into a place where you aren't supposed to be. . . ." His eyes gleamed. And then his gaze came back to me. "And the way Mr. Knowlin was talking about you—"

"Howard Knowlin?" Abigail said, her voice sharp. "You didn't tell me that part. What's he got to do with this?"

Tommy looked alarmed at her reaction. "Nothing . . . he was just. . . . After he got into that fight with that Campbell guy . . . when she"—he nodded his head at me—"left the table with Keisha, he was going on about the people who were giving him trouble. That's when I thought about . . . I saw the keys . . . everybody knows she's the chief's girlfriend. And I knew she was going to be at the marathon. And I thought it would be really cool to go in and look around. I mean, when a guy like Mr. Knowlin was all upset about how he couldn't get her to do what he wanted. . . ." His glance came back to me. "But I didn't intend to take anything. Honest. And I'm really sorry about the dog."

"Boy, you need your head examined," Abigail said. She flashed a glance around the room. "That's our defense. This young man has everything. Good family background, good grades, a star athlete. Big man on campus. And here he goes and breaks into someone's house to look around. An obvious psychological problem. Not a matter for the judicial system." This last was addressed to the assistant district attorney.

"We'll talk about it," he said.

"Does this mean I won't have to go to jail?" Tommy said. "I didn't mean any harm. I just hit the dog to get away." He held up his bandaged wrist again. "I had to do it. He really came at me. It was his fault. That dog was vicious."

Tommy had taken it one step too far. When he glanced at Quinn, he seemed to realize that.

Quinn turned and walked out of the room.

Tommy bit his lip. Then, with tears in his eyes, he said, "He's not going to decide about this, is he? It's not up to him, right? He's the university police chief, not— He can't tell you what to do, can he?" This appeal to the assistant district attorney.

Mayhew said, "You're a damn idiot, kid. Come on, Professor. Let's get out of here."

Abigail followed us out into the hallway and closed the door behind her. "He's a simpering little weasel," she said. "But his parents can take some of the credit for that." She walked over to Quinn, who was standing there with his arms folded. "Thank you for restraining yourself, Chief Quinn. I think you'll agree with me that it's best to resolve this with as little publicity as possible."

"I want him off my campus," Quinn said.

Abigail nodded. "I think his parents can be persuaded to see the wisdom of that."

Mayhew said, "Our sports fans aren't going to be too thrilled to see The Iceman go. Especially the alumni."

And that meant that quite a few people might end up being unhappy with Quinn.

Abigail said, with a wicked little smile, "Hell, Tommy's a southpaw, and even if he stayed on campus, he'd have to be out for the rest of the season after he injured his arm in that nasty fall this morning. The intern in the emergency room said it was nothing serious and that Tommy won't even have to wear that sling for more than a few days. But I have a feeling that when his own family physician has a look, he may think the boy needs to rest his pitching arm for a while. And the truth is, Tommy's been planning to transfer to another university for his senior year. He just hadn't gotten around to announcing it yet, knowing how heartbroken everyone at Piedmont U would be."

I was beginning to like Abigail more and more.

"Of course," she went on. "Everything I've said out here has been intended to serve my client's best interest. That is my only concern. Now, if you all will excuse me, I better get back in there."

Mayhew looked after her. "She's something," he said. "Sure enough old Jebediah's daughter."

"She's his niece," I corrected. "His daughter is Madeline. She—"

"Oh, yeah, the one who runs the shop." Mayhew nodded toward the closed door of Tommy's room. "That one ought to be the daughter."

Detective Williams came out. "Mr. Irving wants to know if this means he won't be able to join his parents in Honolulu for their family vacation."

Mayhew grunted. "Like I said, the kid's a damn idiot. But he sure could pitch."

Quinn said he needed to go into his office to advise the appropriate administrators and the Rockets' coach about the situation before they heard about it from reporters.

I said, "Even if Tommy announces he was planning to leave anyway, will they blame you because it was my house?"

"And my dog," Quinn said. "But since neither one of us coerced Tommy Irving into stealing your key from your purse and duplicating it—"

"Yes, but Mayhew was right. No matter what Tommy did, people are going to be upset about losing him." I leaned back in the Bronco's passenger seat. "Do you really think it'll be all right? That they won't try to hold you responsible?"

"If they do, I'll point out their error."

And consider other career options? I wondered. *Like Wade Garner's offer of a partnership?*

We had really terrific timing. He had an offer on the table. I had one too. And we had just moved into a whole new phase of our relationship.

Not to mention everything else that was going on.

Maybe that was what the cracked heart had been about.

We turned into Quinn's driveway. I reached for my shoulder bag.

"Got your key?" he said.

"Yes, right here."

I'd had a key to his house since December when I'd first kept George. Quinn had said I might need something from the house while he was away. When he returned, I'd tried to give the key back, but he'd told me to keep it. Then he would know where to find a spare. That key had not been on the chain with my house key. Otherwise Quinn would have had to change his locks too.

"Lizzie?"

Halfway out the car door, I turned back. "Yes?"

"Good-bye kisses are appreciated," he said.

"Oh . . . I forgot."

"Absentminded professors." He leaned across the seat. He tasted of the coffee he'd gotten at the McDonald's drive-thru. "Do you regret last night?" His fingers raised my chin.

"No!" I said. "How could you even think that? Last night was wonderful."

"Then stop worrying. We'll work it out. Okay?"

I nodded. "Okay."

He let me go and sat back. "Are you planning on coming into your office later?"

"I thought I might. Why?"

"Because I had facility management change the lock on your office door. Call building security. Someone will meet you with the new key."

I stepped down onto the driveway. "See you later, Chief Quinn."

"You can count on it, Professor Stuart."

I watched him back out of the driveway and turn up the street.

And what had he meant about working "it" out? Working out being in two different cities again if he accepted Wade Garner's offer?

I let myself in and went upstairs to get my overnight bag. The locks at my house had been changed and Tommy Irving was in police custody, so there was no reason I couldn't go home tonight.

Quinn hadn't asked where I'd be later. Had he assumed I'd still be here when he got home? I found the note pad on the kitchen counter and wrote, "Thanks for the hospitality. I'll be at my place. Lizzie."

I scratched out my name and substituted, "Love, Lizzie." Then I checked the refrigerator for fruit. An Egg McMuffin was not my usual morning fare. I found an apple and some grapes. Then picked up the telephone receiver.

What was the number for building security? I could call the university police department and have them connect me. I knew that number.

Or maybe Quinn had a campus directory. If he did, it would probably be in his study.

Crunching my apple, I went up the hall. George's rubber bone—he had two now, one here and one at my house—was in the living room, beside Quinn's recliner.

I'd better stop at the vet's to see George before I went into campus.

But I could still call building security before I left. It was always better to give them a little lead time. Since it was almost noon I'd ask someone to meet me at around one-fifteen or thereabouts.

Quinn's desk was immaculate. Desk pad lined up just so. Desk lamp at the proper angle. Walnut surface gleaming. Not a stray paper clip or balled-up piece of paper in sight. Only two files in his out box, along with a letter to be mailed. His military training seemed to kick in when it came to his desk and his work space, even though he was less prone to white-glove tidiness elsewhere in the house. That was why he had a cleaning woman who came in once a week.

I, on the other hand, could keep my house picked up. But my pretensions to tidiness evaporated in the immediate vicinity of my desk.

I opened the bottom drawer of his desk. Gallagher telephone book, but no campus directory. I tried the drawer above it. The paper clips were there. Along with a book of stamps, sharpened pencils, pens, rubber bands, and a ruler. All arranged in an organizer tray, no less.

I pushed back his desk chair and pulled at the center drawer. It didn't budge. I tugged again. Something must be caught. I squatted down in front of it.

There was a lock. The drawer was locked.

I sat back on my heels, staring at it. If he had something that he didn't want me to see, he certainly wouldn't have given me a key to his house.

But the drawer was locked, so even if I did have a key to the house. . . .

The house had been empty while he was away. If he had important papers, of course, he'd lock them up. I pushed the desk chair back into position and glanced around the room. The built-in bookshelves were filled with books that he'd actually read. I'd been through the books on his shelves, but I had never gone through his desk.

He had a photograph of me in a silver frame on the desk. He'd taken it at a winter carnival we'd gone to, snapped it just as I was about to bite into a pink cotton candy. I had been laughing. At least he hadn't taken that one to the office to display on his desk there.

So what was in the locked drawer? If I had the key, would I look inside? And now I knew exactly how Pandora had gotten into trouble.

Carrying my apple core, I walked out of Quinn's study and back down the hall to the kitchen. The university operator was able to connect me with building security. The man I spoke to promised to have someone meet me at Brewster Hall outside my office door at 1:30.

I was about to leave, when another thought occurred to me. Joyce. Her biopsy was scheduled for tomorrow. I should see if she wanted me to be there.

The telephone at her house rang several times, and then the answering machine came on.

"Hi, it's Lizzie. Just calling to see if you'd like some company tomorrow morning at the hospital. Talk to you this evening."

I hadn't offered before because I had been hoping she'd tell Pete what was going on and that he would turn out to be more sensitive than either of us expected. But if she hadn't told him, she'd need someone to be there.

But right now, I needed to visit George. He was probably wondering what was going on. The police canine unit had taken him to the veterinary hospital closest to my house. It didn't happen to be the one that Quinn used. So George wasn't even with people that he knew.

I stopped to see George, and made it to campus in plenty of time to meet the building security officer. He gave me my new key, and I let myself into my office and tried to settle down to work.

The folder in front of me contained the first hundred pages of my manuscript. Working title, *Gallagher, 1921*. I picked up my red pen and began to edit, using the reading process as a way of getting myself back into the flow of what I was writing about.

But 1955 was the year that kept popping into my head. Verity Thomas and Blanche Campbell in a fight to the death. Blanche Campbell's 10-year-old son, Sloane, now grown up. Sloane Campbell, who had punched Howard Knowlin in the nose over a real estate purchase and threatened to ram a camera down J. T.'s throat if he pursued the documentary Keisha had proposed.

Around and around. All connected. Sloane Campbell and Jebediah Gant. Jebediah convinced Campbell was out for revenge. Campbell owning the plaza where Madeline had her shop. Madeline involved with Doug, who was representing Knowlin, who was Campbell's arch rival.

Even Tommy Irving. Because of what Knowlin had said about me, Tommy had thought it would be "cool" to prowl through my house. Having been busted, Tommy was then represented by Abigail Sims, niece of Jebediah Gant, who had represented Verity Thomas, who had killed Blanche Campbell. Which brought us back to Sloane Campbell again.

It was amazing Campbell wasn't interesting in owning Charlotte's house on Grant Avenue. If he knew Knowlin wanted it, he might be.

I leaned back in my desk chair, tilting it at a daredevil angle, and stared up at the ceiling.

Everything interconnected except RaeAnne Dobb, who was missing.

But Knowlin had met her. As Keisha and I were walking away from the table, he had asked Madeline, "That beautiful young woman I met in your shop?"

And Knowlin had told everyone at Doug's table that I was one of the people who was giving him trouble. Maybe I'd better find out a bit more about Howard Knowlin. The lynching of Mose Davenport in 1921 could wait for a bit. My manuscript wasn't going anywhere. Worse luck.

Knowlin's Maine-based real estate company had a Web site. The site included links to scenic Maine. Bar Harbor and the Acadia National Park.

Knowlin had included a bio on his site. He had been born in Portland, Maine. No year given. Educated at Harvard. Degrees in business and landscape architecture. Skiing, backpacking, white-water rafting mentioned among his pastimes. A rugged outdoorsman.

Nothing in his bio about a wife or children. Victor Newman had him beat on that score. Or perhaps Knowlin preferred to avoid a soap-opera-style listing of that aspect of his life.

Planning commissions and boards of directors that he had served on. Professional memberships. Nothing that sprang out as being unusual.

I checked the other sites which the search engine had generated. A bunch of articles in the *Gallagher Gazette* about Knowlin and Project Renaissance. I had seen those.

Wait. . . . Howard Knowlin's name among a list of guests attending a political fund-raiser. I clicked to the article. It was from another newspaper. A $500-a-plate gathering for a "conservative Republican candidate." Knowlin had been among the attendees.

Back to the search results. Home of real estate developer Howard Knowlin. An article in the Sunday supplement of a newspaper.

Shucks, article not found. But I had the newspaper and date. I could go over to the library and track it down.

I went through the rest of the hits for Howard Knowlin. A few wrong Knowlins. Most of the right ones were about real estate deals and presentations at professional conferences or as a guest speaker. An honorary degree he'd received after giving a commencement address.

I might as well check on Sloane Campbell while I was at it.

He had a Web site too. Campbell Development. Properties acquired. Properties for sale. No bio. No pretty photos of Virginia.

His name was scattered here and there in *Gazette* articles about Chamber of Commerce meetings, the Jaycees, etc.

I tried adding his mother, Blanche, to the search. "Blanche Sloane Campbell." There. "The murder of Blanche. . . ."

I clicked to the site. It was someone's personal reminiscences of life in Gallagher after World War II. Photos of Daddy coming home from the war. School days in the 1950s. "Duck and cover" drills. Sock hops. Crushes on Eddie Fisher and Frank Sinatra. Wanted hair like Debbie Reynolds.

I scanned the article till I finally found something about the trial. The writer's boyfriend broke their date because he had to work late at the newspaper office, helping to get out a special edition about the trial.

"I felt so sorry for that little boy," she wrote. "He didn't cry at all. The sisters cried, but that little boy Sloane never even shed a tear. Such a sad, proud little boy."

I sat back in my desk chair. Touching, but not particularly useful.

I turned off my computer and reached for the index card on which I'd jotted down the newspaper and date for the Sunday supplement about Knowlin's homestead in Maine. Somehow I doubted that the house on Grant Avenue, slashed wallpaper and meager furniture, was up to his usual standards of luxury.

That reminded me that I still needed to call Charlotte Wingate, or her assistant, and mention finding that night guard under the stairs. Right now, it was languishing in my car glove compartment while someone ground his or her teeth and made them loose. Not to mention driving any roommate to distraction.

CHAPTER · 16

THE UNIVERSITY LIBRARY was a gray stone building, four stories with enough corners and cubbyholes so that one could hide out even on heavy-usage days. My favorite spot was a table across from the ancient-history section on the fourth floor. Not a high-traffic area for students.

But today that wasn't an issue. The building was practically deserted, and my destination was the microfilm machines in the basement.

I should have searched "Jebediah Gant" on the Internet while I was at it. Well, I could do it on one of the computers here before I got started with the microfilm. I reversed course and went back up the steps to the first floor. No waiting line for the computers, either, today.

The search found "Jebediah Gant honored by the Virginia Bar Association." I'd seen that. I'd also seen the Verity Thomas case entries.

They Fought for Justice. A book. I clicked to the site.

It was a blurb about a book published by a Richmond press. A book about Virginia lawyers in the twentieth century who "stood up and spoke out." Jebediah Gant, who'd not only served as defense attorney for Verity Thomas, but who had spoken out against the Virginia version of McCarthyism. No mention that Jebediah had taken part in any civil rights demonstrations. But he had represented a black minister and a Jewish rabbi arrested during a rally on behalf of city maintenance workers.

According to a biographical sketch, Jebediah's wife, Frances, his childhood sweetheart, had died at 41 after a brief illness. She was survived by Jebediah, who was 44 at the time, and Madeline, who had been 14. No mention of Abigail, but she would already have been a part of the household by then. So his wife had died, leaving Jebediah with two young girls to raise. I exited Netscape and went into the library catalogue to look for *They Fought for Justice.* The library owned a copy, but it had been checked out. I would have been willing to bet I knew by whom. Keisha. Well, at least, she was learning how to do research.

Time to go downstairs and find the newspaper article about Knowlin's house. The feature article was about Knowlin's "magnificent stone and glass retreat."

Knowlin had designed it himself, had it built to his specifications, and decorated by a young, "maverick" design team.

The feature writer noted that the design team, two gay men, had hesitated at first to take on the project. They disagreed with Knowlin's conservative political views. But he had wanted them and no one else. In the end, it had been "the perfect collaboration." He had given them creative freedom and unlimited funds.

The results—if the grainy photos were any indication—had been worthy of a Sunday magazine showcase.

Not much more in the article. Only a rather coy sentence or two from the feature writer about Knowlin's passion for cleanliness. A state-of-the-art sauna and whirlpool had been installed in the master bathroom, which also included a system for automatically disinfecting the toilet, tub, and sink after each use.

His cleaning woman must thank him every time she didn't have to scrub his toilet.

And undoubtedly Knowlin did not eat suspect shrimp in his germ-free bathroom.

Okay. So all this effort hadn't given me a lot more information about Knowlin. But the next time I saw him, I could ask about his fabulous coastal retreat.

I rewound the microfilm and put it back into the box. Almost four o'clock. The mall was open until six today. I could have another go at finding a dress in case Quinn and I ever got around to our romantic evening out.

Victoria's Secret was having a sale. I glanced at the skimpy pieces of silk and satin and lace. Then chose a bra and a black nightie that was about as daring as I was able to carry off. The dress I found in a department store was black too. Above the knees, with a back that plunged, even if the front didn't.

Satisfied with my purchases, I walked back out to my car, shopping bags swinging.

When I got home, there was a message from Joyce. "Lizzie, thank you so much for offering, but I'm all set for tomorrow." A pause. "I told Pete. He turned several shades of pale. But he says he wants to be there. Probably out of obligation. But it's the least he can do. I'll let you know how it turns out. And thank you again for offering. You're a good friend."

Well, it had been the least I could do too. But I was glad to hear that Pete had come through in the pinch.

And I was starving. I hadn't eaten anything since my breakfast Egg McMuffin and that apple from Quinn's refrigerator. I made myself a tuna salad with lots of celery and added a peach for dessert. I carried the tray into the living room. It was time for the news.

I hadn't heard from Quinn since we'd parted in his driveway. But I suspected that by now the local media had put him on the hot seat about Tommy Irving.

I clicked on the TV, hoping it wouldn't be too horrible.

Channel 13 carried the story third in its lineup. A straightforward recitation of the facts. Piedmont U's star pitcher, known as The Iceman because of his cool under pressure, had been arrested by the Gallagher PD. According to a statement from Detective Marcia Williams, the 21-year-old junior, who had been expected to lead the team to victory this season, had inexplicably and illegally entered an unoccupied house. He had been chased away by the family dog, then apprehended by the police after going to a clinic to receive treatment for dog bites. Tommy Irving was at present at Gallagher Medical Center, where he was receiving treatment for injuries acquired when he attempted to flee police by jumping from a second-story window.

That was it. No mention of my name as the owner—or lessee—of the house. Nothing about Quinn. Only a final comment from the anchorman about the shock and dismay of Tommy's coach and teammates.

I clicked the remote to Channel 6 in Roanoke. Channel 6 reported the story as part of its "Sports Roundup." And gave more or less the same version as Channel 13, adding only that even if The Iceman resolved his legal problems, his injuries would keep him off the playing field the rest of the season.

Obviously someone had been at work to downplay the whole incident. Who? A bunch of possibles—the administration, the alumni, Abigail Sims. Or maybe even Howard Knowlin. He'd seemed to like Tommy.

Not that I was complaining. I was happy not to hear my name on the six o'clock news. But I couldn't wait to ask Quinn how it had been managed. Of course, this might be only the first installment. By tomorrow there might be blazing headlines. But still, the media had had all day to get the details. So maybe we would get through this without major fallout.

Unless the reason Quinn hadn't been heard from was because he was still explaining himself. But President Sorenson had stood behind him during the investigation of Richard's murder. And if Sorenson was thinking of running for political office, he certainly wouldn't want on his record anything that smacked of abuse of power. Such as firing his university police chief because of a criminal act by a student.

Maybe it had been Sorenson's political supporters who'd gotten the story played down.

Yawning, I stretched out on the sofa. Reaction. I'd been holding my breath all day, expecting the worse. I thought of calling Quinn to see if he was home. But he knew where to find me.

The ringing doorbell brought me upright on the sofa. Dazed, stiff, and wondering what time it was. I'd taken off my watch.

My eyes wouldn't focus to look through the peephole in the door. "Who is it?" I said.

"Doug Jenkins, Lizzie."

Doug? What on earth? I tugged at my wrinkled purple T-shirt and rubbed at my eyes.

When I opened the door, Doug gave me an apologetic smile. "I woke you up, didn't I?"

"No . . . I mean, it's all right. I fell asleep on the sofa." I glanced at the sleek watch on his wrist. "What time is it, anyway?"

"A little after nine."

I'd been asleep almost three hours. "I'm sorry, Doug. Please come in."

"I'm here on a mission from Madeline," he said. "Both of us really, but she thought of it. Then Abigail stopped by, and Madeline decided she'd better go with her to talk to her father." He grimaced. "Jebediah's been behaving a little strangely."

"He has?" I said. "He seemed okay the last time I saw him." I was still trying to shake off my sleep-induced fog. "Madeline thought of what? Come into the living room and sit down. Can I get you something? Coffee?"

Although, since Quinn claimed I made coffee like a tea drinker, he might be better off with some other beverage. And where was Quinn anyway?

"Coffee would be great," Doug said, sinking into one of my landlords' big, cushy armchairs. "Or if you happen to have something with a bit more kick."

"Wine?" I said. "Or Irish whiskey?"

"Now, you don't strike me as an Irish whiskey kind of woman." He paused, then grinned. "Aah, the boyfriend."

"I also have Harveys Bristol Cream," I said, ignoring his teasing. "If you would prefer that."

"Let's go with the wine," Doug said. "The whiskey might floor me. I've had a long, hard day."

"Could I be an awful hostess and take you out to the kitchen? I'm dying for a cup of tea."

"Then we'd better go out to the kitchen," he said.

Doug followed me down the hall and settled into a kitchen chair that was not quite as comfortable as the armchair in the living room. I opened the refrigerator. Now that I'd made him move, I should at least give him cheese and crackers with his wine.

He did look tired. Was being Knowlin's public-relations person getting to him? And, of course, he had other clients.

"Why a long hard day?" I asked as I set the bottle of wine and a glass in front of him. "And what were you saying about being on a mission from Madeline?"

"Howard had intended to make a donation to the sports program at Piedmont U," Doug said. "He had been seen with Tommy Irving, our pitching phenom. Had called him a fine young man. As you can imagine, the news about Tommy's extracurricular activities required some damage control." Doug helped himself to the cheese and crackers.

As he crunched, I said, "The tone of the news reports was decidedly low-key."

Doug smiled. "A good PR man has a favor or two he can call in."

"You may have done it for Howard, but I'm sure the university is grateful too," I said.

"I'm a Piedmont U alum," Doug said. "And it may sound hokey, but I really do care about the old place."

"I'm glad you care," I said. "The university really doesn't need any more negative publicity." I set the kettle on the stove. "Quinn and I don't need any more publicity, either."

"Glad I could help," Doug said.

I took a mug out of the cupboard. "Now, about your mission—"

"I'm here with a solution to your other problem."

"What other problem?"

He sipped his wine and held his glass up to the light. "Not bad."

"Another customer recommended it," I said. "What other problem?"

"Your ceramic heart. Madeline knew you were concerned about getting it repaired. And since we both felt bad about not having kept a better eye on your purse—"

"Since you didn't expect Tommy to do something like that."

"No, I can't say that we did," Doug said. "But we did feel some responsibility since it happened at our table. So Madeline—as a part of her excellent customer service—did some checking around. She managed to find a woman up in Blacksburg who also does work in ceramics. Madeline called her and described the damage to your heart, and the woman is willing to try to repair it."

"She is?" I said. "Even though it's another artist's work?"

Doug poured himself a bit more wine. "The truth is, Madeline placed an order with this woman for some of her own work. She's good. Not as good as RaeAnne Dobb, but since we don't know where RaeAnne is. . . ." Doug bit into a piece of cheese and chewed. "Anyway, to speed up the process of getting your Valentine's gift repaired, Madeline will be happy to send it to the artist in Blacksburg. With your permission, of course."

I thought about that as I dropped a tea bag into my mug. "This is going to sound strange," I said, "but I'm not sure I should have anyone but RaeAnne repair it. It doesn't feel right. She made it and . . . I know that sounds superstitious."

"Only when I'm not."

"What?"

"Something my mother used to say whenever anyone accused her of being superstitious. Don't ask me what it means."

I laughed. "I won't. Actually, I think I know. Anyway, I do appreciate the trouble Madeline went to. But RaeAnne may turn up soon."

"Maybe," Doug said. "But Madeline says RaeAnne had—hopefully still has—some problems. You know her boyfriend was a drug addict."

"But from what I understand, RaeAnne isn't. Or is she?"

"Not that Madeline knows about. But her taste in men—"

"Lots of people get involved with the wrong person," I said, taking the whistling kettle from the burner. "But her aunt didn't think she would just go off and leave her son."

"Which raises some unpleasant possibilities," Doug said. "And, in that case, you might be better off going ahead and letting Madeline send the heart to the woman in Blacksburg."

"Yes," I said. "And please thank her for finding someone. But since Quinn is already back and I've already told him about the damage, I think I'll just wait for a few more days and see if RaeAnne does turn up."

"Your choice," Doug said. "Whatever you feel comfortable doing." He emptied his wine glass and got to his feet. "Now, I'm going to get out of here and wind my way home to my bed."

"Thank you for making the special trip," I said.

"Not a problem. Maybe it'll make up a little for our carelessness with Tommy."

I saw him to the front door, then walked back to the kitchen. That was when I remembered it was Sunday. Tommy had been arrested that morning. Doug and Madeline couldn't have found out about it until Abigail did, if then. So how had Madeline found an artist in Blacksburg on a Sunday in the few hours since. . . .

Of course, lots of artists had their studios in their homes. And Doug hadn't exactly said that Madeline had started to look for someone after they heard about Tommy.

Even if Madeline had only contacted the woman in Blacksburg today, it was possible that she'd already had a lead on her. If Madeline had seen the woman's work, she was probably someone Madeline wanted to carry in her shop anyway. And she'd simply asked the woman to do the repair job on my ceramic heart as an add-on to their negotiations.

And Doug could have called to tell me. But the face-to-face, personal touch was always more effective: *We're out there working hard for you. See how tired I am, but here I am on your doorstep anyway.*

No wonder he was such a whiz as a PR man.

I finished tidying up and stood by the sink, considering my options. I could get out my floppy disk with my manuscript and work on that for a couple of hours. I could have a shower, then climb into bed with a good book. Or I could make some popcorn and find an old movie on one of the cable stations.

In the end, the popcorn and the movie won. But I decided to have the shower so that I would be ready to toddle off to bed when I was too tired to keep my eyes open.

I hadn't thought to ask RaeAnne's aunt if RaeAnne had left alone. That occurred to me as I was pulling my nightshirt over my head.

As I was making popcorn, I considered those less-pleasant possibilities that Doug had alluded to. Had her aunt filed a missing-person report yet? Sergeant Burke would have contacted the other law enforcement agencies by now. But it would probably help if her aunt also filed a report.

No matter what child welfare might do, if RaeAnne had been missing for six days it was time to take action.

Unless she had come back by now. Sergeant Burke had checked on Friday. Maybe she had come back and simply not bothered to call Madeline. Or me because I hadn't left my telephone number.

Tomorrow, I could stop by her house again. Or better yet, ask Quinn to check. He would definitely say that would be better.

And surely he wasn't still in his office. Maybe he was mad at me for coming home.

I clicked the remote until I found *Splendor in the Grass*. Natalie Wood had just broken down in class and run out of the room weeping.

I pushed away my comforter and set my popcorn bowl down on the coffee table. Out in the hall, I tapped my fingers on the table, considering. He was being ridiculous if he was angry at me for leaving.

But I dialed his number anyway. The telephone at his house rang until his answering machine came on. I hung up without leaving a message. Should I call his office?

The ringing doorbell sent me halfway to the ceiling. Nerves. A definite bout of nerves.

I edged closer to the door and looked out through the peephole. Quinn.

I opened the door and stepped back to let him in. "I just called your house," I said.

He smiled. He looked as tired as Doug had. "Trying to find me?"

"Wondering where you were," I said.

"Conferring most of the afternoon. Then dinner with the Rockets' coach—who's a sensible guy, by the way. After that, back to the department for a joint press conference."

"I didn't see that," I said. "Has it already—"

"Tonight on the eleven o'clock news. We didn't say a lot. A prepared statement from me that was a masterpiece of evasion. Then the coach outlined the team's strategy for dealing with Tommy's absence for the rest of the season."

"Did whose house Tommy broke into come up during your press conference?"

"Oddly enough," Quinn said, "no one asked."

"Doug Jenkins stopped by," I said. "It seems he called in a few favors in the name of damage control. Howard Knowlin had been too friendly with our young felon."

"That would explain the politeness of the reporters who attended the briefing."

"It's kind of scary to think someone can call in favors that suppress the facts, isn't it?"

Quinn smiled, a twist of his lips. "That depends, Lizabeth, on whether you think your involvement in this is a relevant fact that is essential for an informed public."

I shook my head. "Okay. So much for my ethics. And I did say a very nice thank-you to Doug."

Quinn yawned. "Sorry. So is that why Doug Jenkins stopped by. To be thanked?"

"No," I said. "Why are we standing here in the hall. Let's go—"

Quinn pulled me back against him and nuzzled my neck. "So why did he come by?"

"To tell me Madeline had found someone in Blacksburg who could repair the heart. But I said I'd rather wait and see if RaeAnne turns up. Has Sergeant Burke's request to locate produced anything?"

"Not as of this afternoon."

"Quinn, is there some particular reason why we're standing here in the hall? You're exhausted. Why don't we go sit down?"

"Because I don't want to sit down if I'm going to have to get up again."

I twisted around and put my arms around his neck. "Would you like to stay?"

"If I'm invited."

"Yes." I kissed the corner of his mouth. "This will give me a chance to find out if you snore. I fell asleep last night before—"

He pulled me closer. "Suddenly I feel wide awake, Lizabeth."

CHAPTER · 17

MONDAY, MARCH 19

He was gone when I woke up in the morning. That was annoying because I had never been a sound sleeper, and he had managed to not only leave the bed without disturbing me but to come back at some point and put a note on the other pillow. And I had slept right through it.

And I still didn't know if he snored. But he did write nice notes.

"Eight o'clock meeting with the president. Had to go home for a clean shirt. When I woke up and saw you sleeping beside me, I almost called in sick. Love, John."

Did he want me to call him John? "Quinn" had become so much a habit, so automatic.

And how had he managed to wake up without setting the alarm? He wasn't a morning person either. But after years of getting up in spite of that, he had probably developed some kind of internal clock.

Or maybe he'd set the alarm after I'd fallen asleep, and I'd slept through that too. It was a little unsettling to have someone coming and going when you were asleep and unaware. And probably drooling into your pillow. But I would undoubtedly adjust.

I stopped to see George on my way in to campus. He was much perkier than he had been the day before. When I spoke to the vet on duty, he said that he wanted to keep him one more day to be sure he stayed quiet, but he seemed to be mending well.

That much was good news. In fact, by the time I got to the office, I had almost convinced myself that the universe was settling back into place.

Except for RaeAnne Dobb. But RaeAnne had gone missing before I went looking for her. She was not my responsibility.

But Keisha McIntyre was. The voice-mail message she had left a few minutes before I arrived threw my day right out of whack.

"You've got to come to Richmond, Dr. Stuart. I'm calling from the lobby at the state library. I've found the documents from the Verity Thomas case. The librarian brought out this whole box of papers. And you've got to come read them. There's this letter that her mother wrote. And Mr. Gant's appeal to the governor. And a letter from this man who wrote to the governor that if he didn't execute Verity Thomas, no white person in the state of Virginia would be safe. I'm going to go read some more. But if you come, I'll be home by the time you get here because my mother's expecting me to be there for dinner." She recited her telephone number at her parents' house. Twice. In case I'd missed it the first time. "Then tomorrow morning, we could come back and you could read everything for yourself," she finished.

I had jotted down Keisha's number automatically. The question was whether I was about to drive to Richmond. Yes, she had told me that she was going to look for the documents from the case in the archives. What I hadn't anticipated was being asked to come look too.

I shook my head. No one but Keisha would call a professor and ask her to drop everything and drive for three or four hours to see what she'd found. It was an outrageous request. One that I would never have dared make of any of my professors—even when I was a doctoral student.

But, on the other hand, I did want to know more about the case. I could use it in my lectures. And this was free time. No classes this week. The perfect time for a quick field trip to Richmond to get to know the archives at the state library. If I was going to stay in Virginia, that was something I needed to do. I would be working with grad students who might need to know what was available. It was always better to have seen firsthand.

As for the Verity Thomas case, the documents Keisha had mentioned sounded fascinating. If I went to Richmond, I could swing by and see the postcard Mrs. Cutler wanted to show me. I could drive to Richmond this afternoon, go with Keisha to the library in the morning, and then visit Mrs. Cutler in the afternoon. And be back in Gallagher by tomorrow evening.

I could tell Quinn I was going to Richmond to help a student with some research. And tell him about Mrs. Cutler when I got back.

I was supposed to give Amos my decision about Charlotte Wingate's offer today. But I couldn't tell him what I still hadn't decided. It would be helpful to know what Quinn intended to do about Wade Garner, but since he hadn't brought the subject up again. . . . Not that I intended to organize my life to accommodate his various career changes. But still, if I knew what he was going to do, it would give me some additional information for decision making.

At any rate, I would rather not have to talk to Amos just yet. I could leave him a message saying that I'd been called out of town and I would get back to him as soon as I returned.

It might be easier to leave Quinn a message too. If we talked, he would be sure to notice something in my voice or tone. He heard . . . and saw . . . entirely too much sometimes. It was a good thing I didn't intend to make a practice of trying to deceive him.

But this wasn't deception. It was omission. And I would remedy my omission when I returned.

It took me three hours to drive to the outskirts of Richmond. It was almost four o'clock by then. I found a motel with an in-house seafood restaurant, took a shower, then debated calling Keisha. The problem was that if I called too early, her parents might invite me to come over for dinner. Her parents sounded like the kind of people who would be pleased to open their home to one of the professors who was helping their daughter get her education. At any other time, I would have enjoyed meeting them. But I'd had too much time during my drive to contemplate my visit with Mrs. Cutler tomorrow.

Tomorrow afternoon at four. We had agreed on that time when I called her before I left Gallagher. She had sounded just as she had over twenty years ago. And the muscles in my stomach had tightened in anxiety. This time she was not going to be calling on me in class. But she might tell me something that would turn my life upside down.

So with the prospect of a meeting with my old teacher in less than twenty-four hours, I was not up to playing caring professor with Keisha's parents. I would call after I'd eaten. At around nine or nine-thirty. Then if I got one of her parents on the line, we could exchange pleasantries and that would be it.

"I certainly wish we had known you were here in town," Keisha's mother, Gloria McIntyre, said. "My husband would have come right over there and got you. You could have had a nice dinner here with us instead of that motel restaurant food. And I know how much they charge for it too."

"Thank you so much, Mrs. McIntyre," I said. "I would have enjoyed meeting you and your husband, but when I got in I was just so tired from the drive. . . ."

"I know you must be. I'm just outdone not to get the chance to meet you. I'll be working tomorrow. Keisha talks so much about you. 'Dr. Stuart this' and 'Dr. Stuart that.' She's real proud to see a black woman teaching at that school."

Damn. Now I really felt bad about not calling earlier.

"You and Mr. McIntyre should be very proud of your daughter," I said. "She's a beautiful, intelligent young woman."

"And she's got a lot of get-up-and-go about her," she said. "From the moment my Keisha came into this world, she's had her mind set on letting people know she was here and weren't going to stand for no stuff." She laughed. "It didn't always make her an easy child to raise, though."

"But her determination serves her well now," I said.

"Yes, it does. And listen to me running on like this when you're tired. I'll give Keisha your message when she comes in. You'll meet her in the front lobby of the library at ten in the morning. Is that right?"

"That's right. Thank you, Mrs. McIntyre. It was lovely speaking to you."

"It was real nice speaking to you too, Dr. Stuart. You take care of yourself now. And thank you for all the care you've been giving our Keisha. You don't know how much comfort it gives her daddy and me to know she has somebody like you there at the university to guide her the way she ought to go."

"Thank you. Good-bye, Mrs. McIntyre."

To guide her? I could barely guide myself. Talk about putting on heavy parental pressure. Lizabeth Stuart, professor, role model, and guide. But she had sounded like a warm, caring woman. The kind of mother we'd all like to have. But we got what we got.

CHAPTER · 18

Keisha had been right. The documents in the governor's records were definitely worth the trip. She kept whispering, "See, Dr. Stuart. Read that one."

The documents fell into four categories. Letters from the officers of the court and criminal justice officials, including defense attorney Jebediah Gant, the prosecutor, and the warden at the prison where Verity Thomas had been held while she was awaiting execution. Letters from Verity's family members and the pastor of her mother's church. A signed petition from Chicago. And finally letters from Virginia citizens, most of them supporting the execution, but a couple suggesting that life in prison might serve as well, that this poor ignorant black girl should be shown mercy.

One of the more interesting documents was the letter from the prison physician to the governor. Verity's parents had claimed that she was barely 17, but she had not been born in Virginia. The family had come from the backwoods of Mississippi. They had no birth certificate, there was no record of her birth, and the black midwife they claimed had delivered her was dead. This had prompted the prosecutor to suggest that claiming Verity was 17 was a ploy on the part of the defense. In his own letter, the prosecutor asserted that Verity had all the appearance of "a sturdy well-grown Negro woman of 20 or 21."

The governor had asked the prison physician for his opinion. The physician had responded that based on his examination, "the prisoner is a fully developed woman. It is impossible to ascertain her exact age. However, she may be somewhat older than 17." Thus giving the governor a way to avoid dealing with the issue of executing a juvenile.

But in her letter, Verity's mother had called her daughter, "my poore child." The letter was written in a crude, barely legible hand, but all the woman's pain was there on the page: "Please, sir, you have the power to spar my poore child. Please, sir, I knows she done wrong. But please don't kill her."

The petitioners from Chicago had been more sophisticated in their prose and less temperate in their appeal. Describing themselves as "a group of concerned

United States citizens of both races," they had argued that "taking the life of this young Negro girl will serve no good purpose. Her offense is clearly the result of lack of training and discipline. The fault lies not with this child but with the state of Virginia, which kept her in ignorance, which has failed to educate its Negro citizens. You, Governor, may start to correct this grave wrong by bravely showing mercy to this child."

That letter to the governor of a Southern state which already felt itself under siege from "outside agitators" must have gone over well.

Jebediah Gant had written in his letter of appeal:

> Perhaps I should have put her on the stand and had her tell her own story. But I feared that would only inflame the passions against her. This is a girl who is the daughter of ignorant Negro sharecroppers. The crime she committed was brutal. But I truly believe she acted first in self-defense and then on impulse, and not from cold-blooded deliberation. Therefore, this case lacks the premeditation required for a capital sentence. I ask that you commute her sentence to life in prison.
>
> Please note, Governor, that the girl meant no harm to the baby. Its drowning was a tragic accident. I should also point out that this young girl is feeble in her intelligence. I ask that you take this into consideration as well.

Not brilliantly written, but better than the petition from Chicago in its likelihood of swaying the governor. If Verity Thomas had not died two weeks before she was scheduled to be executed, would the governor have given her a last-minute reprieve? Was there any chance at all that he might have commuted her sentence to life in prison? Or would the racial and political climate have overwhelmed all other considerations?

"We need to know more about the governor," I said to Keisha, keeping my voice low to avoid the wrath of the librarians. "We need to know his party affiliation and whether it was an election year. And if he had made statements about the death penalty. And, of course, exactly what was going on in Virginia at that time with the civil rights movement."

Keisha's grin took up half of her face. And I realized what I had been saying. "I mean, *you* need to know," I said, trying to backtrack.

"But couldn't we work on it together, Dr. Stuart? Couldn't we do a paper for one of the criminal justice conferences? Or a journal article like you have us read?"

I looked from her eager face to the documents on the table in front of us.

"Please, Dr. Stuart," she said. "I promise I'll work really hard on it."

"All right," I said, hoping I wouldn't regret it. "But an academic paper, Keisha. An article, not a documentary. We leave Sloane Campbell out of this other than his role during the trial. We do not climb fences to get onto his property. We do not try to interview him or Jebediah Gant or any of the other still-living participants. Understand me?"

She looked crestfallen. "Then what do we use? Just these letters and things?"

"We use these documents as a starting point," I said. "And then we gather evidence—everything else we can find about the racial, social, and political climate in Virginia, the South, and the rest of the country in 1955. We place the case in that context, then pose and try to answer one question: If she hadn't died of pneumonia, is it possible that Verity Thomas's sentence might have been commuted by the governor from death to life in prison?"

"And that's how you do it?" she said. "That's how you do historical research?"

"That's how we do this case," I said. "Because any other approach will have Sloane Campbell punching our lights out."

She frowned. "But don't we want to . . . I mean, isn't it important to—"

"Keisha, we're social scientists, not investigative reporters. We don't need flash. We need thoughtful research and discussion."

She nodded. But she looked unconvinced.

"That's the only way I work with you on this, kiddo," I said.

Her smile was sheepish. "Okay, Dr. Stuart, I guess you know." Then she grinned. "And maybe somebody will read our article and decide someday to do a documentary."

I laughed. I couldn't help it. I didn't burst her bubble by telling her that the readership for articles published in scholarly journals was mainly other academics. Howard Knowlin might have read one of my articles, but that was because he'd gone looking for it. So we'd be no threat at all to Jebediah's memoirs, especially if we focused on the question I'd posed.

And since Doug said Jebediah was acting strangely, it was possible he'd never get around to doing his memoirs anyway.

Still, Jebediah had brought the case to my attention. As a courtesy, I should tell him what Keisha and I had in mind. But I would worry about that when I got back to Gallagher.

I glanced at my watch and asked Keisha if she wanted to stop for lunch. She shook her head. I was willing to ignore my stomach too.

We got photocopies of what we could and made notes about everything else. Then we found a table out in the lobby and discussed what we needed to do next. Research to commence after spring break.

I was explaining to Keisha why we needed to know more about the signers of the Chicago petition, when I remembered my appointment with Mrs. Cutler.

"Keisha, I've got to go. I'm supposed to visit someone who lives near Williamsburg this afternoon."

"Okay, Dr. Stuart." She grinned. "I've got enough to do to get started."

"More than enough," I said. "Now, can you tell me how to get from here back to the exit that I need?"

"I've got my mom's car. I'll lead you out to the highway."

"Thanks," I said, gathering up my briefcase. "I don't want to be late for this."

"Are you going to visit a friend?"

"My eleventh-grade geometry teacher. Who did not tolerate it when her students were tardy."

Keisha laughed. I was serious. Mrs. Cutler couldn't send me to the principal's office, but her "Lizabeth" would be enough to express her disapproval.

As I had feared, Mrs. Cutler had not changed. Her dark hair still showed only that one V-shaped streak of white in the front. The students used to whisper that she had been born with it. Someone's mother had said that the white streak ran in Mrs. Cutler's family among the women. "Because they're witches," the kid who had reported that had joked.

Whatever she was, Mrs. Cutler had not changed a great deal in twenty years. Her skin, the color of light brown sugar, was still unlined.

"Lizabeth, I'm pleased to see you," she said. "Come in."

Her red brick house featured a lawn that her husband was at that moment tending. His own head liberally sprinkled with gray, he was out there on his knees in a flower bed, surrounded by an assortment of gardening equipment.

It was he who had assured me that yes, I'd found the right house and "Enid" was expecting me.

"Enid" explained that she thought we should speak in private. Therefore, her husband would not be joining us for tea. Or coffee, if I preferred.

I assured her tea would be fine. And suddenly remembered I was supposed to have tea with Charlotte Wingate on Wednesday. Tomorrow.

But even Charlotte, with her servants, would not be able to outdo Mrs. Cutler's style. China and cloth napkins. A silver teapot. Tea served at her dining room table with delicate cucumber sandwiches and poppy seed cake.

I fiddled with the napkin in my lap and hoped I wouldn't spill anything on her white lace tablecloth.

During tea she questioned me about my work. Her first question was, "How did you choose criminal justice as a field, Lizabeth?"

I swallowed the piece of cucumber I was chewing and said, "I . . . uh . . . I had majored in English and history, with a minor in psychology."

"With what intent?" she asked.

"I didn't really have an intent," I said. "That was how I ended up in criminal justice." *Wonderful, Lizabeth. That was crystal clear.*

Mrs. Cutler said, "Because you had no intent?"

"Because I needed . . . I wanted to go to graduate school . . . I had taken a criminology course and it seemed interesting. I thought it was a field in which I could bring together my interests. And do research."

"Yes," she said, nodding. "Would you care for more tea?"

"No." I set down the cup I had just drained. "No, thank you, Mrs. Cutler."

"We are no longer student and teacher, Lizabeth. You may call me Enid."

Yes. When I'm one hundred and two. But I could get to the point and get out of here. "You said in your letter that you had something to tell me about my mother."

She laid her napkin down on the table and stood up. "Shall we go into the living room? The postcards are there."

Postcards? There's more than one?

We went into the living room, and she walked over to a corner desk and opened a drawer.

"You wrote that you and my mother were friends," I said, as she came back with the postcards in her hand.

"Of sorts," she said, using the phrase she had used in her letter. She sat down on the sofa beside me and held the postcards out. "These came a few weeks after your mother left."

My heart was pounding so hard I could hear it in my ears. My hand was shaking when I reached for the postcards.

I jumped as Mrs. Cutler's hand closed over mine. "It was a long time ago, Lizabeth. The past can't hurt you."

But it could. I knew that from experience.

But the gesture, the touch of her hand on mine, steadied me. "Thank you," I said.

The cards were picture cards. Two of them. I examined the first one. The postmark was Chicago. The date blurred. The photograph on the front of the card was of a five- or six-story building. The name on the canopy over the entrance read HOTEL MARTINIQUE. I turned the card over and felt my heart bump again at the sight of the sprawling, looping handwriting that I had seen before in the old school books of my mother's that I'd found in the attic after my grandmother died. My mother had written her name in the front of the books, along with an occasional comment in the margins.

But no clues to where she had gone when she got on that Greyhound bus and left Drucilla. "As you can see," Mrs. Cutler said, "the postmark is Chicago. The caption on the back also indicates the hotel is in that city. Or was. Perhaps it's no longer there."

I stared down at the message my mother, Rebecca, had written: "Here I am in the big, bad city. Not staying at this hotel, but I've been inside. Becca."

That was all. I put that postcard down on the coffee table and picked up the other one from my lap. This was a postcard of a different kind. On the front was a caricature of jazz musicians. One had his head thrown back as he blew his saxophone. Another leaned over a piano. And a sexy chanteuse stood at the front of the stage. They were all black.

I turned the card over. The notation read, JAZZ IN CHICAGO.

My mother had written, "That's going to be me up there singing like that. I've met a man who likes my voice. Becca."

When I raised my gaze, Mrs. Cutler was watching me.

"I didn't know my mother. . . . I had never heard that she wanted to be a singer."

Mrs. Cutler smiled. "She wanted to be a star. A singer. An actress."

I nodded. "Then Chicago . . . I suppose that seemed a better place to achieve that than Drucilla, Kentucky."

Mrs. Cutler said, "For a 17-year-old girl, Chicago would have seemed a city of bright lights and possibilities."

"And there were only these two postcards? You never heard from her again after that?"

"I was somewhat surprised to hear from her at all," Mrs. Cutler said.

"But you said you were friends."

"As much as Becca could be friends with any other young woman." Mrs. Cutler smiled, a twitch of her lips. "She found me tolerable because I was so much in awe of her. Rather like Peppermint Patty and Marcie."

"Peppermint—? The "Peanuts" characters?"

"Marcie is the loyal sidekick," Mrs. Cutler said. "Even calls Patty 'Sir.'"

"But Marcie is the smart one. Peppermint Patty is always blundering." I said.

"And that's where my lighthearted analogy breaks down. As a skinny, bespectacled bookworm, I may have been in awe of her. But your mother was every bit as smart as she was beautiful. And she never blundered." Mrs. Cutler smiled again. This time a full-blown smile that warmed her face. "But she did often dare. I think that was why I was in awe of her."

"And was I a dare?" I said.

Mrs. Cutler's smile faded. "I'm afraid I have no idea, Lizabeth. Your mother never told me how you came to be conceived." Before I could speak, she added, "Or who your father was."

"In your letter you— What did my grandmother say when you took her the postcard?"

Mrs. Cutler glanced away. She reached out to adjust the position of the small stone Aztec figure on the coffee table.

"Please, tell me what she said."

"Your grandmother said that your mother was a slut. She said Becca had brought disgrace on her family. She said she wanted to know nothing about her or where she had gone or what she was doing. She told me to burn the postcard and never speak again of Becca in her hearing."

I swallowed to wet my dry throat. "But you didn't burn it—them."

"No, I put them away in my journal, my own dream book. And now, I'm giving them to you."

"Who do you think—? Did you know the boy . . . the boys my mother. . . ?"

Mrs. Cutler shook her head. "Lizabeth, to be blunt, your mother shared her favors with a number of young men. Or, at least, that was what they said. And she never denied it."

"Then she was—"

"She was a lovely, fun-loving young woman. She resisted your grandmother's efforts to enforce her own puritanical standards, and she rebelled." Mrs. Cutler paused. "But in your grandmother's defense, she was a good woman, a strong woman with great dignity. It was because of their respect for her and your grandfather that people spoke so rarely of your mother after she went away. They cared about your grandparents, and they knew your grandmother was trying hard to raise you without shame."

But she hadn't quite succeeded. There had been the whispers. The taunts from the boys who'd heard their parents talking. The snide remarks from some of the girls.

I had survived because I'd stop listening and retreated into my books. Wild Becca's daughter was a bookworm. Not at all like her mother.

Well, Mrs. Cutler and I had that much in common. Although, she had probably already shown signs of being formidable even when she was skinny and bespectacled.

"Are you sure you won't have more tea, Lizabeth? I'll make a fresh pot."

"No, thank you, Mrs. Cutler. I have to go. I have a long drive."

"As I said in my letter, you are more than welcome to spend the night."

"Thank you, but I'm expected home."

"Then someone's waiting?" she said. "You have a young man?"

"Yes," I said.

"And plans for marriage?" she said.

"No. No plans. Thank you again." I reached down for the postcards. "May I take these?"

"Of course. I want you to have them. They should be yours."

She walked with me to her front door.

"Good-bye," I said.

She took the hand I held out and covered it with her own. "You're an adult now, Lizabeth. Your own woman. Not your mother's creation or your grandmother's. It's your choice what you do with those postcards. Don't let them make you unhappy. Throw them away if they hurt too much."

I nodded. "Thank you for saving them for me. Good-bye."

She smiled. "I hope you'll visit me again. I would like to meet your young man. You have turned out quite as well as I expected, Lizabeth. I was always sure that you would make me proud."

"Then why, Mrs. Cutler, did you terrorize me every day by calling on me in class?" It had popped out. I clasped my hand to my mouth.

She burst out laughing. A tinkling, youthful laugh. "Lizabeth, if I hadn't pushed you, you would never have known your own strength."

I could think of nothing to say to that. I turned and walked back to my car at the curb. Mrs. Cutler's husband, still at his gardening, smiled and waved as I passed.

"Have a good visit with Enid?" he said.

"Yes, thank you. Good-bye."

I missed the exit I should have taken. I was thinking about what my grandmother had said to Mrs. Cutler. She may have called her daughter a slut and said she wanted to know nothing about her. But when she was dying and had thought I was my mother, Hester Rose had said, "Becca, why you come back here?"

As if she had sent her away. Even known she was going. Leaving behind only one person who shared her secret. My grandmother, Hester Rose.

And perhaps the man—the boy—who had fathered me. But since no one had ever stepped forward to claim me. . . .

Had my mother hoped that Mrs. Cutler—her almost friend Enid—would take the postcards to Hester Rose so that she would know Becca was all right?

Or had been all right when she met a man who liked the way she sang. Anything might have happened after that.

But my mother had not been a sweet young innocent. At 17, she had probably known more about men than I knew now at almost 40.

Too bad for Quinn I wasn't a bit more my mother's daughter.

And I was lost, dammit. I had missed my exit. I could get off at the next one and try finding my way back . . . or go on to Williamsburg. I had never been there.

I ended up in one of the resort hotels on the Colonial Williamsburg property. I had taken one of the shuttle buses from the parking lot to the welcome center to use the rest room. That was when I saw the sign for accommodations. Since I didn't really care to drive back to Gallagher right then, I got in line. Minutes later, I had a room across the street. I checked in, pretending to listen as the clerk handed me a map and pointed out the restaurant next door, etc.

Then I walked to my room with my overnight bag bumping against my leg. When I got inside, I dropped my bag to the floor. Then I stripped off my clothes.

The water from the shower pounded over my shoulders. I put my head underneath and reached for the tiny bottle of shampoo/conditioner.

Ten minutes later, hair and body dried, I pulled back the covers on the bed and climbed in.

It was 12:43 A.M. when I woke up. I stared at the dial of the clock radio for several minutes. Then I fumbled for the lamp. My throat was parched. I was hungry. I got up and went into the bathroom for a glass of water.

I came back and sat on the bed, sipping it.

What on earth was I doing? I should have called Quinn. I'd said in my message that I'd be back tonight. He was probably imagining me in a crumpled car somewhere.

Being upset was one thing. Being thoughtless was another.

I took another sip of water. Then I reached for the telephone.

He answered on the second ring.

"Hi, it's me. Did you get my message about having to go help my student with her research? I was delayed, so I decided to spend another night."

There was a pause. Then he said, "So you're still in Richmond?"

"No. In Williamsburg."

"I thought you were going to Richmond."

"I did. But I ended up in Williamsburg. It's a long story. I'll tell you about it when I get home tomorrow. Is everything all right there?"

"I'll tell you about it when you get home tomorrow," he said.

"Quinn, what— Has something happened? Tommy Irving? George?"

"Tommy Irving left the hospital today for his arraignment. He's out on bail, with his parents, who flew back from Honolulu. George is fine. I picked him up this afternoon."

"Then what? Tell me."

"RaeAnne Dobb," he said. "She may have been found."

"Found? Is she—"

"If it's her, she's dead."

"How?" I said.

"The cause of death hasn't been determined yet. Two boys out in the woods with their dogs found the body. It had been doused with gasoline and set on fire. The crime-scene unit recovered metal strips, small nails, and bits of leather from among the human remains. They think the body was in a container— maybe an old-fashioned trunk—when it was set on fire."

It took me several seconds to swallow down the nausea in my throat.

"Lizzie?" Quinn said.

"Yes," I said. "Why do they think it might be RaeAnne?"

"Because the body is that of a young woman. The aunt identified a silver ring that she says is similar to one RaeAnne wore. The ME is waiting for her dental records."

"But why would someone go to the trouble of burning her body but leave behind a ring that could be used to identify her?"

"He might not have been able to get the ring off her finger," Quinn said. "Or maybe he overlooked it. Or panicked."

I swallowed again. "I have to go now. I'll be back tomorrow."

"And then you can tell me what you've been up to," Quinn said.

"Yes," I said. "Good night."

"Good night, Professor Stuart."

CHAPTER · 19

Why would someone want RaeAnne Dobb dead? If she was the woman in the woods, who had done that to her and why?

I thought about that as I drove back to Gallagher in the morning. But I knew almost nothing about her—that she'd had a young child, a 2-year-old son, fathered by a drug addict, now deceased, who had often cheated on her. That in spite of those depressing aspects of her life, she'd designed whimsical, lovely pieces like my Valentine's heart. That she'd been going to school part time. Wanted to be an art teacher. Her aunt said she'd sometimes lacked good sense. Howard Knowlin had remembered her as a beautiful young woman, and if the photograph I'd seen was accurate, she had been.

That was all I knew about her. Except that she might have been murdered, doused with gasoline, and burned in a trunk. That part of it wouldn't be confirmed until the ME compared her dental records.

I jerked the steering wheel, and the car swerved. I eased my foot off the brake and guided it back from the shoulder of the road.

The ME was going to check RaeAnne's dental records. X rays of her teeth. Patient notes from her dentist. Was there even a possibility that her dental records might indicate RaeAnne had been a teeth grinder? Had she ever been fitted with a night guard?

If the owner was dead, then she wouldn't miss her night guard. Wouldn't come back to look for it.

An expensive night guard in a tangerine plastic case. Neither the night guard nor the case had been grimy, even though they'd been under a staircase in a dirty, dusty basement. What if they had been there only a few days?

But I was making a gigantic leap. A leap from dental records to a lost night guard. Even if it was hers, why would RaeAnne have been carrying it around with her? And how would it have gotten under a staircase in Charlotte Wingate's empty house?

I needed to call Quinn.

Dammit, this was another one of those times when in spite of my objections to cell phones, having one would have been convenient. It was almost ten minutes before I spotted a gas station. I turned into the driveway and pulled up to the pay phone.

"Sorry, Professor Stuart, he's not here," the officer who answered told me. "Do you want to leave a message?"

"Yes, I do. Would you tell him to please ask RaeAnne Dobb's aunt if RaeAnne wore a night guard?"

"A what?"

"It's a dental— If she wore one, her aunt will know what it is."

"Okay," he said. "Ask her aunt if RaeAnne Dobb wore a night guard. I'll leave the message."

"And please tell Chief Quinn that I'm en route and should be back in Gallagher in about an hour."

In my car again, I opened the glove compartment. The tangerine plastic case was still there on top of my road maps and car registration card. I picked it up and shook it. Then opened it to make absolutely sure.

An artificial palate with teeth impressions and a wire across the front. The dentist who made it should be able to identify it.

The basement staircase. There had been something wrong with the staircase. The wooden support had been broken as if something had crashed into it. A struggle on the stairs? A body falling against the railing? Or maybe a trunk. Someone losing control of a heavy trunk containing a body. The trunk crashing into the stair railing.

Enough, Lizzie. Just start the car and drive home.

The night guard probably belonged to one of the teenagers who had stayed there with the foster parents. But if it had been RaeAnne's, maybe she had been killed there in that house. Killed by one of the people who had known her and who had access to the house.

RaeAnne and Knowlin. "That beautiful young woman I met in your shop," he had said to Madeline. What if he had said that as a way of planting his lack of knowledge about her whereabouts? What if he had seen RaeAnne, and she had been something else he wanted? He'd said that he had seen the house. Never bought anything without examining it. Had Charlotte agreed to let him look at the house before she decided not to sell it to him?

Or had he somehow gotten a key? Maybe Tommy had duplicated it for him.

No, I was getting too far out there. Knowlin was too shrewd to rely on a flaky kid like Tommy.

But Doug. Doug had been his liaison for the house negotiations. Suppose Doug had a key. Suppose Knowlin had arranged to meet RaeAnne at that house and something had gone wrong in his plan to seduce her. She had been killed. Maybe an accident.

And then the body had to be disposed of. Burned to prevent identification—or to hide evidence of rape.

I jumped as a driver honked at another car in the gas station driveway.

I put the plastic case back into the glove compartment and started the engine. I needed to get home and talk to Quinn.

I was approaching Gallagher from the west, seeing the downtown municipal buildings rising up on the other side of an abandoned railroad bridge, when I remembered it was Wednesday. This afternoon, I was having tea with Charlotte.

So drive straight to campus and see Quinn. Then call Charlotte to confirm my invitation and ask what time I should be there.

Even in my wild conjectures about RaeAnne—if it was RaeAnne who had been murdered—Charlotte Wingate was an unlikely suspect. The house on Grant Avenue belonged to her, but she was a 70-something woman with a touch of gout. It was difficult to imagine her moving a dead body.

And she had emphasized that we would be having tea alone. So there was no reason to worry that any of the others would be there.

The PBS radio program moved from a discussion of a new book about health care to the local news. I reached out to turn up the volume as the reader said, "The gruesome discovery of a burned body in the woods near Blair in Pittsylvania County still has local police investigators baffled. . . ."

The report was a repeat of what Quinn had told me on the telephone. The only new information was that the body had been found late Monday afternoon.

Two days ago. So Charlotte and the others would know about it by now.

But I was not going to Charlotte's to play detective. Amos expected me to go. It was important to the school that I go. I intended to focus on getting more information about Charlotte Wingate's "agenda," so that I could make my decision about the endowment.

So stop at Quinn's office, give him the night guard, then leave it alone. Don't invite trouble, Lizabeth.

Quinn looked up and smiled as I walked into his office, but his attention was on his telephone conversation. Training standards and community policing.

Too antsy to sit still, I got up and began to wander around his office.

It was a generic university administrator's office. File cabinets, bookcases, a work table. Green plants scattered about, including a large orange tree near the mini-blind-covered windows. A conversation area with a beige-print sofa facing a glass-topped coffee table, flanked by two similarly patterned armchairs.

But there were also some uniquely Quinn touches. On one wall, he had framed portraits of Civil War Generals Robert E. Lee and Ulysses S. Grant. A West Point pennant hung between the two portraits. In honor of their shared alma mater. And his own.

When I had first seen that grouping, I asked if it wasn't a bit risky given the fact that he was from Philadelphia and some Southerners were still fighting the Civil War. His response was that it was a "useful starting point" for conversations about the War and regional differences and his own background. And the sport pennant went over well with football fans. And—third point—since Piedmont U had once been a military institute, he was maintaining a proud tradition.

I suspected he had said some of that tongue in cheek, but since the portraits of the opposing generals and the West Point pennant were still there, I assumed it accomplished some purpose.

I had come to realize Quinn did most things with a purpose in mind—with intent, as Mrs. Cutler would have put it. Like his display on his bookcase of a photo of his mother, stepfather, and half sister, all attired in tribal garb, the picture taken at a Comanche ceremonial gathering.

When we'd started officially dating, he had added a framed photograph of me to his desktop. Nothing like the cotton candy one on his desk at home. A simple head shot. Nothing provocative except for the fact it was a photograph of a black woman there on the white university police chief's desk.

But apparently the photograph had served its purpose, because after he'd put it there, his always-polite officers had turned downright friendly. Now, whenever I dropped by to see him, I was greeted with big smiles and told to go right on back to his office.

And then there was my Valentine's Day gift to him. A "cops and robbers" chess set that I had found on the Internet. The chess pieces were straight out of a 1920s gangster movie, featuring a judge in his black robe, a beat cop, a burglar in a black mask, a getaway car. Quinn had discarded the board that had come with the pieces in favor of a chess table. Flanked by two chairs, the chess table had its own corner. I hadn't asked if he or anyone else ever played. There was some reason he had decided it should be there.

Like the Georgia O'Keeffe "Blue River" print behind his desk. And *The Phantom of the Opera* poster (white mask against black background) on the other wall. That was flanked by a movie poster of Gary Cooper in *High Noon*.

Of course, his coffee maker also had been given a table of its own, with mugs and additional Styrofoam cups. And a box of chocolate chip cookies. He'd added a water heater and a box of tea when I pointed out that not everyone drank coffee. But given how long that box of tea had lasted, I was probably the only one who ever touched it. Cops were tough. They drank coffee strong enough to corrode the stomach linings of ordinary mortals.

And he was still on the telephone talking about training standards. How much more could he and the person he was talking to say about that?

By the time I'd made myself a mug of tea that I didn't want, he was hanging up. "Sorry," he said, standing up and stretching and yanking at the tie he was wearing with his dark blue suit. "That was my counterpart at a university in

North Carolina. They're moving toward a community policing program, and he was interested in what it took to implement the model we have here."

He was rather proud of how his community policing program was going, so I smiled and tried to think of something to say. Nothing came to mind. My mind was on RaeAnne Dobb, and I was a little annoyed that his wasn't.

He walked toward me. I took a sip of my tea. He took the mug out of my hand and set it on the glass coffee table.

"That was your cue," he said, drawing me toward him, "to tell me how wonderful my policing program is and what a terrific university police chief I am. But I gather you want to talk about the body in the woods."

"Yes, I would like to talk about that. And I would think you would be more concerned. She was a student here."

"If it is RaeAnne Dobb," he said. "We don't know that yet. As for being concerned, I've asked Sergeant Burke to give all the information he's generated about her to Detective Mayhew, who has been assigned to work with the county sheriff's department and Gallagher PD. I also passed along your rather odd question about the night guard. Sergeant Burke—who has established rapport with the aunt—said he would call her and ask. That was about thirty minutes ago, soon after I returned to the office and received your message, so I don't know if he has reached her yet. However, I did ask him to get back to me with—"

"All right," I said. "You're concerned. You're following appropriate police procedure. I apologize."

"Anything else you want to apologize for?" he said.

"What did you have in mind?"

"Try that damn message you left on my answering machine—at home, where I wouldn't receive it until evening—announcing that you'd suddenly decided to go to Richmond and you'd see me when you got back."

"Am I supposed to check in with you for permission before I leave town?"

"You're supposed to consider the fact that I might worry about you," he said. "Last night, I waited—"

"I called you last night. I fell asleep."

"Why the hell were you in a hotel in Williamsburg in the first place?"

I opened my mouth.

He waited for me to speak.

I picked up my mug of tea and went and sat down on the sofa.

He stood there on the other side of the coffee table, arms folded, silver-gray eyes fixed on me. Waiting.

I said, "Did I ever tell you how much I hate it when you use your interrogation techniques during one of our arguments?"

"Are we arguing?"

I set the mug down. "I wish we were, because then I could get up and storm out, and then we wouldn't have to talk about why I was in Williamsburg."

"It sounds like something we'd have to discuss sooner or later."

"I suppose so. It's not going to go away. It's about my mother. I went to Richmond to help one of my students, Keisha McIntyre, with some research. Then I went to visit Mrs. Cutler, my eleventh-grade geometry teacher. She wanted to talk to me about my mother."

He came around the table and sat on the sofa beside me. "What did she say?"

I told him. Not bothering to delete any of the conversation.

"Where are the postcards?" he asked when I was finished.

"In my briefcase out in the car."

"I'd like to see them later."

"All right."

"Do you want to talk about it now?" he said. "Or think about it for a while?"

"Think about it."

He nodded. "In the meantime, tell me about your night guard question."

I let out my breath. That hadn't been as bad as I'd expected. I wasn't sure what I'd expected. I hadn't actually told him anything that he hadn't known already. Just that the whispered stories about my mother had been confirmed by a reliable source.

I reached for my shoulder bag and took out the plastic case and handed it to him. He opened it and looked inside.

"I found it in Charlotte Wingate's house," I said and told him about discovering it under the staircase.

"So what does this have to do with RaeAnne Dobb?" he asked.

"If it was hers, if she is dead . . . that would explain why no one came back to look for it."

"Maybe they looked and didn't find it," he said.

"Quinn—"

"Okay. So what would RaeAnne Dobb have been doing in that house?"

I told him my theory about Howard Knowlin . . . about how he might have seen her in Madeline's shop and wanted her. "Burning a body would conceal a rape," I said when he looked unconvinced.

"Yes," he said. "But we would have to assume that Knowlin—a millionaire real estate developer—was so hot for this particular woman that he committed rape and murder. And after doing so, he simply went on promoting his development project."

"Dammit, Quinn, you were a homicide detective. You know that people can kill and then go on with their normal lives. Anyone who could kill a woman and then burn her body would have nerves strong enough to go on as if nothing had happened."

"Maybe," he said.

I took a restraining breath. "Will you at least check into—"

"It isn't my case, Lizzie. Even if it is RaeAnne Dobb, the murder didn't happen here on campus. It's outside my jurisdiction. We're simply providing cooperation."

"Then couldn't you have Detective Mayhew suggest to the county sheriff—"

"That Howard Knowlin might have committed rape and murder?"

"All right. Having Mayhew suggest that Knowlin should be a suspect based on my unsupported suspicions would probably not be too bright."

"Probably not," Quinn said. He held the plastic case out to me.

"You're giving it back? But you said that Sergeant Burke was checking with RaeAnne's—"

"He is. But, Lizabeth, since at the moment this night guard could be considered stolen property—"

"Stolen? I didn't steal it."

"You removed it without authorization from someone else's home."

"But I only brought it with me so that I could give it to Charlotte Wingate so that she could return it to the owner. It was there under the staircase—"

"No matter where it was—"

"So you want me to put it back? Or give it to Charlotte?"

"I think for the moment—until Sergeant Burke gets back to us with the answer to your question—if you just tuck it away somewhere and forget that you haven't given it to Charlotte Wingate yet—"

"I had it in my glove compartment in my car. I'll put it back there."

"That'll work. We'll still have a tricky situation if it does turn out to belong to RaeAnne Dobb. But we'll deal with that in the unlikely event it should happen."

"Okay," I said. "You've made your point, Quinn. I'm fantasizing."

"No, you're playing a hunch. Unfortunately, hunches are wrong about as often as they're right." His gaze narrowed as he looked at me. "But in the meantime . . . until we've checked this out . . . don't run around telling people about the night guard."

"What difference could it make, if you think it couldn't possibly be—"

He smiled. "Stolen property, remember?"

I opened my mouth and shut it. Sometimes, he could be incredibly irritating. "I don't intend to discuss this with anyone," I said.

"Good," he said.

Then fairness drove me to admit, "And it is possible that I've got a bug in my head about Howard Knowlin."

"Generous of you to concede that."

"Isn't it, though?" I said. "I'm going to go now. I'm sure you want to get back to work. And I have things to do too."

He laced his fingers with mine. "But why don't we take a five-minute break?"

We did, and I felt a lot better when I left. But my good mood started to erode when I walked into my office and found a voice-mail message from Charlotte.

"Good morning, Professor Stuart," her voice boomed. "I've left this same message on your home answering machine. I'm calling to remind you that I'm expecting you for tea this afternoon. Shall we say 3 P.M.? I spoke to Dean Baylor, and he assured me that you were giving the condition attached to my endowment offer serious consideration. I'll be interested in hearing what you thought about the house."

The next message was from Amos Baylor himself: "Lizzie, I don't know where you are, but I certainly hope you haven't forgotten that Charlotte Wingate is expecting you at her house this afternoon. Please stop by to see me before you go."

I deleted both messages. I clicked on my computer and checked my E-mail to see if there was anything else to deal with.

Nothing relevant. Grad students about their papers.

"What are you going to say to her?" Amos asked, when I presented myself in his office. "We can assume that she'll want to know if you've reached a decision."

"And I'll tell her that because of personal matters, I need a bit more time before I can give her an answer."

"What personal matters?"

"Matters I would prefer not to discuss, Amos. But I will try to decide what I'm going to do as soon as I possibly can."

His frown deepened. "I don't need a prima donna on my faculty, Lizzie."

"At the moment, Amos, I'm only visiting faculty." I stood up. "However, I understand your position, and I assure you I'm not being deliberately obstructive."

"I hope not." He scowled up at me. "Please try not to antagonize Charlotte Wingate."

"I'll practice my best drawing room manners."

Charlotte's maid opened the door when I arrived promptly at three. She was wearing a black uniform with a crisp white apron. I hoped what I was wearing would do. I'd made a quick trip home to change from the blue jeans I'd put on in Williamsburg, but I had grabbed the first skirt and sweater that came to hand.

Charlotte had apparently recovered from her attack of gout. She was walking without her cane when she joined me in the living room.

I stood up to greet her. "Thank you for inviting me, Mrs. Wingate."

"Thank you for joining me, Professor Stuart. The maid will be along in a moment with our tea."

So much for pleasantries, I thought. *Now what?*

She lowered herself into an armchair. I sat back down on the sofa.

"Once a very long time ago," she said, without preamble, "when we were visiting relatives in Florida, I saw a black man hanging from a lamppost."

That got my attention. But the maid chose that moment to walk through the door, pushing the tea cart. When she had served us each with tea and cookies and gone away again, and after we had each taken a sip from our cup, Charlotte said, "Do you know the Billie Holiday song 'Strange Fruit'?"

"Yes, I know it," I said.

"I found that scene in the movie about her life particularly affecting," Charlotte said, her voice lower than its usual boom. "The scene in which she gets off the bus to relieve herself and stumbles on a lynching victim." She took another sip of tea. "Perhaps the first conference sponsored by the institute might focus on images of vigilante violence."

"You seem to have an interest in the topic, Mrs. Wingate."

"I've had some time to think about it," she said. "About the South and about the way we were and are and how the rest of the world sees us. Our graciousness. Our violence. Our loves and hatreds and the crimes they engender."

I stared at her. She gazed back at me, smiling.

"Perhaps you should speak at that first conference," I said.

"Well, I certainly do expect to be introduced," she said. "Now, let's finish our tea, and then I have some scrapbooks I want to show you . . . and some other old things . . . including some newspaper clippings about old murders."

"Did you know Blanche Campbell?" I asked, unable to resist that opening.

"I knew her. She came from a good family, an old Gallagher family. But her husband was a farmer out in the county. A well-to-do farmer, but he came of poor people." Charlotte smiled. "She was considered to have married down. Class differences existed then, Professor Stuart. They continue to exist."

"Complicated by race and gender," I said, putting my teacup on my saucer. "And the Campbell case brought all three factors together."

"So it did. Jebediah tells me he has asked you to collaborate with him on his memoirs."

"He has. But right now I'm involved in several other projects." Including the article with Keisha that I should mention to Jebediah.

"It would be just as well for him not to do it anyway," she said.

"His memoirs? Why?"

Charlotte set her own cup on the small table beside her chair. "Because some stories should be told only when everyone involved is dead. He already has one lawsuit pending."

"When he came to my class to bring the keys to the house, he said Abigail thought he should settle that lawsuit. Actually, he won't have much choice in the matter if his insurance company decides to settle."

"And that'll be a blow to his pride," Charlotte said. She paused, giving me time to focus on what she would say next. "It's always unfortunate when pride or stubbornness keeps a person from acting in his or her own best interests."

"Yes, it certainly is," I said.

"What did you think of the house?"

"The people who lived there before left it in rather a mess. Renovations would have to be done."

"That mess should have been cleaned up. I asked Jebediah to check on the house's condition and make arrangements."

"Well, perhaps they're just getting started," I said. "The kitchen floor had been mopped."

"That hardly constitutes cleaning," Charlotte said, her displeasure plain. "I'll have to speak to Jebediah about this."

Sorry, Jebediah.

"As for the renovations," she said. "Those will be taken care of."

"But what I wanted to mention," I said. "It was the oddest thing . . . when my colleague Joyce Fielding and I were looking around, we discovered that entrance in the pantry to the secret basement. And—this is the odd part—the railing on the basement stairs had been damaged, as if something had hit it. And this is even odder, we found someone's dental night guard under the staircase. You know, one of those mouthpieces for people who grind their teeth."

"You found it under the staircase?" Charlotte said.

I nodded. "Down in the basement. I'm sorry, I meant to bring it with me in case you might know who it belonged to."

"I'm afraid I don't concern myself with other people's dental equipment, Professor Stuart. I think we may safely assume that it belonged to someone among the former residents of the house. Since they are now long gone, you may toss out anything you found under a staircase."

"If you're sure," I said.

"Quite sure," she said. "The stair railing will also have to be repaired. Those young ruffians. I'm lucky they left the house standing."

Somehow I doubted the foster care teenagers were responsible for the broken staircase railing. But, as Quinn would point out, it was just another one of my hunches.

However, I was no longer guilty of theft. *So there, Quinn.* And if Charlotte knew anything about the night guard, her face hadn't given her away.

I said, "Did you hear that really grisly news report about the body the two boys found in the woods? A young woman's body. It had been set on fire."

Charlotte said, "I don't remember that the sex of the corpse was mentioned in the news report I heard."

"It might not have been," I said. "I heard this from an inside source."

Having indulged in that blatant bit of indiscretion, I waited for her response.

She pressed both hands to the armrests of her chair and started to push herself up. "If it was a young woman, that makes the story even more gruesome."

"Yes," I said, rising too. "She might even have been a student at the university. As soon as I heard the report, I thought of RaeAnne Dobb."

Charlotte was standing now. "Of who?" she said.

"A young woman whose artwork Madeline has been carrying in her shop. She's been missing for nine days now. No one knows where she's gotten to." I shook my head. "It's really awful to think that the girl in the woods might be her."

It was fortunate that I meant what I said. I'm a lousy actress. People always see right through me.

"Did you know this young woman?" Charlotte said.

"No, but I had hoped to meet her. I have a beautiful ceramic heart that she designed. It was cracked during the earthquake, and I'd hoped she could repair it."

"Then for her sake and yours, let's hope she isn't the body in the woods," Charlotte said. "Shall we go into the dining room? I've had the items I want to show you laid out on the table."

We spent a fascinating two hours with her scrapbooks and old photos and clippings. Then she announced that we would have to continue another day. She had a dinner engagement.

As I was leaving, she said, "I hope we're beginning to understand each other, Professor Stuart. I want to see this institute go forward."

"You could do that without me," I said.

"Yes, but I doubt that I could find another executive director who would suit my purpose as well."

More purposes and intentions. "What is your purpose?" I said.

"To make up for the fact that I come from people who believed that black man ought to have been hanging from that lamppost," she said.

"Did your people also believe Verity Thomas should have been executed?"

"Of course they did. Blanche Campbell may have married down, but she came from a respected family and she was a white woman." Charlotte smiled. "But I do know better now, Professor Stuart. And one day not too long off, I will be meeting my Maker. I need you to help me get some more points on the right side of the column."

With that she nodded her head good-bye. The maid nodded her head too and closed the door.

Charlotte Wingate had given me something to think about.

But I had learned very little relevant to RaeAnne Dobb. I hadn't even discovered who else had a key to the house on Grant Avenue.

Amos had asked me to report back to him. But by the time I got back to campus, it was almost six o'clock and his office suite was locked up tight.

If I had known Amos would be gone, I could have saved myself a trip. But I did have papers to read for both my grad and my undergrad classes. I decided to take a stack of them home.

When I opened my office door, I saw the red glow of my voice-mail light. I thought it might be Quinn. Or Amos.

It was Keisha McIntyre. She had returned to Gallagher early and she was upset. At Abigail Sims.

"She got me fired," Keisha said. "Can you believe that? She called J. T. She was going on about how if he tried to make a documentary about the Thomas case, she and her uncle would bring legal action to block it. He told her he wasn't going to because of Mr. Campbell. But she scared him, and when I went in this afternoon to let him know I was back, he said he couldn't afford to have me around. He said that I'd gotten him into trouble and he just wanted to make documentaries, not get sued. I tried to tell him she couldn't sue him even if he did make a documentary about the case." Keisha's voice broke. "But he fired me anyway, Dr. Stuart. I wanted that job so much . . . so I could get experience, you know." She cleared her throat. "I'm going over there and talk to her and tell her what she did wasn't right. It's not fair, Dr. Stuart. It's just not fair."

The phone clicked down.

Why on earth would Abigail have done that? How had she even known about the documentary?

I reached for the Gallagher telephone directory. Abigail and I needed to talk.

The telephone in the law offices of Gant and Sims rang three times. Four. I was waiting for the answering machine, when the receiver was picked up. Or knocked off. There was a sound like the telephone falling.

And then a whimper.

"Hello," I said. "Hello, is someone there? Abigail?"

That sound again. Then nothing. Silence.

And then the sound of breathing. Someone listening on the other end.

"Hello?" I said. "Is someone there? Are you all right?"

The receiver was replaced. A gentle click. And then the dial tone.

I hung up my own receiver. Then grabbed it up again.

When the 911 operator came on the line, I said, "I think there's a problem . . . possibly a medical emergency . . . at the law offices of Gant and Sims."

The operator made me go through what I had heard, give him the firm name and telephone number, give him my name. When we were finally done, I grabbed my shoulder bag and ran for the door. Keisha had been on her way to Abigail's office when she'd called. She was going there to confront her. I didn't even want to think about what might have happened.

I had found the address in the telephone book while I was talking to the operator. But I hadn't checked my city map, and it took me longer than it should have to find the street.

I had no problem finding the building. Red brick with black shutters. Distinguished by an empty lot on either side and a paramedics unit and Gallagher police vehicles in front.

More emergency vehicles than spectators. This was a street of law offices and insurance agencies and tax preparers. It was well after six. Either the occupants of the other buildings had already gone home or were too discreet to come outside to see what was happening.

A police officer tried to wave me back as I hopped out of my car.

"I'm the one who called this in," I said. "What—"

"Ma'am, just get your car out of the street. Pull it in there," he said, pointing at the vacant lot.

I got back into my car and drove it onto Sloane Campbell's property. Then I ran back over to the cop. "Please, I need to know what happened. Was someone hurt?"

"I thought you said you were the one who—"

"I did. But I don't know what happened. I could hear a whimpering sound over the telephone. Was someone hurt?"

"The lady lawyer," he said. "Someone shot her. And you'd better wait here. The detectives will want to talk to you."

"Is she dead?" I said.

"She wasn't when I got here. The paramedics are trying to get her ready to move."

"Was there anyone else in the office when it happened?"

He looked at me. "Yeah. The person who shot her."

Keisha. Where was Keisha?

Marcia Williams had told me that she was about to go off duty when the call came through. Now she was back in her office, fortifying herself from a fresh pot of coffee as she tried to gather information about the shooting of Abigail Sims. Abigail had been found on the floor in her uncle's office. A bullet wound to the chest.

I had been there in Williams's spartan office for almost two hours. I had given my statement. She had made me repeat everything and repeat it again. Then she had gone out and left me sitting there. I understood she had her job to do, but I was about ready to walk out into the hall and tell whoever I saw that I was leaving. That I was going to the hospital to see if Abigail was still alive.

Then the door opened, and Williams came back in with Quinn behind her. She glanced at me, then said, "She was shot with her uncle's gun. He identified the weapon found at the scene as the gun he kept in a desk drawer in his office."

Quinn's expression was about as revealing as that locked drawer in his own desk. He accepted the mug of coffee Williams handed him and took a long sip.

Then he looked at me. "What was it you said about working this afternoon?"

"All I did was call her office," I said.

"Lucky for her that you did," Williams said and sat down behind her desk with the files piled high on one side. "I just heard from the emergency room physician that if she hadn't gotten help as quickly as she did, she'd be dead now."

"Then she is still alive?" I said.

"In surgery," Williams said.

Quinn smiled at me, a quirk of his lips. "Okay, Professor, you did good."

"They said you'd gone to Greensboro," I said. Williams had let me call him before she started questioning me, but he hadn't been in. "I'm glad to see you received my message."

His gaze held mine and he said, "Speaking of mentioning to you when I'm going out of town. . . ."

"Of course, Greensboro isn't as far away as Richmond," I said. "And you expected to be back this evening."

He nodded. "But I'm sorry it took me so long to get here." Then he turned to Williams. "Marcia, about done with Lizzie?"

"Yeah," she said. "I'll get back to you, Professor Stuart, if I need to follow up on anything."

I got to my feet, feeling as if everything had stiffened up while I sat there in that chair.

"I want to go to the hospital," I told Quinn. "They brought me here in a police car. My car's still there in Sloane Campbell's vacant lot. If he finds out who it belongs to, he'll probably have it towed away."

Quinn said, "Why would Sloane Campbell have your car towed away if he knew it was yours?"

I was tired. That had been a bad slip of the tongue.

I reached for my shoulder bag on the floor and felt my muscles creaking. "That's another story," I said. "I'll tell you about it on the way to the hospital, if you'll drive me."

"Talk to you later, Marcia," he said and held the office door open.

"Good night, Detective Williams," I said.

I shouldn't have looked back. "This story involving Sloane Campbell," she said. "It isn't something I should know about, is it?"

"No," I said.

Except it might have been the reason Jebediah had a gun in his desk drawer. Because he was afraid of what Campbell might do. Because he really and truly believed that after all these years, Campbell was planning to somehow avenge Jebediah's courtroom assault on his mother's good name.

But since I hadn't mentioned Keisha—hadn't told Williams about Keisha's telephone call to me that afternoon—it was a little awkward to get into a discussion about the Verity Thomas case and whether it might be relevant to this, or whether Jebediah was simply suffering from senility and/or paranoia.

If Jebediah believed Campbell had shot his niece, undoubtedly he would tell Williams himself. If he hadn't said anything when he identified the gun. . . . But he had probably been in shock. Been horrified at the thought that his gun had been used to shoot his niece.

"You're sure about that?" Williams said. "Nothing I need to know." Her coffee mug was suspended in her hand, her gaze fixed on my face.

I had hesitated way too long after my initial "no."

"It's not related," I said.

Quinn waited until we were in the hall and headed toward the side entrance to the building. "Now tell me what isn't related."

If I told it carefully I could even include the encounter with Sloane Campbell at the film studio. Everything except Keisha's telephone call about Abigail. Which wasn't relevant anyway because Keisha hadn't done this. The question was, where was Keisha now?

The surgery waiting room was on the fifth floor of the medical center. The first voice we heard as we walked down the corridor was Charlotte Wingate's. ". . . just been talking to her on the telephone. I was trying to get you, Jebediah, to ask why you hadn't done anything about getting a cleaning crew in to take care of that mess in the Grant Avenue house. Professor Stuart even found a night guard—someone's dental equipment—under the basement stairs. . . ."

I groaned. Quinn stopped walking. I shook my head, trying to silently persuade him that now—within hearing distance of the waiting room—was not the moment for a discussion.

". . . and who knows what else in that house," Charlotte was saying. "I asked you to take care of the matter, Jebediah. That was over three weeks ago, and what I would like to know is what you—"

Quinn and I reached the waiting room doorway as Jebediah said to Charlotte, "Will you please shut your mouth, Charlotte? Just shut your mouth and be quiet." He was slumped in a chair, his head down. He did not raise his head to look at her as he spoke.

Charlotte gasped at him. Doug moved to her side and took her arm. "Come and sit down, Charlotte. It was good of you to rush down here as soon as you heard."

"Someone might've thought to call and tell me. I had to hear it on the news."

"We were all too stunned, trying to deal with it," Doug said. "Just trying to figure out what was happening." He patted her arm. "You understand. But we're glad you're here now. Come sit over here with Madeline."

Charlotte, wearing her wide-brimmed black hat again, shot Jebediah a glance that was almost uncertain. Then she let Doug lead her over to Madeline—who was simply sitting there staring into space, with an open magazine in her lap.

No wonder Doug had taken over. He was the only one of them in any shape to do so.

I took a step into the room, wondering if Quinn and I should be there. "Hello," I said. "I hope we're not intruding."

Doug looked up from seating Charlotte. "Lizzie. John. Come in."

He came and took my hand and kissed me on the cheek. Then reached over and shook Quinn's hand. "Lizzie, we heard from one of the police officers that you were the one who called for help."

It was a question: *How did you happen to do that, Lizzie?*

I said, repeating what I had told Williams, "I called the law offices because I wanted to asked Mr. Gant about a book I'd seen mentioned that included a chapter about his career—"

"*They Fought for Justice,*" Jebediah said. But he was still slumped there in the chair with his head down.

I went on with my explanation. "The telephone rang," I said, "and I thought no one was going to answer. But then someone picked up . . . or knocked off the receiver . . . and I heard this whimpering sound." That much was true. I was on solid ground now. "When no one spoke . . . just that sound . . . I thought something must be wrong. That was why I called 911."

Madeline had turned her head to look at me. She said, in a voice that sounded hoarse, "Is that all you heard? Just the whimpering?"

I hesitated. But I had already told this to Williams, and she hadn't said not to tell anyone. I glanced at Quinn. He didn't shake his head.

"No," I said. "I think someone else was in the room. Someone picked up the receiver. I could hear breathing. Then the receiver was replaced. If Abigail had already been shot—"

"Then the person who hung up the receiver was the person who shot her," Jebediah said.

We all turned to look at him. He had sat up straight in his chair. His eyes burned in his face, and he seemed to have aged another ten or fifteen years, so that his flesh hung slack along his jowls.

He got up from his chair and started to pace; his hands were clasped behind his back.

Madeline got to her feet in a kind of lurching motion. She went over to him. He jerked away from the arm she tried to put around him. "Daddy," she said. "Please, sit down and rest. You're not helping Abigail by upsetting yourself."

"Upsetting myself? Upsetting myself? My Abigail's been shot. She's in there in that operating room fighting for her life. I could have stopped this from happening."

"Daddy, don't," Madeline said, grasping his shoulders and forcing him to look at her. "The person who fired that gun . . . you had no way of knowing someone would use your gun."

He shook his head at her. "I could have stopped it."

I glanced at Quinn. He was watching Jebediah. He said, "Mr. Gant, if there is something you haven't told—"

Madeline whirled around. "Can't you see he's a tired, heartsick old man." She took Jebediah's arm. "Come sit down, Daddy. She's going to be all right. Abigail's going to be all right."

Jebediah let her lead him back to his chair. The energy had drained out of him again.

Doug cleared his throat. "Would anyone like some coffee?" He nodded his head toward the table in the corner on which sat an empty coffee maker. "The nurse said that was broken but to let her know if anyone wanted—"

"Black and strong," Charlotte said. "And tell her to bring some—"

Her order ended in a sputter as Howard Knowlin strode into the room. He glanced around and headed for Madeline, who had sunk down in the chair beside her father and was patting his knee.

Knowlin squatted down beside her to take her free hand. "Madeline, I am so very sorry. I came as soon as I heard."

She looked at him, her eyes blank. Then she shook her head. "Thank you, Howard."

He clasped her hand a moment longer. Then he stood up and turned to Doug. "What about the surgical team? I can have a specialist flown in from—"

"Too late," Doug said. "They've already started. They needed to operate as soon as possible if she was to have any—" He broke off with a glance at Madeline and her father. "But the trauma specialists here are first-rate. She'll be all right."

Knowlin said, "Let's hope so. How the hell could this have happened? This isn't Boston or New York City. It's supposed to be a quiet Southern town. People damn well aren't supposed to get shot in their offices here."

Weren't they? I could have told him that he didn't know quiet Southern towns. But it was probably more an expression of frustration than a real question. Knowlin wasn't that naive.

He noticed Quinn and me. "Professor Stuart," he said with a nod of his head. He held his hand out to Quinn and said, "Howard Knowlin."

"John Quinn."

"I thought you might be. Are you involved in this investigation? I would have thought your jurisdiction—"

"I'm here with Lizzie," Quinn said.

"Lizzie made the 911 call," Doug said. "If it hadn't been for her, Abigail might have died there on her office floor before she was found."

Knowlin turned back to me. "Did you go to her office?"

"Called on the telephone," I said, not caring to explain again. "I heard a whimpering sound."

He frowned. "Abigail picked up the telephone and—"

Quinn said, "Lizzie wasn't there in the office. She has no way of knowing who picked up the telephone. Only that she heard whimpering on the other end."

"And that was why she called 911," Doug said. "Howard, I was about to check on coffee. Would you like a cup?"

He shook his head. "I've got to go back downstairs. I'm donating blood."

"You're what?" Charlotte said, her voice booming.

"Donating blood," Knowlin repeated. "They're using blood for Abigail, so I'm just giving some back."

Charlotte clapped her hands. "Did you remember to announce that to those reporters downstairs, Mr. Knowlin?"

Doug rushed in. "Charlotte, I'm sure Howard's intentions—" He rubbed a hand over his face before turning to Knowlin. "But, Howard, maybe you should rethink this. I'm afraid Charlotte's right. Some people will see this as. . . ." He hesitated before continuing, "As a rather obvious attempt to garner publicity from—"

Knowlin's chin went up. He looked down his narrow nose at Doug. "I don't give a—" he said, using a colorful expletive. "People can damn well think what they want to about it."

I couldn't resist. "So you're donating blood because you really care?"

Knowlin turned to me. He smiled. "Even villains, Professor Stuart?"

We looked at each other. "Yes," I said. "On occasion."

"If you'll excuse me," he said. "I'll check back after I'm done." He nodded his head at Charlotte. "Always a pleasure to see you, Mrs. Wingate."

"Likewise, Mr. Knowlin," she said.

Doug gazed after his departing client. He rubbed his hand over his face again. The life of a PR man was sometimes not easy. He turned to Charlotte and tried to paste a smile on his face. "You were giving me your coffee order, Charlotte."

I touched Quinn's arm. "I think we should be going too," I said. "Madeline?" She looked up at me, and I said, "I hope Abigail will be all right."

"Thank you, Lizzie."

Doug said, "We'll call when we know more."

"Please do," I said. "If there's anything—"

There was a rush of movement at the door. Sloane Campbell burst into the room. "Abby! Is she—"

Jebediah surged to his feet. He pointed a shaking finger at Campbell. "You! You did this!"

Campbell stared at him.

Jebediah started forward, shoving away Madeline's hands. "I should have killed you before you did this. I knew you were trying to destroy me . . . and now you— My Abigail—"

Campbell shook his head. "Mr. Gant, I would never hurt Abby."

"I know what you've been doing." Jebediah weaved on his feet, steadied himself. "You been trying to drive me crazy. I know it. As crazy as that mama of yours." He fumbled for his watch fob. "It would have all come out, except for her family . . . that was why they protected her when your father— There were whispers . . . but they buried him anyway. Your mother . . . she was a violent woman.

She slapped that girl. Beat her own children. Everyone knew it. You're her spawn. You couldn't destroy me, so now you—"

Jebediah staggered. Madeline grabbed for him and sunk to the floor, cradling him. He was gasping for breath. His eyes had rolled back in his head.

Doug ran out into the hall, yelling for help.

Campbell walked over and sunk down into a chair. He buried his face in his hands.

Jebediah had not had a heart attack or a stroke. The doctors—Doug told us when he came back to the waiting room—agreed on that much. They had sedated Jebediah and he was resting.

Charlotte shook her head under her wide-brimmed hat. "I told Abigail he was not himself. All this carrying on about—" She glanced over at Campbell, who was standing at the window with his back to the room. "Although some of it—"

Campbell turned and looked at her. "If I'd wanted revenge, I would have gotten it a long, long time ago, Mrs. Wingate. There is nothing about my mother I've ever cared to defend."

Charlotte harrumphed. "Your mother came of good family," she said. "She made the mistake of marrying into a situation that she had not been reared to deal with."

"It was my father's mistake," Campbell said. "He should have wondered why none of the town boys had grabbed her up." He turned back to the window.

Quinn said, "Ready to go, Lizabeth?"

"Just a minute, okay?" I needed to speak to Sloane Campbell. I went over to him. "Mr. Campbell . . . Sloane?"

"Are we on a first-name basis now? You got her here to the hospital," he said. "So I owe you for that. But I can't deal with you right now, Professor Stuart. I am not going to stand here and discuss my mother's death or Verity Thomas with you."

"I don't want to talk about that," I said. "I wanted to tell you that I'm sorry. I hope Abigail will be all right."

"Me too," he said.

"Mr. Campbell, I wondered if—" I glanced back over my shoulder. Quinn, with one eye on me, was talking to Charlotte.

"You wondered what?" Campbell said.

"Did you tell Abigail about the documentary that my student Keisha and her boss J. T. were thinking of doing about your mother's case?"

"I thought you said you didn't want to talk about—"

"I don't want to talk about the case," I said, keeping my voice low. "It's Keisha I'm concerned about."

"Why?" he said.

"Because she left me a voice-mail message saying that Abigail had called J. T.

about the documentary and threatened to block it with a lawsuit."

"Abby did what?" Campbell said, frowning.

"So you didn't know—"

"You're damn right, I didn't know. I told her to leave it alone. That it was taken care of."

"Obviously she thought more was needed," I said. "She called and made her threat, and J. T. fired Keisha because he said she was getting him into trouble."

Campbell said, "I'm sorry about that. But right now, I can't get real worked up about—"

"I know. I understand. But I don't know where Keisha is," I said. "She was upset when she called. She said she was going to Abigail's office—"

"Are you telling me that she's the one who—"

"No," I said. "Please, believe me, Keisha couldn't have done that. I'm not even sure she actually went there. But I'm worried about her, because I called her boyfriend's apartment from the police station—she's been staying with him—and there was no answer. I wondered when was the last time that you spoke to Abigail and if she mentioned seeing Keisha?"

"The last time I spoke to Abby was this morning over the telephone. I was trying to persuade her to have dinner with me tonight. Out in public like regular people." He turned back to the window. "Not that that was likely. With old Jebediah. . . ." He shook his head. "Of all the things he could have made himself crazy over, me going after him about my mother is about the damn stupidest."

"But some of the things you did . . . why did you buy the property on either side of their law offices?"

He turned and looked me in the eye. "Because those two lots were going cheap. The buildings needed gutting. I tore them down instead. I plan to replace them with buildings I can rent or sell for more money. That's what real estate developers do. If I could have persuaded Jebediah to sell me his building there in the middle—"

"Did you ask him?" I said.

"Months ago. That was my mistake. That was when he started getting paranoid on me. In all those years, we'd never spoken. Having me come right up and knock on the door of his office—" Campbell smiled, a twist of his lips. "He couldn't believe I was just there about his building. But that was the day I got myself a real good look at Abby."

"Thank you," I said, touching his arm. "I hope she. . . . I'm sorry."

"Yeah," he said. Then, more to himself than to me, "Sometimes you get so damn close you can almost taste it. You think this time you might get it right."

"Yes," I said.

Quinn drove me back to get my car. Then I followed him to his house to see George.

I was sitting on the kitchen floor with George's head in my lap while Quinn made hot chocolate. From scratch. He hated the kind that came in envelopes.

He hadn't probed when I'd told him I'd been expressing my sympathy to Sloane Campbell during that conversation by the window. Maybe because I had told him what Campbell had said about Jebediah and Abigail. That might have been all we were talking about.

"Did Sergeant Burke speak to RaeAnne's aunt about the night guard?" I said, more to fill the silence than because it was the most urgent matter on my mind.

"He did," Quinn said, stirring the mixture in the pan. "The aunt says RaeAnne did not have a night guard. She assured him she would have known if her niece did."

"Then it probably belonged to one of the teenagers who lived in the house," I said, feeling tired and deflated.

I needed to tell him about Keisha. It had been a mistake not to tell Marcia Williams from the beginning.

Unless I told Quinn and Williams, no one would look for Keisha. I had a sick feeling in the pit of my stomach that we ought to be looking for her.

I put George's head down on the cushioned mat that Quinn had bought for him. He licked at my hands when I stroked his muzzle. He was drowsy from the medicine Quinn had given him, but he was getting better.

I stood up and walked over to the sink to wash my hands. Then I turned to Quinn.

"I need to tell you something," I said.

"Sit down," he said. "The chocolate's ready."

We sat down with our mugs. I waited until he had taken a sip or two, and then I backtracked and filled in the part of my story I'd left out. The part about Keisha's telephone call.

"Dammit, Lizzie, how could you withhold a piece of information like that?"

"Because I was afraid Williams might jump to the wrong conclusion if I told her that Keisha—"

"How do you know she didn't?" he said.

"Don't be ridiculous, Quinn. Keisha couldn't do that."

"How do you know?" he said again.

"What would shooting Abigail accomplish? She wanted her job back, not Abigail dead."

"If Abigail wasn't willing to help her get her job back, maybe Keisha lost her temper."

"Losing one's temper is not the same as picking up a gun and shooting the person you're angry at."

George whimpered, responding to my raised voice.

"And even if she had," I said. "She wouldn't have stood there holding the telephone receiver while I asked who was there. She would have been running."

"Maybe," Quinn said. "Or maybe she was standing there holding the receiver because she heard your voice and she wanted to tell you what she'd done."

"No," I said and took a sip of the the hot, sweet chocolate.

But the image he had put into my mind was chilling: An exchange between Keisha and Abigail that became so heated that Abigail had been afraid or had reached for the gun as a way of ordering Keisha out of her office. Keisha grabbing for the gun. Getting it away from Abigail. Firing. Then the ringing telephone, and the wounded Abigail reaching up and pulling it down from the desk, but unable to speak. Keisha reaching out for the receiver to hang it up. Hearing my voice on the other side as she stared down at Abigail and realized what she had done. Hanging up the receiver. Dropping the gun beside Abigail's prone body. Fleeing the office.

"Not so sure are you?" Quinn said.

"Yes, I am sure," I said. "She couldn't have . . . or if she did, she didn't intend— Dammit, Quinn, Keisha wouldn't have deliberately shot Abigail. You're just confusing me."

"No, what I'm doing is pointing out that you don't know what happened in that office. So you don't damn well get to pick and choose what you share with the police."

"Have you ever heard of the concept of not going strictly by the book?" I said and got to my feet.

He leaned back in his chair, looking at me. "Yes," he said. "I've been getting a lot of experience with that concept since I met you."

He was almost smiling. I was not in the mood to be teased or humored.

"She didn't do it, Quinn."

"But you still need to tell Marcia about the message she left you."

"All right," I said. I carried my mug over to the sink. "I'm going home now."

When I turned around, he was standing. "Because you're mad at me?"

"Because I'm tired. And because Keisha might try to call me at home if she . . . if she needs to talk."

"And if she does, you'll call me or Marcia."

"Of course. It's my civic duty, isn't it?"

"Lizzie—"

"All right, I'll call. Good night, George."

He raised his head from the cushion and thumped his tail when I reached down to touch his paw. *Yes, getting better.*

Quinn followed me down the hall to his front door. When I opened the door, he reached around me and pushed it closed. "You can go away not being crazy about the fact that I think like a cop," he said. "But you can't go away without kissing me good night. Even George got a good-night pat."

"George never makes me want to—" I threw up my hands and turned around. "Do you really think this is going to work? Us? The two of us?"

"All we have to do," he said, "is make it work ninety percent of the time. We can survive the other ten percent."

"As long as we focus on the ninety?"

"Exactly. It's when it only works the ten percent that you're in imminent meltdown."

I knew from the shadow that passed over his eyes that he was thinking of how his marriage had ended.

"Even when you don't agree with my perfectly logical arguments," I said, "I still love you."

"That's good, because I love you too." He drew me into his arms. "Sure you can't stay?"

"Yes," I said. "Keisha might call. But if you'd like to come to breakfast in the morning, before you have to go into the office, I'll make waffles."

He laughed. "Lizabeth, from a male perspective, waffles don't quite—"

I kissed his chin. "The best I can do, Chief Quinn. Of course, if you came over really early—"

"I'll see you at around six," he said.

"Not that early. Six-thirty or seven."

"I think I'd better just come at eight for waffles."

"I promise to be awake by then," I said. "Good night." I slid out of his arms and opened the front door before I could change my mind about staying.

There was no message from Keisha on my answering machine, and she didn't call. I curled up on the sofa under my comforter and watched an old movie—*Hush, Hush, Sweet Charlotte*—until my eyes were closing and Joseph Cotton's rendition of the theme song was floating in and out of my almost-dreams.

Then I dragged myself up, almost tripping over the comforter, and fumbled my way down the hall to my bed.

And was immediately wide awake. Wide awake and replaying in my head that image Quinn had planted of Keisha with a gun in her hand.

I sat up and turned on the lamp and got out the pen and pad I kept in the drawer of the night table. If I couldn't sleep, I might as well try to do some constructive thinking.

I wrote Abigail's name down on the legal pad. Who would want to shoot a lawyer? Disgruntled clients. Victims or defendants from the other side of the aisle. Paroled ex-cons. After years in practice, that list could be long. Yes, of people who might want to shoot. But not that many who would actually walk into an office and do it.

But she had been alone in the office. Secretary gone for the day. Jebediah gone too. And Williams had said that the offices on the second floor of Abigail's building were unoccupied. For lease. A vacant lot on either side of the building. Most of the professionals who occupied the adjacent buildings on the street gone home. Limited traffic passing by.

Someone might have walked in off the street. A would-be robber or rapist. That would explain why she had gone for her uncle's gun that had been used against her.

Or maybe she had been shot by someone she knew. An acquaintance, a friend, a family member. Her relationship with Madeline was lively, to say the least. If she and Madeline had gotten into an argument about Jebediah or James, Madeline's dead husband. Or an argument about Howard Knowlin. Madeline was dating Doug. Doug was Knowlin's PR man. And cousin Abigail was having a secret affair with Sloane Campbell—who'd punched Knowlin in the eye. What if Madeline had found out about Abigail's affair?

But would Madeline shoot her cousin because they were on opposite sides of two men's turf war? Even if, during an argument, Abigail had suddenly revealed her relationship with Campbell, I couldn't imagine Madeline grabbing up a gun and shooting her.

But, on the other hand, Madeline might very well have known the gun was there in the office. Other people might have known it too.

I imagined Abigail turning around and seeing someone she knew standing there pointing her uncle's gun at her.

But who? And why?

What if Abigail had found out something about Knowlin? Something she threatened to make public unless he got on his jet and left town. Doug had a lot invested in Knowlin. He had joked during the lunch at Charlotte's that he hoped to make enough money in his dealings with Knowlin to persuade Madeline to have him. She had come back with her own joke about only being interested in his body. And he had agreed that, yes, she did have her own money. But Knowlin was probably the wealthiest client that Doug had ever had. He might have been averse to having Abigail—

But what could she have found out about Knowlin? Something about his business dealings. Maybe he'd bribed the city council to get them to go along with Project Renaissance. Or maybe he had—

RaeAnne. I sat there staring at the closed door of my bedroom and telling myself I didn't know how to let go of an idea. Like a dog with a bone.

It had not been RaeAnne's night guard under the stairs.

We wouldn't even know until tomorrow if it was her body that had been burned in the woods. But I kept coming back to what Knowlin had said about getting what he wanted. And what Keisha had said about how he was an old guy who liked to hang out with jocks. Like to pretend he was still young and vigorous.

He wasn't that old. Not as ancient as Keisha'd made him sound. But the basic idea was that he was attracted to youth. And beauty. He had described RaeAnne as a beautiful young woman. He had met her. She was missing. Now a burned body had been found with a ring similar to RaeAnne's. A body that the

ME might tomorrow identify as hers.

Suppose Abigail had stumbled across something that connected Knowlin to RaeAnne—to RaeAnne's murder. Suppose Doug—or Knowlin himself—had been there in her office. She wouldn't have been stupid enough to invite Knowlin in to tell him what she knew or suspected. But Doug? What if she had found this whatever it was that made her suspicious. And she had called Doug and asked him to come over because she wanted to warn him.

But would Abigail care about warning Doug? At the pasta blast, she had seemed angry—outraged—by the fact that Madeline was "bedding" the man who was with James Oliver when he died. Abigail had never given any indication that she held Doug in deep affection. So why would she warn him?

If Abigail had a warning to give, wouldn't she have given it to Madeline rather than to Doug? Her cousin would have been the one she would have wanted to protect.

And when she did, what would Madeline have done?

No, wait—think of it the other way around. Abigail still cares about Madeline. She thinks Knowlin might have had something to do with RaeAnne's murder . . . assuming she somehow knows that the body in the woods is RaeAnne. So she calls Doug to come to her office because she doesn't want to see Madeline hurt. She wants to give him a chance to put some distance between himself and Knowlin, so that he won't be brought down with him.

But Doug already knows what Abigail has called him there to warn him about. They're talking. She turns away for a moment, he opens the drawer and takes out the gun—

No, the gun was in Jebediah's desk drawer, not Abigail's. Abigail was found in Jebediah's office. Why was she in his office?

I shivered at the chill creeping over me. Jebediah himself? Jebediah, somehow finding out about Abigail and Campbell. Jebediah feeling betrayed by the niece he had treated like a daughter. Betrayed by the one person he thought he could trust. Reaching into his desk and pulling out the gun—

I dropped my pen and pad onto the covers and flopped back in the bed. None of my little scenarios were particularly pretty.

Not even the one where Knowlin did it. He had gone downstairs to give blood. And as much as I disliked him on occasion, the man was more complex than a cartoon villain. He might not be a villain at all.

Then again he might be. Someone had shot Abigail and left her there on the floor of her uncle's office to die. Someone had listened to my voice on the telephone and then quietly hung up the receiver.

The lamp was shining in my face. Instead of turning it off, I rolled over on my side away from the light. Quinn was coming for breakfast. I needed to at least try to get some sleep.

CHAPTER · 20

THURSDAY, MARCH 22

"It's her," Quinn said, over the telephone. "The ME has confirmed based on her dental records that the remains are those of RaeAnne Dobb."

I sunk into my desk chair. "I thought . . . I was sure, but to hear you actually say . . . and I don't even know why I'm so . . . I never even met her."

But she had crafted that heart. My whimsical, lopsided ceramic heart that Quinn had given to me on Valentine's Day and made me feel loved.

Now she was dead. And the crack in that heart would never be repaired.

I realized I was shaking. Not enough sleep last night. Too many waffles this morning. An insulin surge from maple syrup.

Someone walking over my grave. *Go away, Hester Rose. Just because you were superstitious—*

"Lizzie? Are you—"

"Yes, I'm all right. I'm just . . . I'm okay."

"Are you going to be there the rest of the afternoon?"

"Yes," I said. "I still have papers to read. Why?"

"Because I might not be able to go all afternoon without seeing you," he said. "By the way, Marcia called me after you called her."

"To complain?"

"No, to update me on the Sims case. Keisha McIntyre is a student at the university. If she's involved—"

"You're involved too. Did Williams say anything about Keisha's status? Does she consider her a suspect?"

"Marcia wants to talk to her."

"I know that already, Quinn. I was hoping for a bit more. Like whether Williams has any witnesses or physical evidence. Who's at the top of her list of suspects. That kind of thing."

"Sarcasm, Lizabeth?"

"Quinn—"

"Lizzie—" He was silent for a long moment, and I waited. "This is off the record," he said. "Do not repeat one word of this."

"I won't. I promise."

"I'm only telling you this because if I don't tell you, you'll be out there asking people questions—"

"I won't repeat it, Quinn."

He was silent for a moment longer. Then he said, "There were no clear prints on the weapon. Wiped clean. Lots of prints in the offices—the secretary's, Abigail's, Jebediah's. So many prints that they're not particularly useful."

"That makes sense," I said. "It's a place of business. All kinds of people coming and going. Including everyone who was in the waiting room last night—"

"All of whom might have been in the law offices during the past few days for legitimate reasons," Quinn said. "So Marcia's not really hopeful she's going to get a break with prints. She has officers out recanvassing the street for information about people and vehicles seen in the vicinity. That's one of the reasons she wants to talk to Keisha. If Keisha was there at some point yesterday afternoon, she might have seen something."

"So what you're saying is that Williams considers Keisha a possible witness rather than a suspect."

"She hasn't ruled Keisha out, Lizabeth."

"But there are other people she thinks would have more of a motive. Who?"

Quinn said, "No one that you're going to encounter while you're sitting there in your office reading papers. And you are going to be there in your office, aren't you?"

"Yes. Unless I have to go out."

"Lizzie—"

"Quinn, I am not going to ask anyone any questions. But I might go out to the library or to have some lunch. However, I will leave this investigation to the police."

"The police appreciate that."

"Quinn, does Williams think the attack on Abigail could be related in any way to RaeAnne Dobb?"

"She didn't mention the Dobb case when I spoke to her," he said, his voice edged with caution. "It's not her case."

"I know that. But doesn't the Gallagher PD coordinate with the sheriff's department?"

"When it seems warranted," he said.

"Quinn, the same group of people who are around Abigail knew or might have known RaeAnne. If Abigail somehow—"

"Lizzie—"

"I'm only saying—"

"I know what you're saying. Marcia is capable of seeing any link between—"

"But if she's focusing on Abigail—"

"Lizabeth." He let out his breath. "When I speak to Marcia later today, I will mention RaeAnne Dobb."

"Thank you. Of course, you're probably right and she has already looked into it. But since we only found out this morning that the body in the woods is RaeAnne, maybe she hasn't really thought about the implications."

Quinn said, his voice thoughtful, "Do you know, Lizabeth, before we met, the dividing line between a homicide investigation and my personal life—"

"I know. Before I met you my life was never like this either. And I promise not to repeat what you told me. I know you need to get back to work. Talk to you later."

"And in the meantime—"

"Promise."

I hung up and sat staring out of my fifth-floor window. That last observation he'd made had sounded serious, no joke: *I'm tired of having to worry about what you're up to, Lizabeth.*

RaeAnne dead. Her body burned. And Abigail, out of surgery, but in a coma. A police guard at her door.

And someone probably feeling very concerned that she would open her eyes and identify him or her as the person who'd held the gun.

And Lizabeth Stuart who was going to sit at her desk and read her students' papers.

Abigail did wake up. Doug called an hour or so later to tell me that she was out of her coma. He had thought I would want to know.

The bad news was that she couldn't remember the shooting.

"Her doctors say that's to be expected," Doug said. "The trauma of the injury, the shock to her system. But the good news is that she's responsive and she recognizes everyone. So her long-term memory is intact." He laughed. "Although Madeline kind of wishes she couldn't remember Sloane Campbell. He demanded to be allowed into the room to see her. The doctor gave in when Abigail asked for him. Since then, the guy's been right there at her bedside."

"What about Jebediah?" I said. "Is he better?"

"Better," Doug said, his voice sober now. "But his own doctor wants him to see a psychiatrist before he's released. Jebediah's still fixated on the idea that Sloane Campbell wants revenge. And now that he knows what's been going on between Campbell and Abigail, he's accusing Abigail of betraying him with his enemy."

I shook my head. "I don't understand how he could suddenly—"

"It wasn't sudden," Doug said. "Abigail had been trying to tell us that he was having spells. But until two or three days ago . . . well, then it got to be hard to ignore. I guess we—especially Madeline—wanted to believe he was just getting old, a little forgetful, a little paranoid."

"A lot paranoid. But he was right about something going on involving Sloane Campbell."

"Just not what he thought," Doug said. "And he's not likely to be able to accept the two of them together."

"Maybe he will eventually," I said.

"I'd like to think so. But I'm afraid Jebediah's problems may run pretty deep." He cleared his throat. "Anyway, I wanted to let you know the good news about Abigail. That she seems to be out of the woods."

"I'm really relieved to hear that," I said. "Thanks for letting me know."

I sat there and thought about Abigail and Jebediah for a while.

Thinking about people's medical conditions reminded me of Joyce. She'd had her biopsy on Monday, and I hadn't even called. Had been too busy running to Richmond and Williamsburg and playing detective to even remember.

I reached for my shoulder bag to dig out my address book with her home telephone number.

One night guard in plastic tangerine case. Right there next to my wallet. I'd taken it out of my glove compartment, intending to throw it away. It didn't belong to RaeAnne, and the other probable owners were long gone. I had meant to get rid of it, but somehow, it had ended up in my purse.

I pushed it to the side and found my address book.

Pete answered the telephone. "She's asleep," he said.

"How did it go?"

"They took out the lump." He cleared his throat. "It was malignant, but they think they got it all."

I closed my eyes. "Is she all right?"

"She's fine. Cracking jokes and giving me a hard time." Then, "She's holding up better than I am, Lizzie."

He didn't sound like a man who thought of Joyce only as his bed partner. Or quite as insensitive as Joyce and I had accused him of being.

"She's going to be okay, Pete. They got it all."

"Sure," Pete said. "Sure, she's going to be fine."

"But call me if you need to talk or something. Okay?"

"Yeah. Thanks, Lizzie. I'll tell her you called."

I was not in the mood to grade papers. I needed to get out of my office. Lunchtime. I could go somewhere and have lunch.

After a stop at Shoney's for the soup and salad bar, I headed for the public library. It had occurred to me that I'd like to know more about the architecture of the house on Grant Avenue.

Joyce had called the place a "pink elephant," but I might be able to sort out the various influences. I found the architecture section and selected several books on Victorian houses. Then I found an empty table.

Victorian homes of San Francisco. Painted ladies. That phrase always made me think of prostitutes. There was probably some connection. I'd have to look it up. Or maybe the name was explained in the book I was flipping through.

Painted ladies were multicolored houses. Well, the house on Grant Avenue was shocking pink with white pillars and black shutters. Did that qualify?

I paused as I saw a house with a Gothic tower. Built in the 1850s. Had the person who designed Charlotte Wingate's eccentric house been influenced by San Francisco architecture? A trip to the West Coast, and then home to build a house that was a hodgepodge of styles.

And why was I sitting here flipping through books about Victorian houses? I should have stayed in my office. If Keisha called . . . but maybe she had gone back home to Richmond. Her parents would be at work, but she might be there.

Dammit, I didn't have the telephone number she had given me. It was at home with the notes and photocopies we'd made at the state library.

So go home and call Richmond.

I started to close the book in front of me, then paused over a photograph of a woman standing outside of a Victorian mansion. Elaborately and elegantly dressed, she was holding a parasol. She was identified as Georgina Hatfield, "whorehouse madam."

Well, if the house was anything to go by, Georgina's girls had lived in comfort. Except for having to entertain the customers.

The author of the book had included an anecdote about the parties Georgina gave. Her kitchen delicacies were as well-known as those of the legendary pleasure houses on the East Coast.

Which had nothing to do with anything. My capacity for being distracted from the matter at hand was incredible.

Wait. Parties. Keisha had gone with her roommate to parties. Who was the girl she had shared the apartment with? She had never mentioned her name. But maybe she had gone back to that apartment.

Or Tommy. Keisha had met Tommy Irving at one of those parties. She had been sitting with him at the pasta blast. Been charmed by his magic trick with the rose.

Except, by now she would have heard about Tommy's other activities. So she would be unlikely to have gone to him. Besides, her boyfriend Marcus was a much more likely choice. She was probably somewhere with Marcus. Or at home in Richmond.

I called Keisha's parents' house in Richmond. There was no answer. I left a message that I tried to make as unalarming as possible asking Keisha to call me if she was still there.

Then I called Marcus's apartment again. And left the same message again. Please call.

Even if she hadn't gone to Abigail's office, by now she must know that Abigail had been shot. So she should be able to guess why I wanted to talk to her. Maybe that was why she hadn't called back.

But the police were looking for Keisha now. And I needed to find her and get her into Marcia Williams's office to tell the detective what she knew. Gloria McIntyre would not think very much of my care of her daughter if Keisha ended up in a jail cell because she had been avoiding the police.

Keisha called at a little before five. I had gone back to my office to try to work. The telephone rang and I grabbed it up.

She said, "Dr. Stuart, it's Keisha. I've got to talk to you."

"Where are you?" I said. "Do you know about Abigail Sims?"

"I know. That's why I need to talk to you. Can you meet me? At the mall."

"Keisha, wherever you are, I'll pick you up. I'll go with you to talk to the police."

"No, I can't go . . . I need to talk to you first. Please, Dr. Stuart, just meet me. At the mall in an hour."

"Keisha, I. . . . All right. At the pet store on the lower level. Do you know where it is?"

"I know. I'll meet you there."

The telephone receiver on her side clicked down. I pressed my hand to the ache in my left temple. Just because she wasn't eager to talk to the police . . . maybe she had seen something, maybe she was frightened.

But in that case, the logical thing to do would be to run to the police as fast as she could. Except people don't always do the logical thing when they're frightened. Especially if they think they might not be believed.

Keisha was a black kid from Richmond. She didn't trust the police and the criminal justice system. Sometimes, I didn't either. Being in love with a cop didn't change that.

Keisha had called me because she wanted to talk. There had been nothing in her words or her tone of voice to indicate that she had picked up a gun and shot Abigail.

But I had told Quinn I would call him if she called. So now what was I going to do?

Too wired to sit still, I got up and paced back and forth between my desk and the door.

As I was about to leave, I called Quinn's house and left a message on his answering machine. He should be home by six-thirty or seven unless he was working late.

My message said that I was meeting Keisha at the mall and then would escort her to Williams's office. Please meet us at the police station.

At the mall, I parked my car and entered through the lower level. The mall was large, but it had only one pet store. Keisha was standing out in front of the store, staring down at the rabbits and guinea pigs in their pen.

A little girl was also staring at the cuddly animals. She squatted and reached her hand down into the pen. "Rabbit," she said.

Her mother, who had been looking at the puppies behind the glass, turned to see what she was doing, and then rushed over to scoop her up. "No, mustn't touch."

Keisha looked at them and then back down at the guinea pigs and rabbits. She was wearing black jeans and a black denim jacket. Her retro-Afro curled wildly around her head.

"Keisha," I said.

She whirled around. "Dr. Stuart, I was scared you weren't going to come. I need to talk to you. I don't know what to do."

I took her arm and drew her away from the mother of the toddler who was listening with interested ears.

"Let's go sit down," I said.

"I can't sit down," she said. "It's really messed up. I think I saw something, but I'm not sure. I mean, it looked like . . . but it was so fast . . . and I don't want to get him into trouble if . . . I mean, I know he shouldn't have, but that's not the same as . . . and if I tell them I saw him there and he didn't . . . maybe he was just there to see her about—"

I held up my hands. "Keisha, wait, wait. Slow down. Who is he, and—"

But she was staring, eyes wide, at something behind me.

Quinn. Coming toward us.

"You told him," Keisha said. "I needed to talk to you before—" She backed away. "I just wanted to ask you what you thought I should do. You shouldn't have told him, Dr. Stuart."

"Keisha—"

She turned and ran. I ran after her. But she had a head start. She was wearing sneakers. I was wearing pumps. She was at the exit and out before I could get there. I pushed past a laughing group of teenagers coming through the doors.

When I got outside she was gone. No sign of her in either direction. Only a bus at the curb. I ran toward it. But it pulled away and moved off down the street.

Had she gotten on that bus? If she didn't have Marcus's car—

Stupid! How could I have been so stupid?

I turned and walked back toward the mall entrance. Quinn burst out of one of the doors. "Where is she?" he said. "Is she gone?"

"Yes, she's gone."

He reached for his cell phone. "What kind of car was she driving?"

"I have no idea. What are you doing here?"

"You left me a message," he said. "That I know you didn't intend for me to receive until after you—"

"Then why did you come here? She had something she wanted to tell me. I was going to bring her to the police station."

He looked at me. Then he said, "I wasn't exactly thrilled with you, Lizabeth, when I got home and found you'd left the message there. You seem to be making a habit of leaving messages that you don't want me to receive right away—"

"So start calling home and checking your answering machine," I said. "Why did you come here? Couldn't you have trusted me to—"

"It has nothing to do with trust," he said. "She could have been dangerous."

"Dangerous? Even if she had shot Abigail, what exactly did you think she was going to do to me? Take me hostage? And I keep telling you, she didn't—"

"So why is she running through malls, instead of talking to the police?"

"Believe it or not, Quinn, some people don't trust cops. Especially when they're scared. If you hadn't shown up here . . . and how did you know where we'd be meeting? I didn't mention the pet store in my message."

"We always meet there," he said.

Yes, the three or four times we'd come to the mall together, I had suggested we meet at the pet store after we'd finished our respective errands. And it hadn't even occurred to me that he'd think of that. But I hadn't expected him to go home early enough to come here.

"Is George all right? Is that why you went home?"

"George is fine," he said.

I closed my eyes and shook my head. "I know I should have called you at your office. But I knew you would insist on doing exactly what you did. And I didn't want to do that to Keisha." I let out my breath. "I was trying to avoid having an argument. But we're still having one, and Keisha's gone."

He took my arm. "Some days, Lizabeth, life is just damn well like that. Come on, I'll buy you an ice cream cone."

"Don't humor me, Quinn. And don't you have to call and report this to Williams?"

"I'll call Marcia later. After you tell me what Keisha said."

"Not much. You showed up."

CHAPTER · 21

THE PEOPLE IN the next-to-last booth were getting reading to leave. Quinn asked for the last booth. Then he waited until our neighbors were gone and the waitress had returned with our order before he asked again what Keisha had said. By then I wasn't quite as annoyed with him as I had been when Keisha ran out the door.

I told him, trying to remember her exact phrasing.

Quinn took a sip of the black coffee he had ordered instead of ice cream. "You're sure she said, 'get *him* into trouble'?"

"Yes, I'm sure." I stared down at the butter pecan ice cream in the dish in front of me and replayed it one more time in my head. "She said 'him' and 'he.' And she must have been talking about someone she knows. She wouldn't agonize about getting a stranger in trouble."

"Any candidates spring to mind?"

I thought about that as I took a sip of water. "One person does. But I may be prejudiced."

"Howard Knowlin?"

"No, Tommy Irving."

Quinn picked up his coffee spoon and reached across the table to help himself to my ice cream. "Why would Tommy shoot Abigail?"

"I don't know why," I said. "Maybe he didn't shoot her. Maybe Keisha just saw him there. Abigail is Tommy's attorney. So he would've had a reason to go to her office. And he would be someone that Keisha would worry about getting in trouble. Kids protect other kids."

"Yes," Quinn said. "But would she feel obliged to protect Tommy, knowing about his housebreaking activities?"

I pushed the ice cream dish across the table toward him. "Assuming she does know. She might have left for Richmond before he was arrested. She didn't mention it when I saw her. And if she's heard about it since getting back, that might be all the more reason she would worry about telling the police she had seen him there."

"Why?"

"Because she might be afraid cops would just naturally assume if Tommy could do one thing he could do the other. She said something like 'I know he shouldn't have, but that's not the same as—' She could have meant that breaking into an unoccupied house isn't in the same category as shooting someone."

"Marcia may have interviewed Tommy already. She knows he's Abigail's client and that he's flaky. Not that being flaky gives him an obvious motive for shooting his lawyer."

"No. But what Keisha said does suggest Tommy might have been at Abigail's office yesterday evening."

"Possibly," Quinn said. He washed down my butter pecan ice cream with another long swallow of black coffee. "Come on, I need to touch base with Marcia."

On our way out to the parking lot, Quinn got Williams on his cell phone and set up a meeting at her office. When I suggested following him there in my car, he suggested I go home. I said if I couldn't come along to his meeting with Williams then I would go to the hospital and visit Abigail. He thought about that for a long moment. I pointed out it really wasn't his decision. He said—looking less than thrilled with me again—that he would see me at my house in a couple of hours. As he walked away toward his car, I considered yelling after him that I didn't remember inviting him.

But there is a saying about yanking a tiger's tail.

I had to stop at the information desk in the first-floor lobby to get Abigail's room number. The woman at the desk hesitated, then she asked me to wait. She got up and walked back to confer with someone. It was then that I remembered Quinn had said that a police guard was stationed at Abigail's door. Which would explain why he hadn't argued more about my visiting her. He didn't expect me to be able to get in to see her.

The woman came back to the desk with an older woman in tow. She said, "Are you a family member?"

"No," I said. "But I'm a family friend. If Ms. Sims's cousin, Madeline Oliver, is upstairs, perhaps you could get her to vouch for me. My name's Lizzie Stuart."

"One moment, please." The older woman went over to a telephone on the other counter. The first woman tried to pretend I wasn't standing there until she came back.

"All right, Ms. Stuart, they say you may come up," the other woman said when she returned. "Please stop at the nurses' station on the fourth floor." She handed me a color-coded card, necessary for anyone attempting to navigate through the medical center's maze of corridors.

When I stepped out of the fourth-floor elevator, I saw Doug Jenkins standing by the counter at the nurse's station. He hadn't noticed my arrival because he was engaged in animated conversation with the two nurses on duty. They seemed to be enjoying the distraction he was providing from the charts stacked in front of them.

Was people-pleasing a talent with which some people were born? There had been a segment on public radio last week about how the parents of attractive infants had numerically more positive interactions with their babies than did the parents of less attractive infants. As a result, attractive infants became attractive children—both physically and in terms of personality—with self-confidence and assurance in dealing with other people.

Watching Doug, one suspected he had been a very attractive baby. And Madeline still found him cuddly. What had Madeline's husband, James, been like?

"Lizzie!" Doug said when he turned his head and saw me. "Thanks for coming by."

"How is she?" I asked.

"Holding her own. Madeline's in there with her now."

I looked in the direction of his gesture. The corridor outside the door was empty. "I thought there was a policeman on duty," I said.

"Last night. But now that the police know Abigail can't remember—"

"But I would think that would be all the more reason to have someone on the door. If she can't remember, then she's vulnerable if this person should try again."

"But apparently the city can't afford to keep a guard on the door. So Sloane and Madeline—in an unprecedented moment of accord—agreed that beginning at midnight tonight a paid bodyguard will be stationed outside her door and be there every night until she leaves the hospital."

"Good idea," I said. "May I go in to see her?"

One of the nurses leaned toward us to answer that question. "I'm afraid not. She needs to rest. The doctor has restricted her visitors."

"To Madeline and me," Doug said. "And Sloane Campbell."

"But not Jebediah?"

Doug smiled at the nurses and took my elbow, guiding me toward the small waiting room. We sat down across from each other. He sighed and rubbed his hand over his face.

"Jebediah's in a room on the third floor," he said. "He has seen the psychiatrist, and they're probably going to release him tomorrow. But when Madeline went down there to ask if he'd like to be brought upstairs to see Abigail, he said no."

"So he's still upset—"

Doug grimaced. "I don't think he and Abigail are going to settle down again to happily practice law together."

"Doug . . . he said you suggested he write his memoirs."

"I thought it might help. When we were discussing it, he seemed more like himself." Doug shook his head. "It's hard to see a man like Jebediah declining, getting on in years, and losing himself."

"Yes, it is," I said. Time for a change of subject. "So, tell me what kind of coverage the media gave Howard Knowlin's blood donation? I forgot to check the news."

Doug smiled. "I managed to keep Howard's altruistic gesture private."

"He really did seem to want to do it because it was a good thing to do."

"I'm sure he did. Howard has a social conscience that sometimes catches people by surprise."

And while I had him chatting about his client, I said, "Tell me the truth about the house on Grant Avenue, Doug. Why does he want it? It doesn't seem to be his style. I read an article about his fabulous seaside retreat on the coast of Maine."

"I've been there," Doug said. "It's more than fabulous."

"So why does he want the Grant Avenue house?"

Doug leaned toward me. "Want the truth?" he said.

"Yes."

He lowered his voice to a whisper. "The Gothic tower."

"What?"

Doug laughed and relaxed back in his chair. "Howard's a history buff. Very into medieval warfare and castles and towers. I happened to mention Charlotte had a house with one—a tower, that is—and as soon as he saw it for himself—"

"So he's willing to buy the house to get the tower."

"He owns a castle in England. The tower on the Grant Avenue house reminds him of that."

I looked at him to see if he was joking.

He shook his head. "No kidding. When you have as much money as Howard does, you can indulge your whims." He smiled slightly. "Of course, that particular house does happen to belong to Charlotte. If he could persuade her to sell it to him—"

"It would be a psychological victory in their little war?"

"Something like that," Doug said.

"On that note, I'm going home. Please tell Madeline and Abigail that I stopped by."

"Madeline knows you're out here," he said. "She sends her best, but she wasn't up to visiting."

"I understand," I said. "Tell her to take care and get some rest."

"You do that too," Doug said, studying my face. "You look a little tired."

"Early morning," I said. "And you're supposed to pretend not to notice."

He laughed. I didn't mention the dark circles under his own eyes.

* * *

As I rode down on the elevator, I thought about Knowlin and his tower. Well, at the pasta blast he had mentioned Richard III. That should have given me some clue.

And, upstairs, Jebediah was enacting his own version of *King Lear*, casting off his daughter-niece for her betrayal. But the shooting seemed to have brought the cousins back together again. Madeline was at Abigail's bedside.

The elevator stopped and I turned toward the front lobby.

Shucks, if Quinn was coming over to my house, I wouldn't have a chance to see George. I couldn't go back with Quinn later because I needed to be at home in case Keisha called again. After the episode in the mall, that wasn't likely, but I should be there just in case.

So I should probably stop by Quinn's on my way home. Except I didn't feel comfortable about going into his house without telling him first. Which was ridiculous when the man had given me a key, and all the time he was in Oklahoma I could have come and gone as I pleased. But he was home now and in residence.

Or maybe it was his locked desk drawer that I kept obsessing about. Or the fact that he hadn't brought up Wade Garner's offer again.

He still hadn't told me what he intended to do.

Of course, I hadn't told him what I intended to do about Charlotte Wingate's offer.

It wasn't as if we'd had a lot of time since he got back to sit down and discuss our respective plans for the future.

But that was another matter—or the same matter. Anyway, I would feel more comfortable telling him I intended to drop by and see George.

I realized I was standing in the middle of the corridor. I stepped to the side, out of the path of a man on crutches.

Public telephone around the corner, according to the sign. An ATM too. I might as well get some cash while I was at it. Then I wouldn't have to write a check at the supermarket.

Or maybe Quinn would rather do takeout. Unless he'd already eaten with Marcia Williams. It was almost eight o'clock.

And he was not answering his cell phone.

I was being silly anyway. I hung up without leaving a message. He'd given me a key. So he wanted me to use it when I needed to. If he didn't, he should take it back.

I fished my ATM card out of my wallet and punched in my PIN and transaction request. As I waited for my money, I glanced over at the bulletin board for hospital volunteers. Annual banquet on April 12 at the Sheraton. Big-band music. Tickets now available.

Hospital blood drive still under way. Howard Knowlin had done his part.

Training seminar on the "new" heroin epidemic and intravenous drug use.

The ATM was beeping. I reached out and removed my cash and declined another transaction. My card and receipt popped out of their slots.

Intravenous drug use. RaeAnne's boyfriend had been an addict. Had OD'd.

Drugs. Shared needles. HIV. Addicts with HIV infecting their partners.

According to Randy, her next-door neighbor and protector, RaeAnne had been crying. RaeAnne didn't cry. He had been disturbed by her tears.

If RaeAnne had found out that she was HIV positive. . . . But Randy had admitted that the next day, she had been her old self again. She wouldn't have just shrugged off a diagnosis like that.

No, not shrugged off. But people reacted in all kinds of ways when they were told they had a potentially fatal illness. Joyce had gone out and bought brownies and sat there in the faculty lounge with tears in her eyes. But by Thursday afternoon, she had been able to make her usual wisecracks, able to go on almost as if everything were normal.

Except, at the time, Joyce's diagnosis had been indefinite. Unconfirmed. If you had been told that you definitely had a condition that might kill you . . . but even then, how you reacted would depend on your personality and your circumstances.

And I was way out there in space again. Just as I had been with the night guard from under the basement stairs that I was still carrying around in my shoulder bag.

There was no reason to think RaeAnne had been HIV positive. She could have been crying for a thousand different reasons. A nasty remark someone had made. A bill she couldn't pay.

Did the medical examiner routinely test for HIV?

But even if RaeAnne had been HIV positive, that wouldn't explain why she'd been murdered and her body burned.

Burned. Why burn a body? To prevent identification. To cover up the means of death or what had been done to the victim.

To cover up evidence of disease? During plagues, dead bodies had sometimes been burned to prevent the spread of disease. But in RaeAnne's case—if she had been HIV positive—if she had told one of her sexual partners and he had struck out in anger. Killed her. Then burned the body. Destroying the evidence. Or expressing his revulsion.

Not Knowlin. He had donated blood last night. If he thought he might have been exposed, he wouldn't have—

But maybe that was exactly why he had done it. He knew he had been exposed. Had already confirmed he hadn't been infected. So a public announcement that he was donating blood. Then later, if by some chance the medical examiner discovered RaeAnne had been HIV positive, Knowlin was above suspicion as one of her sex partners.

I needed to talk to Quinn. Ask if the ME had tested or could test. Would there be a way of doing the test on a burned body? Bone marrow? Did HIV affect the blood cells in the bones?

Quinn was going to say I'd lost my mind. I'd seen a flyer on a bulletin board, and I was off and running again.

I turned from the bulletin board back toward the public telephone. A woman was two steps ahead of me with her change purse out and an expression on her face that said she had got there first, so don't even bother to ask.

Quinn was right. I needed to get a cell phone. I hated cell phones. People walked around as if the damn things were attached to their ears and everyone in the world was just dying to listen to their private conversations.

And ranting about cell phones wasn't helping. *Calm down. Take a deep breath.*

Go back to my original plan. Go to Quinn's house to see George. Call Quinn again from there. Or wait until I saw him. It wasn't as if the ME was going to do the test tonight. If he or she hadn't done it. Or could do it at all.

Or if Quinn would even consider suggesting it.

But when a beautiful young woman is murdered and her body disposed of in such a brutal fashion, her sexual history becomes relevant. The possibility of HIV is a part of that history. Especially when her dead boyfriend had been an addict.

Good, sensible argument, Lizabeth.

I had parked in the garage across the street from the medical center. Aside from access at street level, the garage and the medical center also were linked by a covered pedestrian bridge and a bank of elevators. I decided not to go back out into the night. Veering left in the front vestibule, I made for the bridge. With almost an hour left before visiting hours ended, people were coming and going. I was grateful for that because I felt a little jumpy. I had scared myself with what I had been thinking about RaeAnne.

I wanted to get in my car and lock the doors and drive to Quinn's house.

This was not the moment when I wanted to run into Howard Knowlin.

"Lizzie!" Doug Jenkins said as he trotted up beside me and linked his arm with mine. "I thought you'd left."

Or Doug. I didn't want to run into Doug.

Why was he here? He was supposed to be upstairs with Madeline.

He was smiling. I smiled back. Or tried to. "I did start out," I said. "But then I remembered I needed cash. So I made a detour by the ATM in the lobby."

"So this would be a good time to hit you up for a loan," he said.

"Only if it's under twenty dollars. I've got to stop at the supermarket." My arm, still linked with his, jerked in a nervous movement. I couldn't help it.

Doug looked at me, not smiling anymore. "Hey, are you okay? You just shivered."

"Goose walking across my grave. Actually, it's my grocery list. I forgot it. So now I have cash, but no idea what I need to buy." My voice sounded strained even to my own ears. "So I guess I'll have to get in and out of the store as quickly as I can. When you don't have a list, you end up with a whole cart full of impulse buys. And then you have to go back the next day for everything you really needed and forgot to buy."

He nodded. "Definitely a nuisance."

We had reached the bank of elevators. Doug pushed the button. Somehow we'd managed to arrive during one of those lulls in traffic flow. We had the lobby in front of the elevator bank to ourselves.

"Sure you're all right?" he said.

"Fine," I said as the middle of the three elevators arrived.

He gestured for me to go ahead of him. I stepped inside and punched the button for the third level. He reached over and pressed 4.

I said, "Just one of those complicated days. Including an argument with my significant other."

The elevator slid downward. As it opened onto the fourth level of the garage, Doug straightened from his slouch against the wall. "Now, Madeline and I never argue."

"Don't you?" I said.

"Nope." He stepped out of the elevator, a bearded man with a pleasant face, smiling as he looked back at me. "She tells me what to do," he said. "And I do it."

"I don't think that would work with Quinn," I said as the elevator door started to slide shut.

Doug waved as he turned away. "Have a good night, Lizzie."

Paranoid. I was getting as paranoid as Jebediah.

The elevator stopped on the third level, where my car was parked. Car doors slammed. Several people were in plain view. So undoubtedly I would be able to walk to my car in safety.

I had been so busy letting my imagination run riot, I hadn't even asked Doug where he was headed. Home probably. If Madeline intended to stay with Abigail until her bodyguard arrived at midnight, she was going to be putting in a long day. No point in both of them sitting there for another four hours.

C H A P T E R · 2 2

I PULLED INTO QUINN'S DRIVEWAY. A wooden fence around the house separated it from his neighbors on either side. If you wanted your neighbors to be able to keep an eye on your house, a high fence was not ideal. When I'd mentioned that to Quinn, he'd laughed and said that his neighbor across the street was my Mrs. Cavendish's equal when it came to surveillance. Anyway, the fence had come with the house, and it was a quiet neighborhood.

Right at that moment, it was too quiet a neighborhood. No one was out taking a stroll or walking a dog. And Quinn's neighbor across the street did not have the lights on in her living room.

I stopped to fish the house key out of the pocket of my shoulder bag before I got out of the car—and in the process, had one more encounter with the plastic case containing the night guard. It was there beside my wallet, taunting me.

Irritated, I picked it up and held it in my palm. Not RaeAnne's. But whose? Someone had gone to a dentist and had the thing made and then not even come back to look for it.

Not known where he or she had lost it, Joyce had said.

Looked, but not thought of looking under the basement stairs, Quinn had said.

You had a night guard. So why were you carrying it around anyway? You took it out of your mouth in the morning, and you left it in the bathroom until that night when you needed it again.

Unless you needed it in the daytime too. What if you ground your teeth when you were sitting at your computer working or aggravated by rush-hour traffic? Then your dentist might tell you to wear it during the day. Tell you to pop it in during high-grind times.

But if you were that much of a grinder, you'd be frantic to find the thing if you'd lost it.

Unless you could afford to buy another. Howard Knowlin could afford another four or five hundred dollars. But even if he had been in that house—and he had—what would he have been doing in the basement that would have involved having his night guard fall out of his jacket pocket? Standing on his head on the basement stairs?

Wait. Jacket. Something about a jacket.

I almost jumped out of the seat when it hit me. RaeAnne's aunt. RaeAnne's aunt had said that a kid kept calling RaeAnne about his jacket.

Tommy Irving. Tommy sounded like a kid.

And Tommy had a father who was a dentist. If he had a night guard and lost it, his father would make him another.

What if Tommy had gotten a key to the house, and—

But had Tommy even known RaeAnne?

Parties. Keisha had met Tommy at a party. RaeAnne was their age—a college student—maybe she had gone to parties too.

But Keisha hadn't known RaeAnne. She hadn't recognized the name that night at the pasta blast. Which didn't mean anything. They might even have been at the same party and not been introduced.

Or maybe Tommy had met RaeAnne through Doug or Knowlin.

And what if Tommy had gotten a key to the house on Grant Avenue, and RaeAnne had gone there with him. What if somehow she had ended up dead, and Tommy—

No, that didn't work. If he knew RaeAnne was dead, he wouldn't have been calling her house asking if she had his jacket.

Unless he wanted to make it look as if he didn't know.

Both Tommy and Madeline had called looking for RaeAnne. Leaving two or three messages each. Tommy about the jacket. Madeline because she'd wanted to get some more of RaeAnne's work.

What if Madeline didn't know RaeAnne was dead, but Doug did? That would explain his visit to my house that evening. Doug had persuaded Madeline that she should find someone else to repair my ceramic heart because he was concerned that she had sent me out to look for RaeAnne.

We needed to find Tommy. Tommy and Keisha. The two of them held the key to this. If Keisha had seen Tommy at Abigail's office, then maybe Tommy had seen something too. Maybe he could link RaeAnne to the house. Or to Doug and Knowlin.

Or maybe Tommy had lost his night guard in the house on Grant Avenue, and it had nothing at all to do with RaeAnne's murder. *If* it was Tommy's night guard.

I shoved the plastic case back into my shoulder bag and reached for my door handle. And stopped as my eye caught a movement in the driveway behind me.

A cat. Quinn's neighbor's cat. I watched it slink along beside the fence and disappear around the corner. Out mousing. And giving unsuspecting people heart attacks.

I went inside and found George up and walking. Slowly, favoring his injured leg, but navigating. He came out into the hallway to meet me. I bent down to give him a careful hug. Then I walked with him back into the kitchen. He stretched out on his cushioned mat.

"I really did come to see you," I said. "But I need to call Quinn."

Who answered his cell phone this time. "I'm at your house," I said when he asked where I was. "I stopped by to visit with George."

"Wait for me there."

"No, I can't. I need to go home in case Keisha calls again. Have you and Marcia Williams spoken to Tommy yet?"

"We haven't been able to locate him. He's not at his parents' house or his apartment."

"Oh, dammit, I hope Keisha didn't go looking for him. Quinn, Tommy's father is a dentist. In *The Tattler* article about him, it said his father—"

"And?" Quinn said.

"And the night guard. Maybe it was Tommy's night guard under the basement stairs. Suppose he'd somehow gotten a key to the Grant Avenue house and—" I broke off. "But there's something else. Something more important. Quinn, do you know if the medical examiner tests for HIV?"

"In Virginia, no, not routinely. Only if the ME suspects HIV from the medical history or from something that has turned up in the police investigation. Why?"

I told him. Then before he could say it, I said, "I know it sounds like another one of my flights of imagination."

"But this one might be worth looking into," he said. "Even if Knowlin isn't involved, if RaeAnne had been HIV positive, someone she'd been with might be angry enough—"

"Then you think—" I froze in place. "Quinn," I said, in a whisper. "Someone's outside."

"Where are you?"

"In the kitchen. I can't see anything because of the light. But I heard a thump against the wall outside."

"Get out of the kitchen now."

I backed toward the doorway. "Maybe it's one of your neighbors. With a fence around the house, who else would think of coming to the back—"

"Lizzie, listen to me. Lock yourself in the downstairs bathroom. I'm calling for a patrol car. I'll be there in ten minutes."

The receiver on his side clicked. I stood there in the hall, staring at the bay window in the kitchen. The darkness beyond it.

George. I edged back toward the doorway. He was on his feet, his eyes trained on the window.

"George," I said. "Here, boy. George, come!"

He turned and started toward me.

The telephone in my hand rang. George barked. I almost passed out.

"It's all right, boy. It's probably Quinn." I pushed the button. "Quinn?"

"It's me, Dr. Stuart. Keisha."

"Keisha! Where are you?"

"Outside in Tommy's van. We've been driving around, and he's . . . he says if you don't come out . . . he's got a gun and he says—" She cried out as if she had been struck.

"Keisha?"

Tommy spoke into my ear. "Come outside. Walk to the white van at the curb." His voice was jittery, ragged. "Do it fast or I'll kill her."

I put down the telephone in my hand. Dropped it on the kitchen table en route to the counter. I pulled the pad toward me and wrote.

Tommy has Keisha. Said he'd kill her. Had to go.

I grabbed my shoulder bag up from the table. "It's all right, George. Quinn will be here in a few minutes."

But I needed a head start. A chance to try to talk to Tommy before he was surrounded by police cars with Keisha there in the van with him.

Keisha was on the floor between the front and back seats of the van. Her hands were taped. She had a piece of tape dangling from the side of her mouth. Her face was streaked with tears, one eye swollen half shut.

"I'm sorry, Dr. Stuart," she said. "I told him that I'd called you before I knew that he—"

"Shut up! You get down on the floor too," Tommy said to me. "And don't do anything stupid."

His spiky blond hair was standing on end. He had a gun in his hand that he kept jerking around. I was not inclined to argue with him. Especially since I had probably already done something stupid. If I hadn't come out of the house, he might have shot her. Now he'd probably shoot both of us.

Well, at least I wouldn't have to explain to Gloria McIntyre.

He slid into the driver's seat and started the van. I prayed that a police car would scream up and block his path. But there was no siren. No rescue as he drove us out of Quinn's quiet neighborhood.

"Tommy," I said. "I don't know why you're doing this, but you're only getting yourself into more trouble. The police are on their way. I was on the telephone with Chief Quinn. I told him I heard someone outside—"

"Shut up! I've got to think."

"Think about pulling this van over and—"

He twisted around in the seat. The van lurched. "Shut up, or I'll kill you both right now."

Keisha sobbed. I shut up.

I tried to see what I could from the floor. We were headed back downtown.

I reached over and eased the loose tape from Keisha's face. Then I tugged at the duct tape that was wrapped around her wrists. It was tight, clinging to itself. She moaned when I yanked at it.

Tommy glanced back. "Leave her hands alone. I said, don't do anything stupid." He sounded like a thug in a gangster movie. Tough guy by rote.

"Where are we going?" I said.

"Someplace," he said. "You'll see when we get there."

The van stopped. Tommy glared over the seat. "Stay where you are, you hear me?"

He was gone for only a moment or two. Long enough to unlock the gate. I could see the Gothic tower glinting gray in the moonlight. He had brought us to the Grant Avenue house.

He left us again to close the gate after we'd driven through. Then to unlock the front door. Not enough time to do anything.

Nothing to use as a weapon on the floor of the van. Nothing in my shoulder bag.

And not a lot of good to wish for a cell phone now.

"Out," he said, waving the gun at me. "Bring her with you."

I pulled Keisha up. She lurched as she tried to get out of the van with her hands taped, and fell to her knees on the driveway.

Tommy started to reach out to her. Then he gestured to me. "Get her up," he said, waving his gun. "Both of you—inside."

Keisha was sobbing again, her bottom lip bleeding. I considered simply springing at Tommy and bashing his face in.

But he had that gun in his hand. It was his game for the moment. Abigail had been right, he was most definitely a simpering little weasel.

He made us sit down on the ripped velvet love seat in the living room. He paced back and forth. Looking at us. Shoving his fingers through his hair with the hand that wasn't holding the gun. Still sporting a gauze bandage on that wrist from George's teeth. Good.

Keisha whispered to me, "I wanted to tell him that I'd seen him drive past, Dr. Stuart. I wanted to tell him before I told the police. I didn't think he'd really shot her."

"I didn't shoot her!" Tommy said. "I told you, I didn't shoot her. I told you, whoever shot her must have been in there with her when you knocked on the door. I didn't shoot her!"

Keisha said, "Then why are you doing this, Tommy? If you didn't shoot her, then why are you doing this?"

"Because I—" Tommy bit his lip. "That old woman—old Mrs. Wingate—called when I was there in Abigail's office. She was all upset about the house still being messed up when old man Gant was supposed to have taken care of it. Then Abigail . . . she said something about a night guard, and I started to get scared. And then she said something . . . old Mrs. Wingate was telling her something . . . asked if she knew someone . . . and Abigail said, 'RaeAnne,' and then she said, 'Are you sure, Charlotte? The body those boys found in the woods?' And then I was really scared. I had to get out of there."

And I was beginning to feel sick. Charlotte had called Abigail that afternoon. She had called because of what I'd told her. And somehow it had led to Abigail's being shot.

Tommy said, "It was my night guard. It was in my jacket pocket. I have to wear it. My father—"

I said, "RaeAnne's aunt said someone called about a jacket. That was you, wasn't it?"

He waved the gun. "I didn't know RaeAnne wasn't there. She had my jacket when I left. I gave it to her when she fell."

"Fell from where?" I asked.

"Down the stairs. Old man Gant came when we were hanging out in here. I saw her at the Student Center, and I talked her into coming with me . . . she was acting funny, anyway. And she started getting high when we got here . . . I had some—" He scowled. "We were just having some fun. Playing around in here. Then he came and he was coming up the front stairs and she popped out and said 'Boo!' and he shoved her away and she fell. I thought she'd broken her neck, but she was breathing. So I called . . . I called somebody."

"Who'd you call?" I said. Although I thought I knew the answer.

Tommy scowled even harder. Trying to look mean. "None of your business."

"All right. Then what happened after she fell and you called this person."

"He came over and took care of it."

"Got rid of her body?" I said.

"No! She wasn't dead. She came to. She was all right." Tommy's face twisted in a grimace. "But she died later. Passed out again. Some kind of brain hemorrhage or something. Then he put her in a trunk and got rid of her body because if anyone'd found out, Mr. Gant would have been in trouble. That was why he burned her. So they wouldn't know who she was."

"If you don't go to the police right now," I said, "you're going to end up taking the fall for this—for both RaeAnne and Abigail."

Keisha said, "Tommy, if you just explain what happened. That you didn't have anything to do with burning that girl's body or with shooting Ms. Sims—"

"I'm afraid there could be a problem with that," Doug Jenkins said from the doorway.

Keisha's eyes went wide. My own heart went into overdrive. This was not getting better.

I said, trying to keep my voice calm, "Was RaeAnne HIV positive, Doug?"

"How the hell did you figure that out?"

"That was why you tried to talk Howard Knowlin out of giving blood," I said. "Because you knew he'd been exposed—"

"And I thought it would be just as well if he didn't find out. Not that he hadn't worn a condom. But nothing's foolproof."

"And that was why you killed RaeAnne—"

"You killed her?" Tommy said, his voice hoarse. "You said she died from the fall. You said you—" He shoved his fingers through his hair. "Murder. We're talking about murder."

"Didn't you figure that out when he shot Abigail?" I said.

Tommy glared at me. "He said someone had come in off the street and shot her. That it had nothing to do with this."

"And you believed him?"

Doug shook his head. "Things aren't always what they seem, Lizzie."

"But you did kill RaeAnne because she was HIV positive and you were afraid Howard Knowlin would find out."

"Howard wouldn't have been happy to learn I'd introduced him to Typhoid Mary."

"He might have been willing to forgive and forget," I said. "He might have been concerned about RaeAnne."

Doug smiled. "You think so? I wasn't willing to take that chance. RaeAnne dropped her little bombshell while I was putting an ice pack on her head. She sat there looking up at me and explaining why she had to tell Howard. It was only right, she said, because she should've told him about her boyfriend in the first place. But I'd told her not to." Doug glanced at Tommy, who was still pulling at his hair with the hand that wasn't holding the gun. "Of course, I was also concerned about who else she might end up telling. If the media had gotten hold of it . . . well, you can imagine the tabloid headlines." He shook his head. "A good PR man doesn't let that kind of thing happen to a client. Especially one as wealthy as Howard, who could make a significant contribution to his future prospects."

"So you killed her," I said. "There in the kitchen. That's why the floor in there had been mopped."

Doug nodded. "Not a pleasant experience. She was going on about how she had to tell Howard, and suddenly I had the poker from the fireplace in my hand and I was hitting her with it." He shook his head. "At the time, it seemed like a good idea. Like the only thing I could do that would—"

"And later?" I said.

"Later was too late," he said. "It probably was the only thing I could have done. I offered her money. But she was determined to reveal all. And Howard had been bugging me about hooking them up again. So sooner or later, unless I got rid of her, she was going to cause me problems. Maybe big time. Having Howard Knowlin as an enemy isn't something—"

"So you killed her and put her body in the trunk," I said. "Why did you leave the ring on her finger?"

"Have you ever killed anyone, Lizzie? As I said, it wasn't pleasant. She was lying there with her eyes open—" He took a handkerchief from his blazer pocket and rubbed it across his mouth. "I saw the ring when I came back to get her. But her fingers had gotten stiff. And she— I'd left the trunk on the basement landing. It fell during the earthquake. She was there at the bottom of the stairs. Her hand sticking out from under the lid. I saw the ring. But I couldn't get it off."

"She must have still been wearing my jacket," Tommy said, waving the gun in his hand. "That was how my night guard fell out. It was in the pocket of my jacket. When the trunk fell—"

"Will you shut up about your damn night guard," Doug said. "If you hadn't stolen my keys and duplicated—"

"I just wanted to come back here again when no one was here," Tommy said, a whine in his voice. "You're the one who killed RaeAnne. Even if I hadn't brought her here, you would've—"

"And tonight you decided to take a hostage," Doug said.

"What'd you expect me to do? Keisha called and said she'd seen me. And it wasn't my idea to bring—" Tommy jerked his gun in my direction. "You were the one who told me to go and get her."

"How did you know where to find me?" I said.

Doug said, "You were behaving a little oddly when we walked to the elevator together. I was on my way to see Tommy. But I thought I'd better follow you, just to see what you were up to. When I saw where you'd gone, I called Tommy and told him what to do."

"So now you have us," I said. "But the police are looking for us by now." *And please let Quinn remember what I'd said . . . that Tommy might possibly have a key to this house.* "I think you really do have a problem."

Tommy stared at Doug and said, "You killed her. You killed RaeAnne. So none of this is my fault. I'm not going to—"

"Tommy," I said. "I think he's planning for you to take the fall on this one. If he killed us and then killed you—"

Tommy started toward Doug, practically jumping up and down in his sneakers, gun waving. "Is that what you're planning?"

"Calm down," Doug said. "She's trying to—"

"She's right," Tommy said. "You've been trying to set me up. To frame me. The night guard—"

"Tommy," Doug said, shaking his head, his voice soothing. "Don't be a damn fool. She's trying to trick you. She wants you to turn on me. But you're looking at jail time too. There's a crime known as felony murder." Doug smiled at me. "True, Lizzie? Since Tommy was present, he—"

"That doesn't apply here, Tommy," I said. "You—"

But he was scowling at me. "No, no. Don't give me that."

Dammit!

Tommy turned back to Doug. "What are we going to do with them?"

I touched Keisha's hand. When she looked at me, I mouthed the word *run* and rolled my eyes toward the dining room doorway. The kitchen beyond.

She nodded. I stood up, drawing her up with me.

Tommy whirled around. "Why are you getting up? Sit down."

I opened my shoulder bag. "I just want to return your night guard. You should have it in case he's planning something."

Tommy glanced behind him at Doug.

"Here, Tommy! Catch!"

I threw the plastic case at him. He jumped back as the night guard flew out of the case and clattered to the floor. He fired the gun into the air.

Doug dived toward him. Keisha ran, stumbling as she tried to keep her balance with her wrists taped.

I scrambled in the opposite direction, darting around Doug and Tommy, who were wrestling on the floor. The gun went off again. Tommy fell back. I screamed as Doug came up with the gun in his hand.

He grabbed for me. I dodged him and ran toward the foyer.

But he came charging after me—was suddenly there in front of me, between me and the door.

I backed up. I turned and ran toward the stairs, expecting him to shoot, expecting to feel a bullet ripping through me.

But he didn't fire. I retreated up the stairs, moving out of the light below, into the shadows cast by the moonlight coming through the windows above. Doug followed me. Stalking me.

I stumbled on the stairs, righted myself. I looked down the second-floor hallway. Moonlight and shadows. Empty rooms. The bathrooms. Did they have locks? Could he shoot off a lock?

"Lizzie?" Doug was almost at the landing. I ran toward the narrow stairs leading to the attic. Fell, scrapping my knee, feeling with my hands for the next step, hearing him behind me.

Moonlight again, coming through the window. If I could get out onto the ledge, climb down . . . was there some way to climb down?

The window wouldn't open. I shoved at it. But it wouldn't move.

The ceiling light flared on behind me. "Lizzie, I've had a long, hard day," he said. "Let's just sit down."

The lock! I had locked it when Joyce and I were here before. I twisted the lock and shoved the window up. It rasped and shuddered in its frame.

"Lizzie, come on now. Don't go out there."

I kicked off my pumps and edged my way forward, out onto the ledge.

Then he was there in the window, leaning out. "Lizzie, come on back inside.

This is an old house. That ledge could crumble right out from under you."

A silver-edged cloud sailed across the moon, blotting it out. The wind whipped at my skirt and blouse. A loose shingle on the roof flopped back and forth. I shivered and dug my fingernails into the rough timbers of the wall behind me.

"Lizzie," Doug said, his tone a combination of patience and weariness.

"Keisha got away," I said, hearing my voice shake. "The police will be here any minute."

Doug sat down on the edge of the window sill. "I know they will," he said. "So why don't you come back inside? I'd rather not have to explain to Chief Quinn how I chased you up here and you fell off the roof."

He sounded so reasonable. Almost amused. How could he have killed one woman and tried to kill a second and sound so reasonable?

"Then I suggest you go away," I said. "Why don't you make a run for it? Then I can come back inside."

"I'm too tired to run," he said. "It's been one damn thing after another lately."

"Why did you shoot Abigail?" I said.

"Trying to keep me talking, huh? Not necessary. But, actually, that was not my doing. That was Madeline."

"Madeline?" I twisted my head to look at him.

"Madeline arrived as Tommy was leaving. Abigail was wondering about Tommy's abrupt departure. He had mentioned my name before he ran out of her office. And Madeline knew Tommy wouldn't keep his mouth shut if people started questioning him. That's why I'd been doing my best to speed his departure out of town. I was working on that with Abigail . . . had even found a couple of baseball programs for Tommy to choose from."

"But then Madeline shot Abigail. To protect you."

Doug laughed. "To protect herself. After all, she was the one who'd suggested I provide my clients—jaded middle-age businessmen—with the company of lovely young women like RaeAnne. She never got directly involved except to point out possibles. Like your little Keisha. I think that's why Tommy elbowed Keisha in the nose that evening. RaeAnne hadn't told him about her HIV, but she had told him about me fixing her up with Howard. And Tommy was kind of sweet on little Keisha. So I think he was being chivalrous and getting her away from our evil influence. Mine and Howard's."

"And Madeline's?"

"Not Madeline's. Who'd ever think Madeline could have her dainty hand in something so sordid. But she did enjoy laughing about what a hypocrite Howard was, thinking he was fooling her and everyone else."

"And didn't it occur to Madeline . . . assuming she was so smart . . . that if RaeAnne's boyfriend was a drug addict—"

"Aah, but you see, RaeAnne had been tested. She told Madeline she had been when Madeline was scolding her about her scummy drug addict boyfriend.

RaeAnne even showed Madeline the letter about her test results. What RaeAnne neglected to tell Madeline—undoubtedly for fear of another scolding—was that she'd had one last fling with her old boyfriend after she was tested. That was the time that did it."

"But Madeline must love you, Doug," I said, trying to keep my teeth from chattering. "You were the one who killed RaeAnne. Madeline hadn't actually done anything illegal. Unless suggesting that you become a procurer for your wealthy clients—"

"Yes, but how would it have looked? The scandal. Madeline Oliver's lover on trial. The same man who'd been out there on the golf course with her husband when he died."

I shivered. My nose was running. I didn't dare take my hand from the wall to do anything about it. "Did you have something to do with his death?" I said.

Doug smiled. "He had a heart attack. I did remember after a few moments of panic that I had my cell phone and could call for medical assistance. Perhaps if I'd tried to perform CPR while we were waiting for help . . . but if anything, that was omission. Not commission. And Madeline was pleased enough to have him gone. She told me that she'd put up with his and her father's 'sanctimonious crap' for so long she was 'dying of it.' The truth is, Madeline was just plain bored."

"I see," I said and pulled my hand from the wall for the second it took me to rub my running nose on my sleeve.

"I doubt it," Doug said. "It would be hard for you to fully comprehend a woman like Madeline. She even suggested we let her dear old father take the blame if RaeAnne was found. Of course, that was before Tommy let himself into your house and she shot Abigail."

"The best-laid plans," I said, shivering as the wind whipped around me.

"Don't they, though. And since we were making this up as we went along—"

Sirens.

Doug tilted his head, listening. Then he held out his hand to me. "Come back in and we'll go on down."

I shook my head. "I think I'll just wait up here."

"Suit yourself," he said, a shrug in his voice. "I'll tell them where to find you."

I looked down. Police cars were screeching into the driveway. The door of a black Bronco was flung open. Quinn.

I took a step back toward the window. Then stopped. Better wait until Doug—

Suddenly I was falling, nothing under my feet. I screamed and grabbed out. My hands found the projecting edge of the roof. But I could feel it swaying under my weight.

I screamed for help.

Then Doug was there at the window. "I told you about that," he said. "Here, give me your hand."

I could feel myself slipping. In another moment. . . . I reached out with one hand, holding on with the other. He edged out farther.

The piece of roof I was clutching broke loose. I screamed, then felt a hand close around mine, a hand gripping mine, pulling my arm from its socket, holding me suspended. Then arms closing tight around me, dragging me toward a heart that was pounding as hard as my own.

Doug pulled me through the window, and we both tumbled to the floor and lay there, panting.

Feet came pounding up the stairs. Voices. A few seconds later, Quinn's head appeared. Then the rest of him. He pointed his gun at Doug. "Let her go. Now."

Doug took his arms away. Put his hands in the air. I edged away from him and wrapped my arms around my knees.

"Get up," Quinn told Doug.

A patrol officer, Gallagher PD insignia on his sleeve, took out his handcuffs and put them on Doug's wrists.

Doug turned and smiled and winked at me. "If you'd care to testify on my behalf at the trial," he said.

The patrol officer took him out. I leaned my head on my folded arms and closed my eyes.

"Tommy?" I said. "Is he dead?"

"No," Quinn answered.

"Keisha? Is she all right?"

"Yes," he replied.

"And you're furious," I said.

"How did you guess?" He reached down and pulled me to my feet. "Every time I turn my back—"

"I know. I'm sorry."

"You're going to make me an old man before my time, Lizabeth," he said against my neck.

When we got downstairs, Doug was standing with Detective Williams. She glanced at me, and then she motioned to the two uniformed officers to take Doug out.

He winked at me again as he was leaving. But he looked pale and scared.

And he had killed RaeAnne. He had taken a fireplace poker and killed her. Then he'd burned her body. And he had let Madeline's husband die.

Did saving me make up for that?

"Madeline is involved in this too," I said. "She's at the hospital with Abigail. She shot Abigail."

Marcia Williams cursed.

Madeline looked up when we walked into Abigail's room. She was curled up in the armchair beside her sleeping cousin's bed. A magazine lay open in her lap, but she was sitting with her chin propped on her hand.

Williams said, "I think you'd better come with us, Mrs. Oliver. We want to question you about the attempted murder of your cousin."

Madeline looked from Williams to Quinn. Then at me standing behind them. "Where's Doug?" she said. Was there real concern in her voice?

"On his way to jail," Quinn said.

Madeline stretched and then rose from the chair. But she seemed a little unsteady on her feet.

"It really was an accident." She glanced at Abigail. "I'm not sure how it happened. She asked me about RaeAnne. She said Charlotte had said RaeAnne might be the murdered girl in the woods. She asked me when I'd last seen her . . . RaeAnne." Madeline pushed back her hair. "She was at my father's desk, looking for a pen to write him a note about Charlotte calling about the house not being cleaned. And she was saying it was a waste of time the way he was lately. Then she just stopped and looked at me. She said Tommy had said something strange before he ran out about calling Doug 'when she fell.' She asked if he could have been talking about RaeAnne." Madeline glanced from one of us to the other: "She had the desk drawer open, and the gun was there. I looked down at it, and she saw me looking. And there was this moment when I could hardly breathe. And then I just reached over and grabbed the gun up. And she laughed. She shook her head at me like she couldn't believe anyone as silly and vain as me would even know what a gun was. And even if I did know, I would never . . . and it just went off. I didn't mean to hurt her. She's my cousin, and I do love her." Madeline sighed. "I thought it would be all right when she couldn't remember."

But she hadn't known that her cousin would wake up from her coma with no recollection of the shooting. She must have been sweating that one out. And even after Abigail regained consciousness and said she couldn't remember, Madeline must still have been worried that her cousin's memory would return.

All things considered, it was probably just as well for Abigail that Sloane Campbell had made his presence felt. Otherwise, Madeline might have looked down and seen a pillow and suddenly found herself holding it over her cousin's face.

Madeline walked past me, toward the two uniformed police officers who were waiting to take her away. "Good-bye, Lizzie." There was a touch of sarcasm in her voice.

"Madeline," I said, unable to let her go without asking at least one question. "RaeAnne . . . why did you send me to look for her?"

She tilted her head and smiled. "I thought I was being clever. Why would I send you to look for her if I knew she was dead? I didn't expect you to find anything."

She turned away from me and came face-to-face with Sloane Campbell, who was stepping out of the elevator. He looked at Williams and Quinn. "What's going on?" he said.

"She shot Abigail," I said. "Excuse me."

There was no one in the waiting room. I sat down and took a deep breath.

"It looks like I owe you again," Campbell said from the doorway. He came across the room and sat down beside me.

"I got her shot," I said. "If I hadn't been playing detective . . . if I hadn't told Charlotte about the night guard I'd found and that the body in the woods was probably RaeAnne . . . that was what Tommy overheard. That was why he ran out and why Abigail was suspicious and Madeline shot—"

He held up his hand. "But Madeline pulled that trigger. Just like it was Verity who killed my mother."

"Verity? Why are you comparing—"

"When I was bargaining with God to let Abby live, I said that if she did, I would tell this." His dark gaze was steady, but he paused as if the words were hard to get out. Then he said, "Verity didn't steal that skirt and blouse. She was protecting me."

"Protecting you?"

"She knew I did it. That I'd cut up my mama's skirt and blouse and buried the pieces. A 10-year-old boy's revenge for another whipping." He leaned forward, hands clenched together. "But because of what I did, one thing led to another. Verity ended up killing my mother during that fight. Then Verity died herself. She would have been executed if she hadn't died."

"You didn't know when you took the skirt and—"

"Just like you didn't know when you told Charlotte what you told her." He looked at me. "And, Professor, you can do whatever you damn please with what I just told you. Write it up and publish it if you want to. I'm tired of hiding it."

"I don't want to do anything with it," I said.

He smiled, his face full of shadows and angles. "That's probably just as well. When my Abby got back on her feet she might've come after you and scratched your eyes out."

"She knows what you told me?"

He nodded. "I thought she ought to."

"What did she say when you told her?"

"She cried for that 10-year-old boy. Then she hugged me as hard as she could. Sometimes there's a whole lot of healing in just being held."

Campbell glanced toward the doorway, then got to his feet. He nodded at Quinn as he passed him.

"What did he want to tell you?" Quinn said, coming to stand beside me.

"He wanted to thank me again for saving Abigail. I told him I almost got her killed."

Quinn looked down at me. "That wasn't your fault."

Me and Tommy. Not our fault.

"Wasn't it? And Keisha tonight. I could have gotten her—"

"Keisha said you saved her. She said you risked your life to save her."

"But I shouldn't have let her get involved in the Verity Thomas case in the first place, and then she wouldn't have been at Abigail's office when—"

"Stop it, Lizzie. Do you hear me? You aren't responsible for—"

"All right. Maybe not. As Dr. Cage would undoubtedly remind me, I am not the empress of the universe." I stood up. "People do what they do. And somehow I keep on finding myself in the middle of their messes."

"And that's all you do," Quinn said. "You don't cause what happens."

"Nope, I'm just there when it happens. But there is a lesson in all this, isn't there?"

"What lesson?" he said.

"That you can't escape your relatives. Good or bad, one way or the other, they get to you. Cousins, uncles, fathers, mothers. Sloane Campbell had his mother, and I have mine."

"Lizzie, this has nothing to do with your mother."

"She's a relative. I want . . . I need to try to find her, Quinn."

He said, choosing his words, "That might not be a good idea, Lizabeth. You might find something you'd rather not know."

"Quite possibly. But she and the man who fathered me are a part of who I am."

"But that doesn't mean you have to. . . ." He touched my cheek. "Babe, you have this way of taking in pain, of. . . . What would you do if you found something—"

"Then I would know. I'm going to try to find her."

He stood there, looking at me, trying to see into my head. Then he opened his arms, and I burrowed into them. Campbell was right.

"Okay," Quinn said. "You're going to look for Becca. Want some help?"

"Yes." I leaned back so that I could see his face. "I think having the help of a trained detective would be quite useful. Unless you have other plans."

"All my plans include you, Professor Stuart."

An answer that told me nothing about what exactly those plans were. But it was enough for now. Enough to go on with.

I said, "I have a few plans that include you too. Since I didn't die tonight after all, I think we should do something special to celebrate."

That smile started in his eyes. "What'd you have in mind?"

"I thought I'd make you a Brandy Alexander pie."

He burst out laughing. "A pie? Definitely the way we should celebrate, Lizabeth."

"And we can add some candles and music," I said, kissing his chin and moving up to his mouth. "Some wine for you and a pot of tea for me—"

"This is beginning to sound better and better," he said.

ALSO BY FRANKIE Y. BAILEY

Death's Favorite Child

African-American, thirty-eight, and a crime historian, Lizzie Stuart has spent most of her life in Drucilla, Kentucky. When her grandmother dies, Lizzie decides it is time for a vacation.

She joins her best friend, Tess, a travel writer, for a week in Cornwall, England, in the resort town of St. Regis. Lizzie finds her vacation anything but restful when she becomes an eyewitness to murder and the probable next victim.

"In this combination of a traditional British cozy with a touch of American savvy, Bailey creates an eminently readable story with a likeable cast of characters that I look forward to seeing again."
—Maria Y. Lima, Crescent Blues Book Views

"*Death's Favorite Child* introduces us to a new crime-solving woman of color. The reader is immediately drawn to Lizzie's quick wit and zest for seeking the truth."
—Ty Moody, Editor-N-Chief, The DOE Network

Trade Paper 1-57072-146-7 $15.00 · Hardcover 1-57072-145-9 $24.50

A Dead Man's Honor

Crime historian Lizzie Stuart goes to Gallagher, Virginia, as a visiting professor at Piedmont State University and to do research for a book about a 1921 lynching that her grandmother witnessed as a 12-year-old child. Lizzie's research is complicated by her own unresolved feelings about her secretive grandmother and by the disturbing presence of John Quinn, the police officer she met in England. When an arrogant but brilliant faculty member is murdered, Lizzie begins to have more than a few sleepless nights.

"Frankie Bailey . . . weaves a good tale with a dual mystery and a lineup of characters that simply ooze realism."
—Harriet Klausner, *The Midwest Book Review*

Trade Paper 1-57072-171-8 $13.95 · Hardcover 1-57072-170-X $23.95

www.frankieybailey.com

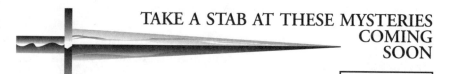